OPERATION GOLDEN DAWN

GEORGE WALLACE

SEVERN RIVER PUBLISHING

OPERATION GOLDEN DAWN

Severn River Publishing
www.SevernRiverBooks.com

ISBN: 978-1-64875-561-3 (Paperback)

Also by George Wallace

Operation Golden Dawn

By George Wallace and Don Keith

The Hunter Killer Series

Final Bearing

Dangerous Grounds

Cuban Deep

Fast Attack

Arabian Storm

Warshot

Silent Running

Snapshot

Never miss a new release! Sign up to receive exclusive updates from George Wallace

severnriverbooks.com/authors/george-wallace

PROLOGUE

12 Jul 1974, 1530LT (1330Z)

The scorching hot sun burned through the dusty haze, painting Mdoukha with a burnished golden glow. The ancient village, little more than a clutch of mud huts haphazardly thrown up alongside a stone road, sat high up on the Eastern edge of the Bekaa Valley, hard against the mountains marking Lebanon's border with Syria. Little had changed since the same road had been trod by Roman legions two millennia ago, save the granite being worn down by generations of wandering feet, ox carts, and recently the stray car.

Twelve-year old Mustaf al Shatar sat on the ground; his back braced against the olive tree. The weathered, scarred tree inhabited a tiny, narrow space between the main street and the open fronted ramshackle cafe. The shop served dark, bitter Turkish coffee to old men who sat and argued the day away. The arguments always covered the same topics, the unbelievable injustice the Western World had visited on the Palestinian people and retribution to be exacted on the Israelis when they regained their rightful homeland.

Mustaf half listened to the chatter as he idly tossed pebbles at an ant struggling to carry its load back to the nest. The hot afternoon sun, barely filtered by the scraggly blue-green leaves, beat down on his shoulders.

The young boy watched the dust swirl in thick clouds behind the cars as they roared up to the bedraggled two-story building across the street. Mustaf counted more than a dozen as they stopped only long enough to disgorge their robed and turbaned passenger's. Papa was hosting an important meeting in their cramped second floor apartment. He sent Mustaf out to watch over his seven-year old sister, Rachel. With so much traffic, it wasn't safe for her to play alone on the street and the apartment was much too small for her and all the important guests.

The Mercedes and Citroens roared off as fast as they arrived. Parking and waiting anywhere near here would only draw the Israeli's war birds. Even the tiny farming village was constantly under their prying eyes.

Mustaf tossed another pebble, smashing the ant just before it reached the fissure in the gnarly old olive tree's bark that it called home. He looked around for another target to vent his frustration. Sitting out here babysitting a little sister was beneath the dignity of a Palestinian freedom fighter. He should be upstairs with Papa, planning another daring raid across the no-mans-land into Israel. He was a warrior, not a child.

Maybe Papa really wanted him to guard the meeting. That was it! Papa knew Mustaf was smart and brave. Papa knew that Mustaf would figure out the real mission. He would sit out here and guard against any surprise attack from the Israelis. If they came, he would shout out a warning and charge into the fight.

His right hand drifted under his robe so that he could feel the soft leather of his sling. He clenched his jaw tightly and looked grimly up and down the road. He carefully selected a half-dozen stones of just the right size and shape, and put them in his other pocket. He was ready.

Rachel scampered by on some imaginary errand, clutching her doll in one hand as she chattered to some make-believe friend.

Mustaf wasn't quite sure what Father did for Uncle Yassir, but he knew it was important and dangerous. Father was fighting for the return of Palestine and the end of the Jewish invasion. Someday Mustaf would be a famous freedom fighter, too.

This house was so very different from the one they had just left in Beirut. A faint smile flitted across Mustaf's young face as memories flooded back; the bustling market, all his friends, the house he loved and the busy excitement of the city.

Then, early one morning, Father appeared unexpectedly, weeks before he was supposed to return. He spoke quietly and quickly to Mama. Words that Mustaf couldn't hear. But he sensed the fear descending over Mama. The family rushed out of the Beirut house, leaving everything behind, even his best soccer ball.

Father drove the small Fiat at breakneck speed, out of the city and across the broad valley. He barely slowed for the military checkpoints that dotted the road. The guards seemed to know they were coming and waved them on through. Still, the trip took all day, jolting over dusty, bumpy back roads, avoiding villages along the way. At last Papa screeched to a halt in front of this house.

Today would likely be the last day in Mdoukha. Then they would be off to some other tiny apartment in some other dusty town. Papa explained to them every move was necessary to protect them from the Mossad and the Israeli bombs. Papa kept them moving too much for Mustaf and Rachel to have any real friends, only make-believe ones and, of course, each other.

Momma complained every time they moved. Mustaf listened through the paper-thin walls as Papa and Momma argued long into the night; Momma complaining that the children had no friends and were not getting any education. Papa yelling back that friends were a luxury they couldn't afford. Except for reading the *Quoran*, schooling would come when they had a homeland of their own.

Papa was a leader in the holy fight to regain their rightful homeland. He was a fighter who had won many battles against the Israelis. Scores of freedom fighters in the *fedayeen* followed Papa on his jihad.

Papa trusted no one outside the family, except possibly a very select few in the Palestine Liberation Organization. The Mossad had agents everywhere. The hated Israeli secret service would search out and kill Papa and the family if they could. Mustaf learned early that a leader in battle had to be as wary of betrayal as he was fearless. In family was the only trust.

Maybe they would be lucky this time and go to Damascus for a few months. Mustaf hoped so. The short time they lived there when he was four or five, when Rachel was born, was the happiest time of his young life.

Damascus was such a big, bustling city. There was always something exciting to do and, for the only time in his life, Mustaf felt really safe. He could explore the warren of streets in the old city; enjoy a thousand adventures as he rushed through the bustling crowds.

"Mustaf, come play with me," Rachel wheedled. She grabbed his hand and tried to pull him upright. "You be the Papa and I'll be the Momma."

She cradled her doll and smiled down at it. "Little Bea will be our baby."

Mustaf growled in his most manly voice, "Silence woman. I am on duty. Father ordered me to guard our house." The boy stood and pulled his sling from under his robe. "No Israeli will sneak up on us."

"Oh, Musta," Rachel giggled. "Father only said that to keep you busy. Now, come play with me."

Mustaf shook off her hand and growled, "I am a freedom fighter. I don't have time to play baby games. I have to guard Papa's meeting."

"Oh, pash!" Rachel cried, tears coming quickly into her deep brown eyes. "You aren't guarding anything. You're just being mean. You don't want to play with me! I'm going to go tell Momma."

Rachel scampered across the street, her black hair streaming behind her just as another large black Mercedes screeched to a halt, barely missing the little girl. The back door flung open. A short, fat man dressed in wrinkled khaki fatigues and wearing a checkered turban clambered slowly out. A grizzled salt-and-pepper beard hid a pudgy face and beady black eyes.

"Uncle Yassir," Mustaf called out.

The little man looked up and glanced across the street just as Rachel darted toward the apartment building. He smiled and waved at Mustaf and headed around behind the car, his arms opened wide to greet the boy.

Rachel ran from the house, happily calling, "Uncle Yassir! Uncle Yassir! Candy! Did you bring candy."

Uncle Yassir smiled and waved at the young girl.

Mustaf heard the roar before he saw anything. Four jets flew low and very fast. They just cleared the ridge top before screaming down the valley directly toward them. Mustaf barely had time to recognize the distinctive shape of an F-4 before he saw the black bombs fall away from under the wings. The vision of the Star of David on each wing burned into his brain as the jets past overhead, the screaming engines shaking the very earth.

Mustaf watched in horror as the bombs dropped away and glided down, right at him. They fell in awful slow motion, coasting over the olive tree and across the street before slamming into the apartment. Piercing the walls and roof of the house, leaving holes where they flew through the dried mud and wood.

Time slowed to a crawl. For a split second, nothing happened. Mustaf dared to hope they were duds. Then the house disappeared in a roaring blast of yellow, orange, and black. It hit Mustaf just a millisecond before the pressure wave tossed him to the ground. His world went dark.

Mustaf slowly shook his head and blinked. The branches of the olive tree came into focus. Something wasn't right. There weren't any leaves on it. Where had the leaves gone? The acrid smell of smoldering rubber and plastic burned his nostrils.

Mustaf eased himself up until he was sitting. The big jets came roaring down the street again. He could see the white Star of David painted on the sides of the American made F-4 Phantom jets as they roared overhead. He thought he saw the pilots smiling and waving.

The pain changed in a flash to pure hate. Someone would pay. He would make the Americans and their stooges, the Israelis, pay. If it took all his life, they would pay. Mustaf yelled in absolute rage, shaking his fist, daring the pilots to come back and fight. He would kill them! He would kill them all!

He looked across the street. Uncle Yassir was just rising from behind his limousine. The car was shattered, torn from shrapnel tossed from the explosion. But where was the apartment? Where were Momma and Papa? There was nothing but a burning, twisted pile of rubble where the old building had once stood. Heavy black smoke swirled and twisted in a massive column reaching toward the sky.

The bitterness of his failure hit Mustaf with a hammer blow. Papa had sent him out to guard the family. He had let the Israelis attack. It was all his fault. If he had been quicker, stronger, braver; Papa and Momma would still be here.

He slumped to the ground, tears welling from his eyes. Then he saw the doll's torn, bloodstained arm. He knew he had lost everything.

He pulled himself erect, using the olive tree to steady himself. The world swayed and whirled for a few seconds. The dizziness passed. He felt a strange burning pain from his cheek and felt the hot and sticky flow of blood running down the side of his face.

Uncle Yassir lifted the boy by the shoulder. "Come, my son. We will fix your first war wound. Then we will teach you how to use that hate. Your battles have only just begun."

1
---

15 Mar 1998, 0130LT (0130Z)

Mustaf al Shatar pulled the black hood over his head, carefully adjusting the cloth. It mustn't block his vision. His smoothly shaved face felt strange. His thick black beard normally hid the old scar, but the angry red welt was plainly visible as it zigzagged across his cheek. Mustaf ran his fingers lightly over the tortured tissue, reflecting that this was only a reminder of a much deeper scar in his heart. Rachel would be avenged.

A fleeting smile crossed his face. A good, devout Moslem should not shave the proof of his manliness, but the exigencies of battle with the infidel necessitated a clean shave. Mustaf was a practical man and knew that Allah would smile on any action that brought grief to the enemies of the true faith. Tonight was a time for revenge.

It felt good to be on an operational mission again, back amongst men of action instead of the political animals that inhabited the PLO headquarters. Uncle Yassir had taught him well, both in the arts of battle and in the political infighting needed to build an army. Mustaf had excelled at both, but only the rumbling growl of an AK-47 or the sight of the enemy's blood brought any joy.

Mustaf glanced around at his small team. These five had been with him in the training camps in Syria and Libya. They had fought with him in the Golan Heights and the occupied territories. They were men he trusted with his life.

Six men in black coveralls crowded in the back of the speeding van. Their pockets bulged with extra clips of ammo and grenades. Each had a wickedly sharp assault knife strapped to the inside of their left calf, just above cloth and rubber combat boots.

Moussiari sat at Mustaf's right, just as he had for the last twenty years, ever since Uncle Yassir had brought the young orphan boy to the training camp hidden high on the Eastern side of the Bekaa Valley. Moussiari was a young freedom fighter then, but already blooded from the fighting in Beirut and a couple of airliner hijackings. Uncle Yassir charged Moussiari with guarding and training the boy. Mustaf learned the techniques of battle at Moussiari's hand and the value of loyalty from the man's devotion. The big man saved Mustaf's life twice on earlier missions.

Moussiari pulled open the aluminum trunk sitting in the center of the van, between their out-stretched legs. Six gleaming new AK-47 assault rifles rested inside, carefully secured in black foam.

He grabbed a weapon, flung the action back and tossed it down the line. The man sitting next to the rear door caught the rifle, slammed a magazine home and slid a round into the chamber. Moussiari picked up the next AK-47 and passed it down. He repeated this until there were only two left. He held one up for Mustaf before taking the last one for himself.

Mustaf snatched the Kalashnikov from Moussiari's hand and worked the action, ramming a round into the chamber. The rough, powerful shape of the Russian automatic rifle felt good. It had been too long since he had last felt the weapon's heavy recoil or heard its deep bark.

Mustaf leaned back against the van's metal side and tried to ease the tension in his taunt muscles. He smiled as he remembered how it was always like this just before a mission, as if his body was coiling to strike.

Where had all the time gone? Had it really been five years since he last led a team of *fedayeen* on a mission of *jihad*? What would his *Wahabi* say if he knew that his star pupil had wasted his time playing political games?

Mustaf shrugged. Such was life. Politics bred power. Power was the name of the game. Righteous causes counted for nothing. Alliances for even less. He would grab as much power as possible, and then the world would feel his pain. He would avenge the murder of his family.

Moussiari asked quietly, his voice heavy with worry, "Are you sure you want to do this, my leader? The team can finish this mission. There is no reason to endanger you."

Mustaf glanced across the van. The big, dark featured Iraqi could always be counted on to be at his side or covering Mustaf's back.

"My friend," Mustaf whispered. "I need to do this. Do you want our men to think I am some weak political animal like Uncle Yassir, ready to bend whichever way the wind blows? The rifle is my right hand, the bomb my tool. Allah must be avenged! Our cause is righteous."

Moussiari glanced around the darkened interior. He lurched forward as the van raced around a sharp turn. Mustaf's hand on his shoulder prevented Moussiari from being thrown into his master.

Moussiari grunted, "These men have served you for years. They know your bravery. Master, I beg you to stay behind. This mission is too dangerous. There is too much to lose."

The van screeched to a halt. The rear doors swung open. Harsh blue-white light shattered the darkness. The lead pair of fighters leaped into the brightness.

Mustaf pushed Moussiari toward the door. "It's too late to back out now. We can only pray to Allah that the Americans know nothing of our mission and that we serve Allah's will."

The pair ran across the narrow alley and followed the group into a darkened doorway. It was peaceful and quiet, beautiful as only an Iberian summer night could be. No shout of alarm, no spray of bullets to greet the fighters, only a warm breeze gently scented with olives and almonds. If they could just make it upstairs and to the front of the building.

Mustaf once again rehearsed the plan in his mind. It all seemed so easy, and so perfect. Israel's Chief of Mossad meeting the American Director of Central Intelligence at the American Embassy in Lisbon. The broad boulevard separated this apartment flat from the Embassy's front entrance. It was an easy shot. A pair of rocket-propelled grenades would smash the cars, then a spray of automatic rifle fire would kill the dazed survivors. Mustaf smiled. A classic ambush in the middle of a safe European capitol.

Mustaf's team quickly dispersed to the three top floor apartments, setting up their killing field. Uncle Yassir's agents rented the apartments years ago, just as they had in most of Europe's capitols, in case they would ever be needed. Two men to an apartment, one ready with an RPG, the other lugging extra rockets and ammunition clips for their AK-47s.

The pink-gold dawn was just lighting the Tagus River when Mustaf slid into position behind the center window. He glanced across the tree-lined boulevard at the white colonnaded façade of the American Embassy. A Marine guard in dress uniform stood just outside the heavy wooden double doors, ready, even at this early hour, to let America's friends in and to stop America's enemies.

Mustaf leaned back and relaxed. There were still several hours to wait. The meetings weren't scheduled to start until ten o'clock. These infidels believed in the comfort of sleep. There was time for him to rest for a few minutes.

The incessant, annoying buzz awoke Mustaf. Why would someone be calling him on the cell phone? Only a very select, very trusted few *fedayeen* knew this number. Mustaf snatched the miscreant device from his pocket, jammed down on the talk button, and growled, "What?"

The excited voice was familiar, a brother from the camps, his source in Arafat's inner council. "Run, Mustaf! You have been betrayed. Arafat sold you out to the Mossad. It's a trap!"

The line went dead.

Mustaf dropped the phone and stared sightlessly at the flyspecked white wall. It couldn't possibly be true. Uncle Yassir was his mentor, his father figure. How could the man who had replaced Papa betray him like this? But somehow Mustaf knew it was true. He had risen to the point where Yassir saw him as a threat to his power. With Uncle Yassir, one thing was certain. If you threatened his power base, you would be destroyed.

The first explosion shattered the apartment to the right and blasted a huge hole in the adjoining wall. Mustaf could barely see through the choking dust and smoke. The shattered shapes of his fighters, blown apart by the missile, were barely visible. Automatic weapons fire poured into the apartment from somewhere across the street. Bullets rhythmically pocked the walls, tearing huge gouges out of the plaster.

A streak of light passed across his vision milliseconds before the second missile smashed into the apartment to the left. The explosion was deafening.

Moussiari stood at the window and opened fire. Mustaf could see the AK-47 jump and buck but, strangely, he couldn't hear the roar he knew so well. The missile blast had deafened him. A burst of machine gun fire found their apartment, stitching a neat pattern across the wall. Another burst tore through Moussiari, spraying the air with a pink mist as the *fedayeen* fighter was slammed back and fell heavily at Mustaf's feet.

"Mustaf, my brother," the older fighter moaned. "Help me. I can't move."

Mustaf knew that they were in a hopeless trap. Nothing left but to escape and fight another day. No sense being a martyr for the cause. That was for the stupid foot soldiers. A leader had to stay alive to lead. He dove out the door and dashed for the stairs just as an explosion erupted in the apartment. Another missile must have found their hiding place. The damned Americans had worked out the angles of attack like a fine science. Bullets zipped through the air like a thousand angry hornets.

Mustaf crawled down the hallway as bullets rent the air above his head. It was only thirty feet, but it felt like a marathon as he struggled to make it to safety. Finally he reached the stairwell and tumbled down the stairs, only to slam into the landing below. In the relative safety of the landing, he tore off the black hood and coveralls, revealing the blue-gray caribinari uniform that he wore underneath. He left the coveralls lying on the landing beside the AK-47 and dashed on down the stairwell. By the time anyone found them, he would be long gone. A pair of explosions and more machine-gun fire erupted above and behind him as he tumbled pell-mell toward safety below.

At the bottom, he pulled the caribinari sergeant's hat from his pocket and jammed it onto his head, completing the look. It was not perfect, but it would do. He took a few deep breaths, clearing his thoughts. When he took the next step and opened the door, he had to be in character. Mustaf was now a harried Lisbon police sergeant suddenly on the front line of a terrorist attack in his peaceful city.

A door on the floor below smashed open. Two figures in black combat garb dove through.

Bulky armored vests and heavy helmets hid their features from Mustaf, but he could easily see that these were the first members of the SWAT team, making their way up the stairs to cut off his escape. Their M-16 rifles danced like deadly cobras as the pair darted forward. Two more team members dove through the door immediately behind them.

Mustaf smiled. These men would be easy prey. One well-placed grenade would take them all out. Either they didn't listen or they were trained by amateurs. Professionals didn't bunch up so they could all die with a single stroke.

Mustaf leaned down the stairwell just enough so the lead gunner could see the uniform and yelled, "Hurry, before they get away. Apartments on the third floor. Hurry!" He waved vaguely upward.

Mustaf barely dared to breathe. He had just about exhausted his command of Portuguese. If the SWAT team stopped to interrogate him, they would easily detect the imposter. His hand dropped involuntarily to caress the butt of the 9mm Beretta in its shiny patent leather holster. He consciously pulled his hand away from the pitiful little weapon. These four would turn him into chopped meat before he fired the first round.

The SWAT team dashed past him with barely a glance as they headed to the ambush.

Mustaf walked slowly down the stairs and out the door. Bright morning sun greeted him as he exited the building that was meant to be his tomb. He slowly strolled down the alley, past the line of police vehicles and out onto the boulevard. American armored cars blocked off both ends. Combat garbed Marines stood behind the vehicles and crouched behind the tall palm trees in the center of the boulevard, their eyes fixed on the smoking apartment. No one even glanced at the caribinari sergeant as he slowly trudged down the sidewalk and rounded the corner.

Mustaf's mind was seething. Everything was changed. There was no going back to the PLO now. It was time for a larger game. The Palestinians could worry about the trivialities of their homeland. It was time for him to free the Moslem world from the tyranny of the American Empire. If he could just make it out of Lisbon and slip across to Libya, Mustaf knew how he would do it. It was all so easy when Allah revealed his plan.

2

***

01 Jun 1998, 0930LT (31 May, 2330Z)

General Liu Pen sat back and listened. The briefing was excruciatingly boring, as usual. Every minor diplomat or small time spymaster laboring in the employ of the Peoples Republic of China seemed to find it vital to report every useless tidbit of information they stumbled across. They didn't seem to realize that the director of Peoples Army Intelligence Corp had important duties to attend to.

Located deep under Tiannamen Square, The Central Command of the Peoples Intelligence Service was not listed on the tourist guide for Beijing. The concrete bunkers, secretly constructed during the sixties, could withstand a full blown nuclear assault from either the Americans or the Russians. Chairman Mao could never quite decide which was the greater threat. Their function to protect China's leaders against nuclear annihilation was largely obsolete, but the bunkers had a new purpose. The massive concrete walls and tons of earth above shielded his command center from any prying eyes. No electronic sensor, no matter how sophisticated and sensitive, could reach here.

From this hidden location, his tendrils reached out to all of Asia and beyond; sifting each tiny bit of intelligence; sorting, evaluating, filing every morsel. And General Liu Pen sat at the center of the spider web.

Liu Pen's eyes drifted away from the briefer and toward the map of Asia, nearly filling the wall to his left. China, of course, dominated the central part of the map, but Liu Pen focused further to the South, to the broad underbelly of Asia.

For untold centuries China's threat had been to the North and West. First from hordes of Mongol barbarians swarming across the empty plains, then from the Russians with their tanks and missiles. In today's world, those threats were gone. The danger was from the South. It was from an odd mixture of Western capitalist economic power and fundamentalist Islamic poverty mixed in the stewing cauldron of the tropics. But, in that boiling mix of greed, hunger, and hate, Liu Pen saw an irresistible opportunity. It was not without risk, but a prize so valuable was worth some risk.

The General sat back and gazed at the map, lost in thought. The giant fans, barely whispering, drew the outside air in, and after filtering it through several levels of defense, delivered a gentle zephyr of jasmine scented air across Liu Pen's cheeks.

"Our friend in Libya has reported in." The briefer finished one subject and moved on to the next.

Liu Pen shifted slightly and turned his stare back toward the briefer. This was a subject that he was interested in. The briefer hesitated before he continued the briefing, almost as if he was tantalizing the General with a morsel before revealing the main course.

"And what does he report?" Liu Pen asked quietly.

There was the barest hint of exasperation in the General's voice. The three other officers, seated around the polished wood table sat upright. These men, General Liu Pen's personal staff, sensed the danger. The briefer was trying the General's patience and he was not known as a patient man.

"He reports that the mission was successful," the briefer droned on. "Mustaf al Shatar received the warning and escaped the Israeli/American ambush. He has safely arrived at the desert camp. He is blaming the PLO for betraying him, apparently as an attempt to remove him as a political threat to Arafat's power. Mustaf has taken charge and broken all ties with the PLO. He is attempting to establish his own operation. From all indications, he suspects nothing of our involvement."

Liu Pen turned to his Chief of Staff, a squat, fat little man with beady black eyes, who squirmed at the General's direct gaze.

Liu Pen held his stare for the barest second before he said, "Have our friend offer Mustaf all the support he wants. We want him deeply dependent on our assistance. Then we will steer him toward our Indonesian operation."

The Chief of Staff nodded and broke into a half smile as he answered, "A perfect match. Bring the Moslem terrorist in to help the Islamic revolution."

He templed his fingers in front of his face. His black eyes beamed out over the tips as he continued. "I shall, of course, hide our presence. The disruption will panic the West."

"But the West are our friends," Liu Pen retorted sarcastically. "Haven't you been paying attention to the new world order? We are all friends now. We live in a time of peaceful cooperation."

His smile shifted to a serious grimace. "Let Mustaf know where his aid is coming from. The man has a pathological hatred for America. He will need to know most of the plan before we can use him. But not all."

The briefer cleared his throat. "May I continue, General?"

"Do you have more drivel that demands my time?" Liu Pen shot back, the heat of his voice betraying the General's annoyance.

"Just one more item," the briefer stuttered, taken aback by the blast. "Our new agent is in place. She arrived in Hawaii from Los Angeles two days ago. She will make contact with our target asset in a few days."

Liu Pen nodded and rose. It was a signal that the briefing was over. The briefer gathered his notes and scurried out of the room, followed by the rest of the staff.

Just as the Chief of Staff reached the door, General Liu Pen called him back. "Two more things for you to do. First, develop a plan to have Mustaf al Shatar meet Admiral Suluvana. We need them to start working together quickly. Time is not on our side."

The Chief of Staff nodded and asked, "And the second thing?"

"That briefer. Get him out of here. I'm thinking command of a border crossing somewhere in the Gobi Desert should be just about suitable for his talents."

07 Aug 1998, 1315LT (0215Z)

Admiral Suluvana grasped the rail and braced his legs against the ship's gentle roll. It felt good to be back at sea again, even if he felt like super-cargo on this new frigate. The starboard bridge-wing of a warship was where he belonged. The sea air blowing through his hair and the afternoon sun warming his skin were just the right combination for a sailor.

The short, middle-aged Indonesian admiral pulled the blue ball cap a little lower so that the scrambled egg encrusted brim shielded his eyes from the sun's glare. Long exposure to salt and sea spray weathered his face to the color and texture of old leather. Years of squinting into the sun carved deep furrows in his brow.

The sea was an unbelievable cerulean that only existed in the deep waters of the tropics. The warm air brought a salt tang to Suluvana's nostrils with just the spicy hint of exotic islands. It was a great day to be at sea.

Suluvana glanced around for a minute. This was the finest ship to ever fly his flag. The *Salawal* and her three sisters joined the Indonesian Navy less than a year ago.

He could not quite understand why the Americans were discarding them. The American *Perry* class seemed ideal for the restricted Indonesian waters, small enough to safely maneuver the many intricate passages, large enough to demand respect, and with enough modern weapons and sensors to handle any contingency.

The *Salawal* was a manifestation of their largesse. The SSQ-56 sonar was fantastic for searching the island strewn waters for submarines, while her radar could search out and track any surface ship within fifty kilometers and any aircraft out to twice that.

The Americans sailed with the *Perry* class frigates for many years before finally coming to the realization that they could safely pass their much-vaunted technology on to the primitive masses. They had only recently decided that their friends in Southeast Asia should have these magnificent ships.

Suluvana well knew the Americans were using the *Salawal* and her sisters as a bribe to ensure Indonesia's continued cooperation. Their secondary motive was to strengthen the current government against the threat of internal revolt.

Just the barest hint of a smile flitted across Suluvana's dark features. The irony was delicious. The Americans were arming the very revolution they so feared. With *Allah*'s will, he would use their own weapons to drive the infidels from his homeland.

Suluvana strode out to the edge of the bridge wing. He grasped the rail and tensed his shoulder muscles against its unyielding steel. This was the little exercise he could accomplish onboard. There simply was not enough room. Even walking around the ship was difficult with the crew snapping to attention whenever he approached. He tensed each muscle separately, holding the tension for a full minute before relaxing. First the arms and shoulders, then the solar plexus, and then moving down to the leg muscles.

While doing his exercises, Admiral Suluvana stared out to sea. It would be interesting if he could spot the periscope before the *Salawal*'s sonar sensed the submarine.

What was that, maybe five or six kilometers out, broad on the starboard bow? Suluvana thought he could just see tendrils of green smoke whisping upward from the sea's surface. He grabbed a pair of binoculars and focused on the spot. Yes, a pair of green flares smoking on the surface and just beyond he could faintly see the smallest white feather caused by a periscope moving through the water.

Captain Balewegal, the *Salawal*'s commanding officer, stuck his head out the bridge wing door and shouted above the wind, "Admiral, we have regained contact on the *JAHIDIR* at a range of three-seven hundred meters. This SSQ-56 sonar is magic. We detected the submarine just minutes after he launched his torpedo attack."

Admiral Suluvana slammed his binoculars down onto the small steel table. An empty coffee cup skittered across the surface and fell to the deck. The white porcelain cup shattered into a thousand shards. He screamed, "You idiot! Don't you have the slightest understanding?"

Balewegal stared at the irate senior officer, not comprehending why he was in such a tirade. With all his previous anti-submarine ships, he had never detected a submarine. Now that he finally could report success, his Admiral was furious. The taller, slightly overweight Captain shrank back, vainly trying to hide behind the bridge gyro repeater.

Admiral Suluvana stopped yelling at the helpless junior officer. The effort would be lost on Balewegal. The man had no real intelligence, he served only as a pawn in this great game. But a loyal one; and loyal pawns are to be valued.

Suluvana turned away to gaze toward the submarine. He smiled slightly. Out there a few thousand meters was the answer to all his problems. These new *KILO* class boats were amazing. They could silently sneak close enough to Indonesia's finest, most modern ships; and deliver a *coup-de-grace* with impunity. Even the Americans feared their stealth and torpedoes. With enough of them, he could control all of Southeast Asia. With the four he had, and with skillful placement, he could easily command all the sea-lanes passing through Indonesia.

"Signal *JAHIDIR* that the exercise is completed," Suluvana said. "Let us return to port and celebrate our successes. Between *JAHIDIR*'s uncontested command of the undersea and *Salawal*'s prowess on the surface, our naval forces are supreme. No one will dare contest our control of the sea lanes that traverse our sovereign waters."

Captain Balewegal nodded in agreement with the Admiral. He added, "And, my Admiral. With this technology in your able hands, we will be victorious in our quest."

Suluvana glowered at the man. He growled, "You truly are an idiot! Did your mother drop you on your head when you were a baby? How dare you mention such a thing! I should toss you over the side and pretend you never existed."

"But, my Admiral," Balewegal sputtered. "We have planned for so long. The time is now near. Why?"

The Admiral interrupted before Balewegal could complete his thought, "Captain, if you would use your meager intellect for just one second, you would understand. Just the merest hint of what we are planning, in the wrong circles, would cause destruction to rain down on all of us. If you survived President Mustisanissal's torture cell, you would spend the rest of your worthless life as a broken man. A forgotten prisoner deep in a Jakarta prison. And I would die a martyr, a victim of your stupidity"

Captain Balewegal sputtered, "But of course, my Admiral. I understand. It is just the two of us here. No one can overhear what we say, and, besides, my crew is loyal to our quest. There is no danger."

Suluvana glared at the Captain. The silence was so intense that Balewegal thought for a moment that the very ocean had stopped its un-ending motion under the Admiral's glacial stare. Finally Suluvana smiled and said, "Of course you are correct. When you signal *JAHIDIR*, tell Captain al Meshidar that I expect he and you at my quarters for dinner tonight."

Balewegal stepped inside the bridge of the frigate.

Suluvana was left blessedly alone as the gray warship made a graceful turn. They would be back in port before the sun slipped below the horizon. There were many things to accomplish before dinner. He pulled General Liu Pen's message from his pocket and re-read the text. So, the old Chinese spymaster wanted to speak with him about some Palestinian terrorist. Where could that lead?

3

Mustaf listened quietly as General Liu Pen spoke.

The summons to Beijing was a surprise. He had known for some time that powerful, hidden players were pulling the strings around the Arab world. As rich and well entrenched as the Saudi's were, he had sensed that someone else was behind the curtain. The hidden player was far more resourceful than those old desert Bedouins. Neither the Syrians nor the Iranians commanded anywhere near the capabilities that he had already seen. That meant someone outside the Islamic world was in the great game.

Mustaf suspected that the PRC was playing power broker in the terrorist world. This was the first direct contact he had enjoyed.

He sat in Beijing, in the People's Army Intelligence Corp's ornately furnished headquarters. The richly carved rosewood paneling nicely accented the pair of ornately inlaid Ming dynasty chests. Low voltage spot-lights discreetly illuminated priceless porcelains displayed along the wall behind the long teak table dominating the central part of the large room. The room screamed of history, wealth, and above all, power.

For an infidel, the Chinese general seemed inordinately willing to aid the *jihad*. He was offering billions of dinar and invaluable intelligence. His assistance would make Mustaf's dream, a killing stroke against the West, a reality. It was almost too good to be true.

Since first climbing off the PRC transport jet at Beijing Airport's military terminal, Mustaf had been given the Chinese military's version of the "honored guest" treatment. The ride into his sumptuous quarters was in a very nice new Mercedes, windows heavily darkened so that no one could glimpse the lone occupant in the rear seat.

His minder, evidently a high ranking PAIC operative, discreetly informed Mustaf that any needs would be fulfilled, but that he should not venture out of his suite.

When the minder came to escort him to the meeting, Mustaf was more than willing to go. He felt like a tiger in a silk cage. But it had been worth the effort. There was very little chance that anyone would be able to tie his operation with the PRC or with Admiral Suluvana's revolution.

Mustaf smiled inwardly. The old spy wasn't being so magnanimous because he had suddenly seen the true path of Allah. His altruism had a hundred hidden catches. But, still, his money and resources were valuable. He was a tool to be used to reach Allah's goal.

"This will probably be the only time we meet," General Liu Pen continued. "The Americans and the Israelis are far too likely to catch some hint if we ever come face-to-face again. Our communications must be infrequent and circumspect."

The General slowly looked at each of the other two men in the room. Admiral Suluvana was watching through carefully hooded eyes. There was no way to tell what the Indonesian was thinking behind that opaque mask.

Liu Pen turned toward Mustaf and said, "I think we have found a weapon to unleash on the West that will exact the blood revenge you demand. It is near perfect and, once we are finished, even you will be satisfied."

Mustaf leaned forward, his attention drawn toward the General. His purpose was obvious; to keep the West occupied while China pursued her own goals in relative freedom.

It required all of Mustaf's will power to suppress the grin. China could do whatever she wanted, as long as she gave him the weapons he needed. Rachel would be avenged! The West would pay!

"We have come across a strain of mousepox that has been isolated and mutated by a group of Australian scientists," General Liu Pen continued.

Admiral Suluvana snorted, "You called us to Beijing to tell us you had discovered a way to make mice sick?"

General Liu Pen raised his hand and smiled faintly. "Admiral, please allow me to continue. What I am explaining is every bit as subtle as employing those new *KILO* submarines we gave you."

Suluvana sat back quietly. The veiled threat didn't escape him. The PRC was supplying him with his weapons and could just as easily stop.

"As I was saying," Liu Pen went on. "The Australians mutated the mousepox during their research. The strain they developed was absolutely immune to any known antidote. We now have a few grams of that virus and, more importantly, a scientist who says he can transfer the genetic structure to a smallpox virus."

General Liu Pen turned to face Admiral Suluvana directly. "Now, Admiral. Do you see where our target is a little more than a few sick mice?"

Mustaf could barely grasp what he was hearing. Smallpox had nearly eradicated mankind several times since the Romans ruled the world. The disease was a horrible scourge, killing millions over the last millennia. Modern science had only brought it under control in the last century. Bioweapons engineers dreamed of using smallpox as the perfect bio-weapon, but until now the weapon and the antidote had been in perfect synchronization.

Now some hapless Australian scientists had found a way to make a totally incurable strain. A weapon capable of destroying most of mankind, a weapon totally without defense.

It was perfect. Revenge was within his grasp. Smallpox had been declared eradicated nearly a generation ago, except for some strains ostensibly kept "for science." Even the vaccination programs had been closed down years ago. A few medical facilities were rumored to maintain some stocks of the vaccine as a precaution, but not nearly enough for an epidemic outbreak.

"You say this stuff, this mousepox, is immune to all antidotes?" Mustaf questioned. His eyes glistened as he rapidly shot out his inquiries. "How virulent is it? What is the death percentage? How contagious?"

Liu Pen held up his hand to stop the verbal onslaught. "There is still some research to complete and some production to finish before the mousepox is ready to use. Then we will be able to answer all your questions with operational proof."

He smiled toward Mustaf, an evil grin that even stopped the Palestinian terrorist. "For obvious reasons, we can't do this in China. We need a location where we can absolutely control the security; a place that allows us easy access."

Suluvana brightened. "I have the perfect place, a tiny island in the Java Sea. Totally uninhabited now, there used to be a small mine there. Bauxite, if I remember correctly. The place is called Nusa Funata. I really pity anyone we put on it. Nothing but mangrove swamp surrounding a mountain jungle."

"Perfect," Liu Pen nodded. "Have it ready to go in three weeks. Doctor Aswal and his team will fly then. Mustaf, gather up a security team. The Admiral's soldiers can guard the island, but we need someone else to guard the facilities themselves. I want people who know how to keep a secret."

With that Liu Pen slammed his hands down on the table and rose. He turned and walked out of the room. The meeting was over. It was time for action.

10 May 2000, 1815LT (0415Z)

"Conn, sonar. Regain contact on Sierra Two-Two, bearing three-one-five."

The 21MC announcing speaker blared in Jon Hunter's ear. The Commanding Officer of the nuclear attack submarine *USS SAN FRANCISCO* was anxiously waiting for this report. But the announcement still startled him. He glanced at the BQQ5 sonar repeater to see a faint squiggle just beginning to appear on the screen, confirming that they weren't all alone in this part of the Pacific.

They had been playing cat and mouse with Sierra Two-Two, the Trident submarine *USS NEBRASKA*, for the last three days. Both submarines were doing their best to hide in the cold, black depths West and North of Hawaii.

Hunter reached over and snatched the 21MC speaker from its holder next to the sonar console. "Sonar, Captain, aye. Looks like he's slowly drawing to the left."

The six foot tall Commander hunched over the screen, his brow furrowed as he stared at the screen. His thick blond hair and fit figure belonged to a young man. Only the crows feet developing around his deep brown eyes belied his forty-two years, nearly twenty of them riding submarines.

Just a few feet forward of where Jon Hunter stood, six sonar operators sat poring over more sonar screens, each trying to draw every possible bit of information from the ocean outside the *LOS ANGELES* class submarine.

Master Chief Sonar Technician Holmstad, the sonar supervisor, took a quick glance over one operator's shoulder and watched the passive broad-band display for an instant. "Captain, Sonar. Sierra Two-Two bearing rate left zero-point-three degrees per minute," he reported while he kept moving over to look at the next display. "Just starting to pick up a two-forty-seven hertz line on passive narrow band again."

Holmstad was a fixture onboard. He had been the sonar chief onboard *SAN FRANCISCO* ever since she was launched, almost fifteen years ago. He made his name aboard the older *STURGEON* class boats when they went up North of the Kola Peninsula to hunt out the Soviet boats.

Hunter flipped the screen on his display over to passive narrow band just as Bill Fagan stepped over. Fagan, *SAN FRANCISCO*'s Executive Officer, was busy supervising the fire control party as they struggled to transform the sonar information into range, course, and speed information for the *NEBRASKA*.

"Captain, we've been picking up that two-forty-seven line at about two thousand yards. That's about two thousand yards closer than our tracking solution has him."

"Well, looks like you'd better move your tracking solution in a couple of thousand yards," Hunter said dryly.

SAN FRANCISCO's control room was so crowded that it was difficult to move. At least fifteen crewmen crushed into a roughly thirty foot square space already jammed full of equipment. The entire starboard side was devoted to the computerized fire control system. Six men, dressed in nearly identical blue coveralls, sat in front of flickering screens, deciphering the hieroglyphics, manipulating data, flitting from display to display as they labored to solve the problem of what was happening in the sea around the sub.

Two large glass topped chart tables filled the aft third of the control room. A team of sailors huddled over paper charts, chewing on every tidbit of information as it came in from sonar, fitting it into a mosaic. Everything to give Jon Hunter another look at what they thought *NEBRASKA* was doing.

From the forward port side of the room, the Diving Officer and his team drove the sub through the depths. Just forward of the Diving Officer's seat, the helmsman and planesman controlled the submarine's depth and course. Two of the youngest men onboard, barely legally allowed to drive a car, were driving the seven thousand ton monster with ease. They handled control yokes that looked very much like the ones that airline pilots used. The helmsman, sitting on the right, turned his wheel to turn the rudder and steer the sub. By pushing or pulling the control yoke, he positioned the fairwater planes to make *SAN FRANCISCO* go up or down. The stern planesman, sitting on the left, controlled the sub's angle by pushing or pulling his control yoke, positioning the stern planes.

"XO, get a quick handle on what *NEBRASKA* is doing. We need to get up to copy the broadcast," Hunter ordered. "Never can tell when Squadron will decide to tell us to do something else."

Fagan nodded and chuckled, "Maybe they'll get lonely and call us home. Don't know about you, Skipper, but I'm getting mighty tired of babysitting these boomers. I'd even settle for a Squadron admin inspection if it meant I could get to the O-club for happy hour."

"Careful what you wish for, XO," Hunter answered. "Commodore Calucci and his boys would probably be waiting at the pier. At least out here we don't have them trying to "help"."

Hunter stepped over to the periscope stand that dominated the center of the control room. Two silver poles of the side-by-side periscopes rose out of the deck and disappeared into the overhead.

"Officer of the deck, make your depth one-five-zero feet, slow to ahead one third," he ordered the young Lieutenant standing by the number two scope. Gold dolphins decorated the right breast of his blue coveralls; a cloth nametag with the name "Miller" embroidered on it was sewn to the left breast.

The submarine angled upward and slowed as it rose up to the new ordered depth.

"At one-five-zero, ahead one-third," Lt Miller reported. "Clearing baffles to the right."

Hunter nodded and answered, "Very well, Weps. We need to be up to copy the 0430 Zulu broadcast. You've got five minutes. Let's ventilate for thirty minutes while we are up. We could use a little fresh air."

SAN FRANCISCO swung around to the right so that the sonar dome in the submarine's bow could look back behind where the boat had been, making sure that no ship was hidden there. Hunter bent over the sonar screen, watching as the previously baffled sector came slowly into view. Nothing appeared on the screen.

"Conn, sonar, completed baffle clear," Master Chief Holmstad's voice boomed from the speaker. "No new contacts. Currently hold one contact, Sierra Two-Two, currently bearing three-zero-four."

"Captain," Miller called out. "Hold one sonar contact, Sierra Two-Two, NEBRASKA. Request permission to proceed to periscope depth to copy the 0430 broadcast."

"Proceed to periscope depth," Hunter ordered.

Miller reached up into the overhead and grabbed the large red ring that circled the number two scope. "Raising number two scope," he called as he rotated the ring.

"Speed five," the Diving Officer called out, verifying that SAN FRAN-CISCO was going slow enough to raise the periscope.

As the periscope smoothly slid upward, Miller squatted down, waiting for the eyepiece to rise out of the deck. "Dive, make your depth six-two feet," he called out.

"Make my depth six-two feet, Aye," the Diving Officer answered. "Proceeding to periscope depth."

The control room fell silent. Everyone's attention was riveted on Miller as he rose with the scope eyepiece. He slapped the handles down and glued an eye to the eyepiece. With any sign of a ship above, either from Miller seeing it or from the sonar, the crew had to instantly respond to get them back down to the safety of the depths.

The submarine slowly rose upward until the periscope broke through the surface into late evening sky.

Miller danced the scope around in a complete circle, peering out in search of any shape that might be a ship bearing down on them. He saw only the Pacific swells illuminated by a full moon shining down from above and the last glimmers of the sun disappearing below the Western horizon.

"No close contacts."

Everyone could relax and breathe again.

"Chief of the Watch, raise number two BRA-34," Miller called out.

The Chief of the Watch reached up on the panel of switches, gauges, and indicator lights in front of him and flipped up on a small toggle switch. "Number two BRA-34 coming up."

The 21MC speaker blared out, "Conn, Radio, in synch on the broadcast."

Miller glanced over at the ballast control panel, where the Chief of the Watch controlled hydraulic, air and trim systems throughout the sub. A small section of the panel was devoted to controlling the various masts that filled the sail above them.

"Chief of the Watch, prepare to ventilate the ship," Miller called out.

The Chief grabbed the 1MC microphone and called out, "Prepare to ventilate."

Crewmen on-watch around the boat moved to align dampers and fans in the ventilation system so that new air could be drawn from outside and old air exhausted overboard.

"Raise the snorkel mast," Miller ordered.

"Snorkel mast coming up," the Chief of the Watch called out as he flipped the toggle switch that pushed the big mast up.

"Torpedo in the water!" The startling announcement came out of the blue, the 21MC reverberating with the information. Someone had shot at them.

Lieutenant Miller reacted automatically. "Torpedo evasion, ahead flank!" He yelled out. "Make your depth six hundred feet! Snapshot, tube two!"

The crew jumped into action. They had to out-maneuver or out-run the incoming torpedo and shoot back. It was the only way to stay alive.

"Torpedo bearing three-one-two!"

Hunter stomped up on the periscope stand and, in a commanding voice, ordered, "All stop. Make your depth four two feet."

The fairwater planes slapped the surface as the boat bobbed upward until the main deck was awash.

"Torpedo bearing three-one-two!"

Fagan called from across the room at the fire control system, "Solution ready on bearing of incoming torpedo; weapon ready, tube two."

Hunter ordered, his voice flat and dry, "Shoot tube two."

A slamming, whooshing noise rushed up from the torpedo room. An ADCAP torpedo flushed out of tube two and raced off toward its target.

"In-coming torpedo bearing three-one-two," Holmstad called out. "Own ship's weapon running normal."

Hunter whispered so that no one but the young lieutenant could hear, "Mr. Miller, you had masts and antennas up that would have been bent over with that little maneuver. I know it's difficult, but in the future please try very hard to keep your head out of your ass."

"But Skipper," Miller pleaded, "We had an incoming weapon. We had to evade."

"You're supposed to be the Weapons Officer," Hunter answered. "What are the chances of out running an ADCAP torpedo with the alertment we had?"

"Probably none, sir," Miller answered sheepishly.

"Then we have to out-smart it," Hunter continued. "NEBRASKA thought they were shooting at a submerged nuclear submarine. They know the standard evasion tactic as well as we do. They expected us to go deep and run. What they got instead was a surface ship stopped in the middle of the ocean."

Miller's face brightened as he understood what Hunter was teaching him, "Of course! He would shoot with Doppler Enable in and submerged settings. The torpedo wouldn't even look at a zero knot target on the surface."

"Conn, sonar, incoming weapon passed underneath and is opening. It missed. *NEBRASKA* is speeding up. Sounds like she is going to flank."

The torpedo launch control operator called out, "Detect! Detect! Acquisition!"

"Own ship weapon speeding up. We got a hit!"

4

---

21 Jan 2000, 1640LT (0440Z)

Tommy Clark stood on the rusty steel deck and watched as the Motor Vessel *Sabinyama* slowly inched away from the pier and headed out from the hustle and bustle of Surabaya toward the Java Sea.

This was his first venture into the mission field. He was determined to bring peace and salvation to the suffering people of Indonesia, just like his parents had tried to, thirty years ago. This mission to Sulawesi was exactly what he had prayed for.

Thirty dedicated young people gathered up from the churches in Australia, Canada, and America, plus a shipload of medical supplies heading out to the outer reaches of Indonesia, an island rocked by religious warfare and grinding poverty. It was exciting stuff for a young man just months out of graduate school at Pepperdine University in Malibu.

It had taken three frustrating months to worm through the bureaucratic maze in Jakarta, before they had permission to head out. The officials seemed baffled by the missionaries' desire to leave the big city comfort for the dangers and hardships on the outer islands. And every one of them had their hand out. Tommy knew they would cool their heels in the capitol city forever unless he paid, so he reluctantly doled some of their meager funds into the clawing hands.

"Tommy, this is too exciting!" Nan Badgett squealed as she leaned out over the rusty old rail.

The pert little red head seemed always to be within a few feet, ever since she joined the group in Perth. That was just before they flew on to Jakarta. She was in her second year in an Australian nursing school. The donors thought that her rudimentary skills might be useful in the villages where they were going. Medical care was primitive. Even a second year nursing student would be useful in handing out vitamins and aspirin.

Surabaya's noise and congestion fell further and further astern. The old inter island tramp steamer chugged and wheezed through thick green waters of the Surabaya Straits, separating Java from Madura Island.

Clark smiled at Badgett's enthusiasm, so near his own hidden emotions. This girl didn't seem to keep anything back, so unlike the girls in Los Angeles. Clark found himself drawn to her open, direct manner as much as he was by her sunny good looks.

"Nan, we're here to do God's work, not to enjoy the sites," he responded with much more sternness than he felt. The responsibility for the success of this mission rested heavily on his young shoulders. It was serious work.

"But the sites are here to enjoy," she countered easily. "Only a fool would ignore the beauty and excitement." She didn't seem the least deterred by his demeanor.

The *Sabinyama*'s bluff bow pushed through the low, easy rollers as the boat entered the Java Sea. The sun slowly dipped into the sea, painting the Western sky brilliant shades of orange, red, and pinks for a few seconds before it dropped below the horizon. The two young missionaries stood quietly as the lights from Paceng and Klampis flickered on, yellow swatches against a black sea.

11 May 2000, 0605LT (1405Z)

He rolled over and smiled. Tony Calucci stretched and felt the warm, comforting flesh sharing the bed with him. Last night was totally unexpected. It all started when he had driven his Porsche down to Waikiki in the hopes of picking up some vacationing house-frau from the mainland just to relieve the tedium of spending another night with the wife.

He was sitting at the bar in the Pacific Beach Club when she walked in, a vision of pure sex. Every man in the bar was instantly erect. Her long tanned legs barely covered by a mini-skirt that bordered on being a wide belt, her ample bosom encased in a halter-top that revealed more skin than it covered. She swayed across the room and stopped at the bar next to Calucci's seat.

Glancing at the bartender she ordered, "Chivas neat with a water chaser."

Her voice was deep and husky, a perfect match to her ravishing dark features. She had just the hint of an accent that Calucci couldn't quite place.

The bartender actually drooled onto the bar as he rushed to pour her drink. His hand shook so bad that he splashed some of the amber liquid onto the gleaming mahogany as he filled the shot glass.

Calucci's jaw dropped. This was a goddess, truly worthy of the chase. He could barely take his eyes off her; they were riveted on her amply revealed cleavage.

She turned and smiled. Then she murmured, "Like what you see?"

Tony Calucci was caught totally off-guard. This girl was out of his league. She wasn't some junior officer's wife out for a good time while she humped to help her husband's career.

"I'm Tareena. Tareena Mustala." She smiled at Calucci and the whole room lit up. "I'm new in town."

Tony Calucci stammered out an introduction. It seemed like she hung on every word he spoke. Lightening flashed from her eyes as an electric current flowed between them. Three drinks later and Tony was telling his life story. Two more drinks and they piled into his red Porsche 944. She directed him to a plush apartment building up in Pearl City, overlooking the sprawling Pearl Harbor Naval Base Complex.

The pair stumbled into her apartment in a maddening flurry of flying buttons and zippers. By the time they fell into her king sized waterbed, Calucci was completely in her power.

12 May 2000, 0042LT (11 May, 1642Z)

The *Sabinyama* glided to a halt. The constant vibration from her slowly turning screw and the laboring of her ancient engines stopped abruptly.

Tommy Clark jerked awake. What was the problem this time? No wonder they got a bargain to ship over on this old rust bucket. A three-day trip was now into its second week. These constant breakdowns were becoming more than an annoyance. His team of missionaries only had a few weeks to build their clinic and get some work done before most of them had to be back for college.

Clark rolled out of his bunk and climbed around and over the clothes, shoes, and other stuff strewn about by the four men who shared his tiny cabin. Outside, the night was warm and dark; a wide band of stars sprinkled from horizon to horizon. Tommy stopped for a moment and gazed upward. The stars down here were so different from the ones he was familiar with. It was one more reminder that this tropic sea was far from the Malibu beaches below Pepperdine.

He climbed up to the bridge just in time to bump into the captain as he stormed out of the bridge house.

"Damn oiler. If I told the Chief Engineer to clean it once, I told him a thousand times," the captain muttered angrily, more to himself than to Clark. "Now the main bearing's gone and seized."

Clark wasn't quite sure what he was talking about, but the grizzled old man was a veteran of forty or so years at sea. If he was in this state, it couldn't be good news.

Clark asked, "This going to delay us long?"

The captain nearly exploded. "If that incompetent idiot really got the bearing seized, we're done. Ain't no way to make the screw go round. I should'a thrown that scum over the side when he first whined his way on to my crew. Damn Flip can't tell a bearing from his ass."

"What do we do?" Clark continued. The thought of drifting out here while the crew tried to repair the ship didn't appeal to him at all.

"We sit here, is what we do. Ain't no choice. We sit until someone comes along that can tow us to the nearest port. Might be a week or two. Ain't much traffic this way. Nearest land is that island over to port. Place called

Nusa Funata. Chart shows it deserted and restricted by the Indonesian Navy.

12 May 2000, 0510LT (1310Z)

Commander Jonathan Hunter greeted the dawn as he did every Saturday he was in port; by racing to the top of Tantalus Mountain and then over to Round Top and back down to the park at the foot of the mountains. It was his favorite run. There was no one to bother him and no way for anyone to intrude. It was a time to think; to rehash the past week and to plan ahead. And a chance to blow the dust out of his system. Hunter always ran alone on this run.

The night was still black when he climbed out of his car at the entrance to Tantalus Park. The houses up on the left were all dark. It was much too early for anyone to be about. The sparsely spaced streetlights pointed the way up the steeply sloping street. The tall blonde man bent to check his running shoes. Satisfied, he reached into the car and grabbed a water bottle before locking the vehicle.

He headed up the road with an easy loping stride. The first couple of miles were steep city streets. His legs were tight and his lungs burned from the exertion. The street snaked back and forth as it wound its way past some of Honolulu's most exclusive addresses. Somewhere a dog barked in protest at having his sleep disturbed.

By the time Hunter had run a couple of miles, he was warmed up and easily shifted to a faster pace. Up this far, the houses gave way to dense forest. The sharp scent of eucalyptus invigorated his lungs. He raced at top speed, up the center of the dark road. Except for the stars dancing through the leaves, he might be running in a cave.

He didn't get to do this often enough. It seemed like he was spending thirty hours a day on the boat. There was always more to do than he had time for. Peg, his wife, only half joking called the sub "his mistress" or when she was really exasperated, that "black bitch." But, to be fair, he had trained his entire life for just one purpose, to command a nuclear submarine. And now he commanded the *SAN FRANCISCO*.

The eucalyptus abruptly gave way to rainforest at the ridge top. Koa, wild guava, and mango trees were washed by a gentle warm mist pulled from the Westerly winds as they were lofted up over the Ko'olau Mountains.

It always seemed there was something demanding his immediate attention. The crew and young officers to train, making sure the never-ending maintenance was up-to-date. But lately the problem seemed to center more and more around one man. Ever since Captain Calucci had taken command of the squadron, he seemed to go out of his way to make life hard for Hunter and the *SAN FRANCISCO*. Hunter had seen Calucci's type before; the ones who would do anything, walk over on anyone, to move up the chain. Calucci was determined to make Admiral, and he didn't care who got hurt along the way.

Sweat poured from his brow as Hunter raced along the ridge road connecting the two peaks. The road swung around a sharp bend and plunged down off Round Top. He suddenly emerged from the rainforest when the road made around a sharp left turn. A sharp right and the road was clinging to the edge of a steep slope. The mountainside fell away sharply to the Moana Valley, a thousand feet below. The panorama of Honolulu from the Ko'olaus, past Diamond Head, to Pearl Harbor, never failed to take his breath away. Hunter always tried to time his run so that he arrived here as the first rays broke over the mountains and painted the Honolulu skyline with gold and rose.

Times like these were meant to be savored. Hunter slowed his pace to a jog for a few seconds. A warm breeze came up from the valley below, heavy with the scent of plumeria and bougainvillea. A couple of rain clouds skirted around Koko Head, watering the gardens over at Hawaii Kai. He could just make out a large white cruise ship heading toward the passenger terminal on Sand Island with another load of tourists to fill the coffers down on Waikiki.

Hunter ran down the road as it circled the slope. Punch Bowl came into view. The bright green lawn divided by row upon row of crosses. On down the slope he ran until he was back on city streets. Traffic was starting to pick up, it was time to be a little more careful.

What to do about the boat? The crew couldn't take much more of the constant criticism from the Commodore before it seriously affected their morale. He had to get them away from Pearl and Calucci before the man did real damage. But how? He had volunteered for every mission that came up, no matter how boring and trivial. Calucci's answer was always the same. *SAN FRANCISCO*'s crew wasn't ready yet. They had to get past the next in a never-ending series of inspections.

Hunter turned the last corner. He could see the car, just where he had parked it an hour ago, a couple of blocks up the street.

He would try again Monday. He would plead for a chance to go up to the Northwest and trail one of the boomers coming out of Bangor. It wasn't much, but at least it would get his team to sea.

Hunter stopped by the car, his lungs heaving as he pulled in great gasps of air. He bent over to unlock the car door.

Something was terribly wrong. The world was spinning at a tremendous rate. His vision closed in to narrow dark tunnel. It felt like he was on a carousel at Mach 3. The ground rushed up to meet him just before everything went black.

Hunter didn't know how long he lay there. It couldn't have been more than a few minutes. He clung to the car, slowly pulled himself upright. What had happened? What was wrong with him?

He carefully opened the car door and plopped into the driver's seat. He held the steering wheel in an iron grip as he fought to control his racing heart. The dizziness slowly ebbed away until he felt almost normal. His hands shook so bad that it took both hands to insert the key in the ignition. The drive home would be difficult. Thank God the roads would be almost empty.

Hunter had no idea what he would do next, but he knew that he wasn't going to go to the Navy doctors until he found out what the problem was. No one, not a power hungry Commodore nor a well-meaning Navy doctor, was going to take him off his beloved boat. The crew needed him and he was going to make sure he was there.

Maybe the civilian doctors up at Kaiser Permanente could take a look and give him a pill or something.

5

---

15 May 2000, 1321LT (2121Z)

"We're saved!" Nan Badgett yelled out.

The pert redhead jumped to her feet and pointed out across the mirror flat water toward the yellow, hazy horizon. The sun, sitting high in the Western sky, burned down unmercifully, turning the old tramp steamer into an oven. The missionaries had long since learned that the wheezy old air conditioner did nothing more than stir the torpid air. A ragged tarp hanging across the fantail afforded some meager shade, and the futile hope of catching any possible whiff of breeze.

Tommy Clark slowly pulled himself up and stared in the direction that Nan pointed. The forbidding bulk of the island, Nusa Funata the captain had called it, loomed closer each hour. Close enough to plainly see the sharply jagged rocks jutting out into the water from the nearly vertical volcanic mountain. Tommy was entertaining visions of being shipwrecked on a desert island, a modern day Robison Crusoe, when Nan shouted out and pointed in the opposite direction.

Sure enough, there, just rising above the horizon, he could make out a warship steaming straight toward them. At first Tommy could only see the high masts and antennas; then the bridge and superstructure. More and more of the gray ship became visible as it raced toward them. Ominously, the big cannon mounted on the middle part of the ship swung around until it was aimed directly at them. Surely the warship wasn't going to shoot. Why would anyone waste time shooting at this old helpless rust bucket. They weren't a threat to anyone.

As the warship charged toward them, Tommy Clark could make out the Indonesian flag hanging listlessly from the mainmast. He breathed a quiet sigh of relief.

"Relax, Nan," he whispered. "The Indonesian Navy is here to rescue us."

Still, the big cannon swung slowly, always aimed directly at them. Tommy could almost feel a bull's-eye painted on his chest.

Finally the great gray warship pulled alongside and slid to a halt only 100 meters from where they bobbed helplessly. A man standing bridge wing raised a loud-hailer to his lips and called out, "Ahoy there. This is the Indonesian warship *Jalawal*. You are in restricted waters. You are forbidden to be here. You are under arrest and your ship is impounded. Stand by while we take you in tow. We will open fire if any attempt is made to escape."

Tommy looked up at his boat's pilot house just in time to see the old captain step out with his hands raised above his head.

20 May 2000, 0900LT (1700Z)

Jon Hunter shook his head ruefully. The Monday morning call to hustle over to SUBPAC for a pre-mission briefing was as a complete surprise. Even more surprising, only he and Fagan were allowed to attend. But a mission, any mission, was an answer to Jon Hunter's prayers. Finally, something real, something to test his crew and prove they were as good as anyone.

The small Special Compartmented Information Facility, the SCIF, briefing room was almost empty when Jon Hunter stepped through the heavy vault door. Rear Admiral Mike O'Flannigan, COMSUBPAC, occupied the seat at the end of the small wooden table. Physically a big, florid-faced Irishman, Mike O'Flannigan had a reputation as both a deep strategic thinker and a superb tactician who really cared about his men.

The Chief of Staff, Capt Sam Hughes, sat at his right, chewing on the inevitable unlit cigar. The only other person in the room was the SUBPAC Special Operations Officer.

O'Flannigan jumped up and bounded across the room to grab Hunter's hand. "Jon, bet you're wondering what's going on," he said in his deep baritone.

"Yes, sir," Hunter answered, flexing his fingers to get some blood flow restored after O'Flannigan's bear-like grip. "I'm hoping this is better than a couple of weeks upkeep and a 3M inspection."

Sam Hughes spat out the well-chewed cigar remnants and chuckled, "Careful what you wish for Commander. You may find this interesting, but probably not fun."

He waved toward the briefing officer. "Let's get started. Time is short here. First off, everything said here is Special Compartmented Information, strictly need to know. No one outside this room is cleared to know the purpose of this mission."

The Special Ops Officer began his briefing. He flashed a slide up on the small screen and spoke, "Essentially, one of the "three letter agencies" has caught wind of someone buying several shipments of specialized laboratory equipment and smuggling it into Indonesia. The equipment; incubators, sterilizers, containment hoods, and the like, is ideal for developing biological weapons."

He flashed up another slide, this one with pictures of several men, some dressed in lab coats, others in ill-fitting suits. The pictures looked like they had been taken without the subject knowing he was being photographed.

"At the same time, several top biological weapons experts from the Middle East and the old USSR have dropped out of sight. What links them together is that they all worked on weaponized smallpox."

Another slide flashed up. This one was the outside of a large red-brick building. It looked like a university classroom.

"And just to make things really interesting, someone broke into the Australian Research School of Biologic Studies. All that was missing was some genetic material derived from some mousepox research. Doesn't sound very threatening until you understand that the material makes the pox resistant to all known vaccines."

The screen went blank.

Capt Hughes spit out his cigar and growled, "It all adds up to give some very high level people some very sleepless nights."

"I don't need to tell you that Indonesia is the home of the world's largest Muslim population," O'Flannigan grunted. "And with the current political unrest there, it is extremely volatile. We have some very dubious HUMINT that points toward a small, uninhabited island in Indonesia called Nusa Funata. You are to go in and check it out. Your cover, for what it's worth, is to be the ESSEX Strike Group's eyes."

Hughes added, "Given the classification and the sensitivity of this information, you are not to brief anyone on your crew until well after you are underway. And nobody is to know anything about possible biological weapons. Ever."

24 May 2000, 1830LT (25 May, 0230Z)

Jon Hunter walked down the long cement pier. They would get underway this evening. On Monday the place had been in lazy tropical torpor. Now the pier fairly hummed with excitement. A lot had been accomplished in the ensuing week, but a lot remained to be finished before SAN FRANSISCO could slip her mooring lines.

The crew worked around the clock for the last three days to get the boat underway. Trucks and forklifts bustled up the pier to stack pallet after pallet of stores. Every carton was laboriously hand-carried from topside to its storage locker somewhere deep in the bowels of the boat. Every piece of onboard equipment was checked, groomed, calibrated, and rechecked.

The crew and the wardroom officers had been told that they were heading out on weekly ops, but the added stores and locked canisters had not gone unnoticed. You just didn't need that many groceries for a week at sea.

The SEAL Team loaded their complete combat stores on Wednesday. Four torpedoes were off-loaded, replaced with lockers filled with weapons and explosives, as well as the myriad of other gear the SEALs would need.

As the sun was descending over the Wainea Mountains, Captain Calucci summoned Hunter and Fagan to his office. Together, the pair took the short, brisk walk down the waterfront to the historic headquarters building overlooking the submarine piers and the vast Pearl Harbor complex. From Calucci's ornately paneled office Dick O'Kane, Mush Morton, Gene Flukey, and a host of other heroes of the great submarine battle of World War II had left to face death. Some returned to report victory, too many stayed on eternal patrol.

As Hunter and Fagan entered the office, the large picture window behind the Commodore framed the sun sinking below the Wainai Mountains in a glorious splash of vibrant oranges, reds, and gold. Calucci did not rise from behind the ornately carved koa wood desk to greet them. He merely grunted and waved them toward two straight backed chairs arranged in front of his desk. Hunter couldn't help but think of respondents before the royal throne.

Calucci dispensed with any pretense of the normal pleasantries and immediately began the briefing. "Let's go over this one more time. SUBPAC is all over me to make sure you don't screw this up."

He idly knocked his large gold Naval Academy class-ring against the gleaming wood. It was a very unsubtle reminder that Hunter was not part of "the club" and Calucci fancied himself as part of the inner circle.

Calucci once again reviewed their mission, emphasizing, for the thousandth time, the need for absolute security. "We have to find out what is happening on that island. If the intel reports are even close, we are playing with fire."

Hunter nodded and watched the Commodore as he ranted on.

"I don't mind telling you, you and your crew are certainly not my first choice for this run. If I had anyone else, I would send them. But you're it."

He fairly growled as he said, "Just the hint of this op getting out and I'll fry you all. There are security leaks all over this island. That's why only you, my ops officer, and I know anything about it. If word of this gets out, you caused the leak."

Underway from Pearl Harbor was set for 0100 with no prior notice. There would be no radio traffic to minimize prying eyes seeing the operation and to allow *SAN FRANCISCO* to be submerged and well away from the islands before dawn discovered her empty berth.

Calucci had no new information, only a rehash of what they all knew. The meeting was mercifully concluded.

Hunter and Fagan rose to leave. Calucci chose not to walk out with them or to wish them luck. Hunter could feel Calucci's baleful eyes burning into his back as he strode out of the office.

As they walked back toward the boat, Bill Fagan was trying to figure out all the millions of details of trying to get SAN FRANCISCO to sea without being discovered. The one thing that he just couldn't answer was the need for tugs. He rubbed the late afternoon bristle on his chin.

With a 0100 underway, they would need the tugs tied up alongside by at least 0015, to allow time for main engine warm-up. They needed to use them for the underway, but arranging for them was a dead give away. How were they going to get around this?

SAN FRANCISCO's huge main turbines needed to be carefully brought up to operating temperature before they were ready to push the big sub through the water. Much like a turkey slowly roasting on a spit, they were turned as they were heated by steam from the reactor until they were thoroughly and evenly warmed. Failure to successfully complete this delicate procedure could result in the turbine blades hitting the casing and sending deadly shrapnel around the engine-room. The problem, though, was that her engines were so powerful, if she was not restrained by the combined power of the tugs; she could rip the bollards out of the pier or snap the doubled Kevlar mooring lines during the delicate main engine warm-up. Older classes of submarines had a clutch installed that allowed for disconnecting the shaft and screw from the main engines, but they lacked the immense power of the LOS ANGELES class. A clutch powerful enough to withstand her tremendous torque would not fit within the confines of her hull, so the decision had been made to forgo the convenience.

"What is it, XO," Hunter asked. "I hear the gears grinding."

"Tugs, Skipper".

Hunter hesitated, nodded, slowly rubbed his chin, and then said, "Let's do this without tugs. We can't afford to announce our underway, particularly in the middle of the night. You've listened on harbor common before."

Both knew that anyone with a marine-band radio within twenty miles would know everything happening inside the harbor by listening to all the radio racket.

They rounded the corner of the headquarters building and walked down the waterfront, past the piers that were temporary homes to *SAN FRANCISCO*'s sisters. Most of the berths were empty. The few boats left from the repeated fleet down-sizing's of the last decade were out on missions.

"OK, Skipper, what are you thinking?" Fagan asked.

"Well, Bill, look at it as innovative ship handling. Let's do it the way the whaling ships did, capstan and lines."

Fagan flinched, "But, Skipper, that's never been done on an *LA* class before. And those whaling ships didn't have a sonar dome to worry about." He didn't need to add how much was at risk if they drove the sonar dome into the pier.

Hunter responded, "We've never been bothered by the fact something hasn't been done on a *LOS ANGELES* class before. Besides, we have the outboard."

Hunter referred to a small retractable and trainable electric motor mounted in *SAN FRANCISCO*'s aft ballast tanks, used to swing the stern around or for emergency propulsion if the main engines failed.

They stopped and sat for a few minutes on a picnic table under the palm trees behind the SUBASE theatre. *SAN FRANCISCO* lay just a few yards away, attended by scores of scurrying sailors. But here was a small, quiet oasis away from the hustle and bustle. The perfume wafting from the dense growth of plumeria behind the old SUBASE Officer's Club enveloped them with the peace of a warm Hawaiian evening.

Taking a scrap of paper out of his pocket, Hunter began to draw, "We'll use simple vector arithmetic...."

LCDR Fagan wasn't entirely convinced but took the scrap of paper and said, "OK, Skipper, I'll brief the line-handlers and put some of the SEALs on the piers to take in the lines."

He didn't need to add how ticklish he felt this idea was. If the boat slid even a couple of feet forward by too strong a pull on the capstan, she would hit the coral and damage the sonar dome. Too much use of the outboard would pull the stern out and push the bow in to the pier, again damaging the sonar dome.

Hunter stood and walked the short distance to the *SAN FRANCISCO*, "Don't see any other choice, do you?"

26 May 2000, 0325LT (25 May, 1925Z)

Mjecka stared at the prisoners.

How dare the infidels parade through Allah's land, bringing blasphemy with them. The young males would pay with their lives. But the uncovered houri females. Didn't the Prophet teach that it was every warrior's responsibility to make them show proper respect, and impregnate them with the next generation of Allah's warriors.

Mjecka grabbed himself and smiled at the red head. *She was the one. The first to feel the real power of Allah's warriors. One of the promised seventy virgins, but delivered before paradise.*

He strode across the room and grabbed the young *houri* by her blasphemous uncovered red hair. He could feel the blood rushing to his manhood. This would be very good; and maybe when he was done he would share her with his friends.

Nan Badgett screamed in fright. The awful, ugly guard, the smelly one with the rotten teeth was trying to drag her off. There was no mistaking his intentions, he meant to have his way with her.

The young missionary lashed out with all her strength, trying to kick and punch her way free. Mjecka laughed easily at her futile efforts as he dragged her toward the door. Tommy Clark jumped up and rushed across the narrow space, fists clenched and ready to strike out to protect her.

Mjecka chortled as he swung his AK47 around. The barrel caught the young missionary leader squarely on the chin. He spun the heavy assault rifle around and slammed the butt into Clark's mid-section. Clark fell to the deck, groaning with pain. Tears ran down his cheeks, more from the frustration of not protecting Nan than from the pain roaring out of his stomach.

Mjecka dragged Badgett out the door and across the narrow passageway, into a small room. He reached up and snapped on the lights. *Light was important. The houri must see the sword of Allah before he penetrated her with it.*

The terrorist grabbed Badgett's blouse and ripped it off. She stood there, futilely trying to cover her breasts. He nodded toward her pants. She screamed loudly and backed further into the tiny room. Mjecka lashed out with his right fist, smashing into her face and knocking her to the deck. He reached down and grabbed her pants, pulling them off in one stroke.

Badgett tried to roll into a ball in the corner, but somewhere in her mind, she knew the inevitable was going to happen.

Mjecka unsnapped his pants and let them drop to the floor. He grabbed himself as he stepped toward the naked, cowering *houri*. He kicked her legs apart and knelt down. It was time to do Allah's work.

"What are you doing, you stupid fool!" Captain Balewegal kicked Mjecka, knocking him away from the prisoner. "When Admiral Suluvana finds out about this, you will wish your mother had consorted with camels."

25 May 2000, 1930LT (26 May, 0630Z)

The sun was just an afterglow to the leeward side of the islands, out beyond Barbers Point. *SAN FRANCISCO* lay quietly alongside the pier, her rounded black shape looking vaguely out-of-place, a creature of the open ocean held captive by the lines reaching to the pier. The brown-green harbor water lapped just a few feet below the deck, hiding most of her massive bulk. The large sail rose imposingly from the deck with wing-like fairwater planes jutting from either side. The only external way to separate *SAN FRANCISCO* from her sisters was the large white "714" attached to the after surface of the sail and the blue banner laced to the brow rail with the large ship's seal and "USS SAN FRANCISCO SSN 714" lettered across it in white letters. Soon these trappings would be stowed below. *SAN FRANCISCO* would be indistinguishable from any other *LA* class sub.

Hunter and Fagan dodged trucks and forklifts to wind their way to the boat. A group of six SEALs carried the last of their gear onboard. Seaman Martinez, one of the most junior men on the crew, brushed by, hands full of boxes. His hands full and not being able to salute, he was flustered, but settled on nodding acknowledgement of the two officers.

Hunter called out, "Martinez."

The young seaman stopped in his tracks.

"How is your girlfriend doing?" Hunter inquired.

Martinez stammered, 'Better. A lot better. Docs up at Tripler say she'll be able to come home in a few weeks."

Hunter clapped the young man on the shoulder and said, "Glad to hear it."

Fagan shook his head. It was amazing how Hunter could keep track of every crewmember's problems, even at times like this.

Topside was rigged for underway. The lifelines, deck lights and all the other paraphernalia were safely stored below decks.

The IMC blared "*SAN FRANCISCO* returning" in the traditional announcement the Captain was back onboard.

Lieutenant Jeff Miller crawled up through the hatch and reported that all was ready for underway.

"Skipper, most of the four hour prior to underway items are done. We are on reactor power. The shore power cables have been removed. The Navigator is reporting some problems with ESGN settling out, but he expects the Schuler oscillations to be adequately damped out by twenty-four hundred, in time for underway. Pre-underway brief in the wardroom in twenty minutes. The Weapons Department is ready to get underway."

"Thanks, Weps. Have the Nav report if he has any more problems. I'll be in my stateroom," Hunter said as he walked to the Forward Operations Compartment Hatch.

The thick rubber acoustic tiles covering *SAN FRANCISCO*'s exterior added a springiness to his step while the gritty black non-skid paint held Hunter firmly to the rounded hull. He dropped through the open hatch and slid down the vertical ladder to the deck below. The narrow passageway led directly to his stateroom and then, beyond, to the control room.

"XO, there's still some stuff we need to talk about," Hunter called through the doors to the shared head that separated his stateroom from the XO's.

Bill Fagan stepped through and took a seat at the small settee that served as the outboard bulkhead of the closet-like CO's stateroom. Hunter remained seated at the small fold-down desk that made up most of the after bulkhead.

The wood-grain Formica-paneled stateroom was a study in compact placement. All of the necessary facilities for the Commanding Officer to live and conduct the day-to-day operations of the complex ship were clustered in easy reach. The settee folded down into a narrow bunk. A large, heavy safe containing classified material and papers sat above the fold-down desk, while the space below the desk contained drawers. Just outboard of the desk were several small electronic panels that displayed vital functions from the ship's systems. Also included was a telephone handset that allowed him to communicate with key stations around the sub.

"Skipper, sure looks like a mission for the books, doesn't it?" the Bill Fagan said as he flopped down onto the upholstered seat.

Hunter glanced up from reading the message boards and nodded, "And my last in the Navy. Wouldn't expect it to be run-of-the-mill. My retirement papers came in today's mail, effective upon relief." He paused. "Any word on naming my relief?"

"Nothing official, but scuttlebutt over at SUBPAC has someone in the next Prospective Commanding Officers Class getting the nod. So, you've made up your mind?" answered Fagan.

"It's time to go," Hunter sighed. "I want to be there as the girls finish growing up. I've already missed too much.

Hunter slowly shook his head, "When I started this business, we were deep in the Cold War. We were scared, but we knew the mission."

He removed his reading glasses and wearily rubbed the bridge of his nose.

"Now it's worse. At least then we had a threat that we could see. We knew that their leaders were logical. Now it's all these terrorist groups and religious fanatics. Don't even know where it's coming from." Hunter sighed. "I don't mind telling you that I'm scared."

After a pause to change topics, Hunter said, "Anyway, we need a list of the problems and how to deal with them. The first thing that comes immediately to mind is security. I sure didn't like what the Commodore was saying about possible security leaks here on the Islands. The group that knows the total picture is small; you and I on the boat, the Commodore at the Squadron, Admiral O'Flanagan and his special intelligence officer over at SUBPAC.

"The larger risk is someone piecing information together. There's not much more that we can do about hiding our underway. I want to dive as soon as we are clear of the buoy Papa Hotel. We'll then head due south for a day before we start to head west. SUBPAC is bringing *CHICAGO* around to delouse us. Anything after that, we'll just have to deal with as it comes along."

Hunter stood and rummaged in his safe. "Let's not brief the wardroom on any part of the operation until we are submerged. Until then, they'll think that this is just another weekly op. We've done enough exercises with the SEALs so the crew might buy it for a little while. The Navigator, communicator and the leading radioman will have to be told something about what to expect, at least where we are headed. Let's get them in the wardroom right after the pre-underway briefing."

"OK, Skipper, I'll set that up," the XO acknowledged.

Hunter continued, "And remember, XO, nobody's to know about the smallpox. That's the really important thing. Remember the SUBPAC briefing. They think the terrorists stole a genetically engineered form from some Australian research lab. A very deadly new cousin to smallpox with no known vaccine. A real panic in the making if any word leaks out. Even to the crew and even after we are underway."

Just then the Weps knocked and stuck his head past the dark blue curtain covering the doorway and reported, "Excuse me, Skipper, XO. All pre-underway checks, up to two hours before departure, are done. The ship's divers have completed their security swim of the hull and the maneuvering watch team members are all mustered in the wardroom for the briefing. Nav says the Schulers are dampening as he expected."

6

Hunter and Fagan walked down the ladder to the Middle Level Operations Compartment passageway. Not much more than shoulder width wide, it was the sub's real center of life. The chiefs' quarters, commonly called the goat locker, and the ship's office were at the forward end. Along the port side of the passageway were the crew's berthing and the tiny dual-purpose signal ejector/Doc's office space. The access to the officers' staterooms and the wardroom was along the starboard side.

The deck was actually the top of a hydraulically operated ramp that lifted up to mate with the upper edge of the forward hatch. When weapons were being loaded, two-ton torpedoes were gently lowered down this ramp to the torpedo room on the lowest deck.

The passageway ended with the crew's mess. Both the crew's mess and the wardroom were really multi-purpose spaces, eating facilities for the crew and officers, as well as a place to study or relax. Both served as meeting spaces for training and briefings.

Hunter stepped into the crowded wardroom to a chorus of "Attention on deck!" Everyone sprang from his seat to stand at attention.

"As you were," Hunter said quietly, making his way to the chair at the head of the table, traditionally reserved for the ship's Captain. The seat to his right was the XO's. A steaming mug of strong, black Navy coffee sat on the table in front of the CO's seat, placed there by the cook.

The wardroom was a study of efficient utilization of a limited space. The large table took up most of the floor space. The inboard bulkhead was composed of storage cabinets with a long counter between the upper and lower cabinets. At the aft end of the counter stood a large coffee machine.

The forward bulkhead contained an upholstered bench where the supply officer sat during meals. Navy tradition held that the supply officer was to be available as the target of verbal criticism by the captain if the meal was not up to his liking. There were numerous sea stories of submarine captains who felt that verbal abuse was not adequate and had found this arrangement of seating convenient for throwing the offending food item at the responsible supply officer. There was a gouge in the Formica above the bench that legend held was the result of a rather heavy gravy boat being heaved by one of the Commander's dissatisfied predecessors.

Above the bench sat a small locker containing operating manuals, a tiny TV, and a VCR.

The outboard bulkhead was made up of a short built-in Naugahyde couch, more lockers, and a collection of small indications and communications (IC) panels similar to the ones in Hunter's stateroom. Even the wardroom chairs were utilized for storage. Under each seat was a heavy metal locker containing an emergency breathing apparatus for use in the case of fire or other toxic contamination of the sub's atmosphere.

Crowded in the small space were the players who would guide the ship safely out of the harbor. The navigation team, led by the Navigator, LCDR Warran Jacobs, and the leading quartermaster, QMi(SS) Buell, would be taking visual fixes through one of the periscopes and backing that up with electronic fixes from the GPS. The sonar team, led by Master Chief Holmstad, would listen for any underwater indications that could help the OOD. The ship's control party would carry out the OOD's orders to steer SAN FRANCISCO safely out of Pearl Harbor. Even the line-handler supervisors were present. It was important that they all performed as a closely coordinated, well-rehearsed team and that they all knew Hunter's plan for the operation.

Sitting down, Hunter looked around the room, casting a critical eye on each person. He then said, "Gentlemen, we are going to brief the underway. The XO and the Nav will cover the details, but first, I want to say a few words. Right off the bat, let me emphasize the security procedures that we will be following. The idea is to sneak out of here without anybody being the wiser. The Commodore wants to see if it's possible to get to sea without it showing up in tomorrow's Honolulu Advertiser."

Hunter looked down the table at Chief Tyler, the leading radioman. "That means no use of the bridge-to-bridge radios on the bridge and no talking on the harbor common frequencies. If Harbor Control challenges us, we will ignore them. I don't expect this to happen, but it may."

The portly Chief busily scribbled a few notes on his pad, not questioning the unusual procedures.

Hunter continued, this time directing his gaze over at QM1 Buell, "The radars will be off and housed. We will be operating without running lights or the sub ID light. Remember, the goal is to leave Pearl without any fanfare."

Buell nodded.

"The second point I want to make is, although this underway is a little different, by and large, it is similar to night underways we've done before. Pay attention to the XO and Nav, and remember what you've learned."

The assembled group fidgeted restlessly as the Nav stood to speak. They had a thousand questions.

25 May 2000, 2315LT (26 May, 1015Z)

The warm Hawaiian night greeted Hunter as he climbed up to the bridge cockpit. High cumulous clouds scurried across the sky, playing hide and seek with the stars. A quarter moon momentarily peeked out of the clouds to the West, out beyond Barbers Point. It would soon drop below the horizon. No one was visible around the waterfront, except three SEALs over on pier Sierra-Nine and three more here on pier Sierra-Five. Even the normally noisy submarine repair facility across Magazine Loch at Kauhua Point was quiet.

Standing in the narrow bridge cockpit, Hunter and Lieutenant

Commander Sam Stuart, officer of the deck, started the long process of getting the large ship underway. *SAN FRANCISCO* was as graceful as a ballerina in her element, submerged out in the open ocean. Alongside the pier her single screw and rudder, together with her long cylindrical shape, made her very ungainly. Any mishap in inching her seven thousand ton bulk carefully out into the channel's relatively open water could cancel the mission before it even started. It was a real test of their combined ship handling skills.

SAN FRANCISCO was ready to get underway. A two-inch Kevlar and Dacron mooring line was passed from a bollard on the neighboring pier to port, over the rounded bow of the sub, and aft to the capstan positioned above the engine-room. Line-handlers stood at each of the four retractable cleats along the ship's starboard side. The reactor was supplying all the ship's power needs, so the large heavy shore power cables were laboriously manhandled off the ship and the brows removed. The last umbilicals to the shore were severed. She was ready to return to her element.

"All right Eng, let's get this show on the road. Lower the outboard, shift to remote and train to port zero-nine-zero degrees" Jon Hunter said.

"Aye, sir," Sam Stuart acknowledged and repeated the order over the 7MC announcing system to the control room supervisor, thirty feet below in the ship's control room.

The order was relayed to the engineering officer of the watch (EOOW) in the maneuvering room, back in the engineroom. He, in turn, relayed it to a watch-stander at the aft elliptical bulkhead, as far aft as you could get and still be inside the boat. The operating station for raising and lowering the outboard was mounted on the bulkhead just to the starboard side of the massive main shaft. The watch-stander pressed a button that actuated the hydraulic controller. Out in the ballast tank, on the other side of the elliptical bulkhead, the outboard lowered smoothly until it extended four feet below the submarine's hull. A green light flashed at the ship's control panel, telling the helmsman that the outboard was lowered and he had control. He held a switch near his left leg in the "Port" position until the dial indicator showed that the outboard had rotated to a position of "Port 90" degrees. Finally, the Helmsman reported, "The outboard is lowered, shifted to "REMOTE" and trained to port zero-nine-zero."

"Eng, single up all lines," Hunter directed.

"Skipper, we can't," LCDR Stuart reported, frustration dripping from his voice. "The lines-forward phone talker just reported that Weps ordered the capstan line put over line one rather than under. They won't be able to cast off line one with the capstan line in the way. They will have to run it again."

He shook his head slowly. "I don't know what Weps was thinking. Just looking at it, even an idiot could see you can't get a line off the cleat with a taut line over top it."

"What the hell!" Hunter snatched the JA handset. "XO, get topside and straighten this mess out. Talk to me about the Weps after we secure the maneuvering watch."

"Yes, sir. I've just sent the COB forward to take care of it. Five minute delay." Bill Fagan answered.

Hunter could already see men straining to move the line. They unwound it from the capstan, lugged the heavy hawser forward and then manhandled it under line one. When it was rewound around the capstan, all was really ready.

Finally, Stuart ordered, "Single up all lines. Slack lines one, three and four. Hold two." This left a single thread holding *SAN FRANCISCO* to the pier at each cleat. All lines draped loose except line two. It was a spring line. Instead of stretching to a bollard directly across from the cleat, it was stretched from a cleat just forward of the sail, aft alongside the ship, to a bollard directly across from number three cleat. It prevented the ship from moving forward into the mud, coral and stone beach scant inches away from her tender fiberglass bow. Line two was held taut.

"Take a strain on the capstan," Stuart ordered. The line stretching from the capstan, forward to the number one cleat and across to pier sierra nine came taut. Seawater sizzled as it was squeezed out of the line. It groaned under the load. .

Slowly, almost imperceptibly, the bow started to swing away from the pier. The large soft inflatable camel that had been wedged tightly between the bow of the massive submarine and the pier floated free, while the after camel squealed in protest as the force of the ship's pivoting movement was felt.

Stuart pressed the key on the 7MC microphone and ordered, "Start the outboard." The stern of the sub started to move ponderously away from the pier.

As soon as motion to port was perceptible, he ordered, "Stop outboard. Ease the capstan." Slowly SAN FRANCISCO slid into the center of the slip and came to a halt with the gentle restraining force of the still singled lines.

"Train the outboard to port one-eight-zero, cast off all lines and back out into the harbor."

Precisely as the last line slid into the water, Hunter heard a faint rustle behind him and looked back to see Old Glory proudly waving in the glow of the pier lights. SAN FRANCISCO was underway.

The black submarine glided silently out of the pool of light between the piers into the inky blackness of the central turning basin. Sam Stuart used the rudder and outboard to turn her so that she faced the waiting ocean. He ordered the main engines warmed as the few men topside carefully, yet quickly, rigged for submerged operations. Every piece of topside equipment was checked twice. Nothing about the examination was cursory; a rattle caused by a loose fixture or the coke-bottle sound of water flowing over an uncovered opening could mean the difference between being the hunter or the hunted.

The required half-hour seemed to stretch to eternity as they sat rolling in the almost imperceptible swell of the inner harbor. In the maneuvering room, Lieutenant junior-grade Rich Baker stood, observing the throttleman spin the large chrome hand-wheel to open the *Ahead* turbine throttle. Just as the roaring steam rolled the turbine, the throttleman flung the hand-wheel shut and spun the *Astern* hand-wheel open. This process was repeated every minute.

Baker, who had just recently finished the difficult qualification process to be an EOOW, reveled in finally having charge of the engine-room himself. This was great, but he really wanted to be up on the bridge, driving SAN FRANCISCO out to sea. He knew that he would have to spend almost another year of qualifying before he saw that day.

Finally LTJG Baker reported, "The mains are warmed and the bridge has control."

Sam Stuart ordered "Ahead one third, steer course three-three-one," over the 7MC from the bridge.

From thirty feet below, the helmsman replied, "Answers ahead one third, coming right to course three-three-one."

Unlike surface ships, where the traditional spoked wooden ship's wheels were still used; the helmsman's station resembled an aircraft pilot's controls. He had no broad expanse of glass through which to gaze at the horizon. His only means of sensing direction and depth was a myriad of gauges and digital readouts set in a blank steel panel.

The great bronze screw turned, leaving a swirling frothy white wake in the glassy smooth harbor water. The huge black warship slowly gathered speed.

Glancing over the side of the tall sail, Hunter saw they were being escorted by one of the large gray hammerhead sharks that frequented the harbor. The hammerheads had discovered that the shallows of the West Loch were a perfect place to mate and give birth to their young. It glided along effortlessly for some distance before lifting its grotesquely shaped head to gaze emotionlessly at the man-made shark of steel. Then, with a flick of its tail, it dove deep and was gone.

"Looks like we have an escort out of the harbor after all," he said, more to himself than anyone else. "Nice to see the professional courtesy."

26 May 2000, 0135LT (26 May, 0935Z)

From the lanai of his official residence on Ford Island, Rear Admiral Mike O'Flanagan watched *SAN FRANCISCO* glide down the channel. He stepped inside and picked up the red secure phone resting beside his bed and dialed a series of numbers. When he received an acknowledgment at the other end, he simply said, "They are on their way," and hung up.

26 May 2000, 0135LT (26 May, 0935Z)

At an apartment in one of the modern high-rise buildings in Pearl City, overlooking the Pearl Harbor Naval Base a similar call was being placed. This one was placed over normal commercial phone circuits, but hundreds of complex switchings and dead ends made the call untraceable. Half a world away, the information was received with a guttural grunt.

26 May 2000, 0210LT (26 May, 1210Z)

The great black ship glided through the night, past Ford Island and the *ARIZONA* Memorial. The brightly-lit white arching monument served as a constant reminder of the bravery and sacrifice needed to defend this country.

On the port side, a little further down the harbor, was the *NEVADA* Memorial, a small granite marker that commemorated the valor of the crew of that brave ship. They fought to get the battleship underway amid the buzzing hornets of the Japanese bombers and then, mortally wounded by Japanese torpedoes, ran her aground to prevent her sinking and blocking the only ship channel. The unlit memorial, little more than a stone's throw across the harbor from the *ARIZONA* Memorial, was all but forgotten.

SAN FRANCISCO steamed onward, rounding Hospital Point and past dry dock four where the aircraft carrier *YORKTOWN* had been hurriedly repaired so that she could play a decisive role in the Battle of Midway. Then past the beautiful officer's club at Hickam Air Force Base, to be greeted, finally, by the long smooth rollers of the open Pacific.

The ship's slow pitch and roll told experienced sailors that they were once more in deep water.

Jonathan Hunter glanced over toward Sam Stuart, then out toward the open ocean. After a few moments of silently staring at the stars, he thought, *This is what makes it all seem worthwhile. A good ship under your feet, a star-filled night sky over your head, and a sense that you are doing a worthwhile job for your country.*

The clamor of Hickam Air Force Base and Honolulu Airport faded quietly into the distance. The golden glow of Honolulu and Waikiki still filled the view behind them, off to the left. Dark rain clouds obscured the view of the Ko'olaus behind Honolulu. Before them stretched the inky black of the Pacific

Hunter sighed, knowing that Stuart was probably thinking the same thing. "Must be something in the night air," he said, breaking the moment. "We're clear of the channel. Transfer the conn below and dive the ship. I'm laying below."

"Aye, sir," Stuart answered, watching the Skipper's head disappear down the ladder.

26 May 2000, 0310LT (1310Z)

Peg Hunter stood at the shore, quietly watching long after the darkened submarine disappeared around the curve of Hospital Point. Tall and dark blonde, she cut a striking figure under the Hawaiian moon.

Finally, she turned away and walked back to the dark house, her hand grazing along the smooth granite surface of the *NEVADA* Memorial. She longingly remembered all the evenings she and Jon had spent there, watching glorious tropical sunsets over the Wainai Mountains. It seemed that she had spent most of the last twenty years waving good-bye to a disappearing black ship and the man it held.

And then the endless, grinding waiting; never knowing for sure if or when he was returning; fearing every time the phone rang.

The first few years had been the worst. Back then, she was a brand new Navy wife and he was assigned to one of the early Poseidon submarines, one of Admiral Rickover's famous "Forty-one for Freedom." This was the Cold War at its most tense. The Americans and Soviets stood nose to nose, each daring the other to blink. The threat of a global nuclear war was the reality of the face-off. The Poseidon boats were at the very forefront of the confrontation. Their movements were very closely held secrets.

She had worried endlessly every day that he was gone. The worst part was not being able to even send a letter. The only communications were four Family-Grams per hundred-day patrol. Forty-word, rigidly censored radio messages that wives could send. They could contain only good news and every ship in the fleet monitored them. They were not a place to share the intimate thoughts of a wife to a husband. There was no means for a return message. It was like he existed only in a dream.

The loneliness had been almost unbearable. But then she discovered the semi-official submarine wives' organization. Years before, recognizing that they all faced the same fears and loneliness, the wives of each boat had naturally banded together for mutual support. Unofficially led by the captain's wife and the chief-of-the-boat's wife, they helped each other through life's trials, whether it was the broken-down car, the stopped-up plumbing or a sick child. Peg first learned how to survive and then to thrive in this environment. The network of support was comforting and the time spent helping the other wives was fulfilling.

As the girls, Megan and Maggie, were growing up and Jon was advancing to more senior responsibilities, the fears never totally disappeared, always lurking in the background. He was riding the fast attack boats. She knew he was out playing a deadly game of hide-and-seek with the Soviets, but the veil of secrecy prevented him from sharing any part of it with her. She drew some comfort from knowing that the job was important and their sacrifice was maintaining a precarious but precious peace.

There would be no sleep tonight, she knew from long experience. There never was on the nights that he departed. Too much to worry about and no one to share it with. He had told her this was a weekly op, but she knew better. Jon never said a word about it, but she sensed his tension. This was important and probably dangerous. *She was so afraid and so tired of being the always strong, always persevering one; the one that everyone leaned on. Didn't they see how weak and scared she really was? She was the "Captain's Wife" and all the wives depended on her. The young wives, some barely old enough to drive, looked to her for advice and support.*

Peg walked inside, and aimlessly puttered around, preparing for this afternoon's Mah Jongg game. The submarine officer wives made the weekly game a tradition. The clicking tiles and conversations were comforting. They made the time pass.

She would have to be careful, though. Brenda Calucci and several CO's wives were expected. Never could tell who knew what or what they would tell their husbands.

Might as well put on a pot of coffee and bake some brownies for this afternoon. She hoped that she could put up a good front. Her wives would need her.

26 May 2000, 2215LT (1415Z)

Mjecka screamed.

His dark, angular face was contorted by the terrible agony. His only world was a living cauldron of pain. He suffered with all his senses. The white hot flashes filled his vision; the screams flooded his hearing. He even knew the taste of pain.

He had no idea who or where he was, only the constant torment. He screamed again, barely more than a gasp. His strength was waning. Death would soon bring a welcome soothing relief to his agony.

Admiral Suluvana stepped back from the observation window. A thin smile flitted briefly across his dark face. The demonstration had gone well. The wretch in the sealed room was only the first of many to feel his wrath, his power. The group of idiots in Jakarta would bend to his will, at last. Just before they too died.

Dr. Aswal sidled up beside the admiral. "Did you enjoy the demonstration, Admiral? Did it meet your expectations?"

Suluvana turned toward the swarthy little biologist, tearing his eyes away from the window. "It looks promising. You say that he was exposed yesterday?"

"Twenty hours ago." Beads of sweat popped out on Aswal's brow. The admiral's icy glare unnerved him. "He was symptomatic in three hours and incapacitated within six. This new strain is magic. The human interleukin-4 gene we inserted in the virus makes it completely resistant to any vaccine. To think, this came from research for a mouse contraceptive."

The scientist almost smiled. "We simply substituted smallpox for mousepox."

The admiral silently turned on his heel and walked out of the cave. Stepping aboard his private helicopter, Suluvana punched the buttons on his cell phone. When it was answered he began to talk. "All is well at the site. We will have enough for a first delivery in a month. Testing confirms that the product is better than expected. The Australians saved us years of research. The genetically engineered smallpox is more deadly than we thought, far better than that Iraqi camel pox."

Half a world away, deep in the Libyan Desert, Mustaf al Shatar listened to the admiral's report. "Good, very good," Mustaf said. "We must discuss the delivery options. I am looking at demanding a ten billion dollar payment for not delivering the virus. Our Chinese partners agree. It will be most interesting to watch the world leaders trying to bargain on this."

Suluvana grunted his approval. Mustaf's description delighted him.

"Now, what about our guests?" Mustaf asked.

He raged inwardly. *They were so close to delivery, so close to all his dreams, so close to making the world pay for what they did to his family. These amateur idiots risk everything on some stupid do-gooders on a rust bucket tramp steamer! Fools! Must he always be saddled with working through such people? But, it would not be good for others to see him so agitated and, besides, Admiral Suluvana was such a head-strong prima donna.*

"They are comfortable in quarantine. The engine on their ship failed and they drifted to the island. We have them all in a separate facility. They didn't see anything. There is no evidence to link them to us. Their ship developed a most unfortunate leak in deep water when we were towing it for repairs. I'm afraid that it was a total loss," Admiral Suluvana replied, his sarcasm evident through the distortion of the scrambler phone.

7

---

26 May 2000, 0630LT (1630Z)

Sam Stuart closed the lower bridge hatch above him and spun the handwheel. Then he turned to LCDR Warran Jacobs, who had relieved him as OOD, and shouted, "Last man down, hatch secured."

SAN FRANCISCO was ready to return to the deep. The Chief of the Watch glanced at his panels to confirm that all hull openings indicated shut before shouting "Straight board," verifying the Engineer's report.

Hunter turned to the Navigator and ordered, "Officer of the Deck, submerge the ship."

The scripted and well-practiced choreography of diving the submarine was played out. There were no superfluous reports or actions. Every operation was carried out precisely and methodically. Every report was made exactly as it was expected, both in timing and wording. Over a century of submarining taught, sometimes with very bitter lessons, this careful, practiced approach was required to operate safely in this hostile environment.

The Chief of the Watch grabbed the green handle of the diving klaxon and pulled it. The loud "Aoooogha, Aoooogha," blasted through the boat. He yelled, "Dive, dive!" into the 1MC microphone. He then reached up, lifted the protective guards and flipped the switches, opening the main ballast tank vents.

Great geysers of mist and spray shot up from each of the vents as the trapped air that had been holding SAN FRANCISCO on the surface escaped. If anyone had been outside the sub, they would have heard the blast of twelve huge air horns of escaping air. SAN FRANCISCO slowly settled lower in the water. Water lapped over the main deck as it dropped below the surface. Then the rudder disappeared. The great ship slipped beneath the waves. All that was left on the surface was a frothing wake ending abruptly where she had submerged. Soon, even that was gone.

The diving officer spent a few minutes pumping and flooding water to and from various internal trim tanks to balance the boat for submerged running. SAN FRANCISCO was ready to proceed on her mission.

Satisfied with the ship's trim, Hunter ordered, "Nav, steer course one-eight zero true. Ahead Full. Deploy the thin-line towed array. Keep your eyes open for any contacts, particularly submerged ones. CHICAGO will try to sneak up on us sometime in the next twenty-four hours. I expect you to find him before he finds us."

The thin-line towed array was a line of sonar hydrophones that trailed for better than a mile behind the sub. When not in use, it was stowed on a large reel in the after ballast tanks. It allowed the sensitive signal processors of the sonar system to listen over vast distances of the ocean to detect the miniscule noises that differentiated a submarine from the many other noises in the ocean.

Hunter continued, "I'll be in my stateroom. Call me if you detect anything." He turned and stepped out of control.

Hunter and Fagan sat across from each other at the small table in Hunter's stateroom. It was time to review the night's activities. Hunter said, "If the Nav thinks that CHICAGO is out here to play games with us, he will make damn sure that we scour the ocean to find every submerged contact inside a thousand miles. That'll make me feel better than any delousing CHICAGO might do."

Hunter put his coffee cup down firmly and, with heat in his voice, said, "What the hell are we going to do with the Weps? Another screw-up topside. He expects me to recommend him for promotion and selection for XO. Right now, I can't."

"Skipper, he's young," Fagan answered, trying to mollify the agitated Commander. "He's got a lot to learn. Give him a chance, lieutenant fitness reports aren't due until we get back."

With an aggravated grunt, Hunter answered, "Alright, XO. We'll give him a chance. You're the training officer. Take him under your wing and train him. I'll decide on the recommendations when we get back."

"I think I'll check out in control one more time before I turn in," Hunter said as he stood and then immediately sat back down, hard.

"What's the matter, Skipper? Are you OK?" The XO asked, his eyebrows knitted.

"Nothing, just a little dizzy when I stood up. Must be more tired than I thought."

Fagan snorted.

Hunter quickly added, "Now, don't you go running to the Doc with this and getting him all in a lather. He can be worse than my wife with this kind of stuff."

"OK, OK. Why don't you just turn in and get some rest? I'll check in control and then I think I'll turn in, too," the XO replied.

"Thanks, Bill. We are both going to need to stay well-rested from here on out," Hunter said as Fagan disappeared through the curtain.

Damn, now Fagan had seen it. Hunter had been hiding these spells for over a month now. The first one really scared him. Enough that he had gone to a civilian doctor at the Kaiser Permanente Medical Center in Pearl City. The tests were finished last week, but in the rush of preparations for the mission, he had not seen the results.

There had been more spells since the run up on Tanatulus. Just last Saturday, he had returned to the house from a long run out to Ewa Beach and back. He blacked out and only came to moments before Peg returned from shopping. There were more since, but none quite so serious.

The test results would be academic anyway. Hunter knew deeply in his being that something was seriously wrong. But whatever it was it would have to wait until he got back. He knew even more deeply that he had to do his job this one last time. If anyone found out, he would be out of submarines. He must be more careful.

26 May 2000, 1145LT (2145Z)

Through the fog of sleep and fatigue, Hunter heard Warran Jacobs knock on his door and enter the stateroom, reporting that he was relieved as officer of the deck by the Weps. Jacobs also reported they were steaming on a course of one-eight-zero true, at a standard bell and a depth of five-seven-five feet. There were no signs of the *CHICAGO* or any other contact. He heard himself answer, "Very well, Mr. Jacobs," before tumbling back into darkness.

It was mid-afternoon before Hunter aroused. He headed aft for an invigorating hour of working out on the Life Rower and Versa Climber, installed in out-of-the-way corners of the engine-room. This was his effort so the crew could get at least a little exercise on the cramped boat. He then showered and headed to the wardroom in search of a cup of the ever present black coffee.

There was a knock on the wardroom door and HMC Pugh, *SAN FRAN-CISCO*'s Corpsman, stepped in.

"Knew that I would either find you here or back on the Life Rower, Skipper. The XO stopped in to talk to me a little while ago," he opened.

"Damn, I told him not to talk to you," Hunter snorted. "Guess I'll have to have a discussion with him about the penalties for insubordination."

"Captain, this could be serious. How long have you been having these dizzy spells and when do they happen?" Doc asked.

"Not very often, only when I am tired and usually when I stand up," Hunter answered.

"Just dizzy, or does the vision tunnel? Have you ever blacked out?" Doc continued his interrogation. He pulled a blood-pressure cuff from his back pocket and wrapped it around Hunter's arm.

"Doc, you really are worse than my wife. I just got a little dizzy, that's all. Don't you have someone who needs a shot or something?" Hunter retorted angrily. He knew he was lying to the Doc and it bothered him greatly, but what was the choice?

Doc Pugh pumped up the cuff, plugged the stethoscope in his ears and measured the Skipper's blood pressure.

"105 over 70," he murmured. "Low, but normal for you. Resting pulse is 50, strong and robust."

"That's what I said," Hunter grunted. "Everything is normal. I'm fine, maybe just a little tired."

Doc Pugh rose to leave, "OK, Skipper. Just tell me if it reoccurs or gets any worse. You need to ease back on the coffee and get more rest. We'll need to do some tests when we get back to Pearl."

"Yeah, sure Doc. Count on it."

27 May 2000, 0737LT (26 May, 2337Z)

"Our Chinese friend tells us that their agent in Hawaii reports one of the American nuclear submarines made an unscheduled late-night departure," Admiral Suluvana began his brief. "Very unusual."

Across the broad expanse of his desk sat the commanding officers of two of his *KILO* class diesel submarines. They were particularly attentive. The portly little admiral had a vicious temper and would not tolerate even the slightest missed detail. Suluvana was ruthless in his drive to power. A mistake could easily cost a subordinate his life.

The Indonesian Navy recently purchased four modern Russian-built export diesel submarines, courtesy of the Chinese Peoples Liberation Army Navy (PLAN). The crews completed familiarization training in the frigid Arctic Ocean off the Kola Peninsula and then made the long transit down the coast of Europe and Africa, around Cape Horn, and through the Indian Ocean, to Java. They conducted anti-surface ship and anti-submarine exercises while en route. By the time they arrived back home, they were very proficient warriors of the deep.

Two of the four boats were placed directly under Suluvana's command. His official assigned command included responsibility for patrolling the Eastern approaches to Indonesia. The other two were homeported at Banda Aceh, Sumatra, where they could control the Malacca Straits and the Western approaches. His *KILO* submarines were key to the Admiral's much more secret plans. They were the weapons that would swing the balance to him.

"We have information that leads us to believe that this American submarine is on a mission to hamper our activities. Evidently our Chinese spy is quite friendly with the American submariners." Suluvana rose and stepped over to the large chart of the Southwest Pacific and Southeast Asia covering one wall of his large office.

He pointed to two ship cutouts pinned to the chart, one a few inches to the West of the other. "There is also the possibility that either the *ESSEX* amphibious group or the *NIMITZ* battle group may be directed against us. They are both en route for regularly scheduled Arabian Gulf deployments," the admiral continued. "You two are assigned to intercept these ships. You will stop them from entering our sovereign waters using all means at your disposal."

He slapped two areas with his pointer. "You will establish patrols here and here. If any of the American ships get past you, you will report immediately. You will remain undetected at all times. If you detect an American submarine, you will attack immediately. I don't care about surface ships, even the American carriers. Submarines are the real threat. Do not let them past you. This mission has the highest possible classification. Do not discuss it even with your crews."

The two commanding officers rose and left the briefing room to return to their ships. Their duty was clear and they were ready to carry out their orders.

As the large wooden doors swung shut, Admiral Suluvana pulled a cell phone out of his pocket and punched in a well-remembered number. The call was answered on the second ring.

"Mustaf, the submarines are on their way. They will deal with the Americans," Suluvana said.

Mustaf al Shatar answered, "That is good, but we need a back-up plan. I've put something in motion in Pearl Harbor, just in case your submarines fail. We will hit this Hunter where it hurts. We will take his family, then see what he does. My people will not fail."

27 May 2000, 0243LT (1243Z)

Warran Jacobs reached for the black JA handset. He pushed the button, energizing a buzzer in Hunter's stateroom. "Captain, Officer of the Deck. Sonar reports a narrow-band frequency on the thin line towed array. Ambiguous bearings are three-four-one and zero-one-nine. Designated sierra two-one and sierra two-two. Frequency equates to a reactor coolant pump line from *CHICAGO*. I have stationed the section tracking party and have a line of bearings. Coming left to two-seven-zero to resolve bearing ambiguity."

Jacobs leaned over the navigation plot, reading the information that his watch team was busy updating. The quartermaster was feverishly plotted each new bearing line as it was called out of sonar. The fire control technician analyzed the same information on the attack computer. The control room hummed with activity.

When sonar detected a contact on the towed array, the relative bearing of the noise signal could be from either side of the array. There was no way to immediately tell which side the contact was on. Therefore, there were always two different possible locations for the contact. The only way to resolve the ambiguity was to maneuver the ship and see where the contact showed back up. The problem was the array acted like a whip behind the sub. During, and for several minutes after a turn, the array was bent, so any signals were meaningless. Frequently, when the array was finally straight again, the signal would be gone. The search had to begin all over again.

Seated at his desk, Hunter digested the report. This would be a good test for the crew, a rare chance to use their skills against another boat.

"Very well, Officer of the Deck. Station the fire control tracking party. Be on the alert for any other contacts in the area. I will be right out," he answered.

As Hunter walked the few steps into the control room, he could hear the muffled bustle of the crew scurrying to their battle stations.

"Steady on course two-seven-zero. Sonar, report when array is stable," Bill Fagan, the fire control coordinator, muttered into his headset while directing the fire control tracking party.

Hunter saw the fire control party had been manned in just under two minutes and was attacking the problem.

Seaman Martinez brushed by, rubbing sleep out of his eyes, hurrying over to the ballast control panel, donning a sound powered phone headset to be the control room phone talker. The control room was calm and quiet despite the crowd of people trying to do their jobs.

Not bad, they are getting 'with the program', Hunter thought as he stepped up on to the periscope stand.

"Coordinator, sonar, array will be stable in five minutes," the sonar supervisor answered Fagan.

Fagan turned toward Hunter and quietly murmured, "Captain, sonar reports five minutes to array stable. The contacts are sierra two-one last bearing three-four-four and sierra two-two last bearing zero-one-six. Frequency equates to *CHICAGO*'s reactor coolant pump line. No other contacts. No contacts in previously baffled area."

Hunter responded "Very well, Coordinator. Any sign that *CHICAGO* has contact on us?"

"No indication, the frequency was stable right up until we turned. We should know for sure as soon as the array is stable," the XO answered.

The sonar supervisor reported, "Coordinator, sonar, the array is stable, integrating."

The array had settled out straight behind the sub again. The system began gathering data on the new course. It automatically integrated all the signals it received over a period of time so that it could maximize sensitivity and separate real contacts from random background noise. The system was so sensitive it would detect signal levels much weaker than the surrounding sea noise and several orders of magnitude below what the best sonar man could hear.

"Coordinator, sonar, regain of sierra two-one. Best bearing three-five-zero. Resolved ambiguity to the Northwest . Attempting to go into ATF on sierra two-one. No other contacts."

Fagan murmured into the phone, "Sonar, Coordinator, aye," and then announced to the fire control party, "Ambiguity has been resolved to sierra two-one bearing three-five-zero. Drop sierra two-two. Going into ATF on sierra two-one."

ATF, the automatic target follower, allowed an electronic tracker to follow the contact automatically as it moved through the bearings. It gave the party a continuous update of the bearing to the contact. To do this, it needed a strong, stable signal.

They gathered and analyzed target data for several minutes to determine the general motion of *CHICAGO* relative to them. The process of determining the range, course and speed of a submarine using only passive sonar was a tedious, iterative one. Bearing to the *CHICAGO* and the received frequency were the only real information. Everything else was inferred. Gather bearing and frequency information for five or ten minutes on one course and then change course. Analyze many different possible solutions. Repeat the process until only one solution remained. Hopefully the correct one.

Through all the maneuvering and data gathering, the sub had to be kept at a range where the hunted would not counter-detect the hunter. Preferably, this was at the very edge of the detection range for the hunter's sonar and far back in the target's baffles; that cone behind his screw where it is difficult for him to hear.

This all depended on *CHICAGO* staying on a straight course. If he changed course, a zig, the process had to start all over again. It often took many hours of excruciating attention to all the nuances of the data before having a solution accurate enough to shoot a torpedo. One wrong move in this cat-and-mouse game and the hunter suddenly became the hunted.

After another hour of tracking the *CHICAGO*, Hunter turned to Fagan and Jacobs and said, "Well, we know where she is and what she is doing. No indication that she has found us. Normally I'd like to stay here and play. But we need to get on down the road. XO, secure the fire control tracking party. Officer of the Deck, re-station the section tracking party."

Stepping over to the navigation chart, Hunter checked *SAN FRAN- CISCO*'s intended track, plotted with green tape.

"Track *CHICAGO* as long as you maintain contact. Be alert for any other contacts. Resume course one-eight-zero. When you get to one-five-five West, one-five North come right to new course two-two-zero. The next waypoint will be one-eight-zero West, zero-zero North."

27 May 2000, 2245LT (2145Z)

"We are on schedule for delivery of the first shipment," Mustaf growled into the cell phone. "It has tested much more successfully than we anticipated. All of the test subjects were symptomatic within an hour after treatment. They all terminated by the third day, most after the first. Much better than the natural product."

In his office deep underground, just off Peking's Tiannamen Square, General Liu Pen, the Director of Special Intelligence Operations for the Peoples Republic, listened to the report of his most important asset. "Good, very good. How was the viability of the virus?"

Mustaf answered, "Even better than we expected. It should last indefinitely in storage. Once dispersed, its soil borne half-life is estimated at twenty years."

General Liu Pen was impressed. "Excellent. We must discuss the destination for the first shipment," he answered. "It is my thinking that we should deliver first to the customer who will advertise our wares to our best advantage."

"Where do you have in mind?" Mustaf queried. "Our partners at the manufacturing site have their own ideas of how best to use the initial shipments. They are thinking of a few free samples in the local area."

"I am aware of their desires," General Pen answered curtly. "I am not interested in their petty little problems. We have a much larger game to play. If they get lost in the shuffle, that is too bad."

The spymaster continued, "But, I am thinking that their simple plots and intrigues may be useful. We will make Suluvana and his traitors the sham front for this endeavor. While we will stay carefully in the background. Make that blustering fool of an admiral think that he is actually directing how this will be accomplished. As long as we can maneuver him in the way we want to go, he will remain useful. When we are through, the West will be in shambles. You will have your revenge and China will assume her rightful place in the World Order."

Mustaf replied thoughtfully, "Maybe there is a way to use our impertinent friend. What if his organization became identified with this plot? They would become the most hunted men on Earth."

Liu Pen snorted. It was as close as he ever got to showing humor. "A marvelous idea, my friend. Great minds sometimes think alike. A note will shortly arrive for the head intelligence officer of each of the members of the UN Security Council. It will demand a very large ransom, just as we planned. The added twist will be that the note will be traceable to Suluvana's people. When the attacks begin, he will immediately be blamed."

Mustaf added, "And, of course, since you will be receiving one of the notes, you can aid the investigation."

27 May 2000, 1445LT (28 May, 0145Z)

"The ship will be conducting angles," the 1MC blared, presaging the anticipated submarine roller coaster ride.

"Officer of the Deck, make your depth eight hundred feet with a twenty down," Hunter ordered from his vantage point behind the diving officer.

The deck tilted precariously downward as the depth gauge reeled off the change from 150 feet to 800 feet. *SAN FRANCISCO* slid silently deeper into the depths, without even the sounds of hull creaking or popping.

"At eight hundred feet, sir," reported the OOD.

"Very well. Make your depth one-five-zero feet using a twenty up."

Like a large, playful porpoise, the submarine flew upward, toward the light. They repeated the procedure at twenty-five degrees and then at thirty degrees. At a thirty degree down, the precipitous angle of the deck demanded a firm grip on any available handhold to keep from sliding painfully into the forward bulkhead. A loud crash emanated from the galley, just below the control room, where a locker full of crockery fell open, spilling onto the deck.

"XO, looks like you need to work on the rig-for-sea some more. That crash would have been fatal if we were near someone," Hunter growled. "Have all the spaces stowed again and we'll repeat the angles. We'll keep doing them until we get the stowage right."

Hunter stalked off forward to his stateroom as Fagan began directing the re-stowage work. Keeping the boat shipshape and stowed for sea took on an entirely different importance for submarines than for surface ships. While surface ships were concerned with appearance and the hazards of adrift equipment in high seas, the submarine was also concerned about the noise generated by improperly stowed gear crashing down when the sub needed to conduct evasive maneuvers. A locker falling open and spilling its contents or even a coffee cup falling from a table to the deck could easily be the difference between being detected or silently slipping away.

Jon Hunter often related the story of how he had been counter-detected by a Soviet Charlie class SSGN because a mess-cook had decided to use a hammer to bend over the clips on a TDU can. The tale of the ensuing active sonar dogfight made true believers out of the crew.

28 May 2000, 0430LT (1530Z)

"Captain, Navigator," The 21MC speaker in the CO's stateroom blared. "Just received the fourteen-forty-five Zulu message traffic. It has a message from CHICAGO to SUBPAC. She did not detect us and had no other contacts either," LCDR Jacobs reported from radio.

Hunter was instantly awake. He had just drifted back to sleep a few moments before, after observing the trip to periscope depth. Bringing the ship to periscope depth was the most hazardous evolution a submarine routinely performed. A quiet ship could easily be immediately above them and not detected until they were on their way up. It required immediate action to avoid collision. For this reason Hunter was always in the control room to observe any trip up to periscope depth, just as his mentors had been when he was still a pup.

Hunter left control after ensuring that they were safely alone in this stretch of the South Pacific and fell on his bunk, exhausted. LCDR Jacobs was going to ventilate the sub with fresh air while copying the radio broadcast and verifying the accuracy of his navigation with a GPS fix.

"Thank you, Nav. Looks like the sound-quieting program is working," Hunter replied, before falling into the oblivion of slumber.

Although SAN FRANCISCO conducted many tests and sound trials to make sure that they were as quiet as possible, the best test was still to have another highly proficient sub try to find them. That CHICAGO could not was a comforting affirmation of their efforts. If the CHICAGO couldn't locate them, chances were very good that no one else could, either.

8

Sam Stuart snatched another pork chop from the large platter. "I'm telling you, Nav, it's a fool proof system."

He slapped the chop on his plate and reached for the sweet potatoes. "You can always tell the main course when you first walk in the wardroom, way before the cook serves. Cooks always put the veggie on the table with the salads. Meat is still in the warming oven. Problem is, you don't know what it is and you want to know whether to pig out on the salad or hold off for the meat. Now, problem solved. Just use my Meat Indicator System."

Warran Jacobs looked up, chewing reflectively. He swallowed and said, "OK Eng, prove it."

"Take tonight as a test case. Pork chops. The meat indicator for pork chops is lima beans, always lima beans. There was a bowl of lima beans on the table when we walked in. Applesauce for sliced pork, mashed potatoes for fried chicken. I've got it all worked out."

Bill Fagan joined in. "You could always read the Plan of the Day. I put the menu in it."

Both Stuart and Jacobs looked at Fagan and shook their heads. In chorus, they replied, "Nah! XO, nobody believes the POD!"

The cooks shuttled in platter after platter heaped with steaming hot food. The good-natured banter died as the men shifted their attention to the meal. Gradually the feeding frenzy subsided. Finally, the cooks cleared the remnants of the meal and served up bowls of freshly made ice cream for dessert.

"Well, Mr. Green, that was another fine meal," Hunter commented to the supply officer as he pushed back from the wardroom table. "Where did Petty Officer Swain get the recipe for that clam chowder? It has to be the best in the fleet. Can't say that I've ever had any better, not even when we lived in Maine."

The evening meal was the one time the officers could gather together in a social setting. Unlike surface ships with their separate Captain's Mess, a submarine skipper almost always ate with his officers. His personality determined the overall personality of the wardroom. Jon Hunter had served with both convivial CO's and ones that bordered closely on anti-social. He was determined that his wardroom would be a close-knit, happy, professional group. He frequently likened this concept to "Nelson's Band of Brothers" after Admiral Horatio Nelson's famous group of commanding officers before the Battle of Trafalgar.

"Excepting, of course, your wife's. It's the standard Navy recipe with some of Swain's special secret spices added," Ensign Green responded.

Hunter chuckled, "Sucking up isn't going to help your FITREP, Chop. Anyway, tell Petty Officer Swain that it was especially good. XO, grab the cribbage board. We've got time for a quick game before wardroom training."

Fagan groaned, "Skipper, you beat me almost every night. Don't you ever get tired of the lack of challenge"

Hunter said, "XO, don't give me that. I have it on good authority you were the finest cribbage player to ever come out of Annapolis." Hunter rubbed his chin reflectively. "And, reviewing the game results, we are about even. I kind of suspect that you are letting me beat you lately so I don't rank you below the Nav on the next set of FITREPS."

Bill Fagan pulled the well-worn board and the limp deck of cards out of the drawer as Petty Officer Swain served two cups of espresso. The two senior submariners played their game as the remainder of the officers quietly left to attend to various details of their duties before returning for the evening's wardroom training.

Hunter made it a policy that all the ship's officers gather together every week day evening for an hour of training on some aspect of submarine operations. Each officer got the chance to present his area of expertise and frequent "guest lecturers" were invited from the chief's quarters to cover technical matters or "leadership from the deck-plate level" issues. Discussions were usually lively; always full of new insights and ideas. Tonight's discussion promised to be no exception, with Warran Jacobs holding forth on the subject of close inshore, shallow water emergency ship handling.

Only those officers actually on watch were excused from the nightly training. Jeff Miller was on duty in the control room as the OOD and Rich Baker was standing watch in the engine-room as the EOOW. Together they supervised the complex operation of the boat as she steamed through the lonely depths of this forgotten part of the Pacific.

As the Navigator began his opening remarks, the deck suddenly pitched upward. Coffee cups tumbled down the wardroom table, slamming into the buffet behind Hunter. One managed to roll directly into his lap, thoroughly drenching him with hot liquid. His eyes shot toward the depth gauge on the wardroom bulkhead. It counting toward the surface at blinding speed.

Hunter leaped from his seat and rushed out of the wardroom, bounding up the ladder to control, with Fagan hot on his heels. The up angle increased to an alarming level, better than forty up. The two crawled, hand over hand, gripping whatever piping they could, to reach the control room.

"Weps, what's the problem?" Hunter shouted as he burst through the control room door.

People were clinging to any available support to keep from falling out the back door of control. The depth gauge was roaring through 150 feet, moving so fast that it was nearly unreadable. The engine order telegraph was answering Ahead Full, confirmed by the twenty-five knot speed shown on the pit-log.

"N...n...n...nothing Skipper," stammered the ruffled young lieutenant.

The sub jumped through the surface and, with a stomach-churning lurch, splashed back down. Hunter machine-gunned orders, "All Stop!

Diving Officer, full rise on the stern planes, full rise on the fairwater planes! Fishtail the rudder! Report when ship's speed is less than fifteen knots!"

Chief Tyler, the diving officer reported, "Dive, Aye. Answering All Stop, full rise on all planes, speed two-zero knots and falling. Depth three-nine feet and steady."

Hunter turned to Bill Fagan and barked, "XO, see what damage we have."

Chief Tyler said, "Speed one-five knots and falling."

Hunter immediately ordered, "Answer Ahead One-Third. Rudder amid ships. Raising number two scope."

Hunter needed to get the scope up to see any immediate danger. Fifteen knots was the maximum speed to raise a periscope without bending it over if they slipped back beneath the waves.

There were almost instant and simultaneous replies from the helms-man, "Answers Ahead One Third, my rudder is amid ships," and from Chief Gonzales, the Chief of the Watch, "Number two scope indicates up."

The tenor of their voices and the crispness of their replies told the story. They knew that they had been parties to a significant mistake and they would soon hear about it.

After a rapid 360 degree sweeping look around, Hunter reported, "No close contacts," and followed this with a thorough visual and electronic search. "No contacts." Hunter snapped the scope handles up and swung the control ring to the lower position. He then stepped away from the scope and looked around the control room. No one on the team would meet his gaze.

He inquired sarcastically, "Weps, do you think that you and this motley bunch can get us back down to one-five-zero feet without incident?"

Miller sheepishly nodded his head and meekly said, "Yes, sir." He had slipped to the port side of control and was standing behind Chief Gonzales.

He gave every appearance of trying to hide behind the bulk of the portly chief. He ordered, "Dive, make your depth one-five-zero feet," but did not move from his supposed haven.

After they had settled out at 150 feet and the XO had reported that the only damage was the loss of the wardroom espresso cups, Hunter began the discussion sarcastically, "Alright Weps, a new world's record. Broaching from eight hundred feet. Could you tell me precisely what you and your watch section were doing?"

"Skipper, we were supposed to come from our transit depth of eight hundred feet up to one-five-zero feet in order to clear baffles for the twenty-two-thirty comms downlink. This was in the night orders," Jeff Miller began to explain.

"Chief Tyler and I discussed it and we wanted to practice some high-speed ship handling. We've never had a chance to do it. We decided to come up shallow at a full bell. We just didn't know how quickly she would respond at that speed. I'm sorry."

Hunter replied, "Well, Weps, you hadn't had a chance yet, because this watch-section isn't ready yet. And now you know why I'm always in control when we do this. That up-angle could have seriously hurt people. You could have caused a collision if any body had been up there when you broached. And if you hadn't hit someone and they were up there counting whales, you would have certainly caused us to be detected. As it was, you were just plain lucky."

Turning to Chief Tyler and the Chief Gonzales, he continued, "And I depend on you two, as the most experienced submariners on watch, to advise the OOD to steer him clear of this type of foolishness, not to talk him into it. You're supposed to operate as a team out here and I'm supposed to be comfortable sleeping while you are on watch. Do we understand each other?"

"Yes sir."

30 May 2000, 1630LT (31 May, 0430Z)

The young petty officer stood at rigid attention in the stateroom doorway. "Captain, Quartermaster of the Watch, The Officer of the Deck sends his respects and reports crossing into the territorial seas of Kiribati. Currently steering course two-two-zero, making two-five knots good."

SAN FRANCISCO entered the first of the proliferation of tiny island nations that constituted the South Pacific. Most contained land areas of a few square miles of coral atolls dotted across thousands of square miles of territorial seas. Kiribati lay across both the Equator and the International

Dateline and was made up of several small groups of islands, with the Gilbert's being the largest. Tarawa, the main island and capital, was several hundred miles off to the Northwest .

The sub's planned track brought them within a few miles of the intersection of 180 degrees longitude and zero degrees latitude, the point where the day starts and North meets South. Nav slipped in a slight deviation to the planned great circle route to allow the crew the bragging rights of becoming that rarest of all mariners, a Golden Shellback, someone who had sailed directly through 180 degrees West and 0 degrees North. Hunter believed these traditions were important for crew morale and to keep them in touch with their naval roots. The few miles of extra transit were easily worth the gains in morale.

Master Chief Hancock and XO, the two most senior Shellbacks onboard, were responsible for planning the elaborate ceremony necessary to properly commemorate the occasion and to initiate new Polliwogs into the Royal Order of King Neptune's Golden Shellbacks. A visit by King Neptune was expected to be the highlight of the ritual. Polliwogs, including Hunter, were forbidden to enter the mess deck as it was transformed into King Neptune's throne room.

All was in readiness when Nav proclaimed, with appropriate solemnity, over the 1MC, "USS SAN FRANCISCO is now passing through one-eight-zero West and zero-zero North in the watery realm of His Royal Highness, King Neptune." He then rang the ship's bell once. As the deep tone of the bell died out, sonar reported a contact close aboard on the bow. They also reported hearing underwater communications that sounded like a trumpet salute and the words "All hail King Neptune."

A loud commotion erupted in the torpedo room as Nav announced on the 1MC, "His Royal Highness and All Powerful Sovereign of the Seven Seas, King Neptune, arriving." He rang twenty-one strokes of the bell.

King Neptune, who bore an uncanny resemblance to Doc Pugh with a ratty fake white beard, emerged from the torpedo room dressed in his royal robes of seaweed, wearing his golden crown and carrying his trident. He proceeded at a regal pace to his throne room as the crew paid homage and looked on with somewhat exaggerated deference.

Once seated upon his throne, which looked suspiciously like one of the stainless steel commodes from the goat locker attached to the top of the after most mess table, King Neptune decreed that only Shellbacks be in attendance at his court. All Polliwogs, as the lowest of life forms, were banished to the torpedo room in order to prepare themselves for the rigors ahead.

Each Polliwog was individually escorted by a Shellback sponsor and brought before the Royal Court. Appropriate tests of the mariner's skills and knowledge were given to ensure that the Polliwog was of sufficient caliber to become a Shellback. Any lack of skill or knowledge resulted in the Polliwog drinking deeply of the Royal Truth Serum, an evil-looking concoction the COB had been brewing from secret ingredients for days. After liberal doses of the Truth Serum, each Polliwog was deemed worthy of induction into the Most High Order of Golden Shellbacks and paid homage to King Neptune. This involved kissing his rather rotund and well-greased belly.

The first Polliwog to submit to the testing was CDR Hunter. After proving his maritime skills, although his initial answer to the number of buttons on Nelson's coat cost him a taste of the truth serum, he laughingly paid homage to King Neptune. The King had struck him on each shoulder with the Royal Trident, proclaiming him the newest and most junior member of the Most High Order of Golden Shellbacks. The Skipper reminded the King that the Doc would be responsible for treating any health problems resulting from the truth serum.

9

"Gentlemen, it's time that you know where we are heading," Hunter started the briefing.

The assembled group included all the officers, with the exception of the supply officer who did not have the necessary security clearances. Also attending were Master Chief Hancock, the Chief of the Boat (COB); Master Chief Holmstad, the leading sonarman; Chief Jones, the leading electronics technician; Chief Tyler, the leading radioman and Quartermaster First Class (SS) Buell, the leading quartermaster. This small group, out of the whole crew, were those who had a "need to know."

"To start off, this briefing is classified Top Secret. It is Specially Compartmented Information and is code-worded "Golden Dawn." The code word is classified Top Secret, so don't let it out of this room."

"Nav, show them the first chart," he directed.

LCDR Jacobs removed the sheet covering a large-scale chart of the Southwest Pacific, Oceania, and Southeast Asia. On it, he had laid out a green stripe showing their projected track. Tapping the chart with his pointer, Jacobs explained, "As you can see, we are heading South through the Solomons, then between Papua New Guinea and Australia. We will then transit the Arafura and Timor Seas. We will pass South of Java and then through the Sunda Straits, between Java and Sumatra, into the Java Sea. Our destination is one of the small islands in the Nusa Tenggara Group."

Hunter stepped over to the chart and took the laser pointer. He put the little red dot on a small area on the lower left-hand side. "This chain of islands, East of Bali, is known as Nusa Tenggara, the Islands of the South East. Geographers call this archipelago the Lesser Sunda Islands, distinguished from the Large Sunda Islands: Sumatra, Java and Borneo." He swept the dot over the three large islands. "Nusa Tenggara consists of hundreds of islands, but is dominated by the five main islands: Lombok, Sumbawa, Flores, Sumba and Timor."

"Right here," he said pointing to the North and West of the small green mass labeled Lombok. "This little fly speck is named Nusa Funata. Until a couple of months ago, it was an uninhabited bit of jungle and volcanic rock. Its only claims to fame were some nearly impenetrable coastal mangrove swamps and a reported extensive system of lava caves."

Hunter gazed around the small room, glad to see that they were all engrossed in the briefing. "That all changed with a CIA estimate. They have been keeping tabs on a number of Eastern European and Chinese scientists that had been associated with the Iraqi weapons programs. Several of them went unaccountably missing several months ago. At nearly the same time, a leading Middle Eastern terrorist named Mustaf al Shatar also dropped out of sight. Coincidentally, pirate activities in the Straits of Malacca, up here, which had been on the increase, suddenly stopped altogether. Based on some other HUMINT, the CIA thinks that there is a link."

This was a polite way of saying that the CIA had an intelligence source, a spy. There was no way of knowing how reliable the source was or how close he really was to the operation.

"Two weeks ago, a small freighter carrying a group of thirty US and Australian missionaries from Surabaya on Java to Unjungpandang on Sulawesi was reported missing.

"What ties this all together is some satellite imagery of Nusa Funata where the NRO analysts found signs of significant construction. Uncover the picture, Nav," Hunter continued.

Jacobs removed the cloth hiding the satellite pictures.

Hunter tapped on parts of the series of pictures. "Here you can see what looks like a pier and some storage sheds under construction. Here is a small airfield. This construction around these caves is as yet unidentified, but by the level of work here, they are assessing this as being the major facility. Also note the weapons emplacements. Clearly, someone doesn't want to be disturbed. And this small ship at the pier is identical to the description of the missing one. The next satellite pass doesn't show it."

A murmur of angry mutterings started around the room as the group reacted to hearing of yet another group of innocent Americans held hostage, or worse. They were all too familiar with the frustration of watching helplessly as terrorist after terrorist got away with these kidnappings.

Commander Hunter took a sip from his coffee before he continued. "The Indonesia government denies any knowledge of anything happening at Nusa Funata. As you know, they have been in turmoil for several years now. The military has all but taken over the country while they are trying to put down several different ethnic revolutions. They have also severely increased the restrictions on navigating their territorial seas. They aren't allowing any warships in right now. This is a violation of the right of innocent passage, but that is being argued out at the World Court.

"Our passage will be submerged and doesn't classify as innocent passage, anyway. Operating submerged in their territorial waters is technically an act of aggression. If we are detected, we should not expect a friendly reception. That is why we are taking the long way around. The passage through the Sunda Straits is the best way that we can get in covertly. The passage is deep and wide, hard for them to patrol."

Hunter walked back to his chair and sat. "Our mission is to conduct surveillance of Nusa Funata to determine what is going on. We will be rendezvousing with SEAL Team Three at sea so we can put people ashore for an eyes-on-target look."

He took out a small notebook and started reading off a list of items.

"Weps, start developing the environmental and intel chart for the area. Post it in the regular place, on the bulkhead outside my stateroom, but keep it covered. I want your people and Nav's people to do a search for whatever intel that is available. This is a passive search though. No queries outside the ship. As far as anyone outside this room is concerned, *SAN FRANCISCO* has no interest in Southeast Asia."

Hunter checked one item on the list and then read the next one.

"We will be joining the *ESSEX* Amphibious Ready Group as their support submarine while we are transiting the Solomons. The *NIMITZ* Battle Group will be a day's sail behind them. They are both ostensibly heading for routine deployments to the Arabian Gulf. Along the way, they will be conducting joint maneuvers with the Royal Australian Navy in the Timor Sea just South of Bali.

"If we find what we suspect and the Indonesians won't play ball, they will be in a position to dash through the Bali Straits and conduct amphibious operations on Nusa Funata.

Hunter slapped the notebook shut. "That pretty much covers it. Any questions?" he concluded.

The team was excited. At last there was a plan to strike back.

"Yes, sir," chimed in Master Chief Hancock. "I'm assuming that we have National Command Authority authorization to go into Indonesian sovereign waters as well as their territorial sea. We're able to hide so no one knows we're there. But what about the *ESSEX* ARG and the *NIMITZ* Battle Group? How will they get in?"

Hunter answered, "COB, I'll leave the political decisions to the politicians. I'm just a broken-down old sailor who goes where he's told. I'm pretty certain that if we need them, they'll be there. With or without the approval of the Indonesian government."

Warran Jacobs asked, "Skipper, what are the Rules of Engagement?"

"Standard peace time ROE, Nav. We protect ourselves. We protect US Nationals and we follow International Law. In other words 'red and tight.' Any more questions?"

Rich Baker had been staring intently at the chart. He broke in, "Captain, I don't understand the track. If we are supposed to get to this island as quick as we can, why are we going all the way East to the Sunda Straits? Couldn't we just duck in by Bali, for instance?"

Hunter looked over at the young officer. "Very perceptive question, Mr. Baker. Yes we could. There is one problem, though. The Indonesian Navy has four *KILO* submarines and a credible surface ASW force. Two of the *KILOs* haven't been accounted for in the last couple of weeks. We have no idea where they are. They could be anywhere. If the Indonesians are setting an ASW trap, we have to be very wary. Those straits are too narrow for even someone as quiet as we are to slip through. The Sunda Straits are the only ones wide and deep enough to give a high probability of getting through undetected."

Hunter looked around the room, "Any more questions? If not, that wraps it up. Remember this has all been Top Secret Code Word. Not a word to anyone, not even the rest of the crew."

With those final words, the group broke up in a babble of excited chatter and charged out of the wardroom to resume their duties.

An hour later, Hunter and Fagan met in the CO's stateroom. Hunter sipped his coffee and said, "That ought to give them enough to start some planning. Should also help to quiet some of the scuttlebutt going around the boat."

"Yes, sir. But you sort of skirted around the issues that all those missing scientists were biochemists and that most of them had worked on Saddam's biological warfare projects," Bill Fagan replied.

"That's right," Hunter shot back, "and if you recall those briefings that you and I attended in SUBPAC's basement, no one is to know about the smallpox. If word of that leaked out, we would have a worldwide panic, particularly now that we know how deadly it is and how quickly it spreads. If those terrorists are working on an improved strain like we think, and if they are successful, it could be devastating. Common smallpox was highly infectious and deadly. Millions died before it was finally eradicated. An improved strain is unthinkable."

Hunter opened his large safe and retrieved a small folder. It was conspicuously labeled in large red letters "TOP SECRET, GOLDEN DAWN".

"You remember that outbreak of West Nile encephalitis in Queens a couple of years ago? There was some media speculation that it was a terrorist attack, but that was quickly dismissed."

He opened the folder and scanned down the first few pages. "The CIA and the FBI both were quick to say that there was no indication of any terrorist involvement. This report speculates that it was a trial run for Mustaf's first attack. His people had isolated the virus and tried it out in Queens. Apparently the strain was not virulent enough and the mosquito-borne vector was too slow to satisfy him. Six dead and about a hundred sick before it was brought under control and we are still dealing with occasional outbreaks. After that he apparently switched to the genetically engineered smallpox for faster results."

Bill Fagan interjected, "I remember reading an article somewhere that some Congressman was lobbying to set up some sort of CIA-directed task force to detect and counteract any terrorists attacks, headed up by some sort of anti-terrorist czar. Seemed like nothing ever came of that."

Hunter handed Fagan the folder, opened to a page headed 'Background'. "Well, that's not quite the whole story," the Commander answered. "The task force was set up under the direction of the National Security Advisor. It is very hush-hush. As you can see, the CIA and the NSA are the primary members, but of course the FBI and DIA are involved. They have thwarted several attempts over the last couple of years that no one ever heard of. They are directing this mission. Read through that report. It'll give you some more background."

02 Jun 2000, 1850LT (0650Z)

The red alarm light blinked on a millisecond before the siren started its ear piercing scream. The startled reactor operator leaped up, cutting out the siren with his left hand, while searching his myriad of gauges for the problem.

Smoke had just started to wisp around the maneuvering room door when the reactor technician stuck his head in and shouted, "Fire in rod control!"

The EOOW shouted into the 7MC announcing system "Conn, maneuvering, reactor scram, fire in the reactor control panels! Class Bravo fire in the reactor control panel!"

Fire was the hazard most feared by submariners. There was no escaping it; the only means of survival was fighting it and putting it out before it irreparably damaged the ship. If not contained, the atmosphere would rapidly fill with toxic gases and the smoke would reduce visibility to zero. No one could go outside to get a breath of fresh air or escape the searing heat.

To make matters still worse, this fire was in the very controls that allowed them to extract the nuclear power that they needed to drive them home.

The fire destroyed the control circuits, which, in turn, caused the hafnium reactor control rods to release from their latching arms. Gravity and giant springs drove the control rods into the reactor core, stopping the nuclear fission that provided the heat to make the steam to drive *SAN FRANCISCO*'s massive turbines. The sub's powerful reactor shut down. That left the sub's lead-acid battery as the only power source. It was only good for a couple of hours before it would be completely discharged and the lights would go out. They needed to get reactor power back, and soon.

"Reactor Scram, rig ship for reduced electrical. Fire in engine-room upper level forward, rig ship for fire! Don EABs in the engine-room!" Warren Jacobs, the OOD, yelled into the 1MC General Announcing System microphone.

Seaman Martinez heard the announcement while he was scrubbing pots in the galley. He looked up, wondering if he had heard the 1MC right. The loud "Bong-Bong-Bong" of the general alarm died out. Martinez heard the words on the 1MC repeated.

All around him, the experienced crewmen were leaping into action. He had never seen them move so fast.

One pair rushed to shut off all unnecessary electrical equipment to save every watt of the precious remaining reactor heat. Another group struggled to rig fire-fighting equipment so that the fire teams could combat the blaze. A third group, led by Chief Richey, donned fire protection clothing and emergency oxygen breathing apparatus (OBAs), a self-contained supply of breathable oxygen that was good for about thirty minutes. They would be charging in to the engine-room to fight the fire.

Hatches slammed shut, ventilation dampers swung closed, emergency lights flicked on while non-vital equipment was turned off. The operations were carried out so quickly and smoothly it was like watching a professional dance team in motion. Every action was carried out with the idea of quickly putting out the fire and restoring the ship to normal operation.

Seaman Martinez watched in wide-eyed, scared amazement as he stepped out of the galley, dishrag in hand. He had only been onboard a couple of months and had never seen a fire before. The teachers at sub school beat into his head that fires were bad, but nothing prepared him for this. He could smell the *FEAR* as the men rushed to do their jobs. The fast pace of the action was just short of pandemonium. He watched helplessly, not knowing what to do, but knowing that he should do something.

Petty Officer Swain grabbed him roughly by the shoulder, shoved an EAB into his hand and pushed Martinez onto a seat. He yelled through his own EAB, "Sit here! Watch and learn something, non-qual!"

Chief Richey yelled out, his voice muffled by the OBA, "Everybody ready?"

Five sailors grabbed the pressurized snake of a fire-hose, while Richey led the way, looking at the screen on a portable thermal imager to see through heavy smoke.

The fire-fighting teams ran into the engine-room from the operations compartment with pressurized fire hoses at the ready. Smoke poured into the mess decks through the open hatch. The smoke curtain draped down over the hatch was only partially successful in stopping it.

Martinez watched as the air slowly filled with a wispy gray haze; building to a dark, impenetrable cloud. He sucked gratefully on the clean, fresh air of his EAB. Fear churned in his stomach as he sat riveted to the bench. *Was he going to make it through this? Would his crewmates put the fire out in time? How could they do their jobs if they were as scared as he was?* He was slowly beginning to realize why the qualified crewmen were so proud of their silver dolphins.

The engine-room watch-standers rushed to carry out their emergency casualty procedures. Several hurried around the engine-room securing unnecessary equipment to save reactor heat, others completed a checklist that ensured that the reactor was safely shut down, while still others fought the fire. It was a well practiced choreography, carried out in a dark gray cloud.

With their EABs, the watch standers had air to breathe but were limited by the length of their trailing air hoses. EABs received their air supply from special red painted manifolds located around the ship. With visibility reduced to zero, the crew depended on memory and training to find the manifolds with life giving air. It was a careful dance from manifold to manifold; suck in a deep lungful of good air, unplug the hose and scurry a few feet, then feel around for the next manifold and plug in the hose. A few deep gasps and then repeat the procedure.

The reactor technician ran across the engine-room and opened the breaker that powered the reactor control panels.

Chief Turston was the first person to make it to the burning panel. Smoke poured out of it as he unscrewed the red-hot cover screws with his bare hands. He screamed in pain as he threw the panel to the deck and emptied a fire extinguisher into the burning circuitry.

Turston collapsed against the railing, holding his charred hands and moaning as tears rolled down his face. He had to be evacuated forward for the Corpsman to treat.

The fire in the reactor control panels was out, but the heat and flames had jumped across the narrow passageway and caused the hull insulation to ignite. Flames licking the thick polyurethane insulation engulfed engine-room upper level and spread to engine-room middle level.

Thick black, toxic smoke filled the compartment just as the hose teams from forward arrived with their fire hoses. The firefighters were blind. They couldn't see their hands, let alone find a fire. Chief Richey used the hand-held thermal imager to search out the blaze.

The heat was searing. A man could only last for maybe ten minutes before he had to be relieved and sent forward to recover.

Three fire hoses and hose teams converged to put out the building inferno. They worked together to beat back the fire with powerful jets of high-pressure water and then to tear the thick hull insulation away with long handled rakes. The insulation was then soaked in buckets of seawater to douse the stubborn blaze.

Forward in the control room, LCDR Jacobs maneuvered the sub around in a slow upward spiraling circle, using the little remaining speed he had to conduct a sonar search. The sonar watch-standers listened intently to make sure that no ships were close. They were all alone in this forgotten part of the broad Pacific.

Jacobs yelled through his EAB, "Diving Officer, make your depth six-two feet."

The sub slowly coasted up to periscope depth, eking out the last bit of forward momentum.

Jacobs spun the scope around as it broke the sea's surface. The picture through the periscope was a calm tropical night with a beautiful full moon low on the horizon. The difference between the calm beauty above and the heat and smoke below disconcerted him.

The EOOW shouted into the 7MC, "Conn, maneuvering, the fire is out."

His words were barely intelligible, badly distorted by the EAB he was forced to wear.

With the fire finally out, the priority shifted to emergency ventilating the engine-room. The emergency diesel generator would provide some much needed electrical power and suck in fresh air, pushing the smoke from the ship. With all electrical loads supplied by the battery, the need for additional power was critical. The sub could not survive without electrical power. They had less than an hour's electrical power left. And they needed to get rid of the toxic, corrosive smoke before any effective repairs could begin.

Jacobs ordered the snorkel mast raised to provide life-giving air to the diesel and quickly followed that with the order, "Commence snorkeling."

The diesel operator, two decks below Jacobs' feet, threw the large brass quadrant lever over to push high-pressure air into the diesel to start it rolling over. He held it firmly in that position with one hand. With his other, he reached across the narrow passageway and held the snorkel safety circuit switch in "over-ride", bypassing the safety shutdowns until the diesel was up to speed. He used his left foot to hold the kick-drain valve open as he watched for the snorkel exhaust valve to slam open, allowing the exhaust gases to leave the ship. After several heart-stopping seconds, the little amber shut light switched to a green open one. He released his grip on the quadrant lever, safety switch and kick-drain. The diesel was up and running.

The rock-crushing sound of the 12 cylinder Fairbanks-Morse marine diesel was music to Jacob's ears. It meant that electrical power was available to supplement the rapidly depleting battery and, more importantly, clean outside air was replacing the smoke filled air inside the sub. They could soon remove the hot, uncomfortable EABs.

The smoke slowly cleared. The technicians could troubleshoot and repair the reactor control system without the encumbering EABs. Most importantly, the electrical loads were shifted to the diesel. They had time to fix the reactor.

After a rapid survey of the damage and a conference with his technicians, LTJG Baker reported to the Engineer that repairs to the reactor control panels would require four hours. His team was drawing parts from the supply system and preparing the procedures for the repairs.

"Engineer, secure from the training drill, conduct a fast recovery start up," Hunter ordered Sam Stuart as they stood together behind the maneuvering room, observing the melee of action around them. The hot, sweating men removed their EABs. The watch-standers began the choreography of conducting an emergency at-sea reactor start up.

"And, Eng, tell your people, 'well done.' XO, we have to work on getting those hose teams back here faster. That took almost two minutes. I want a minute and a half maximum." Training on a submarine never ended.

10

03 Jun 2000, 0400LT (02 Jun, 1700Z)

Hunter walked into the wardroom, finding Fagan sitting by himself eating a bowl of cereal.

Fagan looked up and asked, "How did Baker do? That was his first time to take her to periscope depth, wasn't it?"

Hunter had just stepped down from the control room where he had observed the trip to periscope depth to copy the broadcast. He was planning on enjoying a cup of coffee before heading to the engine-room for his morning workout. Fagan was taking a break from a late night of catching up on the never-ending paperwork, the bane of an XO's existence

Hunter plopped down in his chair. Deep grey lines were etched in his features. He said, "Baker did fine. That kid has a lot of potential. Keep the pressure on him. He should get his dolphins by the time we get back. Have you seen the Top Secret message board yet?"

He poured himself a cup of coffee, the pushed the aluminum clipboard over to Fagan.

"No, not yet. Was there something on the broadcast? We're about due for an intel update. Can't say that they have been flooding us with info."

Tapping the message board, Hunter nodded, "We got an intel update from NSA. They correlated some signal intercepts with what they call 'other sources'. Apparently there is some Indonesian admiral named Suluvana who has been working with the terrorists on Nusa Funata. Seems he commands the naval base at Semarang on the North shore of Java. That's the base where the two missing *KILOs* are homeported."

Hunter sipped from his cup. "This admiral appears to be quite an independent operator. NSA says he ordered the *KILOs* to sortie and intercept any naval units heading toward Indonesia. Of course, this intel message doesn't tell us where to expect them. That would be asking too much."

He sat back in his chair. "Let's play 'what if' for a few minutes. If you were Admiral Suluvana, what would you do, Bill?"

Hunter was fond of these brainstorming sessions. They helped him plan and at the same time to train his officers. Playing "what if" was a challenge to use every bit of submarining knowledge and to think "outside the box."

Fagan steepled his fingers and replied slowly, "If I were in Suluvana's shoes, I would use the *KILOs* in choke points on the routes into the Java Sea." He grabbed a scrap of paper and sketched a quick chart of the Indonesian Islands. "I would put one up in the South China Sea, here off Singapore, to control the approaches from the North. That's our normal route."

Fagan nodded toward his crude chart. "The other is a gamble. Do you put it here, to the South in the Timor or Arafura Seas, here to the North in the Celebes or Molucca Seas, or do you keep it closer to home in the Banda or Java Seas? You just can't cover all the approaches with only two boats.

"I'd keep the boats well hidden. That's key. Anyone trying to get in would have to play under the assumption that one of the *KILOs* was guarding whatever approach they chose. It's like announcing that you had mined all the straits when you only had two mines. Too big a gamble to disregard the minefield although the odds are that it is not there, so you spend a great deal of time sweeping a lot of empty sea."

Hunter nodded, "If he is really cagey, he will throw in some head fakes to really confuse us. It would be simple to take some *KILO* radios and radars to the various possible locations and allow the signals to be intercepted. Throw in a few spurious reports of periscope sightings and the picture gets really confused."

"Do you think that he's that smart?" Bill Fagan queried.

"He didn't get to where he is without being smart and ruthless. He could do something like this or something totally off the wall. We won't know until we play it out. We just need to be on our toes and ready for anything. I think our plan to head way East and duck through the Sunda Straits may throw them off. That's a thousand extra miles out of our way. They shouldn't expect anything coming from that direction. Just the same, I want to be ready to take on a *KILO* by the time we go through the Sunda Straits. Put daily approach and attack problems on the training plan as we cross the Timor Sea," Hunter directed.

"Skipper, is that soon enough to start?"

Hunter answered, "Yeah. Don't want the team to peak early and slack off. I can't see a place where we will have a problem earlier, do you?" He stood and headed for the door.

"No, sir. Probably not."

Hunter ducked through the hatch into the reactor compartment passageway, thinking, *Bill had certainly come along way since he reported onboard. He's thinking more like a submarine skipper now.* Still, Hunter was worried. *How would the XO hold up when it really got tense?*

02 Jun 2000, 2100LT (1900Z)

Mustaf had just drifted off when his cell phone jangled.

General Liu Pen began without preliminaries. "Mustaf, are you still on schedule for the first shipment?"

These Chinese are almost as lacking in the social graces as those barbarian Westerners.

"We have decided on our first customer."

"I must remind you not to use names on these circuits. We don't know how closely we are being monitored," Mustaf chided the Chinese spymaster. "We are still on schedule, but a complication has arisen. As you know, our competition has sent out a mission to stop our production."

"Truly, most unfortunate," General Liu Pen replied. "I am expecting you to counter this move."

Mustaf explained the plan that he had put into effect.

General Liu Pen chuckled, "How ironic. Our first customer will be in Honolulu. With all the trans-Pacific traffic through there, the panic will spread worldwide quickly. I would expect such disruption that the capitalist economy could collapse.

"The delivery must be absolutely on schedule. Timing is very important. As we discussed, the demands will be delivered to selected world leaders with a requirement for payment in seventy-two hours. Symptoms must not be discovered before that time, but within twenty-four hours afterward. That way, if they refuse to pay, the world will blame them. If they pay, the treacherous admiral will be blamed."

"Brilliant," Mustaf almost chortled in reply. "Not only will it be communicated from there, but that pest hole of capitalist decadence will be no more. The virus can live in the soil and be completely viable for years. America's window on the Pacific will be shattered forever."

General Liu Pen replied, "Now it is I who must warn you to be careful, my friend. Please plan the delivery method most carefully. I want our first to be our best."

04 Jun 2000, 0630LT (03 Jun, 1930Z)

Hunter stepped into control and stopped beside Chief Jones, the diving officer. His small bench sat just behind and between the helmsman, Seaman Osterburg, and the planesman, Seaman Lipinski. All three looked at him expectantly.

He asked "You two ready?"

Chief Jones chimed in, "They're ready. I trained them real good."

"OK, then." Hunter turned toward Sam Stuart. "Officer of the Deck, pass the word on the 1MC."

Stuart grabbed the microphone and said, "The ship will be conducting high-speed maneuvers."

The 1MC announcement was met with a chorus of, "Oh, Boy! E ticket ride time!" The crew loved the effect that large rudder angles had at high speeds. It made for an exciting roller coaster ride.

High-speed maneuvers were meant to be used only in extreme emergencies, like avoiding an incoming torpedo. Frequent practice was required to effectively and safely execute the tricky maneuver. Normally when operating at speeds above twenty knots, a limiter was placed on the rudder control that prevented rudder angles above three degrees. It was a safety measure to prevent uncontrolled, dangerously rapid rudder movements. But for these maneuvers the limiter was disengaged. The ship control party strapped themselves into their seats while everyone else searched for a secure handhold.

Hunter ordered, "*Ahead* Flank!"

Back in the engine-room, the throttleman spun the large chrome ahead throttle wheel as fast as he could turn it. The growl of the steam entering the massive turbines grew to a roar as the mammoth shaft spun faster. *SAN FRANCISCO* leaped ahead. The slam of the reactor coolant pumps shifting to fast speed was heard throughout the ship. Past twenty-five knots, then thirty, until finally the ship was speeding almost as fast as a car could legally go. Seven thousand tons of steel racing underwater.

Hunter braced himself firmly against the chromed railing and stanchion and ordered, "Right full rudder."

He knew what to expect next. The sub was like a very large airplane flying underwater. The large rudder angle caused the ship to heel over to starboard as the ship's head swung around. The snap roll that ensued was frightening to the unsuspecting, almost instantly reaching 45 degrees. Everyone and everything not firmly strapped down was violently tossed to port. That was the good news. The bad news was that with the rudder now at a steep angle from its normal vertical orientation, it acted as a stern-plane as well as a rudder. The ship's nose pitched up for a split second, then dropped quickly.

The helmsman and planes man both had to anticipate this and work as a finely honed team to prevent the sub from diving out of control into the depths. Unlike an airplane going into a dive with thousands of feet to use for a pullout, the submarine had only a few hundred feet before it reached crush depth.

Osterburg and Lipinski were the best team onboard. They had to be, there was no time for orders or even communication between them. Osterburg had to pull on his control column so that the fairwater planes went to full rise as he turned the wheel to right full rudder. Lipinski had to immediately yank back on his column to pull the stern planes to full rise. A practiced and skillful team could perform this maneuver with only a few feet of depth change. They had to "catch her" before the nose started to drop. If they were able to keep the nose from dropping, they could maintain depth control throughout the turn.

"Damn it." Osterburg was a millisecond late in taking the fairwater planes to full rise. He stared in horror, his face ashen, as the sub's nose dropped almost immediately to a 45 down angle. The depth indicator hummed as it reeled off the rapidly increasing depth. Everyone who had been tossed to port was now violently thrown forward. The ship's control party was frozen in horror. No one seemed to know what to do. There were only seconds to react as the sub raced uncontrollably to her doom in the depths.

"Oh, my God!" QM1 Buell yelled.

Hunter was thrown violently to port and forward but maintained a death grip on the stanchion. *Was there time to save his ship? Had he asked too much this time? One thing was sure, if this was the end; he would go down fighting.* "All Stop, rudder amidships, full rise on the stern planes, full rise on the fairwater planes,"

She didn't stop. Still *SAN FRANCISCO* dove into the depths. There simply was not enough time for the planes to take effect to bring her under control before they reached crush depth.

Osterburg pulled on the column with all his strength. His jaw was clenched rock solid as he strained uselessly to bring the ship up.

Chief Jones cried out, "Two hundred feet to test depth, Captain!"

"Emergency blow the forward group," Hunter ordered. This was the last resort. If the emergency blow did not work, there was nothing left.

"One hundred feet to test depth!"

The roar of high-pressure air filled the compartment as 4500psi air forced the water out of the forward ballast tanks.

"Fifty feet to test depth!"

Slowly the angle started to come off as the emergency blow began to take effect.

"Twenty feet to test depth! Starting to come up!" Chief Jones yelled exultantly. The men in control cheered wildly.

As more water was forced out of the forward ballast tanks, the bow came up more rapidly until the angle passed through zero and the ship started to rise. Hunter ordered, "Secure the blow." The roar of air stopped. "Vent the forward group, ahead standard, maintain a zero bubble, make your depth one-five-zero feet," the orders came in rapid succession as Hunter fought to save the ship. He did not notice how tightly he had been gripping the rails until the ship had finally leveled out. His white-knuckled death grip on the stainless steel pipe caused his hand to cramp. The first time he noticed the pain was when it was all over.

Osterburg stammered, "Skipper, I'm sorry. I don't know what happened.

"That's the reason we practice, so you don't hesitate next time," Jon Hunter responded evenly to the young sailor. No sense in letting him see how really close they had come. In combat he might choke even worse.

Hunter slipped out of the control room to go to his stateroom before anyone noticed his sweat drenched coveralls or how much his hands were shaking. A fresh pair of coveralls and a cup of coffee and he would be back to normal.

Bill Fagan knocked on the state room door and stepped in. "You OK, Skipper?" he asked.

"That one was close, too close." Jon Hunter replied, his voice still shaking. "We're going to have to be more careful and train harder. Can't afford a screw up like that where we're going. We'll do emergency ship-handling drills every day until we get in the area."

11

Quarters G was really half of a duplex on Hospital Point at the edge of the Pearl Harbor complex. Built in the 1920s, it originally served as quarters for the nurses at the old naval hospital that lent its name to the point. The hospital was long since gone, enveloped by the expanding shipyard in the 1930s. The result was a little known, quiet backwater surrounded by the noise, dirt, and grit of an industrial shipyard activity.

Just before World War II, the house and its neighbors had been converted into quarters for the commanding officers of the ships that sortied out of the Naval Base. Early residents had front row seats to the devastating attack of 7 December, 1941. The USS *NEVADA* had been purposely run aground almost in their front yard to prevent her from sinking and blocking the only exit channel.

A row of large date palms lined the street, adding to the sense of a quiet island paradise. The banyan tree rooted in the front lawn was probably the largest one on Oahu, if not the largest in Hawaii. Its thick branches spread horizontally for almost a hundred feet in every direction. Aerial roots descended to become massive secondary trunks on both sides of First Street and the intersecting alley that ran alongside the lawn. The effect was a large, shady grove that promised protection from the blazing tropical sun.

Across First Street, the squadron commodores had laid claim to the row of Panama style bungalows that backed onto the water's edge. The Caluccis' house was directly across the street. There was no escaping the demands of the job, not even at home, when the boss lived across the street.

Hunter's oldest daughter, Megan, discovered the banyan tree provided a haven away from the trials of being a teenager on Hawaii. The branches made an ideal resting-place above the world where she could find the solitude to read and write. She sat up there now, writing a letter to her father. These letters had long been a tradition between them. She had written her first one at the age of three. She had known even then that Daddy wouldn't see them until he was almost home. They, along with Mommy's letters, met him when he returned from patrol to the Sub Base at Holy Loch, Scotland. Since then, the letters to Dad had become a touchstone between them.

She had inherited his blonde hair and flashing brown eyes, but her beauty came from her mother. More than one sailor had found to his dismay that she was not amused by sailors.

On the lanai beside the old house, her younger, redheaded sister, Maggie, was helping her mother set the dinner table. The place setting at the head of the table was empty, as usual.

Life on the Islands was not easy for the girls. They had left their friends on the mainland behind for this move to a new and different culture, a culture that did not readily accept haoles (white non-natives). Megan was finishing her senior year at Radford High School. Just off base, it had a student body that was pretty much equally military dependents and locals. The friction between the groups left an unmistakable aura of tension around the school.

The normally gregarious Megan had retreated into her studies and a few close friends. She could usually be found either here in her tree reading or on the phone with her best friend, Sally Johnson. On several occasions she had taken the family cell phone up in her tree, but Peg Hunter had yelled at her for that.

Maggie had it worse. She attended the Aliamanu Middle School, a little further from the base. The demographics here were more strongly dominated by the locals. Her fair skin and bright red hair meant that she really stood-out as a haole. The twelve-year old was having a tough time dealing with entering the teen years at the same time she was trying to acclimatize to the new and hostile environment. The turmoil had exacerbated an already rebellious streak in her. Her green eyes often flashed with frustration.

06 Jun 2000, 1430LT (0430Z)

The sub raced to the Southwest on a general course of two-one-zero true. They passed from Tuvalu into the territorial seas of the Solomons. Reaching 165 East longitude and 010 South latitude, the sub changed course to two-seven-zero true and headed for the San Cristobol straits separating Guadalcanal and Maramasika to the North from San Cristobol to the South. The Straits provided a deep-water passage from the Pacific to the East into the Solomon Sea to the West. The site of some of the most savage land, air and sea battles of World War II, the area was now a quiet tropical backwater.

"Damn it, Chop. What do you expect me to do?" Sam Stuart growled in exasperation. "Your people just can't take care of their gear. Swain knew full well that the seal was leaking, but no one told us until the motor burned." Stuart stalked off in the general direction of the engine-room.

The young supply officer muttered under his breath. All Bill Fagan could catch was something about the ice cream machine.

The Ensign looked up and saw the XO standing there. "XO, the ice cream machine smoked."

Bill Fagan ducked his head into the galley where Petty Officer Swain stood by the open back panel of the ice cream machine holding a fire extinguisher aimed into its heart. The charred panel was smoke-blackened. Both the compressor motor and controller wiring were a partially congealed mass of melted plastic and copper. The pungent aroma of burnt sugar mixed with the smell of fried insulation.

Few things affected crew morale more than the ice cream machine. In the cramped confines of a submarine there was little space to be given over for crew comfort. What little there was meant that much more to the crew.

The ice cream machine, with its continuous supply of cold treats, was a mainstay. A supply officer or head cook who allowed the vital machine to fail would be at the receiving end of crew and wardroom hostility.

Fagan completed his brief inspection of the deceased machine. Turning to the dejected young officer, he said, "Well, Mr. Green, I suggest that you get that machine fixed. I gather that the Eng is not enthused about working on it."

"XO, it's not quite that simple," Ensign Green began to explain, reluctantly. "You remember we replaced the ice cream machine a few weeks before we left. The new one was completely different from the old one. Different maker, model and all."

"Let me guess," the XO interjected. "You forgot to put in a COSAL Change Request so you don't have any spare parts."

The crest fallen look on the Chop's face told the XO that his guess was right on target. He continued with a notably sharper tone to his voice, "Mr. Green, didn't they teach you anything at Athens besides golf? You, of all people onboard, should know that to get spare parts you have to tell the system what equipment you have. Let me make this perfectly clear to you. I don't really give a damn if you and Petty Officer Swain have to sit in the freeze box and stir bowls of ice cream mix with a spoon, but the crew will have ice cream. Do you understand?"

"Yes, sir," the supply officer stammered as the XO stalked off.

A few minutes later, Chief Turston and two of his electricians emerged from the engine-room, each carrying a bag of tools and test equipment

"Mr. Green, the Eng told us that you might have a problem. Don't know if we can help, but we'll give it a shot," the Chief said.

Glancing in the innards of the machine and noticing the trail of blackened ooze leading from the leaky seal to the motor, he muttered, "Looks like a real mess. Sure would have been easier to fix before you gave that motor a taste of ice cream."

"Thanks for the advice, Chief," the supply officer said dryly. "Do you think that you can fix it?"

"Well, Mr. Green, don't know yet," the leading electrician said, rubbing the stubble on his chin. "The wiring will take a little time, but we can fix that here. The motor and compressor are an integral unit and the motor wiring is shot. We'll have to try rewinding it on the lathe. Haven't used that jig, don't know if it'll work. I'm guessing two days, if everything works. Better break out a parka and find a comfortable seat in the freeze box."

07 Jun 2000, 2000LT (1000Z)

The chiefs nervously chattered as they assembled in the chief's quarters small smoke-filled lounge. The COB had not told them why when he called this unusual meeting. But, they could sense something important was afoot.

The group gathered most evenings to "smoke and joke" with a camaraderie developed from years of shared experiences.

The chiefs provided a vital "deck-plate" level of leadership and technical experience, bridging the difference from the bright young college kids in the wardroom and the equally bright Navy-trained enlisted crewmen. They were the father figures to the crew and the mentors for the younger officers. Because of their unique position and history, they had achieved a special status and privilege, which included their own berthing space, the chief's quarters, the "goat locker".

The goat locker was the only living area onboard where the smoking lamp was lighted. Everyone else who wanted to smoke was relegated to a short, cramped passageway on the lower level, served by large ventilation fans.

"Guys, we've got a problem," Master Chief Hancock started.

"We've been steaming West for a week now. I think we've all figured out that this isn't some exercise up North putting a bunch of SEALs ashore in Alaska," the COB continued. "Does anyone have any idea of where we are going or what we are going to do there? Can't do much to help the Skipper if we're in the dark."

"COB, what did you guys talk about in that hush-hush meeting you had in the wardroom?" Chief Richey, the leading machinist mate asked.

There was no way to keep a secret on the boat, but no one had even spoken about that briefing.

"I think that's what we are here to discuss," Master Chief Holmstad interjected. "Am I right COB?"

"Exactly," Master Chief Hancock replied. "Let me start by saying that what was discussed in that meeting was very highly classified. Most of you don't have the clearance to even know the meeting even happened. This one tonight didn't happen."

"OK, COB, are you going to have to shoot us after you tell us this stuff?" Chief Jones jokingly chimed in.

"Jones, you keep mouthing off like that, the XO may find out how "Snow White Does the Seven Dwarfs" ended up in the VCR for the dependents cruise. His wife was not happy." the COB replied.

"OK, OK! It was only a joke," Chief Jones responded, raising his hands defensively.

Jones was an inveterate practical joker. His attempts were not always in good taste or well received. A few months ago he had switched a pornographic video tape for a fairy tale that was to be used to entertain the children during a dependents cruise.

"If we can be serious for a minute," Master Chief Hancock continued dryly, "Master Chief Holmstad and I will discuss some things that we never discussed. Am I clear about that?"

The rest of the chiefs understood the rules. The COB and master chief sonar tech were placing themselves on the line so the chiefs would have the information they needed to do their jobs. If any one of them said a word that was heard by the wrong ears, the two master chiefs would be subject to charges of violating national security.

Master Chief Holmstad started, "Weps asked me to build some sonar search plans for the Timor Sea and the Java Sea."

Routine search plans were done by junior sonar men. The master chief did not build sonar search plans unless they were really going to be used. *SAN FRANCISCO* was heading through the Timor and Java Seas. That meant they were going to do something in Indonesia.

The area had been undergoing unrest for years, with several of the thousands of islands experiencing open warfare in attempts for independence. The news was full of plots, counter-plots and terrorist attacks. The mix of ethnic backgrounds, languages, religions and economic tension was so volatile that not a week went by without reports of some new horror.

If they were going in there, it was important and highly sensitive. The

Indonesians didn't have a blue-water Navy to speak of. Relying on hand-me-down ships from the former Soviets or the US, it consisted mostly of patrol craft, with a few old frigates and destroyers for additional firepower. The exception was four front-line *KILO*s diesel submarines that had arrived last year.

Doc Pugh asked, "If we are going into Indonesia, why do we have all that SEAL gear down in the torpedo room? We don't have any SEALs aboard that I know of." Looking over at the rotund machinist mate chief and added, "Unless you've been secretly working out, Richey."

Pointing at one of the buttons on his tightly stretched khaki shirt, Chief Richey retorted in mock anger, "Doc, another comment about my weight, I'll inhale and drive this button clean through your forehead."

Master Chief Hancock stood and refilled his ever-present coffee cup before saying, "OK, you two, enough of the kidding around."

He paused, glancing around the group, and then continued, "I'm not saying what is planned, but you know that no other boat has spent as much time working with the SEALs as we have."

He placed his cup on the table and continued, "If we were to join up with some SEALs from a parachute drop at sea, then it would all fit together. With that in mind, all of us need to check our gear and make sure our troops are ready. A little revision to the training plan for swimmer launch and recovery might be a good idea."

Chief Tyler chimed in, "If we were to meet up with those SEALs by chance and, if, maybe, we were to insert them somewhere, then we would probably be doing a bit of electronic surveillance before we sent them ashore, just to find any threat radars . Might want to put some ESM training in the revision, too."

"Good idea," the COB replied. "Now if each of us looks at our jobs with this possible mission in mind and makes sure that his people and equipment are ready, I think we have a plan. Let me remind you again, this meeting didn't happen. What you learned here was only a possibility based on what you have seen. Everybody understand?"

A round of affirmative nods and Chief Jones piped up, "OK, movie or poker tonight?"

12

Shortly after *SAN FRANCISCO* exited the restricted waters of the San Cristobol Strait, the sensitive BQQ5 sonar hydrophones picked up the low frequency noise of many large ships transiting together.

"Conn, sonar, picking up several heavy screw beats to the West. At least three ships and possibly as many as seven. They are all close to the same bearing. One of them equates to the *ESSEX*. Trying to sort them out now."

Jeff Miller looked at a reference chart taped to the book locker behind the periscope stand.

"Sonar, conn, aye. If it is the *ESSEX* ARG, you should hear the *ESSEX*, two LPDs, the *DULUTH* and the *CLEVELAND*; one LSD, the *PEARL HARBOR*; one destroyer, the *FITZGERALD*, and two frigates, the *RENTZ* and the *GARY*," the OOD responded.

"Conn, sonar, aye. We hold the *ESSEX* and probably the two LPDs. Trying to classify now. Not sure about the others. Have assigned trackers to six noise sources. Sierra Four-Five is the *ESSEX*, currently bearing two-six-nine, Sierra Four-Six is a probable LPD currently bearing two-seven-zero, Sierra Four-Seven is the other possible LPD currently bearing-two six-eight. Sierra Four-Eight is an unclassified noise source bearing two-seven-one. Sierra Four-Nine is an unclassified noise source bearing two-six-seven. There is another possible contact on the same bearing as Sierra Four-Eight, too weak to assign a tracker."

Miller picked up the sound powered phone handset, selected the CO's stateroom and spun the growler handle.

When Hunter answered, the OOD reported, "Captain, we have sonar contact with the *ESSEX* ARG, bearing two-six-nine. Best estimate of range sixty thousand yards."

Hunter grunted, "Right on schedule, I'll be out in a second. Station the section tracking party."

"Aye sir, the party is stationed and tracking the contacts."

Hunter strode into the control room and checked the navigation plot.

QM1 Buell plotted another bearing line and looked up at the skipper. "Captain, the lines are all laying down right here, almost due West." Buell pointed to the chart he was working on. "My best bet is they are out here in the Solomon Sea."

The latest update on the JOTS (joint operations tactical information system) screen agreed with the navigation plot. Both showed the ARG about fifty miles to the West. This equated roughly with the sonar bearings.

He directed, "Officer of the Deck, come to one-five-zero feet and clear baffles. Then proceed to periscope depth."

As the scope broke the surface of the ink-black sea, Miller rapidly scanned the horizon. Nothing was visible except the sea and the sky. Not even a whitecap disturbed the torpid night. The brilliant moon sketched a highway of light to the East while a million stars, carelessly scattered over the black bowl of the sky, filled the night with diamonds.

Miller ordered, "Chief of the Watch, raise number one BRA-34."

As the COW replied, "Number one BRA-34 coming up," the OOD saw a gray and black shape block his vision for about 30 degrees to the right of dead ahead. Some genius of submarine design had placed the two large radio antennas directly ahead of the two periscopes so that when the antennas and scopes were used at the same time, vision was blocked ahead. To top off a poor placement decision, the masts were about fourteen feet taller than the scopes and needed to be fully extended to be used. This made it impossible to see over the top of the masts. The arrangement necessitated either limiting the use of the mast to short periods or frequent course changes to unmask any ships or obstacles that might be screened from view.

Hunter grabbed the microphone hanging from the stanchion by the periscope and said, "Radio, captain, establish voice communications with the *ESSEX*." Turning to the fire control technician of the watch (FTOW), he directed, " Report into the LINK and get us an updated JOTS picture."

Chief Tyler's reply from radio squawked over the 21MC speaker, "Captain, radio, aye. Tuning the antenna now. Give me thirty seconds."

After a few minutes of waiting, Chief Tyler reported, "Captain, radio, we have sat secure voice comms with the *ESSEX* ARG. Admiral Schultz requests to speak with you. Patching through to the conn."

The FTOW turned from his display screen and reported, "We are active on the LINK, receiving the JOTS picture in fire control now."

Hunter reached over and grabbed the red phone. "Admiral, *SAN FRAN-CISCO* reporting. Request permission to join formation."

The speaker crackled with static. "Permission granted. Jon, General Kendall and I welcome you to the *ESSEX* ARG. Glad to have you with us. Is there anything that we can do for you?"

Hunter replied, "Admiral, we are happy to be part of your group. *SAN FRANCISCO* is fully operational and ready to complete all missions. We don't need anything right now. Request instructions and station assignment."

Admiral Schultz answered, "Jon, I've been briefed a little on your mission. No details, just that you will be leaving us for a little while and that we are to give you any assistance that you need. I understand that you are going to be of limited help to us. Looks more like we will be escorting you rather than the other way around. Joe Strang over on *FITZGERALD* is Echo Xray and will be acting as submarine element coordinator. *FITZGERALD* is equipped with BGIXS so you shouldn't have any problems communicating with her. Talk to Joe. He will give you your assignments. Schwartz out."

The secure radio came to life with a new voice. "*SAN FRANCISCO*, this is Echo Xray. Jon, this is Joe Strang. We are directed to pass you around ahead of us and try to keep up. I understand that your speed of advance is thirty knots. I'll assign you the area fifty nautical miles ahead of track and beyond. That should give you plenty of room to run. We'll maintain twelve-hour comms cycle. Does that work for you?"

CDR Hunter replied, "Echo Xray, this is *SAN FRANCISCO*. Would prefer a twenty-four-hour comm cycle, the same as what we have with SUBPAC. Also, recommend that you back up your messages through the SUBPAC broadcast to make sure that we have delivery. Have you been informed that because of operational security, we can not make position reports?"

"We understand," Captain Strang answered. "That should make coordination interesting. Concur with the twenty-four hour comm cycle and SUBPAC back up. Keep us informed as best you can, given the security constraints. Echo Xray out."

"Well, XO, did we piss him off?" Hunter asked as he replaced the red phone. "We just told our erstwhile boss that we were not going to tell him anything or do what he says. Just to make it worse, we don't want to talk but we expect his help. Hope he's understanding."

In *FITZGERALD*'s combat information center, Joe Strang contemplated this new development. His team had some experience in operating with a submarine and even worked with *SAN FRANCISCO* during their pre-deployment work-up training. They knew the basic tenets of operating with submarines and the special procedures needed to communicate with one. Those procedures included assigning the sub to a defined patrol area so mutual interference could be avoided. Frequent communications were also recommended so planning could be enhanced and the sub kept better informed of the Battle Group's intentions. They had just violated both of these tenets for operational security. He had an uncomfortable feeling that trouble was brewing.

SAN FRANCISCO raced ahead of the ARG, passing through the Solomon Sea and the Louisiade Archipelago, entering the Coral Sea. The Group changed base course to 300 degrees to head for the Gulf of Papua. From there, they would turn to the Southwest to pass between Papau New Guinea to the North and the Great Barrier Reef to the South and West as it extended Northward from the Eastern shore of Australia. This narrow, treacherous passage provided a deepwater access though the sharp coral reefs. Many of these reefs lay just below the surface, ready to tear the bottom out of the unsuspecting mariner. Beyond the reefs lay the Torres Strait separating the Northern extension of Queensland, Australia from the Western state of Papua New Guinea.

06 Jun 2000, 2355LT (1355Z)

The *KILO* class submarine slowed to almost a halt.

"Come up to fifteen meters," the commanding officer murmured, "And raise the observation periscope."

He squatted down and met the eyepiece as it emerged from the deck. The old submariner slapped his eye to the rubber eyepiece and easily swung the scope, watching the blue-green haze gradually lighten as the sub came up.

The scope broke the glass smooth sea surface. There wasn't even a cloud in sight to disturb the perfect blue on blue of sea meeting sky.

"We are all alone. Raise the radio mast and report to headquarters."

The destroyer seemed to come out of nowhere. One minute, they were alone in this stretch of sea, the next the destroyer was bearing down on them.

There was nothing to do. Admiral Suluvana was not someone to toy with. If he said to remain hidden to stop the American submarine, then the *JAWAL* had to stay hidden.

"Make the weapons in tubes one and two ready!" the commanding officer shouted out. "Shoot on bearing zero-eight-nine, range two-one hundred meters."

He felt and heard the torpedo tubes impulse as they threw the torpedoes out into the sea. The destroyer turned broadside to him and then away, as if it meant to out run the two weapons. He could just make out the Australian flag flying from the mast head.

The two weapons detonated almost simultaneously, directly under the destroyer. The blast lifted it high in the air, before breaking its back. The two sections settled down and then slipped below the surface.

The sub commander lowered his periscope. The last thing he saw before the *JAWAL* once more descended into the deep was groups of sailors trying to climb into the few life rafts that had broken free.

08 Jun 2000, 0200LT (0700Z)

"We have an intercept."

Fort Meade, Maryland was America's best kept secret. Even most of the senior military officers had only a glimmer of an idea of what happened in the shiny black glass buildings. And the National Security Agency wasn't about to do anything to raise the veil of mystery.

Deep in the bowls of the main building, over a hundred feet below the red clay surface and beneath some thirty feet of concrete and steel, one of the analysts pressed his headphones to his ears and scrutinized his computer screen.

The supervisor rose and stretched. It was a long, slow night and they still had four more hours. Anything to break the boredom.

"What is it?" She growled. "Another taxi driver in Jakarta trying to get lucky?"

"No, ma'am," the analyst replied. "This has the signature of one of those submarines we were told to watch for. I'm sending it to decrypt now."

The supervisor grabbed her red phone and punched the speed dial button. "Sir, we have a hit. We've found one of them."

13

08 Jun 2000, 1515LT (09 Jun, 0115Z)

"Commodore Calucci, this is Peg Hunter." It was not a call that Peg enjoyed making. She always felt uneasy talking with the Commodore. He could not be trusted. Every word had to be guarded.

"Hello, Peg, I've been meaning to call you. My wife and I are having a reception for the wardroom of a Japanese sub that is due to visit this week-end. Why don't you come over to the house? Say nineteen-thirty on Friday?" the Commodore replied.

Looking out the window, Peg could see his home directly across First Street.

"That would be nice, I'll be there," she responded without enthusiasm. "But that isn't the reason for this call. I have a boat full of very anxious wives. Wives who are expecting their husbands back. They were supposed to have been on weekly ops and should have returned yesterday. The wives will be at my house for a picnic supper in three hours. What do I tell them?"

"Peg, didn't my chief of staff call you last Friday?" the Commodore queried, knowing full well that no such call had been ordered. Now he had to figure out what to say without either divulging the true mission or alarming the wives.

Ever since the loss of the *Scorpion* in 1968, the Submarine Force had been particularly sensitive about their families. On that awful day the Navy had allowed the families of the crew to unknowingly stand on the pier from morning until late afternoon awaiting the ship's return. Only as the sun slipped toward the Western horizon did the submarine squadron commodore arrive to tell the wives the dreaded news that the boat was missing. It was several months of intense searching before they found *Scorpion's* final resting place in ten thousand feet of water west of the Azores.

Since then submarine squadrons had maintained a semi-official liaison with the CO's wife to keep her abreast of expected arrival times and some parts of the boat's schedule. It was an expected part of the Commodore's duties, but Calucci had neglected it.

"No, he didn't and I was home all day," she answered coolly. She knew as well as the Commodore did that he should be much more concerned for the crews of his boats.

"Well, the boat has been assigned to a surprise special warfare exercise up in the Aleutian op areas," he replied, without missing a beat. "It came up at the last minute when a San Diego boat had material problems. They'll be out for a few weeks."

This was the cover story that SUBPAC had come up with to explain *SAN FRANCISCO's* unexpectedly long "weekly ops."

"Why don't I stop over at your place this afternoon and meet with your wives? I can get there by 1830. Is that OK? I'll bring family-gram forms and discuss this exercise. I can bring the staff JAG and the SUBPAC chaplain just like we would for a regular deployment briefing."

"1830 is fine. We'll be in back, under the mango trees," she placed the receiver back in the cradle.

Jon had been far too anxious for this to be just an unexpected exercise. The highly unusual midnight underway didn't equate either. Something was happening and it was important enough that SUBPAC had concocted a convincing lie to cover it up. It was too easy for her to double-check this story for the Commodore to make it up on his own. His willingness to drop everything and rush over to a crew wives picnic was equally mystifying. In the past, he had always insisted on a formal presentation at the Sub Base Theater. He obviously wanted to do this quickly and with as little fanfare as possible.

Pondering all this, Peg Hunter began the series of calls that would set in motion the notification process to tell all the wives tonight's picnic would be more than their normal social gathering. She called Bill Fagan's wife and the Chief of the Boat's wife to start the call tree, an established phone calling procedure to disseminate important information quickly. It was almost as fast as the "back fence grapevine" that seemed to spread rumors at lightening speed.

She knew she needed to have the wives hear the official story and to have a chance to ask the Commodore any questions they had, but should she express her concerns about the "official story"? Was it important for the wives to know she felt a great deal more concern than she would about a simple exercise? If not, could she successfully hide it?

08 Jun 2000, 1830LT (09 Jun, 0630Z)

The little white Dodge Neon rolled into the driveway, small blue and white pennants flapping from short poles on both front fenders signifying that the Commodore was aboard. The tiny car was closely followed by a twelve-passenger van. Both had GSA license plates and "Official US Navy Vehicle" stenciled on the front doors.

The driver, dressed in immaculate summer whites, sprang from the car and rushed around to open the Commodore's door and stand at rigid attention as Carlucci exited the vehicle. He answered the driver's snappy salute with a casual wave of dismissal.

The scene would have been impressive if not for the ludicrous little white car. Cost cutting dictated official vehicles be purchased with cost and economy in mind. The Commodore reluctantly turned in his full size Ford for the tiny Neon that his position rated in the fiscally strapped environment. He insisted on maintaining all the accoutrements of office and seethed at being seen in that car. The squadron staff learned, at their peril, not to mention his new car; even in jest.

The side door on the van swung open and a cadre of the Squadron staff piled out. First out was the chief staff officer, CDR Austin, a rather portly former diesel boat commander on his last tour before mandatory retirement. The staff JAG officer, the command master chief, and the SUBPAC chaplain followed him. They closed ranks and followed Carlucci to the cluster of ladies assembled under the grove of mango trees in the large lawn behind CDR Hunter's house.

As they walked into the back yard, several children ran past the group, on their way to play in the small playground across the alley. The narrow alley separated Hunter's house from his neighbor and the considerable industrial activity on a cruiser in Dry Dock 4. A high chain-link fence overgrown with a lush curtain of brightly colored bougainvillea hid the dry dock. It was curious how the Navy inter-mixed housing facilities with shipyard maintenance and repair activities. They lived in Paradise, but with constant industrial noise and dirt from sandblasting ships' hulls.

Peg Hunter rose from her chair and walked out into the late afternoon sun. "Good afternoon, Commodore," she nodded to the others and added. "We have most of the wives here. I have passed out the information that you told me this afternoon and said that you would be over to do a short sort of pre-patrol briefing. Please don't alarm them."

The Commodore looked at her quizzically. *What did she know? Clearly she knew more than the simple cover story that he had used. Better watch his step and tread lightly. Never could tell when one angry wife could upset a career and this one was not currently happy.*

The wives gathered their lawn chairs into a rough semi-circle and listened attentively as the Commodore and his staff made their presentations, the same canned ones that this group had repeated many times to the wives of submarine crews departing on long and dangerous patrols. Many of these wives had attended the briefings before, as well, and knew what to expect.

The JAG officer spoke about powers-of attorney and wills, both superfluous since the husbands were already at sea. The command master chief and the chaplain discussed the various counseling and financial aid services that were available. The chief staff officer spoke about the need for security and passed out family-gram forms.

The only question asked was the one that all the wives wanted to know. When could they expect their husbands back from sea? The Commodore neatly parried the question by answering that the exercise was being delayed by bad weather and that he would keep them informed as it progressed.

10 Jun 2000, 1930LT (0930Z)

"Did you get it in place?" Chief Jones asked the young petty officer.

"Yea, Chief. The relay is up there and wired in. The XO almost caught me, but I managed to hide behind the ductwork in the overhead. He won't suspect a thing. Do you want to test it now?" he replied.

"No, not yet. This is one of those things that you need to wait until the right time to do," Jones answered. "This is between you and me. Anyone finds out about this and your ass is grass. Remember, you're the one who wired this in. You're the one who'll have to explain to the Old Man what's going on, so don't open your big mouth."

"You can count on me, Chief. My lips are sealed," the young petty officer replied.

09 Jun 2000, 2345LT (10 Jun, 1045Z)

He sat up in bed and marveled once again at the beautiful young dark haired beauty that found him so attractive. Nude, she padded across the carpeted floor, opening the drapes so that they could look out over the harbor from their vantage point high on the hill above Pearl City. The view was glorious, both inside the room and out.

He arrived an hour ago, two hours late for their rendezvous. Those damn wives had kept him at that lawn party for hours with their impertinent questions. He had been furious inside by the time he could finally leave, but he managed to keep it hidden.

His anger poured out as soon as he was inside the door of the apartment. The submarine suddenly leaving on a secret mission, disrupting his carefully planned schedule, that insubordinate skipper, the demanding wives. He told her everything. It felt good to unload all of his cares. She listened so attentively and made him feel so important. Commodore Calucci knew that is was a breach of security, but what was the harm? She was only a student down at the university.

14

Joe Strang stormed into combat. "What do you mean, you don't know if they received the message? Those P-3s arrive in five hours. They're already in the air. We don't have time for guessing games."

He blinked several times, vainly trying to adjust his eyes to the dark interior after just leaving the bright morning sunshine on the bridge. The dim blue light barely illuminated a space crammed with equipment and people. Several large display screens mounted on the rear bulkhead displayed the positions of all the ships and planes within a thousand miles.

Lieutenant Garcia, on duty as the submarine element coordinator, looked up from his chart, "Skipper, it's been on the BGIXS broadcast for fifteen hours now. SUBPAC says that they have been backing it up on their SSIXS broadcast." He stepped over to the small communications center. "Petty Officer Han can explain it better than I can."

Radioman Han jumped up from his seat in front of the computer keyboard. "Yes sir. It's really very simple. We download the message to the buffer. It is automatically uploaded to a satellite in geo-synchronous orbit..."

"Just cut to the chase," Strang interrupted. "Did *SAN FRANCISCO* get the message or not?" There wasn't time for those lessons on the complexities of modern communications.

Petty Officer Han replied a little peevishly, "That's what I'm trying to explain. I don't know. I just don't know. We should get a signal from the satellite when *SAN FRANCISCO* queries it to get the traffic. That hasn't been working for several days."

LT Garcia broke in, "Sir, based on their last reported position and a thirty knot speed of advance, they should be clear of the area." The large screen showed the icon for *SAN FRANCISCO* well beyond the Torres Strait.

Strang shook his head. "I just hope they are. Nothing we can do know."

11 Jun 2000, 1130LT (0230Z)

"Skipper, we just received a Top Secret message from SUBPAC." Fagan rushed into Hunter's stateroom. The XO gasped for breath, his face flushed with excitement.

"The *ESSEX* ARG is running the Torres Straits tomorrow. Intelligence reported a probable *KILO* in the area just beyond Saibai Island. They think it is one of the missing Indonesian *KILOs*. Looks like they shot at an Aussie FFG 7 yesterday. The Aussies are reporting distress calls from survivors somewhere to the West of the Straits. Washington is in an uproar. They want us through the area and clear several hours ago. The P-3's are commencing an all-out ASW sweep in two hours. They are under ROE that has all submerged contacts as hostile and their orders are to engage them." Fagan continued his report as he thrust the red message board into Hunter's hand.

Hunter took the board from the XO and read the message. "This damn message is over seventeen hours old. Nothing newer on the board canceling or changing this?"

Fagan answered, "No sir, nothing else. We have accountability for all traffic. We're not missing anything."

Hunter scanned the message again. It read exactly as Bill Fagan had described it. One of the recon satellites had intercepted a message from the *KILO* to its headquarters. Geo-location had placed it in the vicinity of the Torres Strait. The message that Hunter now held outlined an all-out anti-submarine assault on the straits by every asset that the fleet could muster. Clearly, it was no place for a friendly submarine to hang around.

Hunter digested this information for a few moments and then said, "Well, XO, I guess we had better hustle through there so we don't get our asses inadvertently shot off. We need to slip past that *KILO* as quick as we can, before the P-3s arrive. They'll spend three or four days trying to find that boat. We don't have time to wait while they sort it all out. One of those P-3 jockeys just might get lucky."

He rubbed his bristly chin. "Hmmm, remember that time in the attack trainer when we had to get by the *DALLAS* crew playing a *VICTOR*? I think that will work."

Fagan took a deep breath and then replied, "Skipper that worked in the attack trainer because we caught them off-guard." He hesitated, carefully weighing his words. "Trying to outrun the P-3s and blow past the *KILO* is just too risky. I think we should pop up and send a message to SUBPAC."

Hunter shook his head. "There just isn't time. We can't wait around and then still get to the rendezvous on time. We have to get through." He chuckled, "Besides, what's the use in having the best stealth ship in the world if you don't use it once in awhile. Those P-3s don't have a chance of finding us."

Fagan tried one last time, his voice heavy with worry. "Skipper, listen to me. It's dangerous."

"XO, I am very well aware of that. Sometimes you just have to take a chance. Let's just make sure that we are the ones writing the patrol report. Now, how far are we from the entrance to the straits?"

Fagan gave up the argument. "At this course and speed, we will be there in an hour. Then it's twenty miles beyond to clear the *KILO*'s probable patrol area." He knew that Hunter's decision was final. There was nothing to do but help.

"Okay, XO, let's think like that *KILO*'s skipper," Hunter went on. "We think he is supposed to protect this strait and take out anything that tries to go through. We're in his home waters, so stealth is important to him, but he'll feel that he has the advantage. He also doesn't need to move much. Remember, a diesel boat is only a smart semi-movable minefield."

Fagan responded, "He probably knows that the ARG is coming, but he may not know we'll be there first."

Drawing a rough chart of the Strait on a scrap of paper, Fagan continued. "I would expect him to be to the side of the ship channel just beyond the straits, right here," pointing to a spot just to the North of the main channel. "That way he could take advantage of the constricted waters and hide in the close in-shore noise while shooting out toward open water."

"That's about how I see it, too," Hunter replied. "We'll run through the straits hard and fast. Don't give him any chance to react. Have our guns cocked and ready, just in case. How does that sound to you?"

Bill Fagan responded without much enthusiasm, "It just might work."

Hunter called the OOD and ordered, "Man battle stations torpedo silently and make tubes two and three ready in all respects. Load a MOSS in tube four."

The MOSS, or MObile Submarine Simulator, was a small torpedo-like device that was designed to swim out on a preset course and play a tape recording that sounded like its mother sub. This was supposed to give the attacker the confusing problem of deciding which of two subs to attack.

Fagan rose and took a step toward the door.

"XO," Hunter said quietly. "You ever been at war before? Had weapons free?"

"No, sir," Fagan answered, his voice quivering just a bit. "You?"

"Nope," Hunter answered as he rose to follow the XO out to the control room. "Sure should be interesting."

The emergency DC lights, meant to give illumination if the AC lighting failed, blinked three times. The crew rushed to man their battle-stations, but silently. There could be someone nearby who might hear them.

Hunter walked into control. Reports were being fed to the XO that all personnel were at their battle stations. The weapons in tubes two and three were ready to search out their prey.

Hunter glanced at the charts to ascertain the sub's position, then ordered, "Diving Officer, make your depth eight hundred feet. *Ahead* flank."

He stepped up onto the periscope stand and spoke out, his voice resonating with purpose, "Attention in the fire control party, we are at war right now. There's an Indonesian Navy *KILO* out in front of us somewhere. He's already taken out one Aussie ship."

Hunter looked around the control room. Every member of the team was riveted on his next words.

"He isn't our mission. We have more important fish to fry. We're going to blow by this guy before he has a chance to react. If we think he has detected us, but hasn't shot, we will launch the MOSS toward him. If we detect an incoming weapon, we will snap shot a torpedo down the bearing to keep him busy. If we get him, great. But that isn't our priority. The P-3's will handle him."

"First, we need to get through the narrow part of the straits. We have an hour and a half to go fifty miles before the Airedales get here. Remember, our mission is to rendezvous with the SEAL team. It'll get awfully cold and lonely for them if we aren't there to pull 'em out of the water."

11 Jun 2000, 1200LT (0300Z)

SAN FRANCISCO leaped ahead.

The whole ship shuddered when reactor operator shifted the reactor coolant pumps to fast speed. *SAN FRANCISCO* slid into the depths at a twenty-degree down angle. Leveling off at eight hundred feet, she accelerated past thirty-five knots. Her speed was now so fast that the *KILO* would have only seconds to detect, classify the new contact as a submarine, and put a weapon in the water at her before she was past it and gone.

This was exactly what Hunter was banking on. Catch the *KILO* skipper napping and get beyond him before he could react. Then, when the *KILO* went to periscope depth to report the onrushing US *LOS ANGELES* class submarine, he would be a sitting duck for the waiting P-3C Orion ASW aircraft overhead.

Warran Jacobs was concerned. He pulled Hunter over to the navigation chart and pointed, "Captain, this strait narrows down to a few hundred yards at this depth. It's deep, but real narrow and shoals up fast on either side. This will be like threading a needle in the dark. Recommend we come shallow to give us more room."

"Sounding one-five fathoms below the keel," the BQR-17 Fathometer operator reported, confirming the Nav's fears.

"Noted, Nav" Hunter acknowledged. "We can't afford to come shallow. The cavitation will broadcast our approach. Run continuous soundings on the secure fathometer. Set red soundings at five fathoms and yellow soundings at ten fathoms below the keel. Log your concerns."

Cavitation, the formation and collapse of millions of tiny bubbles caused by the screw moving quickly through shallow water, sounded like hail on a tin roof magnified a thousand times. It could be heard for many miles. Down deep, the bubbles couldn't form, so no cavitation. It was a trade-off that Hunter had evaluated and decided that the risk of hitting the bottom was better than the risk of getting shot at. It was the captain's decision, alone. Warren Jacobs had done his job in voicing his concerns to the captain, but now the decision was made. They would charge ahead, deep and fast.

The submarine rushed onward through the inky black depths. The strait narrowed to a vertical wall of hard lava rock on either side. The slightest miscalculation and they would crash into the rock. Even her two-inch thick HY-80 high-strength steel hull would not withstand the crushing force of seven thousand tons of rushing mass colliding with the solid rock wall. The first indication would be the bone-jarring jolting impact followed almost instantaneously by the inrush of ice cold water compressed to steel hardness by the great depth. In a millisecond, a human being unfortunate enough to be inline with the onrush would be smashed into unrecognizable pulp. The flash fire of compression would incinerate the rest in another millisecond. Incredibly, no one would drown. Everyone would be dead long before that could happen.

Eyes flicked nervously from the fathometer to the dead reckoning bug on the chart. Driven by the ship's electro-stabilized inertial navigation system, or ESGN, its small dot continuously displayed the best available estimate of their position on the chart. Both the ship's chronometer and the bug inched forward imperceptibly.

The beads of sweat stood on Seaman Osterburg's deeply furrowed brow as he concentrated to hold the rudder precisely on course. The fathometer watch delivered his reports crisply, but in a noticeably higher pitch. The

Chief of the Watch's hands crept over the emergency blow chicken switches in vain hope that he could react fast enough to save the ship if anything went astray.

Hunter did his best to look calm as he leaned alongside the number two periscope. From this vantage-point he could survey the entire control room while sipping his umpteenth cup of coffee. As he had come to expect, his crew was doing their jobs like real professionals.

There was little for him to do but to watch, wait, and worry. The planning was done; the tactical decisions lay in the future. All that remained was to ponder and second-guess. He knew it was counter-productive, but the temptation was irresistible. *Was this the best way? Had he chosen correctly? Was he up to the task?* All these questions flashed, unanswered, through his mind. He would know the answers soon enough.

After an interminable forty minutes, Jacobs called out that the ship was beyond the narrowest neck of the strait and they were entering more open water.

As if in confirmation, the fathometer watch reported, "Depth under the keel one-zero-zero fathoms and increasing."

With a nod, Hunter said, "Okay, now to blow past that *KILO* skipper before he knows what's happening. Helm, left two degrees rudder, steer two-three-five."

"Left two degrees rudder, steer two-three-five, aye," Osterburg responded crisply as he turned the wheel slightly to the left. The ship heeled over during the turn and then snapped back upright as Osterburg smoothly swung the rudder to stop *SAN FRANCISCO* smartly on the new course.

"Sonar, conn, coming left to two-three-five. Heads up for that *KILO*. I expect him to be to the Southwest and to be shallow." Hunter replaced the microphone.

"Conn, sonar, aye." It was the voice of Master Chief Sonarman Holmstad, the best sonarman in the world as far as Hunter was concerned. If there were a *KILO* out there to detect, Master Chief Holmstad would find him.

A long chain of events that had started at an electronics manufacturer in Des Moines, Iowa, three years previously was about to come to a culmi-

nation. A switch designed to cause a standby lubricating oil pump to automatically start if low oil pressure was sensed had been improperly
assembled by a line worker suffering from a bad hangover. The switch had
somehow passed the quality assurance checks at the factory and later
testing onboard the ship, when it was installed last year during a shipyard
maintenance period.

It had reached and gone beyond the last cycle that it would operate.
Normally this would not be a problem, as the lube oil system was designed
to prevent just about any possible loss of the vital lubrication the massive
bearings needed to allow the powerful steam turbines, reduction gears and
shaft to keep rotating.

The down angle preceding the race through the straits caused a small
nut, left by an inattentive shipyard worker, to shake free from the remote
recesses of the lube oil sump. The nut was now making its way slowly
toward the operating lube oil pump. The close tolerances of the screw type,
positive displacement pumps would not allow a hardened steel nut to pass
through. The nut jammed the pump, causing it to immediately halt. The
huge current surge tripped open the pump circuit breaker.

The first indication anyone saw was a rapidly falling oil pressure on a
gauge on the throttleman's control panel, followed by an alarm horn
sounding and several alarm lights flashing.

The throttleman yelled "Loss of propulsion lube oil!"

He spun the *Ahead* throttles shut with a giant heave. As soon as the
Ahead throttles shut, he opened the *Astern*. The only hope of saving the
engines from catastrophic destruction was to immediately stop them by
using astern steam.

The engine-room upper level and lower level watch-standers rushed to
find the cause while Chief Turston tried to restore the flow of oil to the
bearings before they became red hot and welded themselves to the shaft.
When that happened, the shaft would suddenly lurch to a halt.

An electrician ran to the operating propulsion lube oil pump switches
and punched them on in a vain effort to start the standby pump. The Des
Moines factory worker's hangover was now in the chain of events. No
amount of effort would start that pump.

"Loss of propulsion lube oil, stopping and locking the shaft," the EOOW screeched over the 7MC Announcing System.

At the same time, the throttleman rang up *All Stop* on the engine order telegraph.

"Answer the ordered bell, do not stop the shaft," Hunter immediately replied. "Engineer, lay aft and see what you can do. If we stop now, we are a sitting duck for that *KILO*."

Stuart leaped up and darted out of the back door of the control room. He slid down the ladder to the mess decks, colliding with Petty Officer Swain. Not even delaying to apologize, the Engineer dashed to the engine-room.

Stuart and his team tried frantically to restore oil flow as the temperature of the bearings inexorably continued to rise.

"Conn, maneuvering, high bearing temperature port high speed pinion bearing,"

"Conn, aye. Continue to answer the bell."

"Conn, maneuvering, high bearing temperature starboard high speed pinion bearing."

The temperature-monitoring panel was lit like a Christmas tree, red alarm lights blinking madly. Still the bell had to be answered. Their lives depended on it. The only hope was to get past the *KILO* before the shaft seized.

Then, the inevitable happened. One of the bearings, manufactured slightly closer to the tolerance limits and subjected to higher heat, reached its material limits. The red hot bearing metal welded itself to the shaft. With an awful grinding noise and a powerful lurch, the shaft came to a halt. The sub would race no further.

"Rig out the outboard and shift to remote," Hunter ordered. "We still might have a chance." Ten miles to the boundary, and the outboard could only push them at two knots. But the noise of the outboard might sound enough like a fishing boat to confuse everyone.

"Shift reactor coolant pumps to reduced frequency. No sense in letting the pump noise advertise we're here."

Fast speed reactor coolant pump sound was distinctive. No matter how much the outboard screw might sound like a fishing boat, the reactor coolant pumps would be a dead give-away. Reduced frequency did away with that problem. *SAN FRANCISCO* would look like a tiny diesel fishing boat to any sonar operators in the area. At least, Hunter prayed, close enough to confuse them.

The race had slowed to a two-knot creep. Everything now depended on who detected and shot first. The tactics had been reduced to an old West gunfight, but both with gunfighters blindfolded. The basic rule was, 'He who shoots first, lives'.

15

Chief Holmstad yelled into the microphone, "Conn, sonar, *KILO* bearing two-six-seven. Designate sierra six-three. He is opening his outer doors!"

Even with his years of experience, this was the first time someone was really shooting at him.

Hunter barked, "Snapshot, sierra six-three, tube three!"

Fagan said, "Solution ready."

"Weapon ready" from the Weps.

"Ship ready" from the Nav.

Hunter ordered "Shoot tube three."

Weps threw the large brass knob first to the left, "Standby", and then to the right, "Shoot."

The ship lurched as four thousand pounds of high-speed death impulsed out of tube three. The roar of high pressure air venting through a muffler drowned out everything as the large air powered piston forced water to literally flush the Mark 48 ADCAP torpedo out the tube. Ten seconds after Holmstad's report, the torpedo raced toward the *KILO*.

"Conn, sonar, indication of outbound weapon running normal in high speed."

Weps reported, "Captain, normal wire clearance maneuver, weapon running in high speed."

Hunter asked, "Sonar, what is the *KILO* doing?"

This was what they had spent years training for. Everyone was working at the peak of their abilities. In one part of his mind, Hunter reflected on how proud he was of these men. The rest of his mind was devoted to getting them through this in one piece.

"Conn, sonar, he is being masked by our weapon now."

"Wait! I'm hearing something over our weapon! Torpedo in the water! In-bound torpedo bearing two-six-five."

"Launch the MOSS from tube four," Hunter ordered. "Launch evasion device from the forward signal ejector and reload. All stop."

Blackness started to close in around the edges of Hunter's consciousness. *Not now!* He fought it with every ounce of his being. The whirling sensation was overpowering. He reached out to grab the chrome handrail and steadied himself.

Bill Fagan yelled fearfully, "Captain, we're dead in the water! We need to get some speed on!"

Running clear of the torpedo's acquisition cone was the normal torpedo evasion tactic. Everyone knew that. But there was no way to do it.

Fagan's voice filtered through the misty blackness. With pure raw will power, Hunter forced himself back from the edge. He glanced around, hoping they hadn't seen. All the crew saw was the Skipper calmly, nonchalantly resting against the rail.

He managed to keep his voice normal. "I know that, XO. I'm banking on him shooting with a doppler enabled torpedo this close to shore. If that's true, that torpedo won't even see us. It will go for the MOSS because it's moving."

Doppler is the frequency shift that sound makes as it comes from a moving object. By sensing and tracking only sonar returns that show doppler, the torpedo could sort out the moving submarine from the stationary erroneous returns. The MOSS was making ten knots almost directly toward the incoming torpedo.

Hunter queried, "Sonar, bearing to the torpedo?"

"Still bears two-six-five. Zero bearing rate."

Weps yelled out, "Detect. Detect. Acquisition. Our weapon has acquired the *KILO!*"

Feedback along the hair thin copper wire connecting the ADCAP to the *SAN FRANCISCO* showed that the torpedo had found its prey.

Sonar reported, "Indication of our weapon acquiring. Weapon in close-in re-attack. Incoming torpedo still bearing two-six-five."

The incoming torpedo was coming straight at them. There was no bearing drift.

The control room was absolutely silent. The normal bustle of men working had stopped. All eyes were glued on the sonar repeater watching the trace, praying for the slightest change in bearing.

"Shit, this is going to be close" Fagan groaned.

Hunter glanced over to see his XO, pasty white and shaking uncontrollably.

Everyone else bent intently to their tasks, mentally willing the incoming torpedo to accept the bait.

"Loud explosion on the bearing of the *KILO*. Breaking up noises."

The sonar report was superfluous. The noise of the explosion came through the hull. It was a terrible sound to hear. Death had reached out and touched their adversary. Now it was dancing with them.

"Torpedo bearing two-six-five. It didn't go for the MOSS. I think it has us!" Holmstad shouted, fear thick in his voice.

There was nothing between them and the incoming torpedo. *Was there a way out?* Hunter was stymied. *Could he fool the torpedo or get out of its acquisition cone?* The tendrils of uncertainty were starting to envelop his thinking. *There had to be a way out. What was it?*

Then it hit him. They couldn't out race it horizontally, but if they timed it right, maybe they could out race it vertically. He would need to let the torpedo get close enough so that it did not have enough time to react and chase them to the surface. If he waited too long, the sub would not have enough time to get out of the acquisition cone before the torpedo hit.

"XO, range to the torpedo?" Hunter asked.

He expected immediate response and didn't hear it. Looking over at Fagan, he saw that the XO was clutching desperately to a pipe stanchion with tears streaming down his face, oblivious to everything except his fear.

Fagan was not going to be any help. Hunter would have to do this on his own. He figured that he had about two seconds of leeway. Not much at all.

What was it his old Skipper on WILSON always said? "Better lucky than good."

Looking at the sonar trace of the incoming torpedo, he waited stoically. *Couldn't let the crew see the emotions seething inside. That was the path to panic. Just a second longer, wait. Wait. Now!*

Hunter shouted, "Shoot evasion devices from both signal ejectors. Chief of the Watch, emergency blow to the surface,"

The Chief of the Watch squeezed the releases and threw the two large brass handles up. A rush of high-pressure air deafened all other sound in control. The ship began to rumble. The diving officer reached up and sounded the diving klaxon three times, the signal for an emergency surface. The roar of high-pressure air drowned out all possibility of conversation in the control room. At first the depth gauge barely moved, then it began to accelerate, then accelerate more, as more 4,500 psi air dumped into the ballast tanks, forcing the water out. The depth gauge was going so fast that the numbers were a blur. The sub's up-angle grew to forty degrees up when the bow finally jumped free of the surface and splashed back down with a stomach-churning crash.

No sooner were they on the surface than they felt an explosion beneath them. The sub jumped and shuddered.

"What happened? What was that?" could be heard around the boat.

To quiet the rising panic of the crew, Hunter announced over the 1MC, "The jolt you just felt was the incoming torpedo detonating on the evasion device below us. When we emergency blew to the surface, we came up fast enough to get out of the torpedo's vertical acquisition cone before it could react. It went for the only target left, the evasion device. We are now on the surface with only the outboard for propulsion. We will establish communications with Alpha Xray on the *NIMITZ* and with the P-3s that are incoming. The engineers will be repairing the main engines so that we can continue on our mission. We're OK."

Loud cheers answered his words.

But the fight was not over yet.

Hunter directed in rapid-fire sequence "Raise number two scope and number one BRA-34 mast. Energize the IFF to squawk mode 4. Raise Alpha Xray on SATCOM secure voice. Officer of the Deck, man the scope and report any contacts. Be on the lookout for any low flying aircraft."

Hunter replaced the microphone and stepped over to where Fagan was standing. Fagan was attempting desperately to regain his composure, tears streaming down his face while his whole body convulsed uncontrollably. Hunter quietly told the XO to go to his stateroom. Hunter would talk with him later.

Warran Jacobs jumped to the periscope, reached up and rotated the large red overhead ring to raise the scope. It slid smoothly upward. As soon as the handles cleared the deck, he snapped them down and glued his eye to the eyepiece.

Chief Tyler reported that the IFF was operating and had today's crypto installed.

Warran Jacobs reported, "No close contacts."

There were no surface ships inside four thousand yards.

He spun the scope around more slowly, carefully searching the horizon, "No contacts on initial low power search."

The afternoon sun beat down on the calm blue waters. A few white, puffy clouds danced across the sky. Everything was peaceful.

"Wait, I have an airborne contact. High power. Low on the horizon. Bearing three-one-zero. Shifting to twenty-four power. Looks like a P-3 down low. Estimated range thirty thousand yards. He is headed this way."

Chief Tyler reported, "Captain, I have Alpha Xray on Satcom. Patching it to the conn."

Hunter picked up the red telephone handset and noted that the green light was lit, signifying that it was operating in the secure mode. "Alpha Xray this is *SAN FRANCISCO*. Status report follows. Over," he said in the curious flat tonality that seemed to be reserved for military radio communications.

"*SAN FRANCISCO*, this is Alpha Alpha. Jonathan, this is Admiral Smith. What the hell is going on out there?"

The *NIMITZ* battle-group commander, Alpha Alpha, had pre-empted his ASW commander, Alpha Xray, to get a direct report. He wanted to know what was going on and fast.

"Admiral, presently on the surface. Have sustained a loss of propulsion lube oil and seized main engine bearings. Unable to make way on the mains. Initial inspections in progress.

"We took out the *KILO*. Have a P-3 closing us rapidly. Request you have him mark on top and then take station to provide us some air cover. Also, sure would be nice to have a surface escort," Hunter reported.

"Jon, the P-3, call sign Xray Papa Three, has your mode four squawk. He holds you visually. He has sighted an oil slick about 10,000 yards from your position and has a stationary magnetic anomaly below the slick. We will confirm your *KILO*. Good work," Admiral Smith replied

He continued, "I will detach *LAKE ERIE* to make best speed to rendezvous with you. His ETA is twenty hours from now. Will you require a tow?"

"I hope not. I won't know until the inspections are completed. My best speed with the outboard is two knots. But we are making preparations to receive a tow as a precaution," Hunter replied.

"Roger, keep me updated. Alpha Alpha out."

Hunter replaced the handset and turned toward Jacobs.

"Well, Nav, you heard him. Tell the COB to break the towing gear out of the sonar sphere and have it ready. I really don't relish the idea of being pulled backwards all the way to Darwin. That looks like the nearest friendly facility that could work on us," Hunter ordered.

"Radio, switch me to the P-3's frequency."

"Captain, radio. You are on the P-3's freq. Clear voice. Our call sign is Foxtrot Four Tango."

With a nod, Hunter said, "Xray Papa Three this is Foxtrot Four Tango, over."

"Foxtrot Four Tango, this is Xray Papa Three. Hold you visually. Have received instructions from Alpha Alpha to stay in the neighborhood. Over," the P3 pilot replied.

"Xray Papa Three, thank you. Request you establish patrol area twenty miles around charlie-charlie. Charlie-charlie will advance corpen two-six-five, speed two. Going sinker. Will stay at papa delta and monitor this freq. Over."

"Foxtrot Four Tango, roger. Establishing patrol area now. No contacts to report. Six hours on station time. Will have hot relief from Xray Charlie Two. Monitoring this freq."

"Radio, Captain. Station a man monitoring the P3 freq continuously."

"Radio, aye," came the reply.

"OK, Officer of the Deck, submerge the ship to periscope depth," Hunter ordered.

Jacobs immediately ordered, "Diving Officer, submerge the ship to six-two feet," initiating the well-rehearsed ritual of turning the wallowing surface target into an undersea warrior again, if a very slow one.

The diving officer responded, "Chief of the Watch, "Dive, dive" on the 1MC and two blasts on the diving alarm."

The Chief of the Watch stood and grabbed the microphone. His voice blared from 1MC, "Dive, Dive!" He pushed the operating lever on the diving klaxon. "Aooogha, Aoogha". He then reached forward and flipped up the switches marked *Vents Forward* and *Vents Aft*. The green bar lights above the switches changed to amber circles. He reported, "All vents indicate open."

The diving officer ordered, "Full dive on the fairwater planes, ten degrees down angle on the stern planes."

Warran Jacobs rapidly looked for the blast of mist rising from the forward and then the after main ballast tank vents to confirm that water was rushing in the bottom of the ballast tanks, forcing the trapped air out the top. "Forward group venting. After group venting," he reported.

"Three-six feet, three-eight feet, four-zero feet" the diving officer called out.

Jacobs reported, "Decks awash," followed quickly by, "Decks under."

Slowly the great ship slid beneath the waves. "Five-four feet, five-six feet. Zero angle on the stern planes. Zero the fairwater planes."

"Six-two feet and holding," the diving officer reported.

Hunter stepped off the conn and headed forward. He found Fagan sitting quietly in his stateroom. He had washed his reddened face and changed into a fresh pair of blue coveralls. His head hung down as he wrote on a piece of paper at his desk.

"OK, XO, just what the hell happened out there?" Hunter asked.

"Skipper, I froze, I panicked. I was so scared that I couldn't do anything," Fagan replied plaintively. He didn't look up from his desk.

Hunter answered hotly, "We were all scared. Do you think that I wasn't scared? Everyone else did their job, you froze. I can't have that. I have to have someone I can depend on backing me up, not some coward shaking like a leaf and crying like a baby. What do you think the crew is saying?"

Bill Fagan finally looked up, pleading with his eyes. "Skipper, I know all that. That's why I'm writing my resignation. If I can't handle the pressure, I don't belong here."

Hunter reached across the desk and grabbed the paper. "So that's your answer, just to run away? I won't accept it. Having an XO that that freezes is bad enough, but one that's a coward is too much. You will do your job and the next time, you'll do it right." Hunter tore the offending page into bits and threw them on the deck.

As Hunter turned to leave, Fagan jumped to his feet, both fists clenched in tight balls at his side. "You sanctimonious son of a bitch! How dare you call me a coward!" he spluttered. "You and your ego. You're so driven, you almost get us all killed making a stupid play like that. Just so you could strut around like some big hero!"

Hunter didn't even respond. He slammed the door and stormed back to his stateroom. He slumped down into the leather chair and put his head in his hands.

What had he done? He had almost blacked out at the worst possible time. Was Bill right? Had his desire to go on this mission, his arrogant knowledge that no one else could do it, brought everything to this? His ego had almost killed his crew tonight.

16

The engine-room was a bustle of hurried activity. One team of machinist mates built a clean tent around both propulsion turbine reduction gears; draping up large sheets of a material called Herculite to form a small room around the reduction gears. Everything inside the room not welded or bolted to the deck was removed. After this was completed, every item that entered the clean room, even Chief Richey's thick eyeglasses, would be logged in and logged out again. Then they unlocked and removed the casing covers.

Two other machinists started to purify and cool down the hot oil remaining in the system. They found several large pieces of bearing material in the lube oil strainers, telling them that one or more of the bearings were severely damaged.

Number one pump would not rotate when they attempted to turn it by hand. It was jammed, but number two rotated freely. Why hadn't it started?

"Eng, here is the reason that number two didn't pick up. Look at this switch. Damn thing failed and jammed open. Talk about Murphy's Law; we have probably tested it fifty times since overhaul, worked every time. When we really need it, the damn thing fails," Chief Turston reported as he held up the offending relay for Sam Stuart to scrutinize. "My guys are drawing a new one from supply. We'll have this baby up and running in a couple of hours," he stated as he rose and stretched to relieve his aching muscles of the tension from working in an impossibly cramped space. "The Navy needs to issue electricians that are ten feet tall with eight foot arms and not more than six inches around. No bones would help."

"Sure Chief, just send that suggestion up the chain," Stuart chuckled as he turned to check on the machinists.

Stuart picked up the sound powered phone. "Captain, Engineer. We have found the cause of the loss of lube oil. Looks like a nut got caught up in the screws for number one pump. Really messed up the pump. We won't be able to fix it. Out of commission for the duration. Number two has a faulty loss of pressure relay. We'll have it out and replaced in two hours.

"I won't know which propulsion train bearings are damaged until we can get into the reduction gear casing to inspect them. I'm hoping that all the damage is on one side. Then we can slip the shaft coupling on that side and operate with one main engine. If we have damage to one of the large main shaft bearings, we're screwed. We can't fix those. If we have damage to the same reduction gear bearing on both sides, we're screwed again. We only have one of each bearing type. If we can repair the bearing, rolling it out and replacing it will take at least twelve hours. Bottom line, best case, I will be able to give you one main in about three hours. Worst case, we get towed home. Anything in between is negotiable."

The SAN FRANCISCO had two identical main engines and two sets of reduction gears that were completely independent. Although normally operated together to drive the single main shaft, they could be separated in an emergency and one used for propulsion while the other was repaired. The two systems joined to drive the huge final reduction gear and then the main shaft. Any casualty to these components meant that SAN FRANCISCO would be without her engines to drive her home.

"Very well, keep working at it," Hunter grunted.

Turning to the OOD, Hunter directed, "Officer of the Deck, reload tubes three and four with Harpoons, just in case we get any surface company."

"Aye, sir," the OOD acknowledged. He then reported "The air charge is at two four hundred pounds. I expect another two hours on it. I still hold

Xray Papa Three visually. No other contacts. Making two point one knots good on the outboard."

Hunter leaned against the stanchion and rubbed his eyes, his mind racing.

So much to do, so much to think about. The blackouts were definitely worse now. How to prevent more of them and hide them from the crew? How do we get the ship fixed and back in the fight? And, maybe most troubling, what to do about Fagan?

10 Jun 2000, 2000LT (11 Jun, 0700Z)

"I can't believe he forgot again." Megan Hunter sat on the limb of her favorite banyan tree, the cell phone covered so that her mother might not see it. "He's always gone for my birthday. I'll bet that Mom buys a present for me from him and he won't even know what it is." Tears of frustration and anger poured down her cheeks.

Across the water on Ford Island, Sally Johnson lay across her bed with her phone clutched against her ear. "Yeah, Dads are like that. Mine does the same thing." She rolled over and grabbed the large fluffy teddy bear that rested on her pillow. "He tried to make up for it this year. Bought a stuffed bear at the Exchange on his way home from the office. Guess he didn't know that I had asked Mom for it the week before. Still got home late and forgot my party."

"I thought mine would remember this year," Megan complained angrily. "It's my sixteenth. But he's off on some silly exercise." She shifted around on the limb, trying to find a more comfortable position. "I hate the Navy. I'll never marry a Navy man when I grow up. I won't even date a sailor, as if Dad would let me date."

11 Jun 2000, 1810LT (0910Z)

Sam Stuart and the chief machinist, Chief Richey, pulled white Tyvek coveralls and booties over their poopie suits while discussing the inspection and repairs they expected to make on the main engine bearings. A lanyard attached every item that they needed to the belt on their suit and everything that could come loose was double secured with tape.

Stuart said, "Chief, you take the starboard reduction gear and I'll take the port. Here's hoping we can get a side back up."

They squeezed through the small access covers into the tight recesses of the reduction gear covers. They saw that they had a problem right away. Both high-speed pinion bearings were firmly welded to their respective shafts. After an hour of sliding around inside the hot, oil coated housing, they emerged, the Tyvek coveralls coated with a thick golden layer of warm oil. They didn't find any other damage.

Chief Turston stuck his head inside the clean tent and reported that repairs were completed to number two oil pump and they were ready to start it.

"Good, just in time to check normal oil flows to all the bearings. I'm still worried about the shaft bearings. If those are damaged, we are SOL," Stuart replied.

Minutes later the reduction gear covers were back in place and the pump started. Oil flowed through the system. Watch-standers carefully checked every bearing to make sure that it had a normal oil supply. Both too little and too much was bad. Too little meant that the bearing was damaged and had restricted flow. Too much meant that the heat had melted off the babbit material in the bearing leaving nothing to support the shaft. The bearing would need to be replaced. Fortunately, all bearings including the vital main shaft bearings had normal oil flows. The only exceptions were the two high-speed pinion bearings. Neither had any oil flow to them.

11 Jun 2000, 2030LT (1130Z)

Stuart wearily reported, "Captain, I have good news and bad news." Sweat dripped from his brow, forming a large puddle on the steel deck.

"Go ahead."

"First, the good news. All the shaft bearings and main reduction gear bearings are fine. We have normal oil flows. Number two lube oil pump is back on line.

"Now, for the bad news. Both high-speed pinion bearings are seized. We only have one replacement onboard. It will take us about twelve hours to roll one out and put in the new one. I am disconnecting the port main engine now and making preparations to replace the starboard bearing. After starboard repairs are complete, we will be limited to twenty knots until we can fix the port bearing."

"Very well, Eng. Keep me posted as you go. If I can get you another bearing, is there anything else that you will need?" Hunter asked.

"No sir. We checked that. We have all the other parts here. What kind of magic do you have in mind? The nearest replacement is at the Pearl Harbor Shipyard," the Engineer replied.

"Don't know yet, but we'll see what we can do. Come forward when you get a chance. I want to sit down with the department heads and plan out the next couple of days."

"Aye, sir. I'll have things rolling here in about an hour."

11 Jun 2000, 2050LT (1150Z)

"Well XO, the first combat submarine kill since World War II. I wonder how Dick O'Kane felt after his first kill on *TANG*. I can tell you that it sure isn't what I always imagined," Hunter said thoughtfully.

The two were standing in the passageway outside the XO's stateroom. It was almost like nothing had happened between them. Almost, but not quite.

"I know what you're saying about the kill, Skipper. I always thought that it would be like running in a touchdown to win the Army-Navy Game or something. But there's just this feeling that we've done something not quite clean, but something that had to be done," Fagan answered after a moment.

Both pretended that the shouting match had not occurred, neither was quite successful.

"That *KILO* skipper must have had ice for nerves. Even with an ADCAP screaming in at him, he stood and shot an accurate counter-fire. Didn't even try to run. I would have liked to meet him under different circumstances. But, all said, it's good to be alive. I'd rather be lamenting his passing than vice-versa. Let's get the department heads in the wardroom to discuss the plan for the next few days," Hunter concluded.

Fagan commented, "One thing that I still don't understand."

"What's that?" Hunter asked.

"How did that *KILO* know we were coming? He fired an ET-80 Alpha at us."

Hunter shook his head. The ET-80 Alpha was strictly an ASW torpedo. The *KILO* skipper was expecting a US submarine.

11 Jun 2000, 2145LT (1245Z)

"The time/distance problem just doesn't work. The Engineer says that he needs twelve more hours before we get one main engine and then we are limited to twenty knots. If we work this out, from here to the rendezvous is twenty-five hundred nautical miles. With this timetable, we will make twenty-four miles good while we are fixing the bearing and then one hundred and twenty-four hours or five days and five hours to get there. That will be a full day after the SEALs arrive." LCDR Jacobs completed his briefing as the assembled department heads pored over the large-scale chart laid out on the wardroom table. "That doesn't even take into account time to come to periscope depth for comms or any delays. We'll either have to delay or abort."

Hunter directed his first team, "Unfortunately, neither of those options are possible. We have to get there and deliver those SEALs. Too much depends on it. Give me another option. Think outside the box."

The room fell silent. No one had an answer.

They had come so far, accomplished so much, only to be stopped here. It didn't seem possible, but there didn't appear to be any alternative.

"Just a minute," the normally quiet weapons officer jumped up. As the most junior and least experienced of the department heads, Jeff Miller was much more inclined to sit back and listen than to initiate any ideas outside of his departmental responsibilities.

"Eng, didn't you say that the nearest bearing was in Pearl?"

"Yeah, that's where it is. Doesn't do us any good over four thousand five hundred miles away," the exhausted Engineer shot back sarcastically.

"Just a minute, Eng. Give Jeff a chance. He may have something," Fagan interjected.

Jeff Miller started out hesitantly, afraid that he would be laughed at or his idea rejected as too far fetched. "Remember that exchange duty I pulled with the Air Force after my junior officer sea tour? I flew as a watch officer on the Airborne National Command Post. You call it Kneecap after the acronym, ABNCP. One thing that we always tracked was the KC-10 tankers around the world. We always had the capability to set up a tanker grid across the Pacific on a one-hour notice."

LT Miller continued, "Now, remember that squadron of F-15 Eagles that the Hawaiian Air National Guard maintains at Hickam? They maintain two birds on a ready fifteen for air defense. Suppose that we put a bearing in an F-15 and flew it to Guam. Have an F-14 from the *NIMITZ* meet it there. The F-14 does a hot turn around to the carrier. Then one of *ESSEX's* OSPREYs brings it to us. If the fast flyers pour on the coal, shouldn't take more than, say, six hours."

"Weps, you're a genius. If you weren't so ugly, I'd kiss you," Hunter shouted over his shoulder as he ran to the control room.

"Radio, Captain, get me Alpha Alpha on the horn."

The reply was quick. "Captain, radio. Alpha Alpha is on the net. The watch officer is notifying the admiral. I have patched you through to the conn."

"Alpha Alpha, this is *SAN FRANCISCO*, over" Hunter started over the red phone.

Admiral Smith answered, "*SAN FRANCISCO* this is Alpha Alpha. Jon, you just called me out of a full house in the staff poker game, so this had better be good."

"Admiral, I probably just saved you from a big loss to your chief of staff. Remember, Captain Butler is an old submariner and we can't be trusted.

"I have a problem and a solution, but I need some help," Hunter continued as he briefed the battle group commander on Jeff Miller's plan. The admiral signed off, saying that he would see what he could do, but clearly unconvinced that the huge multi-service bureaucracy could react that swiftly for one lone submarine, half way around the world.

11 Jun 2000, 0355LT (1455Z)

An hour later, an Hawaiian Air National Guard major briefed his flight of two F-15 Eagles. "I don't know what the skinny is on this, but the general himself was just on the horn. We are flying those two boxes at max cruise to Guam. KC-10s are taking station 500 miles Southwest of French Frigate Shoals and a thousand miles West of Midway. We're to take off ASAP, point West and go fast. ETA Guam, three hours. Sure must be something important in those boxes to turn us into FedEx. Saddle up, time to fly."

At the same time, two F-14D Tomcats were thrown into night sky from the forward catapults on *NIMITZ*. They pointed their noses East-North-East and made maximum speed to rendezvous with the Westbound Eagles on Guam.

"*NIMITZ* control, this is tango bravo flight of two. Outbound zero-three-zero, angels four-five, mach one point two. Verify KC-10s on station, over"

"Tango bravo, *NIMITZ* control, roger. Blue suiters report filling stations available as briefed."

The round trip with two refuelings each way took a little over six hours. The pilots and NFO's didn't even have the time to climb down out of their cramped cockpits into the tropical heat of the Guam night. The F-15's landed as the Tomcats taxied to the hot refueling station. The two packages were stowed as the F-14's tanks were topped off for the high-speed return flight. Then they were out on the runway and gone into the night sky with a brilliant blaze of afterburners.

17

---

12 Jun 2000, 0653LT (11 Jun, 2153Z)

"*SAN FRANCISCO* this is Alpha Alpha. Jon, you were right. Chief of Staff was sitting on four Queens. You saved me a bundle. Someday you have to tell me what is going on. You are clearly doing something other than just escorting the *ESSEX* ARG. I picked up the phone with COMPAC Fleet to tell him your crazy idea and the next thing I know, the whole Pacific Air Force is scrambled to get you not one, but two bearings. They are inbound to *NIMITZ* now. An OSPREY is onboard and ready to deliver them to you. I'm sending you a couple of cases of beer for your crew. They've sure earned it. ETA over *SAN FRANCISCO* in one hour."

"Thanks Admiral. The crew will appreciate the beer. Wish I could tell you what we are doing. I know you understand the security and 'need to know' associated with this. All I can tell you is that the orders start out with the words "matters of highest national priority." We should have one main available in four hours. Estimate another eight hours for both engines. *SAN FRANCISCO* out".

12 Jun 2000, 0830LT (11 Jun, 2330Z)

The dark gray painted twin-engine aircraft flew low and fast just above the placid sea. The grotesquely over-sized propellers kicked up a trail of mist and spray behind it. Just before passing directly over the surfaced sub, the plane executed a maneuver impossible for any other aircraft. The pilot rotated the plane's twin turbo prop engines, located at the ends of stubby wings, until the huge propellers became overhead rotors. In seconds, the fast moving aircraft had been transformed into a hovering helicopter. The large rear ramp rumbled down and a net filled with several boxes was lowered by a single line to the waiting submarine's deck.

As the OSPREY came to a hover, four blue coverall clad sailors emerged from the submarine's deck hatch into the brilliant morning sunshine. The downdraft from the hovering OSPREY tore at their poopie suits. They were quickly drenched from the spray.

The sailors unloaded the boxes from the net and lowered them carefully down the open hatch. In less than five minutes the exchange had been completed. The OSPREY resumed normal flight and disappeared over the horizon as the submarine slipped below the waves. Not even a ripple remained to show that anything had happened at this lonely point in the ocean.

12 Jun 2000, 1810LT (0910Z)

"Alpha Alpha, this is *SAN FRANCISCO*. All repairs are complete. Answering bells on both main engines. Able to answer all bells. Will be running deep and fast to next op area. Out of communications for next 20 hours. Will be standing by for any bell ringers for tasking changes. Detaching *LAKE ERIE* to return to battle group and the P-3 escort to other duties. *SAN FRAN-CISCO* out." Hunter placed the red phone back in its holder.

Turning to the Jeff Miller, who peered out the periscope, Hunter directed, "OK Officer of the Deck. Let's go deep and fast. We have a rendezvous to make. Make your depth eight hundred feet and answer *ahead flank*."

Turning his attention to Warran Jacobs, bent over the chart table checking their progress, Hunter asked, "Nav, how does it look to get there on time?"

"Well Skipper, the Eng cut it real close. If we run at flank and only come up to copy the broadcast every twenty four hours, we should just skid in on time," Jacobs replied, looking up from the chart for a second.

Finally free of the restricted waters of the Torres Straits and able to fly once again, *SAN FRANCISCO* lunged ahead. They raced through the Arafura and Timor Seas, out into the Indian Ocean. Altering course to the Northwest , they headed toward the Sunda Straits, the only passage deep and wide enough to allow them submerged access into the Java Sea without the fear of being detected.

14 Jun 2000, 0330LT (13 Jun, 2030Z)

Bill Fagan sprang up, wide-awake. Normally a light sleeper, especially at sea, and troubled by the recent past, he was instantly jarred from his slumber. The lights in his tiny stateroom suddenly blinked on.

No one else was in the confined space. Grumbling under his breath, he walked over to the switch and flipped it. Nothing happened. He flipped it again and still nothing. The lights stayed on. *Damn it, what was causing this?*

He picked up the MJ phone and selected the OOD's station. When Sam Stuart answered, he requested, "Officer of the Deck, have the auxiliary electrician report to my stateroom to check a faulty light switch."

Within minutes, the young electrician was at his door. Bill Fagan explained, "The light came on by itself and I can't get it to turn it off." He stepped aside to give the AE room to investigate. The electrician reached over and flipped the switch. The lights went out. Another flip of the switch and they came back on.

The petty officer turned to the XO and said, "Switch seems to work fine. Must be MES. Magic Electric Shit."

As the AE left, Chief Jones peeked around the corner and smiled.

· · ·

CDR Hunter yelled through the doors that connected their staterooms, "XO, read this "Personal for" from SUBPAC. Do you believe this! What a tangled tale."

Hunter was sitting at his desk, reading the message traffic from the last communications download.

"This message says that Admiral O'Flanagan is the subject of a Congressional investigation for recruiting irregularities while he commanded CRUITCOM. The most serious infractions were apparently in South LA. Now we find out that Chief Richey was a recruiter there and he recruited Seaman Martinez. SUBPAC Chief of Staff thinks they falsified the enlistment contract and has directed us to investigate."

Bill Fagan rose from his desk, stepped into the CO's stateroom and looked over Hunter's shoulder to read the offending message. Finally he flopped into a seat at the small table against the outboard bulkhead.

"This is great! Just great! Our best chief petty officer and a young kid that we are just beginning to turn into a good sailor caught up in a Congressional witch-hunt. As if we didn't have enough to worry about, they add this BS," Fagan ranted.

"XO, conduct a formal Article 15 investigation and give me the results," Jon Hunter ordered, handing over the message.

"Yes, sir. I'll appoint the Navigator as the investigating officer. Neither one works for him and he has the experience to do a good job," the XO replied as he returned to his desk.

16 Jun 2000, 2200LT (1500Z)

The specially configured black MC-130 Combat Talon II flew over the dark empty ocean, just above the wave tops. After hours of tense, low altitude flight, the pilot heard faintly over the low probability of intercept (LPI) radio, "Night Train, this is Black Shark. I hold your IR light bearing one three zero from me. Range twelve. Come left ten degrees. Standby to mark on top."

After a brief pause "Standby, mark, mark, MARK! Night Train you passed one hundred yards to the Southeast. Ready to receive."

"Roger, Black Shark. Climbing to angels five to send," The pilot replied as the big bird climbed and banked through a 180-degree turn.

The huge aft door rumbled down as ten of the twenty black clad figures silently rose and sauntered toward the gaping opening. The faint red light high up on the right side of the door went out and the green one just below it illuminated. The ten casually walked off the end of the ramp and dropped into the blackness.

No sooner than the last figure had dropped, the plane again banked around in a 180-degree turn to repeat the procedure for the other ten passengers. As the last figure dropped, the ramp rumbled shut. The pilot dove the bird back down to wave-top height and sent, "Black Shark, delivered twenty."

The immediate reply came back, "Night Train, acknowledge receipt twenty. Thanks, good trip home."

"Black Shark, good hunting. Night Train out."

"XO, who thinks up these corny call signs? Sounds like something out of a cheap spy novel," Hunter commented as he stepped back from the scope.

"I don't know," Fagan replied as he replaced the red radio handset in its cradle. "My guess is that there is some over-paid, under-worked GS-15 in a closet at the Pentagon whose only job is to come up with these. Hadn't we better pick up our guests before they think that we are neglecting them? I have the Chief of the Boat with his party standing by in the forward escape trunk."

"Right. Let's get this show on the road. Officer of the Deck, *All Stop*. Prepare to surface," Hunter ordered and returned to staring through the scope eyepiece. "I can see their IR Chem-lites about a hundred yards off the port bow."

"Answering *All Stop*. Ready to surface," the OOD replied.

The huge submarine glided to a halt a scant few yards from the cluster of men in the water.

"Surface! Surface! Surface!" blared over the 1MC, followed shortly by the blast of high-pressure air forcing the water out of the ballast tanks.

· · ·

Twenty men huddled closely, clustered together, alone in the black water of the vast empty ocean.

Suddenly they weren't alone. A massive black shape appeared a few yards away, blocking out the starlit sky.

"Wow, I never get over how they just suddenly appear out of nowhere," one of the swimmers commented.

"It's a damn good thing they do. Otherwise, it's an awful long swim home," another replied dryly.

"Knock it off and start swimming," ordered a third.

16 Jun 2000, 2215LT (1515Z)

"On the surface and holding. One inch pressure in the boat," the Chief of the Watch reported.

"Very well, equalize the ship," Jeff Miller directed.

The crew realigned the ventilation system so that air came in through the snorkel mast to equalize the air pressure internal to the ship with the outside air pressure. Otherwise, the one-inch pressure differential, which equated to about 250 pounds of force across the escape trunk hatch, was enough to launch anyone trying to open it forcefully out of the ship.

"Zero pressure," reported the Chief of the Watch shortly.

"Send the party topside," Hunter ordered.

The coverall-clad figures scurried out the hatch into the moonlight. One threw a short rope ladder down the slick curved rubber coated side of the sub to the swimmers waiting in the water.

Master Chief Hancock reached out to help the first black-clad SEAL up the ladder. "Welcome aboard the cruise ship *SAN FRANCISCO*. Cocktails are being served on the promenade deck. The shuffleboard tournament will commence on the fantail in twenty minutes."

"Thanks, COB," chuckled one of the hulking figure as he scrambled up the ladder, "but where's the chow and did the Skipper beat my record on the Life Rower?"

"Welcome back aboard, Lieutenant Roland. Hot chow is waiting for you below decks. Saw the Skipper coming forward the other day from using the Life Rower grumbling something about "Damn young upstart SEALs" and

"Teaching them respect" so I would venture that your record is gone. Sure wish I could eat like you guys do," he chortled as he pointed out the slight paunch over his belt.

"You could eat like us if you had just jumped out of a perfectly good airplane into the cold dark Indian Ocean, with every expectation of swimming all the way home," the SEAL lieutenant retorted.

"Lieutenant, water temperature is eighty-four, so don't give me that "cold dark ocean" crap," Master Chief Hancock joshed good-naturedly.

All of the figures quickly slid down the ladder and the hatch swung shut. The sub slid beneath the surface, leaving no sign that anything had just happened in this lonely part of the ocean.

On the mess decks, the SEALs sat before heaping plates of hot food, eating with the gusto of exceedingly fit men requiring constant caloric intake. They had exchanged their black wet suits for camouflage uniforms, contrasting sharply with the submariners' blue poopie suits.

Chief Boatswains Mate Sergiavich, the platoon's second in command, asked, "Lieutenant, are you ever going to tell the Skipper that you were All American in single sculls back at Brown?"

"No, Boats, I won't," commented the lieutenant. "Besides, to a man like the Skipper, it wouldn't make any difference. Just like when he beat me on the last Super Frog Triathlon. Didn't make any difference that he is almost forty."

"He beat you because he is a sub-three-hour marathoner and you run like a duck. As I remember that race, you had a ten minute lead coming off the swim," Boats said, relating the annual SEAL Half Ironman Triathlon. "You were about even after the bike race. He caught you at mile six on the run and then ran away from you. Besides, he's forty-four," Boats continued, forking another helping of mash potatoes into his mouth. "I can see this competition ending with you two having a swim race to Zamboango and back."

"That might be an even race. How far is that?" questioned the massive lieutenant.

"About a thousand miles North of here," Boats answered and returned his attention to the plate before him.

17 Jun 2000, 0530LT (16 Jun, 2330Z)

"Injured Man in engine-room lower level! Corpsman lay to engine-room lower level! Captain is down!"

The 1MC announcement caused the crew to spring into action. Doc Pugh jumped from his bunk in the goat locker, grabbed his bag of emergency medical supplies and sprinted aft. He passed the stretcher team picking up a stretcher and additional supplies. They would follow him aft.

ENS Green and Petty Officer Swain had already stopped breakfast preparation and were well into transforming the wardroom into an emergency operating room.

Doc Pugh ducked through the low hatch into the condensate bay in lower level engine-room.

Hunter was sitting on the deck shaking his head and yelling at Sam Stuart. "Damn it Eng, why did you have to go and call away an injured man? Now we've got the whole boat in an uproar!"

"But Skipper, you passed out. One minute you are inspecting the hot well level controller and the next you are laid out on the deck," Stuart retorted, a hurt and offended note in his voice.

"Captain, sit back and let me take your pulse and blood pressure," Doc interjected. "Eng, please call control and tell them to stand down from 'Injured Man'. I won't be needing the stretcher or any other help for now."

He wrapped the black rubber sleeve around Hunter's upper arm, inflated it and listened to his pulse as the sleeve slowly deflated.

Removing the blood pressure cuff from Hunter's right arm, Doc reported, "Well, your pulse is slightly elevated. I expect that after the excitement. Your blood pressure is low, normal for you. I warned you about this. Want to tell me what happened?"

"Not much to tell, Doc. I had just finished my normal morning routine on the exercise equipment. The Engineer wanted me to see the level control for the port hot well. It had been controlling erratically and we were discussing the need to repair it. I squatted down to watch it operate and then started to stand up. Vision went black. The next thing I know, the Eng is shaking me and everyone is rushing about," Hunter replied.

The Corpsman said, "Well, I think that it is only the combination of your low blood pressure and the stress of the long hours you keep. Add that to your "normal morning routine" of two hard hours on the exercise gear and I can see why you went down. If I had an EKG machine out here, I would hook you up, but I don't have one. We will definitely have to schedule you for testing when we get back. In the meantime, try to take it a little easier, and don't jump on the Engineer. He did exactly what he should have."

"OK Doc, thanks and I guess I owe the Eng an apology," Hunter concluded, slowly rising to walk out of the compartment.

17 Jun 2000, 1440LT (0840Z)

Bill Fagan was seated at his desk working down the endless stack of paperwork, the bane of an XO's existence. More redundant reports required by desk jockeys who probably had not set foot on a ship in years. Most likely they were not even read, just filed in some musty closet.

Suddenly the stateroom went dark. He flipped the light switch. Again the switch didn't work. Nothing but darkness.

He stepped out into the passageway and walked to control. The AE again came to troubleshoot the problem. Again the switch worked perfectly for him.

The XO was mystified. He certainly understood the simple lighting circuit. An Electrical Engineering degree from the Academy and the Nuclear Power Training pipeline insured that. This should not be happening. There had to be a logical explanation to this. But, what was it?

18

---

18 Jun 2000, 0045LT (17 Jun, 1845Z)

The sinister black shape slid silently through the warm tropical night. The only sound of its passage was the faint lapping of the torpid waves against the steel monster.

A gentle land breeze mixed the fetid smell of rotting vegetation and the earthy smell of a freshly plowed field with the salty tang of the sea air. Clutches of stars peeked quickly through the fleeting clouds scurrying across the sky. The twinkling lights from several small fishing villages were visible around the periphery of the wide bay. The lights were the only sign that the bay ended and the island began.

All was darkness around the black hulk, as if it sucked in all light like a sea-going black hole.

The unexpected message had arrived early in the morning. Orders from COMSUBPAC were to make best speed to this remote bay on the North side of Java. Rendezvous with the agent at 2230. But no one had shown.

Hunter stayed at the mouth of the bay for an hour past the rendezvous time. When no one showed, he elected to drive slowly into the bay, as far as he dared, in hopes that the agent was merely delayed and he could be met on the way.

Loitering on the surface within spitting distance of land was not a smart move. They had stayed in the confines of the bay as long as they dared. Too many things could happen, all of them bad. Patience was not Hunter's strongest characteristic and this was trying him to the limit. They should be a hundred miles closer to their destination and hours closer to completing their mission.

There was nothing to do but turn around and head out to deep water.

"Captain, Nav reports one-five feet under the keel. He recommends turning now. The bottom is coming up fast, four hundred yards to shoal water." Jeff Miller's whispered voice came out of the darkness.

Hunter looked around once more and whispered, "Very well, Weps. *Back one-third*, left full rudder. Train the outboard to port nine zero and start the outboard. Let's get out of here."

Hunter was already drafting the message to SUBPAC in his mind as he anxiously paced the tiny deck. Maybe the agent had been compromised, possibly his boat had failed, or he just had cold feet and didn't show. There was no way of knowing. But they had wasted eight priceless hours in this futile effort, what with the deviation from the planned track and the wait in the bay. And for nothing. What should have been a source of precious information had turned out to be a dangerous waste of time. Hunter was not happy and he intended to let SUBPAC know it.

Jeff Miller nudged Hunter with his elbow. "Skipper, look. Call it two points off the port bow. Out about five hundred yards. Thought I saw a glimmer of a light."

Hunter looked out into the blackness. "Don't see anything but black, Jeff. Come to *ahead one third*. Steer course zero-two five."

Dark clouds were moving in and obscuring what little starlight was available. The light breeze carried the promise of rain.

"There it is again," Miller all but shouted, pointing excitedly.

"I see it now." Hunter answered. "Steer for the light. Let's get a little closer before we answer. Could only be a fisherman out here, fishing. No sense letting him know we are here until we are sure."

Miller looked through the alidade on the compass repeater, reading the bearing to the faintly visible light. He ordered, "Helm steer course three-one-three." He continued to stare in the direction of the light. "Skipper, the light is flashing now. I make out two shorts and two longs repeated every thirty seconds."

"That's our signal," Hunter replied. "Come to *all stop* and drift up to him." He took the little penlight from his coveralls pocket and answered the signal.

The little perahu pinisi almost bumped against the *SAN FRANCISCO*'s hull before they could see it. Its low dark wooden form was all but invisible in the blackness of the night.

Large droplets of a warm rain began to sputter down.

SAN FRANCISCO slid to a stop as the fishing boat came abreast of the sail. Someone could just be seen sitting in the stern. Hunter reached for his Beretta, just in case.

"Captain, sorry I'm late. Permission to come aboard." The jaunty Australian drawl was unmistakable. "Oh, yeah, password is 'matey'."

Hunter slid the 9mm Beretta back into its holster when he heard the password. He really didn't remember drawing it, but he saw Jeff Miller holstering his Beretta, too. Tensions were running high.

Hunter reached down into the cockpit and grabbed the coil of knotted rope lying on the teak grating. After checking to make sure that one end was firmly tied to a stanchion, he tossed the coil down to the waiting agent. "Quick, grab the rope and get up here. We haven't got all night."

The agent grabbed the rope and climbed up the vertical side of the sail. He stepped onto the port sailplane and then hoisted himself up the last few feet to the lip of the cockpit as Hunter reached over and yanked him in, head-first.

The agent regained his footing and stood next to Hunter. He stuck out his right hand and jauntily said, "Durstin Turnstill. Sorry to be a bit late. Bloody motor on that boat. Had to paddle all the way out."

Turnstill looked to be a middle-aged, medium height, slightly over-weight Australian, dressed in jeans and a Foster's beer tee shirt.

Hunter ignored the proffered hand and growled, "Time for pleasantries later. Get below. We have to get out of here."

Turnstill ducked below the cockpit coaming and disappeared down the ladder.

Hunter grabbed the 7MC microphone and said, "XO, our guest is coming below. Get him in dry clothes and make him comfortable in your stateroom. I'll be down as soon as we are out of here.

"Nav, course to deep water?"

Fagan promptly replied, "COB has him now, looking for a poopie-suit. Nav recommends course zero-one-zero. Fifty fathom curve in thirty miles. Twenty fathom curve in twenty-five. Recommend ahead one-third. Visibility down to one hundred yards."

The little perahu pinisi was left to drift ashore in a few days, one more mystery of the Java Sea.

The rain quickly grew from a gentle shower to a torrential downpour. The drops were hitting so hard that any exposed skin stung painfully. Hunter and Miller gave up all pretense of trying to look out ahead. The driving rain made that impossible. They tried to find a little shelter below the cockpit coaming.

Hunter grabbed the 7MC microphone. "Chief of the Watch, get two pairs of arctic goggles up here quick. Quartermaster, you'll have to keep a good look-out through the scope."

"Captain, Navigator." The tinny speaker was barely audible above the hammering of the driving rain. "Recommend making bare steerageway until this clears. Petty Officer Buell reports visibility down to twenty-five yards. We won't be able to see anything in enough time to avoid it."

Jacobs gave Hunter the "by the book" answer. Maritime law requires bare steerageway when visibility is nil to reduce the risk of running into something or someone. Hunter understood that it was the Nav's job to give him the "by the book" recommendation.

Hunter listened to the recommendation and hesitated the barest instant. "Nav, log your recommendation. *All ahead full*. Where are those goggles?"

There were times when the book just didn't work. There was no telling when the rain would clear. It might be ten minutes, it might be after daybreak. Then they would be stuck twenty-five miles from the nearest water deep enough to hide in. Ordering Jacobs to log his recommendation would prove that Jacobs had done his job if they hit anything. The responsibility rested solely with Hunter.

The tiny speaker squawked, "Nav, aye. Goggles on the way up. Answering *ahead full*."

The fur lined arctic goggles looked incongruous when they were barely four hundred miles South of the equator, but they protected Hunter's and Miller's eyes from the driving rain. Hunter peered out over the top of the sail, willing himself to see anything out there. He could barely make out the white curling wave that washed halfway up the side of the sail before collapsing on its self. *SAN FRANCISCO*,s eighteen knots, added to the twenty knot wind, drove the rain until it felt like gravel thrown against their flesh.

Miller took station on the port side of the tiny cockpit and stared ahead. He yelled above the wind, "Skipper, I can't see shit. How about you."

Hunter yelled back, "About the same. Keep looking."

A white blur flashed toward them and slammed into the sail just forward of Miller. They were both splattered with feathers and blood, which the driving rain washed away. Hunter shouted, "Seagull. He couldn't see either."

They charged through the blinding storm with the wind howling in their ears. Hunter prayed that no fisherman was desperate enough to challenge this storm or any tramp steamer was trying to make way up the coast.

Finally the tinny speaker squawked, "Captain, Navigator. Twenty fathoms under the keel and dropping fast. Recommend we dive now."

Hunter yelled into the microphone, "*Ahead one-third*. Nav, take the conn. Weps and I will rig the bridge for dive. Have personnel stand by in the trunk to hand down gear."

18 Jun 2000, 0445LT (17 Jun, 2145Z)

SAN FRANCISCO slid silently beneath the waves and dove into the depths. The wild driving rainstorm was forgotten, three hundred feet above them.

Hunter walked forward to meet their guest. His shoes squished wetly, leaving puddles on the tile. He reached into his stateroom and grabbed a towel. Vigorously drying his hair, he walked on down the passageway to the XO's stateroom.

Sniffing the air as he walked, Hunter smelled the acrid odor of cigarette smoke. Stepping into the XO's stateroom, he found Turnstill leaning back in Fagan's chair, his feet propped up on the desk. He was nursing a cup of coffee and a cigarette. Turnstill was dressed in a dry poopie suit. His tousled reddish hair, ruddy complexion, and grey-blue eyes gave him a devil-may-care air.

Hunter snapped, "Please put that out. Smoking is not allowed here."

Turnstill slowly dropped his feet to the floor and slipped the cigarette butt into the remains of the coffee. "Sorry, Skipper. Didn't know the rules. Glad you happened along when you did. Didn't relish going back to the island. Landlord was getting upset. When he finds out his daughter's in the family way, my welcome is shot."

Hunter exasperation boiled over. Risking his ship and the mission for this low life was too much to bear. He answered back sharply, "You had better have something useful for us. If we pulled you out just to avoid an irate father, I'll have your ass nailed to a mast!"

Turnstill raised both hands in surrender. "Captain you have no idea how upset one of these Muslim fathers can get. It could mean my head! But I do have a little information for you. I have worked for Suluvana. I know about Nusa Funata."

Hunter pulled up a chair and sat. "All right start talking. You have my attention."

Turnstill leaned back again and began to talk. "Captain, for some reason, I get the feeling we started out on the wrong foot. Let's start over."

Hunter answered drily, "That depends on what you have to say. Tell me what you know about Suluvana."

Turnstill folded his arms across his chest and leaned back in the chair, again. "Fair enough. Let's say that I'm a bit of a free-lancer. Someone wants something done, I do it. Not too many questions. Suluvana wanted mining equipment. Needed it delivered to Nusa Funata quietly and quickly. I found what he wanted and had it delivered. Whole boat load of stuff. Enough stuff to do some major rock moving. Funny thing about delivering it to Nusa Funata. There's nothing to mine there. Most God forsaken piece of rock you can imagine. Insisted on delivery at night and the crew was not allowed off the boat while his people off-loaded the stuff."

Hunter stood as Bill Fagan walked into the stateroom. There wasn't room for three chairs in the cramped space. Hunter folded his chair and leaned against the bulkhead. "When was this?"

Turnstill scratched the stubble on his chin for a second. "Call it a year ago. Yeah, it was just before the monsoons. He was real anxious to get the stuff in before the rains hit."

Fagan chimed in, "Did you get to see any of the island?"

Turnstill looked over at Fagan. "Only what I could see from the deck at night. Just a short cement pier and a little metal warehouse."

Hunter responded, "Anything else? A little more recent?"

Turnstill fidgeted in his seat. "Not much. Just rumors of some troops being reassigned to some unknown location. The enforcers from some local gangs dropping out of site. That sort of thing. Nothing that you could put your finger on."

Hunter glared at the erstwhile agent. "Mr. Turnstill, I hope your memory improves. What you have told us so far has certainly not been worth the risk of pulling you off Java. Until either your memory improves or we can drop you off *SAN FRANCISCO*, you will confine yourself to this stateroom and the wardroom for meals.

"XO, draft a message to SUBPAC telling them that we retrieved Mr. Turnstill. Relate what he has told us. Add a CO's summary that says I don't think his information is worthwhile or timely."

18 Jun 2000, 0800LT (0100Z)

Chief Jones stepped into the radio room and selected the XOSR on the MJ phone growler. He spun the crank once and stepped back out again. He hurriedly passed through control and dodged into the sonar room. He scurried through the computer space and peeked around the corner toward the XO's door. He was just in time to see the XO storm out of the door and charge to control. The room behind him was dark.

Chief Jones hurried back to the radio room and again spun the MJ growler dial. The relay hidden behind the ventilation ducting above the XO's stateroom received its signal and returned the light circuit to normal.

This is working perfectly, he chuckled to himself. *A few more days and he would have a truly memorable gag to brag about. The XO was smart. Pulling this off would prove that he really deserved the age-old description of a Chief "devious and cunning, bearing watching at all times."*

Once again, the auxiliary electrician found the switch working perfectly, to Bill Fagan's growing irritation.

Ensign Green stuck his head into the CO's Stateroom, "Skipper, the wardroom is set up for Mast."

"Very well, Chop. I'll be right down. Tell the OOD to pass the word on the 1MC and have the COB muster the parties in the middle level passageway," Hunter said as he closed the report folder.

Tucking the folder under his arm he sighed and rose to leave, muttering to himself, "Might as well get this over with. Some parts of this job just aren't any fun."

"All quiet in the vicinity of the wardroom while Captain's Mast is in progress," the OOD intoned solemnly over the 1MC.

The announcement was made as much to inform the crew that the meting out of justice in the age-old Navy tradition of Captain's Mast was in progress as to actually instruct them to be quiet.

Dating back to the early days of the British Navy, carried forward from the very beginnings of the US Navy and firmly entrenched in maritime law, the concept that the Captain of a ship at sea had absolute authority over all aboard was steeped in naval tradition. From Captain Bligh to Captain Queeg, the caricature of the despotic sea captain was a popular literary figure. In reality, far from home and out of communications, sea captains were expected to mete out justice for all onboard. The term "Mast" came from the tradition on sailing ships of holding the proceedings before the main mast.

This power and duty had undergone modification in modern times. Rapid communications, a more centralized command structure and a more liberal social environment resulted in limiting the commanding officer's prerogatives to investigating possible offenses and taking action to correct those that he deemed minor and administrative. Serious offenses were passed on to higher command that had court-martial convening authority. This still allowed wide latitude and discretion on the captain's part as to deciding if cases should be sent off for courts-martial or to the form of administrative punishment that was appropriate. But even this was subject to review by higher authority.

Hunter strode down the centerline passageway, passing by the accused without a word or a glance as they stood in their best dress uniforms, nervously waiting. He entered the wardroom, devoid of all furniture save the table and one chair for him. The table had been covered with a deep green felt cloth embroidered with a set of gold dolphins and a gold command star in the center. Neatly assembled on the green felt were a copy of the Manual for Courts-Martial, the charge sheets, the investigation results, and a glass of water.

As Hunter took his seat, the XO, COB and the chain of command for the two accused crewmembers entered and arranged themselves around the table. The XO stood at Hunter's right hand, the COB took station at the door. They had all exchanged their normal underway blue coveralls for dress khaki uniforms.

"XO, are we ready?" Hunter asked.

With that, the arrayed officers and chiefs came to parade rest.

"Yes, sir. All parties are in attendance," Fagan replied crisply.

"Very well. COB, call the accused," the Commander ordered.

The two forlorn sailors marched in to the wardroom and stood before the green table at rigid attention. At the COB's sharply barked order, the pair rendered a crisp salute and then removed their covers.

CDR Hunter read solemnly from a prepared script. "Chief Petty Officer Richey, Seaman Martinez, you stand before me accused of a violation of article 132 of the Uniform Code of Military Justice, in that you knowingly and willingly submitted a false official record, to wit, an enlistment contract for Seaman Martinez that falsely stated that Seaman Martinez had graduated from high school. As you have been advised by the executive officer, a Captain's Mast is not a trial by court martial and the rules of evidence that apply in a trial by court martial do not apply here. You have each been advised by the Executive Officer of your rights. Do you understand these rights?"

The pair chorused, "Yes sir!"

"How do you plead, guilty or not guilty?" Hunter questioned.

Staring rigidly straight ahead, they both stammered, "Guilty, sir."

"Very well, before I pass sentence, are there any mitigating or extenuating circumstances that I should take into account?" Hunter asked.

With a slight hesitation, they answered, "No, sir."

Putting down the script, he peered up at the two sailors standing before him. "You two have seen the report of the investigation that the Navigator conducted and read all the findings. Do you want to tell me, in your own words, what really happened?"

Chief Richey swallowed hard and spoke up, "Skipper, this is all my fault. Seaman Martinez was only doing what I told him. He shouldn't be here in front of you."

"Chief, I admire your leadership and forthrightness for saying that, but, as you have both admitted, you both submitted a false official statement and the fact that you told Martinez to do it, does not change that. Now, please explain to me how my best chief petty officer, who I just recommended for early advancement to senior chief, is standing here before me?" Hunter queried.

"Captain, when this happened I was still a first class petty officer and I had been assigned to the Thirteenth Recruiting District working in South East LA. We were having a terrible time trying to meet our quotas everywhere and I think that South East was the worst. When I first reported there, I busted my butt to make quotas and did everything exactly by the book. The first quarter I made it, barely. The second I didn't and the Senior Chief who ran the place called me in to his office. He had a stack of records from all the guys that I had interviewed and rejected. He chewed my butt royally and then started going through the stack, marking them up. Every mark changed something that was a mandatory reject into an acceptable recruit. I asked the Senior Chief what he was doing. He looked up and sort of smiled and told me he was showing me how to make quota. I said something about how all these kids would get kicked out in basic training. He told me that was boot camp's problem, not his. I told him that I couldn't do that. He let me know that if I didn't make quota, my career was in the tank.

"Well, next quarter I didn't make quota, again. He made life really miserable for me. Even threatening Mast for dereliction of duty. He had me in a real bind. I knew that all the other recruiters were doing it. I was the only hold out. He called me into his office again. Told me that I was on my way out as a second class, but he was going to give me one last chance.

"The next interview was Martinez. He'd dropped out of high school and started to run with a pretty tough street gang. I told him to answer that he had a high school diploma. After I had processed him, I felt so bad that I went to the Senior Chief and told him that I wanted a transfer back to the fleet. He did it, but really screwed me on the transfer eval."

"OK, Chief. Now Martinez, what's your story?" Hunter said, turning his gaze to the young sailor.

"Captain, I grew up in South East. Mom was trying to raise us four kids alone. She is a good lady and she worked hard to keep us out of trouble. I dropped out of High School because of the gangbanging and the drugs. I couldn't handle that scene. I had to get out of there. The Navy seemed like a good way to go. I called the recruiting office and talked to Chief Richey. When I went in to sign the papers, I read the part about having to have a high school diploma and I told him that I didn't have one. He said not to worry, he would fix it. Go ahead and say that I had one. So I did," the young sailor concluded.

"And you both ended up here purely by chance?" Hunter asked.

"Yes, sir. When Martinez reported onboard, I was more surprised than anyone," Chief Richey replied.

Hunter carefully placed the report on the table in front of him and thoughtfully gazed down at it for a few moments. The two accused sailors locked their eyes rigidly on the bulkhead behind the Commander. The moment of truth had arrived. Beads of sweat popped out on their brows.

They were clearly guilty and freely admitted it. The both expressed regret for what they had done. Most importantly to Hunter, one of them was an outstanding chief petty officer. And Hunter had a gut feeling that Martinez could be turned around into a good sailor, given enough time and effort. If he found the charges to be serious or criminal, Hunter would have been bound to hold the two for trial by court-martial when they returned.

Hunter looked directly into the eyes of each one, then he said, "I find you both guilty as charged. Furthermore, I find these violations to be minor and administrative in nature."

Picking up the Manual for Courts-Martial and turning to the marked page, he read aloud, "The maximum punishment that could be meted out for this violation is a reduction in rank to E-1, forfeiture of half of all pay and allowances for six months, confinement for up to ten years and a dishonorable discharge."

Turning his gaze up to the two sailors, he continued, "I further find that there are mitigating and extenuating circumstances here and will weigh them accordingly. Chief Richey, what you did is without excuse. I understand the pressures that you were under, but you are expected to withstand those pressures and maintain the highest moral integrity. You didn't do that and that is a deep disappointment. However, in the time that you have been onboard, you have developed an excellent reputation. Your chain of command, standing here before you, has uniformly praised you.

"Taking that all into account, Chief Petty Officer Richey, I find you guilty as charged and assign the following punishment. You will receive a punitive letter of reprimand that will become part of your permanent service record. Additionally, you are confined to the ship for the next thirty days. Because of your expressed remorse, I am suspending the letter of reprimand for a period of six months. The Executive Officer will explain your rights of appeal after this Mast.

Turning his gaze to the young Seaman, Hunter continued, "Seaman Martinez, have you appeared here at Mast before today?

"Yes, sir. Twice. Once for fighting and once for UA," he answered.

"As I remember, you were involved in a fracas with the leading torpedoman during a weapons load just after you reported aboard," Hunter stated.

"Yes, sir. He called me a 'lazy no good taco eating wetback' and I punched him. You yelled at us and let us off with a warning," Martinez replied.

"And why was that?" Hunter asked.

"You said that I had just got here and deserved a chance. You told me to grow up and learn to control my temper. You lectured us both about how we were all one crew and you would not tolerate any of that racial stuff," Martinez answered.

"And the second time?" the Commander questioned.

"Captain, that was when my girlfriend tried to commit suicide and I needed to get to LA to help her. I just left without telling anyone. You found me at Honolulu airport trying to get a flight out," Seaman Martinez stated.

"And what happened in that case?" Hunter questioned.

"The crew took up a collection and flew my girlfriend to the Islands. Doc got her in treatment at Tripler. She is getting better. We are getting married as soon as I get back. The boat really came through for us," Martinez said.

"Now you are here in front of me a third time. In addition to whatever punishment that I deem appropriate for this charge, I could order the Executive Officer to process you for an admin discharge as a habitual offender. Is that what you want?"

"No, sir," the young sailor answered, his voice quivering. "I want to stay here on the boat. I belong here."

Retrieving the charge sheet from the table, Hunter looked at the seaman. "Seaman Martinez, I find that you have committed the offense as charged. I sentence you to a reduction in rate to E-1 and forfeiture of half pay for two months. Additionally, you are confined to the ship for thirty days. I am suspending the portions of the sentence for the reduction in rate and the pay forfeiture pending your completion of your General Equivalency Degree for a high school diploma in the next six months. Dismissed," the Commander concluded gruffly.

After the offenders and everyone else had filed out, Hunter turned to Fagan, "You know, XO, this mast will ruin Chief Richey's chances of making senior chief for at least ten years and BUPERS will void Martinez's enlistment contract. He'll be out on the streets of LA without a job or any prospects of getting one.

"I want you to draft a reply to that message from SUBPAC and tell them what the investigation found. Make sure that you tell them about that Senior Chief and the climate at LA. I want SUBPAC to know that, in at least that one office, falsifying records was normal and accepted. The Navy needs to investigate to determine if it went any higher. Tell them that we held a Mast and that the results will be sent through normal admin channels."

Hunter picked up his coffee cup and took a sip. "You know how screwed up the ship's office is. I expect that they would probably lose the paperwork before it was ever sent."

"Skipper," Fagan protested. He was proud of the ship's office. It was his personal responsibility and they worked hard. Hard enough to be awarded Squadron "Admin A" last year. They had never lost a report or even submitted one late.

Hunter gave Fagan a look. He then said, very slowly, "XO, you're not listening to me. The ship's office would probably lose that report and not be able to find it."

The light came on for Fagan. With exaggerated emphasis, he said, "Yes, sir, you are right. The situation in the ship's office has become intolerable. I'll have to tighten up on our admin practices because of all this lost paperwork."

18 Jun 2000, 2325LT (1625Z)

The island rose menacingly on the horizon.

Peering through the periscope, Hunter could clearly make out the rising hump of Mount Guishu, the dormant volcano that constituted the only prominent geographical feature. Although still too distant to make out any details, the sense of dread was palpable.

"XO, we'll circumnavigate the island at this range conducting a visual and ESM search before we close it anymore," Hunter said to Fagan.

He stepped back from the periscope and rubbed his tired right eye. Buell took the scope and started to slowly rotate it, continuing the search.

Hunter continued, "I want to know if there is any emitter that might be a threat before we get in close enough to do a good surveillance. We'll probably need to get inside three miles to see well enough to get any information usable by the SEALs. That's too close to suddenly find out there's a high-resolution radar on the island. Make sure ESM's on the ball and knows what to look for."

Hunter turned to Jacobs, standing by the navigation stand, "Nav, the charts around here aren't very good. I don't want to find us high and dry on some uncharted coral head either. Have the secure fathometer manned and run continuous soundings."

As they circled and closed the island, more of its features became visible. Mount Guishu rose almost in the center and sloped smoothly down to the shore on the East and South. On the North side of the island, the slope terminated in shear cliffs that dropped several hundred feet to the surf lapping gently below. This side was not accessible to approach by small boat. The West side appeared to be indented with a small bay. The headland prevented viewing the shoreline on the North side of the bay. A line of breakers was clearly evident across its mouth, hiding a reef that guarded the entrance. Dense mangrove swamp seemed to be the predominant feature near the water line all along the West and South sides of the island. There was no visible sign that man had ever visited this forsaken place.

19 Jun 2000, 0410LT (18 Jun, 2110Z)

Bill Fagan's eyes blinked open. The damn lights came on again. He wearily jumped from his rack and again stormed off toward control.

He bumped into Jon Hunter, dressed in his sweat clothes, heading aft for his morning workout.

"XO, what's so important that you're running around in your underwear?" Hunter asked.

Fagan told him the tale of the mysterious light switch. Hunter chuckled as the story unfolded. Playing practical jokes on the XO was a time-honored tradition amongst the enlisted crewmembers on the boats. The XO was in charge of discipline and generally seen as the "heavy," compared to the Captain's "nice guy". The normal trick was to steal his stateroom door and hide it onboard somewhere. He was then challenged to find it. The crew had tired of that game with Bill Fagan many months ago. This was a more advanced challenge.

Hunter said, "I haven't seen that gag pulled since I was a JG. My electrical division chief showed me how to set it up. If you did some really good exploring and hand-over-handed the lighting circuit wiring, you would find a relay that the schematic doesn't show. That relay will lead you to an MJ growler somewhere onboard. That would be a lot of work. If I were you, I would talk to the COB and ask him to talk with Chief Jones. I bet this problem will just go away.

"How is our guest doing?" Hunter queried. Turnstill had been maintaining a really low profile since the night he came aboard.

Fagan answered, "Just eats and sleeps. Speaking of Chief Jones, Turnstill found out about his library of crotch novels and has become a voracious reader."

Hunter snorted, "Figures. In character."

19 Jun 2000, 1510LT (0810Z)

"Skipper, we received a batch of family-grams," Chief Tyler said as he stood in the CO stateroom door. "Got one for you here."

Hunter took the narrow slip of folded paper that Chief Tyler handed him. The short forty-word message was the only tie he had with Peg and the kids back in Hawaii. Each word had to be savored to its fullest. He knew the squadron had censored it and every radioman in the fleet had already seen it, but it didn't matter. He could almost smell Peg's perfume and feel the touch of her hand as he opened the family-gram. Gazing at the small, framed portraits of Peg and his two daughters, he slowly read the message. The words were sweet, telling a story of a peaceful life at home. It was all summed up in the last few words, "Girls and I are fine. We send all our love."

20 Jun 2000, 1210LT (0510Z)

Thirty-six hours of circling and monitoring the island produced little new information. A powerful low-frequency surface search radar intermittently swept the sea-lanes approaching the island. An air-search radar was also detected. Neither presented any threat to *SAN FRANCISCO* as long as she remained submerged, but would warn the inhabitants of the approach of any surface ship or aircraft. No communications were intercepted. Whoever was on the island didn't want surprise visitors and was not interested in advertising their presence.

LT Roland and Chief Sergiavich worked closely with Bill Fagan and Warran Jacobs to plan the insertions, missions and extractions of the teams.

The detailed work occupied most of the last two days. Turnstill relayed the little information he knew about the harbor.

The four presented the plan to Hunter as they gathered around the wardroom table, liberally strewn with charts.

"We need to do two insertions and extractions," LT Roland began. "The first will be tonight to put Boats and a squad of ten ashore to do initial recon. They will be looking for landing sites, defenses and locations for the hostages. We estimate that the recon will take two nights. Recovery will be on the third night. The next insertion will be the complete platoon on the night before the ARG arrives. The mission will be to prepare the beach and helo landing zones. We will also be disrupting the defenses, take out the radars, and establishing a cordon around the hostages for their protection."

Jacobs continued the presentation. "With those radar sites operating, we will not be able to do a surface launch of the teams. They would detect us as soon as *SAN FRANCISCO* broke the surface and we would lose the element of surprise. With the radar on top of the mountain, they should be able to search out to about a hundred miles."

Hunter walked over to look at the charts. "It's too far to even use the RHIBs to get to shore."

Jacobs nodded. "We agree. That leaves a lockout submerged as the only option. We know it is a high-risk operation and has only been successfully done once before, by *SAN FRANCISCO* as a proof of concept. As we see it, though, there is no other alternative."

Fagan took over, "The first squad will use the inflatable boats stored in the after escape trunk. We'll give them a ride to close in-shore with a snag and tow. Using *SAN FRANCISCO* to tow them will save several hours of transit time and allow us to do the lock out after dark and still get them ashore before first light. The men should still be rested when they get ashore."

Roland said, "They'll hide their boats and scuba gear. They'll need them for recovery the same way on the third night. Once ashore, they will maintain comms with their PRC134 low-power Satcom transceivers."

Hunter took a sip of coffee. "Have we done a comms check? I don't want to count how many times that comms have screwed up an operation"

Jacobs answered, "We have checked to make sure that the radio room here on *SAN FRANCISCO* and the squad has synched up on both frequencies and crypto. The squad will initiate a comms check every four hours and will send any reports as they can. *SAN FRANCISCO* will be continuously monitoring that circuit."

Roland continued. "The second insert will also be a lock-out but with the entire platoon. We will use the RHIBs that are in the supply shapes stored in the torpedo room. The RHIBs are capable of thirty knots so we can get ashore much quicker. That will allow *SAN FRANCISCO* to stand off, out of the way of the ARG."

A RHIB was a Rigid Hulled Inflatable Boat. This design had long ago replaced the floppy "Zodiac" boats for most SEAL operations. With one exception. Because the rigid hull of the RHIBs could not be loaded onboard or unloaded from a sub, the "combat rubber raiding craft" of World War II fame lived on. When the deficiency became evident, Roland and Hunter had worked together to developed a design for a RHIB that would work for these operations. The hull was hinged so that it folded and then fit into a torpedo like cylinder called a "shape." It could be shot out a torpedo tube and float to the surface. Once on the surface, a few latches were sprung and the RHIB was ready to go.

"Any more questions or suggestions?" LT Roland concluded.

Hunter pored over the charts for a few minutes. "I think that we had better do the lock-out here," he said, pointing to a spot about twenty miles out from the island. "That way, if we accidentally broach it might not be detected from the surface clutter. It makes the tow longer. Does that present any problems?" he asked.

"No, sir. The time line works so that the squad will have plenty of time to get ashore and hidden before first light. With the depth of water we have, the XO tells me that you can tow into about a thousand yards from shore. That significantly reduces the time to paddle ashore," Roland responded.

"The one thing that we really could use is an intel update," Bill Fagan added. "We haven't seen anything in a week. The latest satellite imagery would make the SEALs' job a lot easier."

Sweat poured off Hunter's body. It formed a rapidly enlarging pool on the steel deck below him. Just another minute and he would have it. His heart was thumping so loudly that he felt sure that the watch-standers could hear it even over the gasping of his breath. *Don't slack off now. Just thirty more seconds. Keep hammering.*

Finally, the timer started ringing. "Not bad, for an old man," Roland said from behind him.

Hunter stepped off the Versa-Climber and grabbed the towel hanging from a convenient valve hand wheel. The two were on a small platform in the after part of the engine-room. In the cramped space of a nuclear submarine, this was the only place that Hunter had found to fit in this piece of exercise equipment. The Versa-Climber was suspended off the deck by rubberized mounts designed to prevent any vibration from transmitting from the equipment to the submarine's hull and then out into the water. Similar rubber mounts supported the top of the climber. It was crammed into a corner at an oddly skewed angle. The user had a scant few inches clearance on his left from a chill water pump. A large seawater valve was a couple of inches from his right knee. The view in front was entirely taken up by the dark metal after end of the port main condenser.

He had placed exercise equipment in various places around the engine-room soon after reporting aboard. He hadn't bothered to ask for official permission, knowing the Naval Reactors' official policy frowned on any such "frivolity". When Commodore Calucci saw the equipment, he threw a fit and ordered it removed. The Commodore told COMSUBPAC of the problem, but when the admiral decided that he liked the idea, it suddenly became the Commodore's idea. Hunter was ordered to submit the plans for his installation to the squadron engineer so all the boats could enjoy the benefits of the Commodore's idea.

"What do you mean, not bad?" Hunter shot back, attempting to keep his breathing under control. "That is a new world record for a Versa-Climber on a submarine. Twelve thousand vertical feet in an hour."

"Maybe in the over-forty class," Roland kidded the Commander. "I'm afraid that I did fifteen thousand yesterday."

"You're up and about early," Hunter commented, turning the direction of the conversation.

"Yes, sir," the SEAL leader answered seriously. "I always have trouble sleeping before an operation. This one bothers me worse than most, probably because I'm not going in with the first group."

Hunter nodded. "I know where you are coming from. You worry a lot more when you are sending your men in and you aren't going. You trust Boats and your men, don't you?"

"Absolutely. Boats is as good as they get and the men all know their jobs. They're like your crew. All professionals," the SEAL platoon leader responded.

"Then you have to trust them to get the job done. You have planned it out, rehearsed it to perfection. There is nothing for you to do but sit back and wait. That's the hardest part," Hunter said. "Is there anything left that we need to work out?"

Roland answered, "No, sir. We have looked at all the contingencies that we can think of. What is left is the truly unexpected. That always comes up."

"And that is why you trained and coached them so well," Hunter concluded, climbing the ladder to engine-room upper level. "Have a good work-out. See you at breakfast."

20 Jun 2000, 1530LT (0830Z)

Hunter stood beside the number-two periscope, a step behind the diving officer. "Jones, you are just about the poorest excuse for a Chief Petty Officer that I have ever laid eyes on. I still can't believe that stupid stunt you pulled when the Commodore was riding. You know that he is the ultimate prude and yet you show skin flicks in radio. And to make matters even worse, you invite the Squadron Master Chief to watch. Do you have a death wish for your career? If you weren't the best Diving Officer in the Navy, you wouldn't even be here. You'd be a Second Class Petty Officer counting blankets in Nome, Alaska."

Jones replied easily, "Skipper, if I weren't the best Diving Officer in the Navy, you wouldn't be here, either. Without the two of us, this mission would be impossible. Besides, it's common knowledge there is no love lost between you and the Commodore. The crew thinks he's a spineless weenie, particularly after he nixed your chances of making O-6."

Hunter answered, "OK Chief, let's review the bidding here. If I hadn't gone to bat for you, I would be home in bed with my wife right now under a beautiful Hawaiian moon. Instead, I am out here, just off some God-forsaken island that's full of people with big guns who want to do bad things to us. I am about to start a maneuver that has never been done in combat before and has every likelihood of getting our asses shot off. For this I am supposed to be thankful, because you are the best Diving Officer in the Navy? My judgment must be faulty. Now strap on this boat and make her dance."

"Yes sir!" Jones replied as he settled more comfortably into his seat. Reaching out with both hands, he boxed the helmsman's and planesman's ears. "You heard the Skipper, let's make her dance."

"XO, are we ready to go?" Hunter questioned.

Fagan answered, "Yes, sir. The first four swimmers are ready to enter the forward escape trunk. Their gear is stowed in the after trunk. It's flooded and equalized with sea pressure. A watch is stationed at the ESGN to report velocities. The ship has a good zero speed trim. The crew is standing fast so that their weight doesn't mess up the trim. A hose has been rigged from the forward trunk drain to the machinery one bilge. We'll have to do three cycles to get all ten men out."

Fagan seemed to have recovered from the *KILO* affair, but Hunter wasn't totally convinced. He would have to be watched closely for any more signs of cracking.

Hunter said, "Let's get this show on the road. Officer of the Deck, proceed to periscope depth and take a look around. We will be doing the lock-out from eighty feet, just like we practiced."

Sam Stuart ordered, "Diving Officer, make your depth six-two feet." He then raised the search periscope. As *SAN FRANCISCO* started her ascent, Stuart began the slow sweep around to make sure that they were not coming up under any quiet ships that sonar had failed to detect. This was a real concern, particularly in these island waters where fishing from sailing smacks was a way of life. They had expected to see a great deal of fishing, but strangely, had seen none since arriving at Nusa Funata.

Initially rotating the scope's field of vision up to almost directly over-head, he slowly lowered it as the diving officer shouted out the decreasing depth. A few brightly colored tropical fish flashed in and out of his field of vision. Other than that, all he saw was the deep blue of open water.

As the scope broke the surface, Stuart lowered the field of vision until he felt the slight click of the handle detent, telling him he was looking straight out at the horizon. He had not seen any telltale shadow that would foretell an underwater collision. After a quick sweep around, he reported, "No close contacts." Another, more careful search and he reported to Hunter, "Completed initial search, no contacts."

Hunter acknowledged the good news and ordered, "Very well. Make your depth eight-zero feet."

Stuart brought the sub down to eighty feet. The slow, delicate procedure to turn a warship designed to fly effortlessly through the depths into a rock solid launch pad for the SEALs began.

Zero velocity, both horizontally and vertically, was essential. The force of any water flowing past the hatch would tear a SEAL out of the sub as he emerged or exhaust him as he tried to keep up with the moving ship. To make matters worse, the escape hatch on *SAN FRANCISCO* opened forward so that it had to be held open against the flow of water for any forward motion. Too much speed could slam the one ton steel hatch shut on any SEAL unfortunate enough to be emerging just then.

Any vertical motion would result in pressure changes too rapid for the SEALs to equalize. At best they would have ruptured eardrums, at worst, the terrible pain of an embolism.

Forward motion had to be maintained at less than a tenth of a knot while vertical motion had to be kept at less than a foot per second. Depth had to be maintained in a six-inch band. This required an inherent sense of anticipation of the forces acting on the great ship and an uncanny talent to counter them precisely. Chief Jones was truly unique in his ability to, almost unconsciously, integrate the input from the ship's sensors with his own "seat of the pants" feel for the ship's response. Flood a few pounds of water into one trim tank; pump a few pounds out of another. Watch the water temperature and depth gages with an eagle eye. Listen to the reports of ship's velocity in the X, Y and Z-axis. And maintain very careful track of the vital lockout evolution happening thirty feet aft and a deck below his location. Doing all this instantaneously, precisely and for a four-hour period was not something that anyone could be trained to do. It required the one individual in a million who was born with these unique talents.

"All right, Chief. We are at eighty feet. I'll slow to two knots. You trim the ship," Hunter said. They had learned through many hours of trial and error the tricks that made this impossible maneuver possible. One key trick was to slow down incrementally to a hover and to trim the ship very carefully at each speed.

As the sub slowed, the stern started to sink. The ship came to rest with a three-degree up angle.

"Damn, Skipper, we're heavy aft. Pumping one thousand pounds from after trim to forward trim," Chief Jones commented.

The angle gradually eased, but the ship had sunk several feet in the ensuing minutes.

"Pumping from Auxiliaries to sea, one thousand pounds."

The descent slowed, then stopped.

"Depth nine-zero feet coming to eight-zero," he reported, as he used the little remaining speed to plane back up to the ordered depth. She settled out at precisely eighty feet. "Skipper, I'm ready to go to one point five knots."

Hunter ordered, "Maneuvering, make one point five knots."

The EOOW in the maneuvering room acknowledged "Make one point five knots, aye."

The sub slowed to one point five knots. The tedious, yet delicate procedure was repeated. Feel the sub's response. Pump a little, flood a little. Carefully correct the minor imbalances of weight. Then slow again. Repeat the procedure. Slow some more. Repeat; until finally speed was down to almost zero.

At these very low speeds, just the turning of the great bronze screw caused enough torque on the ship to disturb the delicate balance. As each blade tip passed through the low pressure near the surface on the top of its rotation and then bit in to the higher pressure water on its downward travel, it would push the stern down and to port. This resulted in the bow moving to starboard and up. The inevitable result was for the sub to broach.

"Lower the outboard and shift to remote," Hunter ordered. "All Stop."

He grabbed the 7MC microphone. "Maneuvering, Captain. When the shaft is stopped, put the main engines on the jack."

The mains would be warmed and ready if they were suddenly needed, but for now the outboard and its small electric motor and tiny screw would be used in quick bursts to gently move the ship.

The first four SEALs entered the cramped dark space of the escape trunk and dogged the lower hatch shut. The space was so small they could not don their scuba tanks but, rather, had to place them under their feet and stretch the regulator hoses to breath.

Boats climbed a little higher in the trunk and spoke into the intercom, "Swimmers ready, commencing to flood the trunk."

The noise was deafening. The rush of water under pressure into the steel confines of the trunk drowned out all possibility of communicating. The swirling water rose to the swimmers' knees, then their waists, until finally three of them were completely under water. Only Boats had his head above water. A small steel skirt, attached to the underside of the upper hatch combing, provided a tiny air pocket for him to use while operating the trunk controls.

As the water rushed in, Chief Jones pumped water from the Auxiliary Tank located in the submarine's bilge almost directly below the escape trunk. Experimentation and careful practice had taught him how to precisely pump water from the sub at the same rate that it was being flooded into the trunk. Pumping too fast would result in the sub bobbing quickly to the surface and embolising the SEALs, while pumping too slow would result in the sub descending and exposing the SEALs to unendurable pressures. Chief Jones performed his balancing act carefully and precisely. The great ship barely quivered as the trunk flooded. The SEALs did not notice any changes in pressure.

Just as quickly as it began, the rush of water ceased. In the almost unnatural quiet, Boats reported, "Flooding was completed. Equalizing with sea pressure."

The squeal of pressurized air destroyed the stillness. The tiny air pocket quickly came up to a pressure equal to the outside sea pressure. The SEALs popped the upper hatch open and swam free of the submarine.

The SEALs left the dark confines of the escape trunk and emerged into the blue of the open ocean. Below them the blue darkened into blackness;

above it was an iridescent turquoise. In this blue, their only touch with reality was the hard black shape of the sub.

As soon as the last swimmer exited the forward trunk, the crew pumped the upper hatch closed and started the procedure to drain the trunk for the next set of swimmers. Within minutes the next four SEALs entered the trunk and the difficult, tedious procedure was repeated.

The four swimmers sprang to their well-rehearsed tasks. Boats tied a line to the sub and inflated the attached buoy with a small CO_2 canister. He freed the buoy to float to the surface.

The second swimmer, EN2 Stuart, tied another line to the sub and swam to the after escape trunk. There he tied the other end, forming a guide rope for his teammates to follow.

The third swimmer, HT1 Jankowski, began opening the after escape trunk upper hatch so that they could retrieve their equipment. As his three teammates joined him, he started to lift out the first ungainly bag and allowed it to drift to the surface while holding on to the guide rope. As the bag broke the surface, it automatically inflated into a small six-man raft.

"Control, maneuvering. We hear activity in the after escape trunk. Sounds like the SEALs are unloading it."

"Maneuvering, control Aye."

Up rose the second bag to become a second raft. The rafts were tied to the floating buoy to keep them from drifting away. The four swimmers began the laborious task of transferring the rest of the equipment from the after trunk to the waiting rafts on the surface.

After four hours, Chief Jones and his team sat in pools of sweat, reduced to exhaustion by the constant unbearable tension.

Ten SEALs were seated in the CRRCs. As the cool night air wafted around them and the gentle swell of the sea rocked them, the SEALs rigged a line between the two small boats and paddled a few feet apart, leaving the line to float on the surface.

19

The top of the mountainous island was just visible as a darker blotch on an already darkening sky. Black cumulous clouds blotted out the brilliant stars, leaving that whole quadrant a study of deep grays and blacks. A tropical shower deluged the land.

Overhead and to the West, the night sky was filled with stars. The Southern Cross just peeked over the horizon to the Southwest. The setting moon outlined a river of silver off to the Northwest. Waves gently lapped against the side of the boats. Warm tropical winds carried earthy scents of jungle out to the SEALs.

The ten SEALs were alone in the glory of the tropical night. A shape suddenly appeared, blacker than the night, moving silently toward them. An arrow of phosphorescence trailed behind as it glided through the water, closing the distance to the SEALs' tiny rubber boats. The men paddled to move their boats perceptibly further apart to increase the separation. The shape seemed to aim for the space between them, as if undecided as to which boat to encounter.

As it approached closer, the shape could be seen to be two small vertical tubes moving side-by-side, about a meter apart. Although small on the surface, like an iceberg, the shapes had the unmistakable aura of an ominous power just below the surface. Silently the tubes moved forward until they snagged the line connecting the two small boats. The boats swung around and met in a towing position behind the shapes.

Thirty-four feet below the surface, Hunter grinned, "Split the middle. Snag completed. Commencing to tow the SEALs to the beach. Nice driving everyone." Hunter eased back from the number two periscope and rubbed his eyes. "Nav, how far to the drop off point?"

"Captain, twenty-two miles to the twenty fathom curve. At five knots, we will be at the drop off point at zero-four thirty. That leaves the SEALs an hour to paddle the last thousand yards before first light at zero-five-thirty-two," LCDR Jacobs reported.

"Captain, flashing infra-red light from the SEAL squad leader," Petty Officer Buell said. He was watching through number one scope. "He reports snag and tow satisfactory. Speed is good. His people regret missing pizza night."

Hunter smiled and said, "Send back, ' ETA drop off zero-four-thirty. No new intelligence on targets. Will advise if received. Do you want pepperoni and sausage? We deliver'."

Petty Officer Buell grinned as he lifted the infrared equipped Aldis lantern to the periscope eyepiece and flashed the signal.

On the surface, Boats, using IR goggles, could just make out the narrow beam of red light emanating from the scope head window.

"Message understood. Order is for two large pepperoni and mushrooms, one large anchovy with extra cheese," he flashed with his IR light, carefully aimed at the scope head window.

With a mischievous glint in his eye, Hunter said, "XO, time to practice that special tactic for passing 'small time-critical logistic components and sensitive intelligence' to the SEAL Team that we discussed."

"Yes, sir," Fagan replied and hurried off to supervise the operation.

At some time in the misty past, the traditional Saturday midrats on all US submarines at sea had evolved into pizza night. Each crew claimed their cook made the best pizzas in the Navy. A submariner didn't miss pizza night unless there was a very serious reason.

A cheer erupted from the gathered crew as the first large pie emerged from the galley to the awaiting throng on the mess decks. That is, until the XO requisitioned it and had the slices, along with an infrared Chem-lite, placed in zip-lock plastic bags. The crew watched with increasing curiosity as the bags were loaded in the signal ejectors.

Fagan picked up the MJ phone handset, spun the growler handle and reported to Hunter, "Captain, signal ejectors loaded. Looks like one whole pizza per load. You can tell the SEALs that this is one of the cook's special pepperoni and sausage pizzas."

Hunter picked up his MJ handset and said, "Thanks XO. Quartermaster, signal the SEALs that first delivery is on its way."

Turning to the Chief of the Watch, he ordered the forward signal ejector fired.

The signal ejector cylinder cycled and the baggies containing the pizza slices floated to the surface, emerging alongside the waiting SEALs. A brief scurry and scuffle was visible as the SEALs vied to retrieve their piece of this unconventionally delivered pizza.

A flashing light signal came from the Boats, "Compliments to the chef, but you screwed up the order. Should have been mushroom."

"Captain sends his apologies. No charge for the order," Buell flashed back.

21 Jun 2000, 0020LT (20 Jun, 1720Z)

The strange convoy traveled on through the night. Barely a ripple marked their passage toward the dark, ominous island.

The ESM sensors on the sub still detected the powerful low frequency surface search radar and the chirp of the giga-hertz band search-while-track air search radar. Neither was capable of detecting them and had not changed in any way from what they had been monitoring for days. There was no sign that their arrival was discovered.

"XO, send a message to the Intel weenies at SUBPAC and give them the latest parameters on the radars. Also tell them that we are still not receiving any comms intercepts. Nothing unusual at all. Looks like all is quiet for our reception. Ask them where the hell the latest satellite imagery is and the latest assessment of mission locations. Don't those idiots realize that we have the SEALs in the water already? They will be on the beach in a couple of hours."

The lack of intelligence support was grating on Hunter's nerves. They were supposed to have the highest priority possible for this information. It should be flooding in, but nary a trickle came out of radio. Hunter was anxious to get the information that his team needed to successfully complete this mission.

"Yes, sir. We'll have that out on SSIXS in a minute. Nice to have Spec-Op priority so we have our own channel and direct routing from the Comms Center over to SUBPAC's basement. The weenies should have the message within minutes."

Both were well aware of the glut of radio traffic, a large percentage of it routine administration and reports, clogging the limited capacity of the submarine communications system. To allow very high priority missions, SPECial OPerations, to bypass the traffic snarl, they were allocated their own channel. This made immediate delivery from the SUBPAC comm center, located adjacent to the intel center but through a different set of double cypher-locked doors, possible. The use of the code-word priority on the message would jar the on-watch communications officer into action to deliver it as soon as it came off the secure high-speed printer.

20 Jun 2000, 0700LT (1800Z)

Unbeknownst to the submariners on *SAN FRANCISCO*, Rear Admiral O'Flanagan was standing in the emergency command center and closely observing the operation from there. Within seconds of the message arriving, it was in the admiral's hand.

"Sounds like Jonathan is getting a little antsy. Can't say that I blame him," he said to his aide, Lieutenant Pyler. "Get Admiral Pequot at NSA on the STU for me."

The young Lieutenant picked up the red encrypted phone and dialed a series of numbers. After listening to the high pitched whine of the two encryption devices syncing up, he spoke briefly into the handset and then handed it to COMSUBPAC.

"Admiral, I have Admiral Pequot on the line. He is at NSA's Command

Center," LT Pyler reported. "He has the JCS Command Center on line as well. He says that all the Joint Chiefs will be listening in."

"Damn, just what I wanted! An audience of thousands when I have to yell at a senior admiral," COMSUBPAC muttered under his breath as he picked up the bright red phone.

LT Pyler and the rest of the staff backed discreetly away from the admiral's centrally located command chair.

"Jack, this is Mike O'Flanagan out in Pearl. Just received the latest update from *SAN FRANCISCO*. They have the SEALs in the water and are approaching the island. No sign of any alertment yet. The CO reports that there are no comms intercepts and only routine surface and air search radars. He needs the latest KH-II imagery and assessments for the teams. It's zero-three-fifteen out there now and he expects to release the SEALs at zero-four-thirty. He needs that imagery right now."

"Mike, wish I could help," replied the country's top military spook. "Tell your skipper the cloud cover he sees over the island has been there for three days. It's been playing havoc with the visual imagery. As you already know, the oblique angles and definition that we need for this makes even the millimeter wave radar imagery unusable. Visual spectrum photography is the only thing that will get us the info that we need. He is going to have to go with what he has or abort the mission."

"Mike, Jack, this is General Schwartz," the Chairman of the Joint Chiefs interjected. "What is the estimate if we don't get the imagery? Do you recommend that we still go or abort?"

Mike O'Flanagan replied, "General, I want to leave that decision to the on-scene commander. I think that we have learned enough times that trying to micro-manage an operation from Pearl or the Pentagon ends up FUBAR. I know the Skipper out there and he is one tenacious son of a bitch. If this mission can be done, he will get it done. On the other hand, he is no fool. If the mission can't be done or the risks are too high, he is not afraid to say so and high-tail it out of there."

Jack Pequot chimed in, "I have to agree with Mike. Leave it up to the on-scene commander. NRO will continue to try to get the imagery and pass it to *SAN FRANCISCO*. On the last KH-II pass, SIGINT concurred exactly with what the Skipper reported. A low frequency surface search radar and a SHF frequency air search, both located on the mountaintop. No PHOTINT, of course. The next pass is at zero-five-seventeen. Maybe we'll get lucky then. I know that the SEALs won't have a picture, but, at least we can tell them what to expect."

"Thanks Mike, Jack," growled the General. "We will play it your way. Just make damn sure that this works and that we get out with no egg on our face. Now there are some new developments that we have to discuss."

He proceeded to explain that things were happening much faster than they had previously expected. CIA resources were talking of delivery with in the next two days. Once the pathogen was off Nusa Funata, it would be almost impossible to contain.

"Mike," Schwartz concluded, "you had better tell your boy on-scene that he has a job to do by himself. Otherwise we'll have to vaporize that place, hostages and all."

21 Jun 2000, 0235LT (20 Jun, 1935Z)

The periscope stand 21MC squawked. Hunter instinctively reached out and grabbed it without taking his eye from the periscope.

It was Chief Tyler. "Skipper, high priority off-line eyes only traffic coming in from SUBPAC. Request you come to radio."

Hunter answered, "Be there in a second, Chief. Set up the off-line crypto. XO, take charge in control. Call me in radio if anything happens. Hope this is the intel update."

Hunter stepped out of the control room and through the aft door, ducking around the ESGN gyros hanging from the overhead before stepping through the cypher-locked door into the combined radio/ESM space.

In the forward half of the cramped, narrow space the Electronics Technicians were bent over a series of small screens, watching and listening intently for any sign that SAN FRANCISCO was at risk of detection.

The after half of the space was dedicated to radio communications. The bulkheads of the whole space were covered with a multitude of black boxes connected by a myriad of multi-colored wires and cables. Many of the "black boxes" were actually painted red, indicating that the signal being passed through them was encrypted.

Every inch of available space was used. Even the narrow passageway, barely the width of a man's shoulders, was filled with bench lockers that doubled as both storage for immediately needed parts and manuals as well as seats for the watch-standers.

Hunter stepped into the crowded space and took a seat in front of a small, strangely shaped typewriter like device on a retractable shelf, now fully extended. After entering his special memorized password, he turned to Chief Tyler and said, "Alright Chief, pass the "Eyes Only" message over here."

The radioman chief pressed a few buttons and the garble of the encrypted message was passed electronically to the little box. Almost immediately a clear text message began to appear from the high-speed printer at the Commander's feet.

TOP SECRET, GOLDEN DAWN, Special Handling required
EYES-ONLY: CO USS SAN FRANCISCO

From: COMSUBPAC
To: CO, USS SAN FRANCISCO

Subj: Intel Estimate and Mission Tasking
BT

1. Intel Estimate:

1.1. No further photo imagery available beyond what you hold due to heavy cloud cover over objective. SIGINT receipt and analysis for period 0017LT to 0321LT concurs with your estimate.

1.2. Reliable national assets provide following:

1.2.1. Estimate that production completion and delivery within next two days.

1.2.2. Hostages still held under heavy guard at unknown location on island.

1.2.3. Estimate battalion strength resistance with heavy weapons and some armor.

1.2.4. Possible anti-ship and anti-aircraft missile launchers sited at lat: 06:35.151S long: 116:15.145E

1.2.5. No sign of alertment but security forces on high state of readiness. Anticipate that this is due to pending delivery.

2. Revised Mission Tasking:

2.1. Stopping delivery and destruction of product is of highest national priority. Take what ever actions CO *SAN FRANCISCO* deems necessary. Use of all weapons available is authorized.

2.2. Hostage rescue to be attempted only after tasking in 2.1 successful.

2.3. Penetration into sovereign waters authorized for execution of this mission.

2.3.1. While inside sovereign waters remain undetected.

2.3.2. If detected, remain unidentified as US submarine.

2.4. CO, USS SAN FRANCISCO, as on-scene commander, authorized to abort mission if determined to be not accomplishable or of too high a risk.

3. Open and review Special Sealed Appendix to OPORD. Will advise if implemented.
4. Good Luck
5. COMSUBPAC sends
BT

20

"Well, that lays it out. Don't know what we are going into." Fagan laid the message board on the table.

Hunter and Fagan were seated in Hunter's stateroom.

"No sign that they know we are coming, yet they are in a high state of readiness. Are we walking into a trap here? And what about this "hostage rescue only after we destroy the product." How are we going to tell their folks that we let them die but we destroyed the virus? Most of them are just kids and they are all out here to help make life better for the locals," Fagan demanded

"XO, life isn't fair." Hunter answered. "You and I both know that if we don't take out the virus, in the best case these people use it to blackmail the world. In the worst case millions will die a very ugly, painful death. Not a whole lot of options in this one. We have to take it out."

The emphasis was on "have to."

Hunter shook his head ruefully. "Unfortunately, the hostages have to be second priority. We will do everything that we can to get them out, but if the choice comes up, they lose. We need to make sure that we don't have to make the choice."

Hunter watched Fagan closely. *This was where the rubber met the road. If there was any time in this mission where he needed Fagan to be clearheaded and calm, it was now. Was the stress building? Would Fagan be able to handle it? Still had to be careful. Watch his every move.*

"What's this Special Sealed Appendix to the Op Order?" Fagan asked. "I don't remember seeing any sealed parts of the OPORD when we picked it up at SUBPAC."

"It was delivered later by special courier," Hunter replied. "This one is very specifically "CO Eyes Only" so I can't show you. It's in my inner safe. If anything happens and you need it, you know the combination. I don't know what is in it yet, myself."

Hunter continued, "Now what do we pass on to the SEALs and how do we plan this out? Let's get Roland in here and discuss it. But remember, no one is to know about the smallpox , not even the SEALs."

21 Jun 2000, 0302LT (20 JUN, 2002Z)

The ramrod stiff SEAL Lieutenant stood at the stateroom door and barked, "LT Roland reporting as ordered, sir."

"Come on in. Close the curtain and have a seat." Hunter pointed to the pot of coffee and stack of cups. "Grab a cup of coffee."

Roland sat down at the table and poured himself a cup.

"Things have changed. We can't wait for the ARG to complete the mission. Not enough time. The terrorists are apparently about ready to make a shipment. We need to do some planning," Hunter said. "I want to go over some options with you and the XO."

Hunter pulled his chair over so the three sat around the small table in the cramped stateroom. A large-scale chart of the area, the latest message and the now obsolete plan that they had so recently labored over were spread out on the tabletop.

Hunter started the discussion. "Timetables need shifting. We expect the weapons to be shipped within the next two days. We are tasked to stop it before the virus is off Nusa Funata. The Marines will be out of range for a week, at least. We'll have to do this with what we have. Any ideas?

Roland and Fagan looked over the charts while Hunter wrote on a pad that he had pulled from his desk. Roland commented, "Looks to me like we have two missions, the terrorists and the hostages. Can we do both?"

Hunter looked up from his writing. "Lieutenant, the team topside has digital imagery communications capability, doesn't it?"

The SEAL Lieutenant answered, "Yes, sir. They have gear to get intel for the Marines so they can do their Twelve Step Planning Process. They need as much intel as they can get and imagery is always the best way to give it to them. It's also useful for strike planning. The ARG will use it for both aircraft and Tomahawk strike planning. Are you thinking of a Tomahawk strike?

Hunter began to write out a timeline. "That's one step. I'm looking for a way to bring off both missions simultaneously. We think that the production facilities are in those caves Turnstill's mining equipment dug. We can't get TLAM's into them. We don't have any with penetrator warheads. But you can get demolitions in under the cover of contusion from a strike at their pier facilities and disruption from your snipers. Those .50 caliber sniper rifles can raise some havoc.

"I want to re-task the squad to goo locate and image the pier facilities, airfield and the missile facilities for TLAM strikes. I also want them to find and verify the hostage positions. Our best intel is that they are under heavy guard but have not been moved. Also, looks like we are looking at a heavy weapons equipped battalion with some armor."

"What missile facility? We haven't been briefed on that," barked LT Roland anxiously. *Was there a threat to his team that he was kept in the dark about?*

Fagan answered, "Latest estimate from NSA. They have found a possible anti-ship and anti-aircraft missile facility on top of Mount Guishu. Shooting from up there would command all sea-borne approaches."

He pointed to the location on the chart. "It has to go before we can even get close with the amphibs or if we have to do any surface operations."

Hunter continued, "This new mission timing, though, will have to go before we can exfiltrate anyone. I think the sniper teams should set up to provide some cover fire in the vicinity of the hostage location. Meager protection, but the best we have.

"To timeline this out, the squad topside goes ashore in about two hours.

They get their targeting done tomorrow night and get their sniper teams in position. We conduct the strike the next night. Does that timetable work out?" He showed his rough draft plan to the other two officers.

Roland looked at the plan and replied, "We can make it work. First, we need to get the new intel and re-tasking to the people topside. Next, there won't be enough time for them to complete this mission and then to recover them for the strike. We will have to leave them on the island for the duration. Not a problem; they have the equipment and supplies for that. It means that the strike team will just be the ten of us still onboard. We'll carry the C-4 and the rest of the weapons ashore in those two RHIBs down in the torpedo room."

Roland turned to Hunter with a frown. "The tough question is how do we extract both squads and thirty hostages. You have to assume that we will be under fire. To extract to *SAN FRANCISCO* would be very risky. It would take at least three round trips for each RHIB. Probably a minimum of two hours if *SAN FRANCISCO* was close in and surfaced."

Hunter answered, "Good question. You're right about extracting to *SAN FRANCISCO*. I'm thinking of a couple of OSPREY's with a squad of Marine Force Recon for the extraction. That is the only thing from the *ESSEX* ARG with the legs to get here in time."

"That works," replied LT Roland, exhaling deeply.

Hunter concluded the meeting, "Good. Now we have a lot of work to do. Lieutenant, get your guys topside briefed on the new mission. Use the signal ejector method of delivery if you need to get anything hard copy to them, flashing light for everything else. I don't want to use a voice radio this close to shore. XO, get a message ready to send to the ARG commander and the Marine Expeditionary Force commander. Tell them what you need. If you have any problems, get SUBPAC involved. He can raise it to the necessary level to get what we need. Send it as soon as we are back out in deep water." Hunter glanced up at the clock. "We're getting close to the drop off point. I'll be on the conn."

After the two officers left his stateroom, Hunter turned to the large safe above his desk and quickly spun the dial. Swinging the heavy steel door open, he confronted the smaller inner safe. Opening this safe, he removed a manila envelope. The envelope was sealed with heavy library tape and prominently marked in two inch high red letters, "Top Secret Golden Dawn, CO Eyes Only, Open Only Upon Instruction From COMSUBPAC." In the corners were additional instructions indicating that this document required special handling and was exempt from declassification.

Slitting open the envelope, Hunter removed the three-page document it contained. As he read, his face became ashen as the color drained out and his breath came in short gasps.

"Oh, my God. I can't believe that someone even thought of this, let alone planned for it," he gasped.

The Appendix provided a contingency plan if the *SAN FRANCISCO* failed her mission. A B-2 Stealth Bomber would depart Elmendorf Air Force Base, Alaska at 1600Z on 22 June. In its belly would be two armed nuclear air launched cruise missiles. It would fly over 9,000 miles and arrive at its launch point at 0800Z on 23 June. Its mission would be to conduct a nuclear strike against Nusa Funata.

They had until 0800Z on 23 June to destroy the facilities on Nusa Funata or they would have front row seats to watch the first use of nuclear weapons in over half a century.

It was suddenly apparent that their time was limited by more than the delivery schedule of the smallpox. They had to destroy the facility and the existing stores of the contagion with enough time to report before the nuclear missiles could be launched. Once the missiles were in the air, they could not be called back. The knot in his stomach got very much tighter.

21 Jun 2000, 0416LT (20 Jun, 2116Z)

"Skipper, request that you come to radio when you get a second," Chief Jones asked over the MJ sound powered telephone.

"On my way," Hunter answered.

Entering the combined radio/ESM space, the Commander found several of his electronics technicians huddled around the AN/WLR-8 intercept receiver and an attached tape deck. While Chief Jones was carefully adjusting the digital tuner and watching the waveform of the incoming signal, the others were listening to an intercepted conversation. The voices had a tinny, not quite natural quality to them. It appeared to be little more than two soldiers idly conversing to kill the endless boredom of a long night's guard duty. Nothing important was being said, only a rambling discussion of life on the island. The discussion was in English, which had become the common language among terrorists, given their polyglot of mother tongues. One of them had a distinct Eastern European accent while the other had a Middle Eastern one.

Chief Jones looked up from the receiver and saw the Commander standing behind him. "Here Skipper, listen to this," he said, turning to the tape deck. "We picked this up a few minutes ago. Same two that are still talking. Their communications security really sucks. Must think they are safe with a simple commercial streaming encryption algorithm. Took us about five minutes to crack it. Thought you would want to hear it right away."

Putting on the head set, Hunter could hear the two terrorists talking. The first few minutes appeared to be a precursor to the meaningless conversation that they were currently listening to. Suddenly the Commander's ears perked up.

Terrorist number one was talking. "Did you hear what happened to Mjecka after the Major found out that he tried to rape that American girl? The Major gave him to Dr. Aswal to experiment with. I hear Dr Aswal put him in one of those glass cells and sprayed in some of the new smallpox NX. He was dead in twenty-four hours. The screaming was horrible. The body wasn't even recognizable as human.

Terrorist number two chimed in, "I hear that there is no cure. If you get it, you die. I sure will be happy when that stuff is gone off the island. Any word on when the ship will be here?"

"What I hear is that it arrives tomorrow night. Hope we don't get assigned to load it. The farther I stay away from that stuff, the better."

Chief Jones reached over and turned off the player. "Skipper, that's the part that I wanted you to hear unless you want to hear more barracks rumors."

The Commander put down the headset and digested what he had just heard. This verified both the presence of the smallpox and the delivery schedule. And it looked like it was going to be transported by ship.

How was he going to deal with this information getting out among the crew? Although submariners are renowned for their silence outside the pressure hull, there is very little secrecy among the crew. The best that he could hope for was to warn the electronics technicians and hope that they at least passed the level of concern along when they inevitably talked with their crewmates.

He turned to the four people assembled there and said, "Guys, what you heard here didn't happen. This does not go beyond here. This is extremely sensitive and highly classified. Understand?"

They had all routinely been involved in working with information that was classified at a much higher level than Top Secret and fully understood the implications of the Captain's words. They all nodded affirmatively.

21

---

21 Jun 2000, 0430LT (20 Jun, 2130Z)

This was the blackest part of the night, that time just before dawn. The sun was still well below the horizon, not even a faint glow to the East. The moon had set hours ago. The night darkened into near total blackness as they came under cloud cover that obscured even the faint starlight.

The island was darker even than the night. A looming, haunting presence. It was difficult to shake the feeling of dread that grew as the team approached the beach. They could just barely make out the white surf line against the black volcanic sand. The fetid smell of rotting vegetation drifted out to greet them.

The long tow was at an end. After the excitement and exertion of the lockout and the periscope snag, the squad was attempting to get what rest they could in the cramped and uncomfortable inflatable boats. In the manner of battle-hardened warriors, they were resting to store energy because they knew that they would soon need every bit of it. Their survival and the mission success depended on it. A microsecond delay caused by fatigue could be the vital difference between success and failure; between life and death.

The comforting presence of the two periscopes disappeared below the surface.

"All right, start paddling. This is a little too far out to swim in yet," Chief Boatswain Mate Sergiavich hissed, his gravelly voice barely above a whisper. "And keep the noise down. Sound travels forever over water this quiet."

Silently the two CRRCs full of deadly professional killers approached the black sand shore. When they were 500 yards from the beach, the SEALs rolled into the tepid water. The last man in each CRRC pulled lanyards, dumping the CO_2 from the floatation tubes. The now useless, weighted boats slid quickly beneath the surface; settling on the bottom some 200 feet below.

The SEALs descended below the surface themselves, but only a few feet. Their Draeger LAR V re-breather systems fed them pure oxygen and, most importantly, didn't leave the telltale stream of bubbles inherent to scuba regulators. Grabbing their wrist compasses, they swam on until the bottom came up to meet them.

They then followed the bottom until Boats, in the lead, had his head just above the surface. He was at the surf line, just a few yards from dry sand, an almost invisible black head amongst the crashing waves. He spent almost half an hour there, scanning carefully for any sign that they had a reception committee. The remainder of the team stayed fully submerged, lying flat on the bottom, awaiting his signal to either cross the beach or scurry back out to sea.

20 Jun 2000, 1100LT (2200Z)

Commodore Calucci was in a quandary. His normal weekly staff meeting was set for noon. Yet she called just minutes ago to say that her classes had been canceled for the rest of the day and she was hot to see him.

What was a red-blooded guy to do? The staff meeting would last for hours. That fat bore of a Chief Staff Officer would argue every last detail of every agenda item. But he couldn't just miss it without raising suspicion. His irritability was reaching entirely new heights.

His yeoman knocked on the office door and stepped inside, "You wife is calling on line two, sir."

He picked up the receiver. "Yes, dear. What do you want?"

He held the phone away from his ear as she yammered. *Her incessant jabbering drove him insane. What had he ever seen in her? True, her father had been an admiral when they met. That had been useful, at least until the old goat retired. Now she was of no use to him.*

Then his ear picked up words that registered on his cortex when nothing else had. "I need you to come home and talk to your son. He skipped school to surf, again."

He answered, "Dear, I'll be home as soon as I can. I have a lot of things that need to be wrapped up here before I can leave."

He replaced the receiver back on the hook and grabbed his hat as he walked out the door. "Yeoman, I'll be out the rest of the day. Family emergency. Tell the Chief Staff Officer to call me on the cell phone if anything is really important."

He jumped in the Porsche, revved the engine and headed out the North Gate and sped on to the Nimitz Highway. The run to her apartment in Pearl City was only ten minutes. He had the whole afternoon with her. The wife and that brat of a son could wait.

21 Jun 2000, 0600LT (20 Jun, 2300Z)

Boats lay in the surf line watching. Nothing moved ashore. Just the normal jungle sounds. He was so familiar with them that they were comforting. Not the slightest sign that anyone was expecting their arrival. No movement in the trees, betraying an ambush. He raised his hand slightly and waved the all clear signal.

In a carefully orchestrated and practiced maneuver, one black-clad team member scurried across the sand and into the tree line while being covered by team members crouching in the surf.

The sun peeked over the horizon as the last of the squad crossed the sand, carefully erasing any traces of their passage. In the growing light, they buried their swimming gear in shallow holes scooped out of the sand. Shouldering their combat equipment, the team moved inland to find a place to hide for the day.

They slipped through the heavy coastal mangrove swamp undergrowth.

Several groups of patrolling soldiers passed them by without ever seeing the moving green shadows. The SEALs heard the nervous chatter and smelled strong pungent smell of tobacco smoke from the passing guards long before the guards were even near.

These were not highly trained combat soldiers. Even so, they could be very dangerous. They were anxious about something and were nervously patrolling. The squad would have to be extremely cautious not to accidentally encounter a random patrol or to leave telltale traces that would betray their presence.

Avoiding the few built up trails, the SEALs slithered through the swamp. They soon learned why the Nusa Funata mangrove swamps had a reputation for being impenetrable. Wading in brackish water, frequently up to their necks, they struggled silently inland, toward higher ground. The tangle of mangrove roots constantly blocked their progress. The slippery, thick volcanic mud sucked them down. Hordes of biting and stinging insects voraciously attacked any exposed flesh.

They frequently spied snakes either slithering through the tree branches or swimming in the brown water. Boats hated snakes. He had hated them ever since the encounter with a fer-de-lance in Costa Rica during an exercise early in his career. He had nearly died and his left leg still bore the scars from the necrotic actions of the venom. Nusa Funata was home to Sea Kraits, Taipans, Deaths Adders, Tiger Snakes and a host of others, some yet to be named. This was not a hospitable place.

Onward they labored, measuring their progress in scant feet. The heavy packs seemed to snag on every obstacle. Each step involved tripping over a submerged root. Bubbles of methane and hydrogen sulfide burst under their noses, kicked free by their passage. The humidity was cloying, the heat stifling. The fetid odor of rotting vegetation surrounded them like an annoying cloud. No gentle sea breeze could possibly penetrate that maze.

21 Jun 2000, 1400LT (0700Z)

After hours of exhausting slogging, the team finally reached semi-dry ground. The sun was already passed its zenith when they discovered a small hummock, providing good cover and reasonably visible approaches.

Boats laid out the guard positions so all the approaches could be covered with a murderous crossfire if need be.

While the men settled in to get what rest they could before the upcoming night's activities, Jankowski set up to the SATCOM transceiver to communicate with Roland on *SAN FRANCISCO*. The communications were quick, concise and to the point. Just a report that they were safely ashore. No sign of detection. They would be in position tonight for their missions. The chosen approach route could not be reused. A more direct route was needed.

As they settled down for a short rest, the sky opened with a late after-noon deluge. The downpour reduced visibility to inches and seeped into every seam of their raingear. The uncomfortable bivouac was all the SEALs could expect. They simply huddled a little deeper in the undergrowth, secure in the knowledge that the rain that made them uncomfortable also kept the guards from patrolling and drove away the bugs.

21 Jun 2000, 1845LT (1145Z)

All too soon, the day ended as the sun slipped behind the shoulder of Mount Guishu. It was time to move out again.

Rain still dripped from the umbrella of leaves as Boats gathered his small group for a last review of the plan. Spreading out a small map of Nusa Funata, Boats deployed his men. "Jankowski, take Meyer and Cooke. Target the pier and warehouse complex and then the airfield. Stuart, you take Wood, Tagamond and Heigle. Find the hostages. First locate the factory cave. Then set up sniper hide holes to protect the hostages when the strike goes down. I'll take Johnson and Manuelo up Mount Guishu to find that missile and radar complex."

The squads departed on their separate paths. Exhaustion was not an option for these men. Rest was something for after the mission.

Squad One slogged silently through the mangroves again. They headed West for about a mile until they came to the edge of the small bay. Staying hidden in the mangrove, they peered out across the black water. The dark-ened pier and warehouse area was clearly visible through their night vision goggles. The pier was empty but inside the warehouse were several pallets of silvery cylinders.

Meyer tapped Jankowski on the shoulder and pointed. "There it is, just like that Aussie said. Looks like those super-hardened NBC canisters like Sadam used. It'll take a direct hit to blast them." he whispered.

They could see heavily armed men patrolling or standing guard around the complex. The gate through the high chain-link fence surrounding the facility was protected by a sand bagged heavy weapons bunker. The snout of an armored personnel carrier protruded out of the warehouse door, its machine cannon pointed down the pier in their direction.

Jankowski raised a digital camera and took several pictures of the facility as Meyer took a GPS fix of their location. RM3 Cooke had set up the portable Satcom data link. Within minutes, the three had transmitted the visual and position data back to *SAN FRANCISCO*. Confirmation of receipt was immediate. Just as silently as they arrived, they slipped back into the swamp and headed toward the airfield.

Boats, Johnson, and Manuelo headed North. They had to climb to the summit of Mount Guishu. After the first hour, the mangrove swamp gave way to a lush tropical rain forest. They climbed through groves thick with strangler figs enshrouding massive teak, meranti and ramin trees.

In the shade of a particularly large meranti tree, they encountered the horrid smell and awesome beauty of an *Amorphophullus Titantium,* the Corpse Flower. At nearly a meter across and two meters tall, the short-lived blossom was the world's largest orchid. The carrion-like smell attracted insects which, in turn, attracted a swarm of feeding fox bats. There wasn't a single sign that man ever walked here before.

The gentle lower slope of the extinct volcano grew progressively steeper as the team climbed. The red lava soil turned into a greasy, clinging mud with a passing evening shower. Burdened by their heavy loads, they slipped and slided up the slope. The last hundred yards turned into a near vertical climb up a rock face. The only other access was a narrow road carved out of the side of the mountain, but the heavy patrols prevented its use.

Razor-sharp lava rock made progress slow and difficult. Each new handhold bit into the flesh, every slip left cut and flailed skin. The team finally lifted themselves over the edge and found meager concealment in the scree laying in heaps around the cliff edge. The radomes were plainly visible under the camouflage netting further up slope, but the missile launchers and command facilities were not to be seen.

Carefully snaking around the cliff edge to the North, the trio conducted an inch by inch surveillance of the mountaintop. The top of the mountain was crawling with troops. It seemed that every few feet they encountered another patrol.

They could not afford to be discovered. Although they might win a firefight up here, the mission would be compromised. Reconnoitering became a process of slipping forward a foot or two, stop and listen for several minutes, carefully move forward another foot. It was excruciatingly slow and nerve-wracking.

Manuelo almost stumbled over a sleeping guard sitting with his back propped against a boulder and his legs sprawled out in front. He managed to stop just short of stepping on the guard's legs and slowly backed away. The guard muttered incomprehensibly in his sleep and rolled over. Manuelo slid the razor sharp combat knife back in its leg sheath and slipped around the other side of the boulder.

Johnson finally found the command trailer and the missile launchers in two adjacent small gullies cleverly camouflaged to appear as a continuous hummock. A faint glimmer of the coming dawn was just visible on the horizon as Boats transmitted the digital imagery and location data back to *SAN FRANCISCO*. They slid back over the edge of the cliff face to descend in the last bit of cover from the darkness.

The third squad also left the mangrove swamp for the lush tropical rainforest. But instead of climbing higher, they skirted around the base of Mount Guishu to the Northeast.

A few hundred yards beyond the mangrove swamp, they happened on a well-used single lane dirt road. The team concealed themselves in the underbrush for fifteen minutes, carefully watching to see if the road was patrolled. Nothing moved. Finally, Stuart signaled Tagamond to cross. Crouching low, the SEAL scurried across the road and disappeared into the undergrowth. The muzzle of his H&K machine pistol was just visible, pointed down the road.

Stuart signaled again and Wood scurried across. He rolled under a small tree and guarded up the road. Another signal from Stuart and Heigle ran across the road. Finally, Stuart crossed, checking carefully to make sure there was no sign of their passage.

Stuart moved the team about twenty yards up slope. They slipped forward, paralleling the road, but several yards further up the slope so they could stay hidden. The team moved quickly.

They covered almost a mile of thick jungle, occasionally catching glimpses of the road off to their right through openings in the trees. Twice they saw the headlights of trucks driving down the road toward the harbor. Each time they froze, relying on their camouflage to keep them concealed.

Finally, the team halted. The road made an abrupt turn to the left, up the mountain slope. They could see a flickering light coming from a guarded checkpoint. Beyond the checkpoint, arc lights illuminated what appeared to be a military compound capable of housing several hundred troops. Parked in the central courtyard were several armored personnel carriers, each sporting a 23-mm machine cannon.

They skirted around the checkpoint and climbed to high ground. From this vantage point, they could look directly down into the compound and beyond it.

Troops moved around the brightly-lit inner area. The center courtyard was dominated by a large wooden building that appeared to be a headquarters and possibly a barracks. A smaller wooden building stood to the left of the main building, separated by a tall chain link fence. Stuart could see men dressed in white smocks walking in and out of it. Several sat on the front porch of the building, smoking.

A few yards beyond the small building he could see the opening of a large cave with bright lighting inside. Around the entrance the terrorists had placed sandbag emplacements containing Chinese made four-barrel Zu-23 anti-aircraft machine cannons and shoulder-fired SA-7 Grail surface-to-air missiles. A number of people, some in military uniform and others in civilian clothes, were entering and leaving the cave.

They had found the factory complex.

The digital targeting information for the command compound and the cave location were rapidly passed to *SAN FRANCISCO*.

As the team maneuvered around the complex to determine the defensive measures that were in place and the extent of the facility, they passed above the cave entrance. Here they crossed a footpath that they had not previously seen. The footpath headed over a low ridge.

Carefully paralleling the footpath, they crested the ridge and peered into the gully beyond. Even with night vision goggles, it was difficult to discern any human mark in the gully. The path seemed to suddenly end at the edge of some heavy undergrowth. It just didn't appear natural. Why would a well-worn path suddenly end abruptly with some brush? The team spent the next hour working carefully around the uphill side of the gully to try to get a better view. They settled in to observe the mysterious end of the path.

22

21 Jun 2000, 0300LT (1400Z)

The dark shape emerged from the water and crouched under the low rock ledge at the water's edge. As he removed his scuba equipment, three more men joined him. They buried their equipment in a hastily dug shallow hole. The men removed their weapons from waterproof pouches, then slithered across the damp grass to the edge of First Avenue.

The little community was nearly silent. Only the sounds of the night insects and the gentle lap of the water broke the stillness. Not a soul was out for a late night stroll, nor was there any traffic on the quiet street. The sweet scent of plumeria hung heavy in the moist night air.

The four black-clad intruders slipped quickly across the street and hid in the deep shadows under the banyan tree. There they briefly reviewed the plan.

All had gone better than expected so far. The Hawaiian spy had passed the information through several cutouts to Mustaf.

He had planned the action and handpicked these four for this mission. They were his best, most ruthless followers. The four had rehearsed this mission many times on the shore near Benghazi and at their desert camp. They even built a full-scale mock-up of the house and street to practice with. Mustaf had given them the high honor of giving them their final briefing himself.

The four arrived in Honolulu two days ago, coming in on four different flights from different US cities. Before that, they had flown, under different names and passports, from various Middle Eastern cities.

Security at the American airports was laughable. Ashad, the leader, had a moment of panic when a Customs Inspector at New York's JFK Airport reviewed his passport and visa. The Inspector held out his hand to stop Ashad. "Just a minute."

Ashad's heart nearly stopped. *Had someone betrayed them? Were the Americans wise to their plot? His documents were flawless and he wasn't carrying anything that would incriminate him. It must be the Jew loving Americans harassing Arabs. They would pay for this!*

The garrulous Inspector then added said, "Welcome to America." For the rest, cursory inspections of their documentation and then they were through.

The more difficult arrangements were those to smuggle in the weapons. Hawaii had some of the toughest gun control laws in the world, with registration of even ammunition, so locally acquired weapons were out. Smuggling the weapons into the Islands was the only alternative. The weapons were purchased openly in Los Angeles last month. They were modified, adjusted and sighted in by Mustaf's weapons experts in the desert East of Los Angeles. The machine pistols arrived in Hawaii on schedule yesterday in a container manifested as hardware onboard the new Matson liner, *President Reagan*.

They had slipped into the water from the public footpath near the COMPACFLT Boathouse just after midnight. The swim around Ford Island, under the new Ford Island bridge, was uneventful. The only near call was an unexpected late boat running from the Merry Point Landing to Iroquois Point. Ashad broke the surface to check his navigation almost directly in front of the launch. No one onboard saw him quickly dive back below the surface just inches before its keel cleaved his head.

From under the banyan tree, Ashad sent his team to their assault stations. One man took cover under a plumeria bush at the rear corner of the house, giving him a clear field of fire down the rear and side. Another set up at the front corner under one of the banyan's massive aerial roots. His field of fire was down the front and interlocked with his companion down the side. The third moved to the lanai door and quickly picked the simple tumbler lock. No resistance was expected, but weren't all Americans armed? Better safe than sorry.

The door was opened just enough for the four to silently enter the house. Downstairs was empty and quickly secured, the phone lines cut and the breakers for the electrical supply opened. Anyone upstairs was now isolated from the outside world.

They silently padded to the stairs and moved upward. The corner tread, halfway up the stairs was creaky. Hunter had promised to fix it at least a dozen times, but it had never come to the top of the "honey-do" list. The first terrorist stepped on it and it creaked loudly. They instantly froze. *Had the sound warned the quarry? Were they armed? Would the next step be met with a hail of bullets?*

They waited, frozen in place but poised for instant response, for five minutes. No sound. They proceeded up the stairs much more cautiously.

The hallway was laid out exactly as they were briefed. Doors to the left and right opened onto small bedrooms, the door at the end of the hall opened onto the master bedroom. A terrorist stopped by each door waiting for a signal from the leader.

Simultaneously they jerked open the doors and rushed into the rooms. The occupants were each jerked out of their slumber and hauled to the floor. The two girls were roughly shoved into the master bedroom where the wife was defiantly facing the leader.

"Mommy, what's happening? Who are these men?" the young redhead asked in a quavering voice.

""Quiet, dear. Don't be afraid," Peg Hunter answered.

"That's not very good advice," the Ashad growled, menacingly brandishing the dangerous looking machine pistol. "You should be very afraid. If you don't do exactly as we say, you won't live to see the sun rise."

Unnoticed, the oldest daughter slipped behind her mother. The cell phone that she had earlier used to talk to her best friend was on the bedside table. She pressed the "mute" button and then the "send" one. *Don't let them see her. Please let Sally wake up and understand what is happening.*

21 Jun 2000, 0330LT (1430Z)

Over on Ford Island, in Colonel Johnson's house, the phone rang. At 0330, Colonel Johnson was not amused as he reached across his sleeping wife to pick up the phone. As well as being Sally's father, the Colonel was also PACOM J-2 Special Intelligence Officer. He was one of only a small handful of people who had an idea of what was currently happening off Nusa Funata.

No one answered his gravelly greeting so he thought that it was another call from a drunken sailor who had dialed the wrong number.

He had just started to replace the receiver when he heard something that made him pause. He thought he heard a threat in an accent that he had not heard since he left Iraq at the end of the Gulf War. Immediately, he was wide-awake, all senses on peak alert.

21 Jun 2000, 0332LT (1432Z)

Ashad ordered the three hostages to sit on the double bed. The calm dark night outside gave a sharp contrast to the awful tension in the master bedroom.

The three underlings took defensive positions; one at the master bedroom window, one at the window in Megan's room and the last downstairs.

"Now listen very carefully," he began. "Whether you live or die depends on how well you follow orders. We are soldiers of Allah and Mustaf al Shatar. Life is meaningless to us. We don't usually make war on women and children, but your husband has forced this on us. He is trying to stop our great revolution. You will stop him. When the sun rises, we will call your Master of Submarines. You will tell him to order your husband to surface and go immediately to Surabaya. If he has not complied within twelve hours, one of you will die. We will kill one of you every six hours until he complies. Do you understand me?"

The three women huddled even closer together and Peg shook her head in acknowledgement. Maggie put her arms around her mother and whispered, "Don't worry, Mommy, it'll be alright. I won't let them hurt us."

21 Jun 2000, 0340LT (1440Z)

Colonel Johnson picked up his cell phone and dialed a special number. When the duty officer at PACOM answered, he gave the code word for a hostage situation and rapidly explained what he thought was happening. His orders to the duty officer were precise and measured.

Camp Smith, high above Pearl Harbor, erupted in a bustle of controlled activity. The trace on the call to Colonel Johnson proved his supposition that it originated from Peg Hunter's cell phone. Calls to the house on Hospital Point went unanswered.

A security guard drove by the house on routine patrol. He reported the house was dark and there was no sign of unusual activity. Externally all seemed normal, but the cell phone still gave the listeners a ringside seat to what was really happening inside the house.

The PACOM Command Center changed its emphasis from watching the events in Indonesia to directing the response to this hostage situation.

Across the Ko'olau Mountains, at Kaneohe Marine Station, a clanging alarm bell roused the Marine Force Recon anti-terrorist team from their slumber. They jumped from their bunks, donning their combat outfits as they raced toward the flight line. The black jump suits contrasted sharply with regular Marine cammies. The Kevlar vests under the combat harnesses gave them a bulky, sinister appearance.

Three large green MH-53 Sea Stallion helicopters were warming up for the quick flight from Kaneohe to Hickam Air Force Base, next to Pearl Harbor. The fully outfitted teams ran out onto the flight line and jumped in the choppers just as the pilots completed their pre-flight checklists. Within minutes of first receiving the alarm, the ungainly birds were enroute.

The small Marine barracks on Pearl Harbor Naval Station also got a call from the PACOM Response Team. They rushed out of their barracks, grabbing their weapons from the Armory on their way to set up roadblocks. They sealed access to Hospital Point, controlling all activity entering or leaving the Point. This was easily accomplished since there were only two roads leading to the small, isolated housing complex.

The gates to Pearl Harbor slammed shut. No one could enter or leave. All ship traffic in the harbor was stopped.

So far the activity had all been scripted. The hostage response plan was designed to get everything in place as quickly as possible to contain the situation.

The next part would not move so quickly. They had to gather as much information as possible and plan the response. The only constant that they all knew for certain was that there would be no negotiation.

There had been no contact from the terrorists. The waiting game began. This was the hard part. Waiting ground on the nerves as they sat, unable to do anything to rescue the family of one of their own.

Evacuating the small isolated community began. The first few houses were easy. Marines in full combat garb rushed into the houses without bothering to even knock. The surprised residents were shuttled on to launches waiting at Charlie Landing on the windward end of the Point. The launches carried them up the harbor, past the shipyard and the submarine base, to Merry Point Landing, well away from the danger zone.

The houses within view of Quarters G presented more of a problem. Brenda Calucci was awakened by a Marine pounding on her back door. She and her son, still in their nightclothes were hustled down the shore, through a hole cut in the fence, to Dry-dock Four. They joined the residents of the last five houses on First Street, huddled together and chattering nervously, trying to find out what was happening.

Two Marines managed to approach the other side of the duplex from the terrorists' blind side to evacuate the family that lived there. They implanted two sensitive listening devices on the shared wall, but so far nothing had been heard.

21 Jun 2000, 0430LT (1530Z)

"What do we know so far?" Admiral O'Flanagan demanded as he stormed into the command center.

The admiral had been enjoying a few hours of rest at home when the call arrived. The boat ride from his home on Ford Island to the SUBPAC landing had been at full throttle. He had not wasted any time in the short dash to the SUBPAC Building or the hurried descent into the basement.

His aide and most of his senior staff were already in the command center. Some of them had been there to monitor the events off Nusa Funata; the rest had just arrived after being summoned to deal with the latest crisis. They were all focused on the house over at Hospital Point. The high priority communications lines between SUBPAC and PACOM up at Camp Smith were humming with activity.

LT Pyler answered the admiral's question, "PACOM is in command of the situation. The cell phone is still working but the batteries appear to be dying. They have heard all three of the family and at least three terrorists. The one that we think is the leader, some character named Ashad, was heard telling Peg that they were going to demand that *SAN FRANCISCO* divert to the nearest Indonesian port. PACOM has some voice experts coming to help determine their country of origin."

He continued, referring to a large-scale map of the base. "The area is surrounded and cordoned off, here, here and here," pointing to the road-blocks. "I don't think a centipede could sneak through. No direct contact from the terrorists yet."

"Alright, we let PACOM worry about this. What about *SAN FRANCISCO*?" The admiral continued.

His operations officer turned from his desk and answered, "Last communication was about four hours ago. They were working on setting up the relay of targeting information to the *NIMITZ* for the Tomahawk strike. Everything appears to be working OK so far."

Admiral O'Flanagan turned to his Chief of Staff and, in a low voice, asked, "Chief of Staff, what do we do about telling Jon Hunter what is happening here? Clearly we don't divert him anywhere."

Captain Hughes was a senior submariner who hoped to occupy the admiral's seat in a couple of years. He thought quietly for a few moments. He answered in a carefully measured tone, "Admiral, this is a tough one. Jon has every right to know what is happening with his family. It's the humane thing to tell him. Normally we would HUMEVAC him back here as fast as possible. But this isn't a normal time. It is absolutely vital that this strike be carried off. He is the only one in position to do it in time. We can't afford to call him off station for a HUMEVAC. If we tell him and then don't HUMEVAC him, the worry may affect his judgment."

He took off his glasses and began to wipe them with a tissue. This was a ploy that he long ago developed to buy time while he formulated his thoughts. He began slowly. "Remember back in the Cold War days when we both were commanding boats. If something bad happened at home, we weren't told until we came home. Cold, calculating and cruel. But it kept us at our job. That's what we have to do here. Don't tell him until everything is resolved and he is on his way home from the mission. It's the only sensible thing to do."

Hughes let his glasses fall to his chest, hanging from a long black cord draped around his neck. The finality of this small act was a more effective emphasis than anything else.

"He can't do anything about this except worry over it. We have to have him working at his peak. It's far too important."

Admiral O'Flanagan acquiesced, "You're right, Chief of Staff. That is what we will do. Make sure that no message goes to SAN FRANCISCO about this. Get PACOM involved so that Jon doesn't find out through some inadvertent slip somewhere."

Captain Hughes shook his head just a bit. "It's going to leave Hunter mad as hell. When he gets back and finds out about his family, no matter how it turns out, I wouldn't want to be in the blast radius."

O'Flanagan answered, "I guess that's my job."

21 Jun 2000, 0520LT (1620Z)

The hostage response plan was swinging into high gear. A temporary headquarters was set up in the harbor control tower, atop a water tank high above the Pearl Harbor Shipyard. This afforded the local commander a panoramic view of the house and all approaches, without being seen by the terrorists.

Colonel Johnson was in command of the local team. His boat from Ford Island rushed across the placid harbor water, landing at the shipyard docks. A staff car hurtled down the narrow shipyard streets to deliver him to the water tower. He charged into the command center just as the MH-53's from Kaneohe landed at nearby Hickam Air Force Base. Two huge C-17's roared down Hickam's runways to cover the noise of the incoming MH-53's.

Johnson busied himself setting everything in place for the long slow process that would, hopefully, result in the release of the hostages. He could not afford to think of the hostages as friends and neighbors. Megan and Maggie had slept over with Sally many times. He and his wife had been frequent guests at the house he was now observing. That all had to be set aside; forgotten for now. It would only cloud his judgment.

Looking down at the house, he could see that all the windows were still dark. This was unusual. On a normal morning, the lights would be coming on as the household arose to greet the coming day. They should be listening to the sounds of a happy family making plans for the day's activities from the microphones that his people had planted. There were no lights and no sounds.

"Colonel, we have the infrared scan results" one his assistants reported. "We are seeing seven hotspots that equate to seven people. Looks like four terrorists and the three hostages." Looking toward a computer monitor, he continued, pointing out blobs of bright yellow-white against a background of darker reds and blues. "Look here. This is the master bedroom. Looks like three people close together. I'm guessing they're sitting on a bed. Someone's standing over here by the back window and someone else by this side window. When we move to the front bedroom, we see another person standing by a front window. One last person downstairs. Over here in the enclosed lanai."

"That gives us some idea of what we're up against," Colonel Johnson answered. "I make out the three women are sitting on the bed, two guards at the windows in that room, a guard covering the front of the house from upstairs and one guard downstairs. Neat and efficient, professional. Looks like the women are all still alive. You can see movement. Still no contact?"

"No, sir. Not a word out of there, yet," another member of the team answered. He was wearing earphones and sitting in front of a bank of switches and dials, monitoring the telephone circuits into the house and the dying cell phone. Other people were setting up high power tripod mounted binoculars and sensitive directional listening devices. The makeshift command post was taking on the look of a high tech bunker.

"I think it's their move. For now we sit and wait," the Colonel said, more to himself that to anyone in the room.

21 Jun 2000, 0800LT (1900Z)

"It's time," Ashad told Peg, pulling a cell phone from his pocket. He dialed a number that was supposed to be known only to a very few top submariners.

The private red phone in Admiral O'Flanagan's office began to buzz loudly. Mike O'Flanagan reached for the receiver. He was not expecting a call on this line. It was almost never good news when it rang. The last time had been over a year ago. That time had been the report of a submarine in trouble off San Diego.

Peg Hunter was on the other end. She sounded tense, but in rigid control. "Admiral, they are holding us hostage. They're armed and tell me that they will kill us if you don't do as they say."

Another voice, male and heavily accented, replaced Peg's. "You will order your submarine *SAN FRANCISCO* to surface and head immediately for the nearest Indonesian port. It will contact Indonesian Naval Control as soon as it surfaces. You have twelve hours. Then we will kill a hostage every six hours until we hear that it is in port."

Admiral O'Flanagan answered, "But *SAN FRANCISCO* is in the Aleutians, off Alaska. She is conducting exercises up there. We can't even contact her until her next communications cycle in ten hours. We can't…"

"Don't play us for fools, Admiral," the terrorist interrupted. "We know that Hunter and *SAN FRANCISCO* are in Indonesia. We know their mission. You have twelve hours!" The phone was slammed down.

Admiral O'Flanagan turned to his Chief of Staff and Commodore

Calucci. "You heard what he said. I doubted very seriously that they went to all this trouble to carry out a bluff.

"I see that we have two problems to solve. One is how to get Peg and the children out of there. PACOM will handle that problem. Commodore, you coordinate with them and give them all the assistance that they need. You have my authority to use every asset in SUBPAC."

Calucci answered, "Yes sir." *This was a plum. If all worked well, he could be a hero.*

Admiral O'Flanagan continued, "The other problem is to find out where the security leak is. They have information on a mission that has the highest possible classification. Not a dozen people in the country know about it. Chief of Staff, you take charge of finding the leak. Don't leave a single stone unturned. I want to find the bastard who leaked this and then fry him. Do you two understand me?"

The two nodded as they rose to leave. Commodore Calucci felt the cold, clammy sweat of fear trickle down his back.

23

22 Jun 2000, 0430LT (21 Jun, 2130Z)

The targeting information from the SEAL squad on the island arrived as a data stream on *SAN FRANCISCO*. The pieces were correlated and passed to the Tomahawk Afloat Targeting Group onboard the *NIMITZ*, still racing across the Timor Sea. The targeting group took the information and revised existing mission profiles to refine the target locations on Nusa Funata. After four hours of number crunching, a Mission Data Update (MDU) message flew back to *SAN FRANCISCO*. The revised data and imagery gave each missile the information that it needed to precisely locate its assigned target.

Two of the three elements needed to conduct the strike were in place. The last step was to insert Roland and the rest of his squad with the weapons and explosives needed to attack the factory cave.

21 Oct 2000, 1120LT (2220Z)

She wasn't answering her phone. He had tried a dozen times. He had to know for sure. He had to see her again. The horrible feeling in the pit of his stomach was getting worse. It was gnawing at his ability to think.

Commodore Calucci slammed the phone down in disgust. He stalked out of his office, growling at his yeoman that he was going to lunch.

Her apartment was only a ten-minute drive in his Porsche 944. The spinning tires peppered the guardhouse with gravel as he accelerated out the Supply Depot Gate onto Nimitz Avenue. He parked in the "Residents Only" underground garage and ran to the elevator. Sweat blurred his vision as he punched the button for her floor.

Somehow he knew, as he slipped his key into the lock, that she was gone. But he didn't expect to see the Chief of Staff sitting on the couch under the broad window looking out on the bay, polishing his glasses. The same couch that he had shared with her so many times.

"Thought it might be you," the Chief of Staff said as he stood. "She's gone."

A pair of plain-clothes Naval Investigative Service agents stepped out of the bedroom, handcuffed Commodore Calucci, and shoved him roughly out the door.

22 Jun 2000, 0645LT (21 Jun, 2345Z)

Dawn was just breaking over the mountain ridge behind them when Stuart spotted a squad of soldiers ambling down the path from the compound. The men were smoking and talking as they leisurely strolled along the mountain path. Their automatic weapons were slung across their backs, out of reach for quick use. The dirty, unkempt appearance of their motley uniforms completed the picture of a ragtag outfit.

As they approached the end of the path, another equally ragtag squad emerged from the brush. The two squads met at the end of the path and carried out an exchange that appeared to be a changing of the guard. The first squad then entered the brush while the second ambled up the path toward the compound.

The team had found something that warranted the need for a continuous guard. Perhaps they had found the hostages. The only way to know was to go down and take a look.

Silently Wood and Tagamond slipped off into the waning darkness while Stuart reported this new development back to *SAN FRANCISCO*.

Moving scant inches at a time, the two slithered through the under-growth. They were approaching from two different directions to better observe and to provide each other cover fire. By noon they had almost reached positions to observe what was beyond the path.

Unexpectedly, another squad came over the ridge from the direction of the compound. Stuart and Heigle watched in dread from their observation point over 500 yards away. The squad approached the end of the path and the SEALs hiding places. It must be time for another changing of the guard. Would the two scouts be detected? Each of the two watching SEALs slipped a massive 50-caliber shell into the breach of their sniper rifle and slid the bolt home. Placing the cross hairs of the 10X Redfield scope on the head of the lead and trailing man, they waited for any sign of alertment.

The off-going squad emerged from the underbrush and headed back toward the compound as the on-coming squad entered the underbrush. Amazingly, the whole exchange had occurred within inches of the two scout's hiding places, but they were never noticed. The squads of terrorists would never know how close they had come to death that hot fetid morning.

The two SEAL scouts slid through the underbrush a few yards, only to find a lava cave hidden behind it. Just inside the mouth of the cave, the soldiers had built a comfortable campsite. Beyond this, further into the cavern, was a group dressed in civilian clothes, separated by steel bars set into the cave floor and ceiling. Observing the activities inside the cave, the SEALs counted all thirty of the hostages and ten guards. A line of fire for the snipers to control inside the cave was all but impossible without endan-gering the hostages. The only way to handle this was up close and personal.

Just as silently as they had approached, the two disappeared and made their way back to their teammates. Meeting up with their two companions, they moved higher up the hill and made a temporary bivouac.

Stuart radioed back that the hostages had been located. The four settled in to wait and watch.

21 Jun 2000, 2000LT (22 Jun, 0700Z)

Ashad led the young girl down the stairs and out onto the small front porch. There he stood, framed in the doorway with her, still in her night-clothes, standing in front.

With theatrically slow movements, Ashad raised the Tec-9 to the side of her head. Maggie stood absolutely still, frozen by the terror of the moment.

The silenced round found its mark with a barely audible "phfutt". The little girl fell forward as the blood splattered her nightdress.

Ashad hurtled backward into the living room as the silenced .308 caliber match grade bullet smashed through his nasal cavity into the frontal lobe of his brain. Death was nearly instantaneous. A sudden, blinding flash and then nothingness.

It happened so quickly and so unexpectedly that his mind never sent the order to his finger to squeeze the trigger. His blood splattered widely as the hydrostatic pressure from the bullet impact caused his head to explode. The Tec-9 clattered uselessly to the ground, landing beside the prone girl.

Maggie rolled over and started to stand. Her hand accidentally fell on the Tec-9. Picking it up was an automatic reaction. The terror and the rage of the day welled up inside her and took control.

The downstairs guard ran to the stairs and started to climb.

He's going to kill Mom and Megan! Her mind screamed.

She raised the weapon and, from the classic kneeling position, emptied a full clip into the fleeing terrorist. He fell down the stairs as the slugs stitched across his back. She dropped the gun and ran, crying, into the waiting arms of the Marine sniper who had shot Ashad.

In the master bedroom, the remaining two terrorists were confused. The gunfire sounded as if it came from the leader's weapon. They expected that. But they did not expect to hear a long burst of automatic fire. Ashad would have used three rounds. More was a waste. Possibly his gun malfunc-tioned. That was not uncommon with these shoddy American weapons.

Still, all did not seem right. Ashad had not come back upstairs. There were no sounds from downstairs, either. They were on edge; every nerve tuned to the slightest hint of danger. Their instructions had been simple. Guard the hostages and prevent their rescue. They understood that the success of their mission depended on keeping the hostages alive until Ashad said otherwise.

21 Jun 2000, 2005LT (22 Jun, 0705Z)

Colonel Johnson was frantic. The shooting had been totally unexpected. Preliminary reports were that the youngest daughter was safe, although badly shaken. At least two of the terrorists were down.

"Get the gas in there. NOW! NOW! NOW!" he roared over the command circuit.

His team had a small store of a special, newly developed and very secret, crowd control agent that was designed especially for these kinds of situations. A colorless and odorless gas, it rendered anyone exposed to it unconscious in seconds. Better still, it was absorbed through the skin almost as quickly as by inhaling, so gas masks were only of limited usefulness. The effects wore off a few minutes after the exposure ended, but it should give Col. Johnson's team a few critical minutes to act.

They had not used it until this time since it could have some very nasty side effects, particularly if the exposed victim had allergies or was asthmatic. Maggie Hunter had both problems, but she was no longer a hostage. If Peg or Megan suffered an allergic reaction, at this juncture, that was better than the alternative.

Two small, black canisters rolled in through the open front door. The gas spewing from the open valves wafted silently up the stairs. Two more canisters were lowered from the roof so that they were hanging from strings by the inlet of the window air conditioning unit that was laboring to keep the upstairs cool in evening's heat.

Within seconds, all four occupants of the house were unconscious. They lay slumped over where they had sat. A dozen heavily armed figures outfitted in whole-body NBC suits raced up the stairs. Two bodies were unceremoniously hauled off to an interrogation facility. The two women were treated much more courteously. They were tenderly placed on stretchers and lowered to a waiting ambulance for the quick ride to Tripler Military Hospital. This crisis was over.

24

The sun was still well above the Western horizon when the lock-out started. The risk of discovery was necessary to allow the squad as much of the night as possible to get ashore. There was simply too much that had to be accomplished under the veil of darkness.

Once again, Chief Jones and his team performed the delicate balancing act that brought *SAN FRANCISCO* to a rock solid hover 80 feet below the surface. Again ten SEALs exited the submarine in three groups. As the sun dropped below the horizon, the last SEAL broke the surface.

SAN FRANCISCO came up to periscope depth and fired number one and number two torpedo tubes. Two torpedo shaped black objects bobbed to the surface a few yards from the waiting SEALs. They immediately swam toward the shapes. They popped open several spring releases on each shape. Inside was a small rigid hulled inflatable boat capable of carrying ten passengers. It included a powerful, specially silenced outboard motor to drive them to shore. The SEALs boarded the RHIBs and pulled them alongside a third torpedo shape that bobbed to the surface. Opening this shape, the squad loaded their weapons and equipment into the RHIBs. The three now empty shapes were scuttled into the deep water below.

The two low black boats swung around toward the shore and picked up speed. *SAN FRANCISCO* turned toward the open sea and dropped from view.

Aboard *SAN FRANCISCO,* the ship was humming with activity. In the torpedo room, the reload team rushed to drain the three empty torpedo tubes and reload them with TLAMs. The torpedo that was in tube 4, the normal self-defense torpedo, was back-hauled to allow a fourth TLAM to be loaded. There would be no self-defense weapon immediately ready if *SAN FRANCISCO* came under attack.

The wardroom was transformed into a tactical strike planning center. Warran Jacobs and Jeff Miller led their teams of quartermasters and fire control technicians in charting the over-water portion of the TLAM flights.

To maximize surprise, it was necessary for the TLAMs to all arrive at their targets at very nearly the same time and to be closely coordinated with LT Roland's attack. They needed to arrive from different quadrants so that the enemy could not concentrate their defenses. Because the TLAMs required about ten minutes to launch, including gyro spin-up, targeting data download and stabilization, plus the time required to shift from launching one tube to the next, the over-water flight planning for each bird was a complicated balance of air speed, timing, and geographic constraints. At mach 0.8, over 600 miles per hour, the birds required a good deal of real estate to eat up the time differences and to get into position to attack their targets. The missiles were flying at wave top height, so this real estate could not include land. To minimize the chance of detection, the missiles could not fly near any air search radars.

Forms and charts littered the wardroom table, spilled over onto the deck and festooned the bulkheads. Several laptop computers were in feverish use.

The torpedomen and fire control technicians hurried to load the tubes and check the communications to the missiles. Two of the tubes were loaded with TLAM-D's, a Tomahawk variant equipped with hundreds of small 2.2 pound bomblet sub-munitions, while two tubes were loaded with TLAM-C's, containing a single 700 pound Bullpup warhead.

"Sonar, conn. New contact, designate Sierra two-four-seven. Best bearing three-four-two. High speed screws. Classify warship, possible FFG

7 class." The announcement from sonar over the 27MC caught everyone off guard.

Sam Stuart was standing watch as OOD. He stepped over to the sonar display panel and glanced at the white track that was just starting to develop out of the snowy back ground clutter.

"Where did he come from? He's not one of ours," he questioned Bill Fagan who was standing beside him on the conn.

"We sold several FFG 7's to the Indonesians back in the mid 90's. It's probably one of those. Weren't you paying attention during the mission brief? We covered all the expected combatant platforms," the XO replied. "We'd better tell the Skipper."

Stuart called Hunter, who was in the wardroom observing the strike planning, on the MJ phone and informed him of the new development.

"He's going to pose a problem with this strike package. Not likely he would sit by and idly let someone fly TLAMs over his head in his own territorial waters. He might even be coming in to give the terrorists some more cover. Do you have a rough range on him?" Hunter questioned Stuart.

"Not yet sir. Wanted to report him first. Range of the day is two-five-thousand yards for an FFG 7 broadband. Performing a ranging maneuver now," Stuart replied.

The range of the day was an estimate of the range for a fifty- percent detection probability given the particular acoustic environment for that location that day. It gave a very rough starting point to begin the iterative process of refining the range.

Hunter turned to the assembled group in the wardroom and said, "Plot a point at 25,000 yards on bearing three-four-two. Put a fifty nautical mile circle around it. Are we currently planning on flying any birds into that circle?"

"Yes, sir," Warren Jacobs immediately replied. "Our launch basket is just outside the edge of that circle. We had planned all four to fly inside it."

"Well, like all good plans, it has to change," Hunter responded. "That FFG isn't worth anything for ASW, but it does have a good AAW suite. It's not a threat to us, but it is to our birds. We can't afford to have any of these birds detected or knocked down. Give me your revised flight plan ASAP." He left the wardroom and went up the ladder to control.

"Captain, the best estimate of range based on the last maneuver is two-two-thousand yards. Looks like he is headed for the island and in a real hurry." Sam Stuart reported as Hunter stepped into control.

"Very well, we haven't got time to waste watching him. Come to course zero-two-seven and Ahead Full. We need to be at this point in two hours," Hunter said, pointing to a position 100 nautical miles to the Northwest of Nusa Funata and 50 nautical miles from their present position.

The OOD ordered, "Helm, right ten degrees rudder, steady course zero-two-seven. Ahead Full." The sub raced for the launch basket.

23 Jun 2000, 0048LT (22 Jun, 1648Z)

LT Roland's squad pointed their two RHIBs toward the shore. Making thirty knots, the ride was short but rough and wet. At full throttle, they literally skipped from wave top to wave top.

As they neared the black beach, Roland yelled above the wind, "I see the signal, off to the left. Come left twenty degrees." He pointed toward a large log that had washed up on the beach. "Aim for that log."

Boats had scouted the best landing place for them and placed the IR Chem-lite signal on the log. Roland removed the IR goggles as the two RHIBs roared up onto the black sand. Boats met them at the tree line as they pulled the RHIBs under cover.

They quickly unloaded the contents of the two boats and silently followed the Chief into the mangrove swamp, leaving the RHIBs where they lay. No need to waste time hiding them. By the time any casual patrol stumbled across the RHIBs and raised the alarm, the whole island would know they were there anyway.

Slogging through the mud and slime, they arrived at a small raised hummock where two more members of the first assault squad waited. Boats explained, "We've found a good, quick route to the factory. Jankowski, Cooke and Meyer are watching it now. We'd better get humping. The TLAMs are due in an hour and it'll take us almost that long to get there."

This time the SEALs didn't bother with concealment or staying in the swamp. They didn't have the time. They ran down the sides of the road right up to the point where it turned into the compound. Here they split up and moved around the perimeter from both sides.

LT Roland placed his two Squad Assault Weapon (SAWs) marksmen so that each overlooked one of the anti-aircraft emplacements. He placed his two M-60 machine guns so that they could rake the entrance to the cave and the path leading down to the compound. Two of his team were busy planting a series of Claymore mines, detonated by trip wires, along the path down to the compound to make life just that much more interesting for anyone rushing to reinforce the factory's defenders.

22 Jun 2000, 0610LT (1710Z)

Peg Hunter slowly clawed her way through the mist back to consciousness. The fear slammed back. "Where were the girls? Are they all right? What happened?"

She opened her eyes to find the morning sun pouring through the window, filling the unfamiliar room with a warm golden glow. Moving her head to take in her surroundings brought on waves of nausea. She lay back.

"Take it slow, Peg," the familiar growl of Admiral O'Flanagan came from somewhere off to her left, out of her field of view. "That gas can knock your socks off."

"The girls?" She asked querulously.

"They're okay," O'Flanagan assured her. "Molly spent the night at the Johnson's and Megan is in the next room."

He came into view as he walked over to the bed. The inevitable stub of an unlit, well chewed cigar firmly projecting from the side of his mouth.

"Megan woke up a few minutes ago. She is busy attacking breakfast. Molly had a bad night. We are scheduling counseling for all of you."

O'Flanagan turned and pulled a chair over to sit beside Peg's bed. He sat down and squirmed into the hard-backed hospital chair in a vain attempt to get comfortable. Peg figured that he was buying time, delaying the discussion of something that was more uncomfortable than a hospital chair.

"Peg, there's something that we need to discuss," he began. "You've probably already figured out that Jon is not on exercises up in the Aleutians."

Peg started to speak, but Admiral O'Flanagan raised his hand. "Peg, let me continue. Jon is in Indonesia doing something that is very important and very dangerous. I'm not going to tell you what it is exactly, but it is one of those missions that no one will ever know about. You'll have to trust me on that."

The anger rose quickly. Peg exploded, "You expect me to trust you! You almost got my family killed. Don't talk to me about trust."

"Peg, calm down." O'Flanagan raised both hands, palms out in supplication. "I know you're angry, but it won't help you, Jon or us. Just hear me out, please."

He went on to explain the terrorist plot that had been uncovered. As the sordid plot unfolded, Peg began to grasp the implications of any part of it becoming known.

Admiral O'Flanagan concluded, "So you see, we have to make everything look like business as usual. We have already told the press that all the activity on base yesterday was a scheduled exercise. We were testing our new hostage response team tactics with a full-scale dress rehearsal. I need you to support that story. Can I count on you?"

He paused for a second and then threw in the low blow that she couldn't counter. "Jon needs you."

23 Jun 2000, 0040LT (22 Jun, 1740Z)

As *SAN FRANSICO* neared the launch point, the IMC blared "Man Battle Stations Missile for TLAM Strike!" followed by the "Gong, gong, gong" of the General Alarm. The announcement and alarm were anticlimactic. Nearly everyone was already at their battle station making the preparations to launch the Tomahawks.

A quick trip to periscope depth ensured that no one was around to see or interfere with the launch. A careful search for any sonar contacts further ensured they were alone in this particular part of the ocean. The sound of the underwater launch transients, especially the ignition of the booster rocket, carried for many miles and was unmistakable. To add to the risk of detection, once the booster was airborne, it left a smoky arrow pointing back down at the sub. It was important to make very sure that they were alone in this part of the Java Sea.

The launch sequence began. Hunter ordered the missiles in tubes one and two made ready in all respects. A final check of the mission data loaded in those missiles verified all was loaded and functioning correctly.

Jeff Miller reported, "Tubes one and two ready in all respects."

Hunter immediately ordered, "Shoot tube one."

Miller flung the large brass firing lever to 'standby' and shouted, "Stand by," and then flung the lever to 'shoot', shouting "Launch permissive" to the people in the control room.

There was no hint of activity for about forty-five seconds as the gyros in the missile silently came up to speed and the missile performed a series of internal checks. When the checks were all completed, a series of electrical interlocks made contact, porting torpedo tube firing air to the torpedo tube flushing cylinder. The 1500-psi air forced the flushing piston down the cylinder, pushing high-pressure water through a series of passages, up into the after part of the torpedo tube. Meanwhile, in the torpedo tube, the missile canister had opened a series of ports around its after part. The high-pressure water literally flushed the missile out of the canister and torpedo tube. The missile accelerated rapidly out of the tube and clear of the submarine. A lanyard attached to both the missile and the canister yanked taut, igniting the rocket motor attached to the tail of the missile. The missile roared up, out of the water and into the sky.

As the rocket engine burnt out and dropped away, a sequence of events began that transformed the missile into a small robot airplane. An air scoop dropped open beneath the missile. Two small, stubby wings scissored out from inside the missile's body. The turbo-fan engine, now supplied with air from the scoop and ignited by a small explosive squid, came up to speed to give the missile power. The bird then dropped down to wave-top height and flew to the North, beginning its pre-programmed flight.

In rapid succession, three more missiles joined the first one flying over the Java Sea; each one on a flight pattern designed to have them all reach Nusa Funata at the same time. Receiving encrypted Global Positioning System fixes from a constellation of NAVSTAR satellites, the missiles were constantly updating and refining their positions. With each missile having a radar cross-section about the size of a hummingbird, and with the four missiles approaching from four different directions, the terrorists on Nusa Funata did not have a chance of detecting the attack.

23 Jun 2000, 0052LT (22 Jun, 1752Z)

The last canister swung over and landed on the helo deck. The handling crew was still busy lashing it down as the Commander Balewegal ordered all lines cast off. The quicker he got *SAWAL* away from this God-forsaken island, the better. And the sooner he got rid of those three gas canisters, the sooner he could breathe again.

It was an easy trip, really. Admiral Suluvana had assured him. Just run out to *Nusa Funata* and load three canisters of the NX toxin. Then deliver the stuff to the Jakarta piers. From there, the stuff would be loaded into shipping containers and join the vast stream of cargo heading across the Pacific. One night's work and he would be a hero of the revolution. His grand-children would repeat the tales of how he wielded the terrible sword that brought *Allah*'s victory to Indonesia.

The FFG's screw churned up muddy brown-green water as it headed away from the rickety pier and out of the tiny harbor.

22 Jun 2000, 0800LT (1800Z)

The ugly black bird started its take off roll out. There was nothing sleek or sexy about this plane. It was designed for only one purpose, to fly to a well-defended target without being seen and deliver a nuclear weapon. The B-2 Stealth bomber, with its crew of two, headed down the 12,000 foot long runway and used nearly every inch before it lumbered into the morning sky.

Even though it was fully loaded with fuel and carried a relatively light bomb load, the big bomber would rendezvous with four different KC-10 tankers on the long outbound flight and three more on the return trip. Resting in the onboard rotary launcher were two air-launched cruise missiles (ALCM's). Each contained a single W-88 nuclear warhead capable of a "dial a yield" detonation of from 20 to 200 kilotons.

The bomber gradually gained altitude until it was well above the commercial aircraft traffic. It headed out over the cold gray North Pacific and toward a launch point 500 miles North East of Nusa Funata.

As it went "feet wet" over the Gulf of Alaska, the stealth bomber disappeared from all air traffic radars. The pilot merely switched off the IFF and the bird was invisible. The copilot shifted the radio transceivers over to special National Command frequencies reserved for just this mission. They would not acknowledge any traffic on any other frequency. The strike mission was on its way.

23 Jun 2000, 0106LT (22 Jun, 1806Z)

The first missile climbed steeply as it crossed the beach at Nusa Funata. A camera in its belly took a digital picture and compared what it saw to what it expected from the SEAL's pictures. The comparison was close, but not quite exact. The missile made a minor course correction to arrive precisely on target. It made one pass over the weapons facility on top of Mount Guishu, dispensing 2.2 pound bomblets in a path across the radomes. After a wide sweeping turn, it made another pass to sow a path of destruction across the command center. Another wide turn and it crashed into the missile launchers. The remaining jet fuel started explosions that instantly spread to the missiles in the ready launchers. The resulting conflagration spread to the standby missiles. Within seconds the entire mountain top was a blazing inferno.

The troops stationed on the mountain had no idea what had happened. One second they were enjoying the quiet tropical night. The next second they found themselves in the middle of an exploding hell and they couldn't find what the cause was. Those that survived the attack panicked and ran pell-mell down the steep mountain road.

At the same instant, the second missile verified its position and plunged through a window into the warehouse at the head of the pier. The 700 pounds of HBX detonated, obliterating the building and its contents. The APC was shoved out the door and into the water. The canisters containing the pox ruptured in the intense overpressure. The virus inside was destroyed in the heat of the explosion and fire.

Unfortunately for the small team of guards and workers still on the pier, not all the virus was instantly destroyed. Just enough was released in an aerosol from one canister to infect them. None of the aerosol spread beyond the little pier, but their fate was sealed. They would be highly contagious in about twenty-four hours and dead in thirty-six. They had no indication of this. They only knew that Allah had spared them from the sudden death that those inside the warehouse had met.

The third missile plunged into the command center; completely devastating the building and spreading fire to the adjacent buildings. The command center and all communications to the outside were gone.

The last missile flew down the center of the flight line of the small airfield. The bomblets buried themselves in the runway and then detonated, cratering the field down its entire length. No conventional aircraft would be using that field in the near future. At the end of its pass, the missile turned and plunged into the only building near the field. The building exploded into flames as the jet fuel stored inside ignited.

23 Jun 2000, 0107LT (22 Jun, 1807Z)

Wood and Tagamond retraced their torturous snakelike approach and were once again just outside the cave mouth. They lay in the underbrush for several hours, their positions so close that they could easily overhear the guards' conversations. Arrayed beside each of them were two flash-bang grenades and two extra clips for their H&K MP-5 9mm machine pistols.

At the sound of the first missile exploding, they each lobbed a flash-bang grenade into the cave entrance. The excruciatingly loud noise and brilliant light momentarily stunned the guards. This fleeting second was all the two SEALs needed. All ten guards fell to carefully aimed three shot bursts from the H&K's.

As the two SEALs rushed into the cave, they heard the unmistakable bark of the 50-caliber sniper rifle from somewhere behind them. It was repeated almost instantly.

Stuart and Heigle had set up their hide holes about 500 yards above the trail where it crossed the knife-edge of the ridge between the two valleys. This gave them a clear field of fire for anyone attempting to use the trail from either direction. They could hear the short firefight at the cave, but the screening over-growth prevented them from lending their teammates any support.

As the sounds of the firefight died down, a squad of defenders came down the trail from the compound at a dead run, determined to help their friends in the cave. Stuart placed the cross hairs of his night vision scope on the head of the squad leader and while Heigle targeted the last man. Raising the aim point about six inches to allow for drop in the 500 yards to the target, they gently squeezed the triggers of the giant rifles. At two pounds of trigger pull, the hammer snapped forward, activating the 360-grain powder charge. The 265-grain match grade bullets began their journeys at 2600 feet per second. Each bullet found its mark in 0.6 seconds. The heads of the targets literally exploded and disappeared in a red mist.

The rest of the squad stopped where they were, bewildered by what had transpired. Their comrades lay dead at their feet, their heads exploded from no apparent cause. An additional 3.5 seconds elapsed before the sound of the shots reached the squad. They began to react, diving for what cover they could find. By this time the two snipers had each slammed another round into their rifles, selected targets, aimed and sent two more rounds down the mountain. Two more heads disappeared from the bodies. The survivors tried to return fire, but had no idea where the attack was coming from. They were pinned down, with no escape route in any direction.

The two snipers waited patiently. The desultory return fire wasn't coming anywhere near their holes. The squad survivors were uncovering themselves for only a split second to fire a random burst before diving back for cover. There was not enough time for an aimed, accurate return shot.

After several minutes, one of the squad was brave enough to aim a burst up the mountain slope. Unfortunately for him, his time exposed from cover was a half-second too long. A .50-caliber slug tore through his chest and kicked him backward ten yards.

All of the fight was gone from the squad. They simply cowered behind the meager cover, waiting for the snipers to go away.

The first burst of gunfire jerked Tom Clark awake. He jumped up from his meager pallet and rushed toward the prison door. *Maybe, just maybe, someone had finally come to rescue them.*

The shooting and explosions increased in intensity. The blasts nearly deafened him, but he couldn't see anything outside. *Did the rescuers know that they were in here? Would they blast down the doors and come in shooting? Were they even winning, driving away the terrorists? Or would the terrorists come back and kill them all?*

Tom's mind raced. He had to let someone know where they were. He had to protect his little flock. He had to find Nan and protect her.

Tom pounded on the heavy steel door and shouted at the top of his lungs, "We're in here! Help us! We're in here."

After a few seconds, the other missionary men joined in the chorus. Suddenly a deep growling voice penetrated the door. "Get back from the door. Get on the floor with your hands on your head. We are going to blow the door. Anyone standing when we come in will be shot. Do you understand?"

Tom dropped to the floor and waved everyone else to do the same. He called out, "We understand. We're on the floor. Praise God you're here."

The door blasted off its hinges and fell in as two heavily armed men charged through the opening, their rifles dancing around the room like cobras ready to strike. The leader pointed at Tom. "Who are you? Are there any more?"

Tom looked up and smiled. "I'm Tom Clark. This is my missionary group. Are we ever thankful to see you!"

He waved toward the next steel door. "The women are locked up there. Please get them out. Can we get up now?"

25

Roland had just finished assembling his strike teams when the TLAM attack began. He could see the flames and hear the explosions atop Mount Giushiu. The command post a hundred meters to his right suddenly disappeared in a blinding flash. He could easily see troops running from the burning structure. A scant few attempted to fight the fires.

It was time to start the attack on the factory. Roland pointed a small laser designator at one of the machine cannon emplacements. The tiny red dot appeared on the slide mechanism. One of the SEALs manning a SAW fired a grenade from the integral M-203 grenade launcher into the sandbagged emplacement. The other SAW followed suit, almost instantly. He aimed at the other emplacement. The near simultaneous blasts knocked them both out. The 23mm cannons lay, blackened and silent, in the smoldering ruins on the emplacements.

The two M-60 machine-gunners raked 7.62mm NATO rounds across the few guards who were standing around. The covering fire protected the rest of the SEALs as they worked their way toward the entrance of the factory cave. The murderously accurate crossfire knocked any fight out of the remaining terrorists. They fled into the jungle.

Three guards stationed inside the cave entrance came running. The sounds of the firefight drew them out to help their comrades. They ran, pell-mell, down the trail only to fall in a hail of 9mm rounds from the approaching SEALs' H&K machine pistols.

Rushing into the cave entrance, the SEALs were confronted with a heavy steel door firmly implanted in a reinforced concrete wall. Roland shouted, "Jankowski, get up here."

The big SEAL breacher ran up, removing three small charges from his pack as he ran. He taped one over the lock and the other two on the hinges. After turning the timers to give him thirty seconds, he took cover with his teammates, yelling "Fire in the hole!"

The small packets of C-4 plastic explosive left the door hanging loosely open.

As the smoke cleared, the SEALs could see a laboratory facility that had been spotlessly clean, but was now covered with a cloud of settling dust and plaster. A half-dozen white smocked workers picked themselves up off the floor, dazed from the explosion. Confronted with very menacing looking blackened faced SEALs brandishing H&K machine pistols, they raised their hands high over their heads and babbled surrender in several different languages.

One of the scientists, obviously the leader from the manner in which the others deferred to him, approached LT Roland. In a heavy Eastern European accent, he said, "You American fools. You'll kill us all. Don't you have any idea of what this place is?"

"Suppose you tell us," Roland retorted. "Looks to me like we've found a terrorist lab making biological warfare agents. My guess is that you're in charge. That makes you a terrorist. How close am I?"

"You arrogant idiot! Of course this is a laboratory!" the enraged scientist shouted, his face burning crimson. He pointed to a large glass and steel enclosure in which several people dressed in containment suits were standing and said, "In that isolation booth is the most virulent form of smallpox ever produced. It will kill you in three days and there is no cure. Have you ever seen anyone die from pox? A most painful way to die. I suggest that you leave now so that you don't inadvertently expose yourselves."

Lieutenant Roland replied, "Oh, we'll leave all right, but we need to leave a few things here first. You will order those people in the booth to leave immediately and accompany my men outside the cave. You have five minutes to get them out and to evacuate. If you choose to stay, it's OK with me."

Turning to his squad, Roland ordered them to place the explosives that they had lugged up from the RHIBs. The placement was precise, designed to destroy the cave's contents milliseconds before collapsing the roof onto the remnants. The facility would be buried under tons of volcanic rock; sealed forever from the outside.

The agitated Dr. Aswal ordered his workers to exit. He gathered his team at the cave exit. They huddled under the watchful scrutiny of two heavily armed SEALs.

As the last of the charges were being placed, automatic weapons fire erupted outside the cave. The staccato rattle of M-60s was interspersed with the louder, lower rumble of a heavy machine gun.

Several grenades exploded as the SEALs exited the cave. A fierce fire-fight was underway. An armored personnel carrier and a squad of infantry were trying to force their way up the main road. They had the SEAL gunners pinned down under a fusillade of fire from the 23-mm automatic cannon and light machine gun fire. The SEALs were returning fire at a furious rate. Several of the attacking infantry lay sprawled on the ground and a grenade explosion blackened the side of the APC.

With no time to waste before the explosive charges brought down the mountain, Roland surveyed the situation from behind the cover of a large rock.

Boats yelled, "Lieutenant, we got to get moving! Can't hold them much longer. We're running out of ammo."

The added firepower from the SEALs at the cave entrance stalled the assault. The terrorists scrambled to find cover and return fire. The fight was approaching a standoff. Tracer fire from the APC stitched across the rock face. The SEALs had to get out, but the way they came was blocked.

Boats, shooting from behind a tree five feet to Roland's left, signaled that there was an escape route in that direction. Roland rallied his troops and began a covered withdrawal down a narrow footpath.

There was no time to herd the prisoners away. The scientists were on their own. Aswal and his cronies skittered off to the right, away from the escaping SEALs.

The squad leapfrogged down the mountain, away from the entrance. Roland and Boats were the last two to leave. "Get movin', Lieutenant, I'll cover!" Boats yelled. He turned and opened fire. As Roland started to slither across the ten feet of open ground to the next cover, he saw Boats fall. "You okay?" he yelled.

No answer. Roland crouched low and ran back to Boats. He lay sprawled behind the tree, holding his blood-soaked side and vainly trying to reach for his weapon.

Roland threw the Chief over his shoulder and ran toward his retreating squad. They were using the last of their precious ammo to give him cover.

Crossing the open ground took an eternity. Bullets kicked up dust around him and showered leaves and debris on him. Roland's lungs burned like they were afire. His knees felt like rubber. He ran down the trail past the rest of the SEALs until he reached a protected clearing.

He could hear the firefight continuing as the rest of the SEALs executed their covered withdrawal. All but the last person provided covering fire while he rushed several feet ahead of the squad. This process was rapidly repeated several times, until they were all clear of the cave area.

A sudden blast and cloud of dark gray smoke billowed from the cave. The cave roof collapsed on the remnants of the factory, entombing everything under tons of rock. The massive shock loosened a rocky outcropping above the cavern. The rockslide buried the entrance and upended the armored personnel carrier.

Left without their heavy weapons and badly out-maneuvered, the terrorists ran back toward the compound.

Roland checked the wounded Chief. The bullet had passed through his side, leaving a neat little entrance hole an inch below and outside his right nipple. The exit hole, just below Boat's right clavicle, was not so tiny or neat. His blouse was saturated with blood.

"Boats, you alright? Stay with us now!"

A pair of pressure bandages staunched most of the bleeding. A shot of morphine took the edge off the pain. Better medical attention would have to wait until they were back on *ESSEX*.

Boats groaned, "Damn it, Lieutenant. That was a damn fool thing to do. I've told you a hundred times, you run like a duck."

23 Jun 2000, 0115LT (22 Jun, 1815Z)

SAN FRANCISCO raced at flank speed to return from the Tomahawk launch basket to Nusa Funata. Hunter was worried about the FFG that they encountered on the outbound journey. He had an uneasy feeling about it. Nothing that he could really put his finger on, but...

If it was aiding the terrorists, it could lend supporting fire against the SEALs or, more importantly, prevent the OSPREYs from reaching their landing zone. These birds were easy targets for the AAW systems on the FFG-7, which were designed to attack supersonic jets and low flying cruise missiles. Without the OSPREYs, the SEALs and hostages were stranded on Nusa Funata, to share the fate of the terrorists there.

The empty missile canisters remaining in the torpedo tubes from the launch were jettisoned. The torpedomen rushed to reload tube one with an ADCAP torpedo and reload the other three tubes with more Tomahawks.

The torpedo room was starting to look empty. Out of the twenty-six stowage positions available in the room and tubes; with the *KILO* attack, the SEAL equipment and the Tomahawk strike, they had ten empty spaces. They still had two Harpoon anti-ship missiles, six ADCAP torpedoes and eight Tomahawk missiles. When the tubes were loaded, the torpedo gang rearranged the rack-stowed weapons so that there was a torpedo ready to be rapidly loaded behind tube one and a Tomahawk ready behind each of the other tubes. They were betting that these would be the needed weapons. Loading a Harpoon would require moving several of the two-ton behemoths around the room to get one in line to load.

The mission planners were back at work in the wardroom, planning re-strikes on all the missions that had been flown just in case they were needed. This time the launch basket would be much closer to the coast of Nusa Funata to shorten the flight time. There was no need for surprise or simultaneous arrival of several missiles. If the SEALs needed a re-strike, they would need it now. There would be no time for fancy maneuvers.

Hunter looked at the digital time display on the bulkhead behind the periscope stand. *The B-2 was airborne by now and 1500 miles into its 9000-mile journey. Could he and the SAN FRANCISCO/SEAL platoon finish the task in time to turn the bomber around before it delivered its awful load?*

26

The FFG was steaming away from Nusa Funata. Hunter could see the bow wake it was kicking up. He estimated that it was doing at least twenty-five knots. Hunter lowered the scope.

Chief Holmstad confirmed his guess. "Conn, sonar. Sierra two-five-one has increased speed. Turn count for twenty-seven knots of one five-bladed screw."

Hunter spoke into the open microphone to sonar, "Chief, that equates to the frigate. Agree with the speed increase. His bow wave is half way back his side. Real bone in the teeth. Probably doing flank."

"Conn, sonar, aye.

Hunter turned to Fagan, standing on the starboard side of control with the rest of the fire control party. "Still nothing we can do. He hasn't done anything that constitutes a hostile act. I don't know if he is helping the terrorists or just out on patrol. We'll continue to track him until we know his intentions or we have to help the SEALs."

Fagan nodded. "Yes, sir."

Hunter watched Fagan closely. He appeared to be acting normally. No sign of breaking. Yet.

Time for another check on the frigate. Hunter ordered, "Raising number two scope for a look around."

The flight of four F-14s came roaring over the horizon. The OSPREYs air cover had arrived.

"Conn, ESM. The frigate's fire control radar has shifted to targeting mode. Looks like they are getting ready to fire on the F-14s."

Hunter quickly lowered the scope and turned to the fire control party, "That pretty much answers the question of the frigate's intentions. They've locked onto the F-14's with fire control radar. That constitutes a hostile act. We'll attack the frigate and we need to be quick, before they get a bird in the air."

Hunter shouted, "Observation, number two scope, on the frigate."

The litany signaled to everyone in control the Captain was going to be looking at the frigate using the periscope. It was time for absolute silence. The whole cycle of raising the scope from its well, making the observation and lowering the scope back to the well would take less than ten seconds. The scope would be exposed above the water for only about three seconds. It was vital to gather all the available information from that three-second-mind picture without any distraction.

"Up scope," he ordered as he squatted at the base of the stainless steel ring guarding the hole in the deck that was the scope well.

The smooth greased cylinder of the periscope moved rapidly upward in front of him. As the optics section cleared the ring, he slapped down the two handles, spun the scope around to look down the bearing toward the frigate, placed his right eye to the eyepiece and began to rise with the scope.

As he rose, Jon Hunter's vision dimmed and tunneled in from the outside. Darkness surrounded him and an incredible feeling of dizziness and disorientation overcame his senses. The tunnel of light in his vision narrowed until all the light disappeared. With a low moan, he slid down the front of the scope to lay prostrate on the deck.

Petty Officer Buell grabbed the 1MC microphone hanging on the bulk-head behind the periscope stand and shouted, "Corpsman, lay to control! The Captain is down!"

A brief moment of pandemonium broke out in control as they all realized that Hunter lay on the deck unconscious.

Fagan reached over to lower the periscope and said in a loud commanding voice, "Quiet everyone. The Skipper is out. Doc will take care of him. We have a target that we need to attack. Engineer, you take over as Fire Control Coordinator. I will do the approach. Carry on."

Doc Pugh rushed into control carrying his emergency equipment bag. Kneeling beside Hunter, he checked over the downed Captain. Although still unconscious, Hunter's vital signs were near normal. Enlisting the aid of two sailors, Doc carried Hunter out of control and laid him in his stateroom bunk.

Hunter began to slowly regain consciousness, although he was still very groggy. "WWWhat happened?" he questioned as he came around.

"I warned you," Doc said. "You passed out in control. Too much coffee, not enough rest. It was bound to happen. Something's lowering your blood pressure and it's not doing it all the time. You are going to lay there for awhile."

"Nonsense, I have an attack," Hunter said as he started to sit up and immediately fell back on the pillow. "Ohhh, dizzy," he said.

"Now, maybe you'll do what I tell you. The XO will handle the ship. You rest for awhile," Doc Pugh ordered.

23 Jun 2000, 0940LT (0140Z)

"Observation, number two scope, on the frigate," Fagan announced, squatting by the scope base.

The scope slid silently upward with Fagan dropping the handles and swinging it to the correct bearing.

"Bearing mark," he said as he pushed the small red button on the right handle that sent the bearing to the fire control system.

"Range mark! Down scope."

The scope slid silently down. The whole evolution had taken just ten seconds. Now all the data that he had absorbed in that three-second mental picture had to be related to the assembled party so that they could use it in prosecuting the attack.

"Point five divisions in high power," Fagan announced. The frigate had taken up half the distance between two of the small horizontal marks on the scope optics.

Knowing the height of the frigate from the waterline to the top of the mast, Petty Officer Buell whirled the little circular slide rule that hung around his neck to compute the range. "Range one-two thousand yards," he said.

"Range checks," replied LTJG Baker, sitting in front of one of the fire control computers analyzing the incoming data to compute the fire control solution.

"Angle on the bow, port four-three," Fagan said. This indicated that the frigate's bow was pointed forty-three degrees to the left of the submarine or that the submarine was forty-three degrees to the right of dead ahead of the frigate.

"Indicates port three-one," said LTJG Baker. The solution in the fire control system said that the angle was narrower than the XO had estimated.

"Set port four-three," Fagan ordered decisively.

Fagan was confident of his estimate and needed the fire control party to share his confidence. A submarine periscope approach, probably more than any other situation in combat, depended on the vision and percep-tions of just one man, the Approach Officer. The rest of the party had to rely on him and they had to have complete confidence in his abilities. Inde-cisiveness was not an option for an Approach Officer.

"He had a white bird on the rail," Fagan continued, relating what he had seen.

White birds were warshot surface-to-air missiles. They were loaded on the launcher rails only seconds before a launch. The rest of their life was spent protected in the environmentally controlled missile magazine deep in the bowels of the surface ship. The frigate was preparing to shoot at the incoming F-14s. SAN FRANCISCO needed to press the attack. The F-14s might be able to out maneuver the missiles, but the inbound OSPREYs would be sitting ducks.

The periscope observation sequence was repeated to check the solution just prior to shooting. Even though the ADCAP torpedo would sweep out a large section of the ocean in searching for its target, it would take almost seven minutes for the torpedo to reach the target. In that time, the frigate would cover over three miles. Correctly calculating the geometry of the attack was vital to achieve a hit. A minor adjustment to the range and the solution was ready.

It was time to shoot. One final check to make sure that everything was ready.

"Firing point procedures!" Fagan ordered.

"Solution ready," Sam Stuart replied. The solution about to be sent to the torpedo was the best that they had.

"Ship ready," Warran Jacobs reported. The ship was ready to launch the weapon.

"Weapon ready," Jeff Miller reported. The weapons system and the ADCAP torpedo were ready to launch.

"Shoot on generated bearing!" Fagan ordered.

"Set," LTJG Baker reported. He punched a button to send the best solution and bearing to the target to the torpedo.

"Standby," Weps reported as he took the large brass firing switch to the STANDBY position. Interlocks on the torpedo tube aligned to start the firing sequence.

"Shoot," the Weps continued, throwing the firing switch to the FIRE position. The resounding double thump of the tube firing was heard and felt throughout the ship. The ADCAP torpedo was on its way, racing toward the surface ship.

It was time to make sure that nothing had changed and the solution was still tracking.

"Observation, number two scope on the frigate," the XO ordered.

As the scope broke the surface he saw a brilliant streak of white light rise from the foredeck of the frigate. He watched as the missile arced high into the sky. "Shit, the son of a bitch has a bird in the air! He's shooting at the F-14s," Fagan announced.

The missile unerringly tracked until it intercepted one of the Tomcats. There was a dirty puff of smoke as the flaming remains of the Tomcat headed for the water below. Fagan could see only one parachute deploy from the doomed two seat aircraft. The downed airman would land several miles from the sub.

Fagan lowered the periscope. "Plot this point," he directed. "Bearing zero-two-seven, range two-zero thousand yards. Label it as estimated position of downed pilot. What is the status of the torpedo?"

"Estimate one minute to acquisition, solution still tracking," LTJG Baker reported.

The next minute was an excruciatingly long wait. They couldn't run to the downed airman's aid until the attack was finished. Unless the frigate was put out of the fight, the rest of the plan and the people on Nusa Funata were doomed.

Finally, Jeff Miller yelled out, "Weapon acquisition!" The ADCAP had detected the frigate and was in final attack.

"Conn, sonar. Our weapon is in high speed. It is in attack."

"Observation, number two scope on the frigate," Fagan announced.

The scope slid smoothly up as the XO looked down the bearing toward the frigate. "Bearing mark, range mark, down scope."

Everything was just as he expected it. The frigate didn't yet know that it was under attack and now it was too late for it to evade. He lowered the scope.

The ADCAP made its final run at the frigate. It came up in depth to twenty feet below the surface and passed directly under the keel of the warship. A small upward looking hydrophone detected an object above the torpedo as an interferometer detected a large metal object within its sensitivity field. The two pieces of information activated the firing signal, which detonated the 1,000 pounds of PBNX explosive in the warhead. The explosion lifted the center of the hull and formed a large bubble of hot gases under it. As the bubble cooled and collapsed, it would not support the weight of the warship. The center portion of the ship fell into the bubble while the two ends were still supported by the water. This broke the hull in half just behind the bridge.

A loud explosion reverberated through the hull of the submarine.

"Conn, sonar, loud explosion on the bearing to the frigate," the report from sonar was redundant.

"Raising number two scope," Fagan said. Peering through the periscope, he could see the two ends of the frigate rise out of the water as the center section sank below the surface. Survivors were leaping clear of the rapidly sinking warship.

"Down scope. Best bearing to the pilot?" the XO inquired.

"Best bearing zero-three-eight, range one-nine-five-hundred yards," LCDR Jacobs replied.

"Come right, steer course zero-three-eight. Make your depth 400 feet. Ahead flank," the XO ordered in rapid succession. "Nav, you have the conn. Head to the point for the pilot and come to periscope depth. Get the search and rescue detail ready. I want to get that pilot aboard as quickly as we can. I'll be in the Captain's stateroom."

23 Jun 2000, 1025LT (0225Z)

As Bill Fagan stepped out of control, he heard Warran Jacobs making preparations to rescue the downed Tomcat flier.

Fagan knocked at the stateroom door and parted the curtains to enter. "Skipper, how are you feeling?"

He took a seat in one of the folding chairs, carefully bypassing the over-stuffed office chair that was the Captain's domain. Hunter lay on the fold-down bunk.

Hunter growled, "Still a little dizzy. Damn fine time to get weak at the knees." He raised his head from the pillow. "Sounds like you did a great job though. Well done, Bill. I take it that you are heading for that pilot?"

"That's what I intended, but I wanted to check with you before I surfaced in a war zone," Fagan replied as Doc Pugh entered the stateroom.

"Get over there and get ready," Hunter replied. "I'll be out there in a few minutes."

"You aren't going anywhere," Doc protested. "You are staying right here. This is one case where the Doctor's orders supersede. The XO can handle this. The next time you pass out, you might not be so lucky."

Slumping back down in his bunk, Hunter grudgingly acquiesced, "Doc, for once I have to agree with you. This dizziness is just not clearing yet. XO, you run this. I'll advise from here. What's your plan?"

Fagan explained, "Pretty simple, really. Thought we would run over there. Take a look around and blow to the surface. Pull the guy aboard and then dive." Fagan started on a new tack. "I'm concerned with what to do about the survivors from the frigate. They're too far from land to swim and the longer they stay in the water, the more that will not make it."

Hunter responded, "Locating the pilot will be the hard job. You need to get in the area as quickly as possible. He should have a sonar SAR transponder, so search on that frequency with sonar." Hunter hesitated for a moment. "I don't recall the exact frequency, somewhere around 15 kHz, I think. Ask Chief Holmstad, he'll know."

Gazing up at the overhead, Hunter continued to discuss the anticipated rescue. He was thinking through the process as he talked. "We don't know the condition of the pilot. If he's conscious and he knows we are in the area, he may be making noise in the water, too. The easiest way, though, is to call him on his SAR radio.

"Tell Alpha Alpha on *NIMITZ* what you are doing. They can give you the SAR frequency and ID info on the pilot. They can also tell you if the other F-14s have contact with him. They'll be buzzing around him like a bunch of mad hornets," Hunter said. "Tell them that we intend to pick up as many of the survivors as we can once we have the pilot onboard. You'll need air cover the whole time. Tell them to set it up."

23 Jun 2000, 1035LT (0235Z)

Roland mustered his platoon at the prison cave's mouth. The battle-hardened SEALs were doing their best to help the missionaries prepare for a dash to the airfield. There wasn't much time and a lot of ground to cover. And there was no telling if they would have to fight their way out.

Boats was in a bad way. He was losing a lot of blood and slipping in and out of consciousness. The SEALs had done all they knew how to help him. The only way to save him was to get him to the *ESSEX* as fast as possible.

A good looking young red-head emerged from the cave and rushed over to where Boats lay. She threw open a small first-aid kit and then rolled the SEAL over on his stomach.

"Help me out here," she said to Roland. "I'm a nurse and if we don't do something quick, he'll die."

"What do you need?" Roland grunted. He knelt down beside her.

"Water, I need clean water," she answered, pointing at the gaping exit wound. "Wash that out so I can see."

Nan plunged her hand into the wound and felt around. Boats groaned in pain.

"There. Got it," she called out. The bleeding stopped almost completely. "Severed artery. I'm holding it shut. He's going into grade four shock. We need to keep pressure on this and get lots of fluid into him. He needs an IV right now and surgery real quick."

Tom Clark grabbed a couple of saplings and fashioned a make-shift stretcher. "Lieutenant, we'll carry your man. Nan will look after him."

Roland nodded. "We'd better get going. I sure hope those OSPREY's have a medivac kit onboard."

As the group headed down the trail, Tom murmured to Nan, "I didn't know you were a nurse."

Nan smiled and answered, "Not yet. But I will be in a couple of years."

23 Jun 2000, 1043LT (0243Z)

The curtain parted, Buell stuck his head into the stateroom. "Excuse me, Skipper, XO. We're at the estimated position for the pilot. XO, the Nav requests that you come to control."

Fagan excused himself and stepped back out into control.

"XO, no sign of him yet," Warren Jacobs reported as Fagan stepped up to the periscope stand. "I can see a couple of F-14s orbiting to the East. I think that we need to establish contact with them." He never took his eye from the periscope eyepiece.

"OK, Nav. Does radio have the frequencies to talk to them? Tell them to monitor the SAR freqs, too. If they have him, we can vector in on that," the XO replied.

"The pilot freqs are already set in to the red phone. Their call sign is Victor Six Foxtrot. We are Sierra Lima Four," the Nav replied.

"Victor Six Foxtrot this is Sierra Lima Four, we are standing by to pick up your team mate. Do you hold him?" Fagan spoke into the secure phone.

"Sierra Lima Four, this is Victor Six Foxtrot authenticate golf whiskey seven," the orbiting Tomcat pilot replied.

He couldn't see any other US ships or planes and probably did not know that there was a US submarine in the area. He was clearly concerned someone might be on the circuit that did not belong there. The authenticator procedure guarded against this by requiring the initiator to give a code that changed daily. The receiver had to correctly reply to it. If either side gave an incorrect code, the other would immediately break contact.

Bill Fagan checked the codebook with the Navigator and answered "Authenticate yankee three."

"Sierra Lima Four, this is Victor Six Foxtrot; we do not hold you visually. Where are you?" the F-14 pilot inquired.

Fagan answered, "Victor Six Foxtrot, we are a US submarine about four miles Southwest of your orbit. We're the guys who sank that frigate that was shooting at you. We are ready to pick up your downed comrade. Do you hold him?"

"Sierra Lima Four, roger. We have him," the pilot responded, clearly relieved.

The close-knit naval air community went to great lengths to take care of their own. When one of their number was downed, they would stay on station and do everything in their power to protect him and to effect a rescue.

"He is injured and has been passing in and out of consciousness. I think that he is out right now. We are orbiting about three miles to the East of his location. Suggest that you surface and I will vector you to him. If I can get him to respond, I'll have him pop a flare. We have had no contact with his NFO. Didn't see a second chute either. Think he went down with the bird."

"Roger, we will be surfacing momentarily. Request you provide SUCAP while we are surfaced. Sierra Lima Four standing by," Bill Fagan concluded.

SUCAP was the acronym for Surface Combat Air Patrol. Fagan was asking the F-14's to be his eyes for encroaching surface ships while *SAN FRANCISCO* was busy picking up the downed flier.

Turning to LCDR Jacobs, Fagan directed, "Nav, get a quick sitrep off to SUBPAC and Alpha Alpha. Tell them about the frigate firing on the F-14s and us taking it out. Attempting rescue of the pilot. Also tell them we intend to attempt rescue of frigate survivors. We'll need a SUCAP until we can off-load them somewhere. Show it to the Skipper before you send it."

"OK, I'll get it out right away. The ship is ready to surface," the Navigator replied.

The XO turned to the diving officer and ordered, "Diving Officer, surface the ship."

"Surface the ship, aye," the diving officer responded. "Chief of the Watch, on the 1MC, "Surface, surface, surface." Conduct a normal blow to the surface."

The Chief of the Watch stood and announced on the 1MC, "Surface, surface, surface." He then reached for two large toggle switches on the upper section of the forward ballast control panel. When he flipped them up, a roar of high-pressure air filled the boat. The sub's depth stayed steady for a few seconds and then slid smoothly to the surface.

"Three four feet and holding. The ship is surfaced," the diving officer reported.

23 Jun 2000, 1134LT (0334Z)

With *SAN FRANCISCO* safely bobbing on the surface, the XO snatched the 21MC microphone from its holder and ordered Master Chief Hancock, "Search and rescue party lay topside. Be ready to recover the downed pilot."

The search and rescue party raced up the ladder through the forward escape trunk.

A fresh breeze had picked up out of the East. White caps were starting to form as the wind pushed the water to near a sea-state three. The protected Java Sea did not build the long deep rollers of the open Pacific, but an erratic chop made working on the round slippery hull interesting. A group of silvery flying fish broke the surface, skittered across the bow and disappeared back into the waves.

The two rescue swimmers donned wet suits, fins, and masks and reported to Master Chief Hancock that they were ready to enter the water for the rescue. First aid supplies and a stretcher were passed topside to a pair of emergency medical technicians. Two riflemen with M-16s also rushed up the ladder to give some limited protection from sharks.

Doc Pugh and two of the cooks set up the wardroom as an emergency operating theatre. The wardroom table became a make shift operating table, complete with high intensity operating theatre lights in the overhead. Bottles of oxygen were standing by, Doc's instruments were arrayed neatly on the buffet.

Doc was ready to handle anything but the most complicated emergency procedures. If necessary, communications could be set up with the doctors onboard either *NIMITZ* or *ESSEX*. They could talk him through the procedures that he could not accomplish on his own.

The circling Tomcat directed *SAN FRANCISCO* toward the downed pilot. Finding a tiny bobbing head in the vast expanse of the open sea required vigilance and patience. Even with the F-14 above pointing the way, the man in the water was all too easy to miss as he rose and fell in the swells.

Finally, Petty Officer Buell, looking through the periscope yelled, "I see him! About one thousand yards, dead ahead." A tiny yellow one-man inflatable raft came into view. The pilot was lying in the miniature boat, not moving. It was impossible to tell if he was unconscious, dead, or merely resting.

When *SAN FRANCISCO* was about three hundred yards from the flyer, Fagan ordered, "Ahead one third." The churning wake behind *SAN FRANCISCO* eased to a narrow white ribbon. At one hundred yards, he ordered, "Back one third." At fifty yards, he ordered, "All stop." The submarine quietly slid to a halt a scant few feet from the small boat.

Both swimmers leaped over the side into the water and pulled the life raft the final few feet alongside. The little inflatable raft was lashed to the side of *SAN FRANCISCO*. The party gently lifted the injured flier onboard. Doc Pugh checked his vital signs and examined him for any easily apparent injuries. The unconscious pilot had a nasty bleeding gash across his forehead and his right leg jutted at an odd angle, obviously broken.

Dead in the water, *SAN FRANCISCO* wallowed in the seas. The action of the wind and waves pushed her around until the seas were from dead astern. Waves rolled up the stern as the pilot was strapped into the stretcher and carefully lowered into the boat.

Doc Pugh followed the stretcher down the ladder just as a large wave rolled up the stern and poured down the hatch, thoroughly soaking him. He cursed loudly for the rest of the climb down. The topside party followed him down the hatch and the submarine once more slipped beneath the waves.

The flier, whose flight suit bore the name "LCDR 'Red Dog' Jones, was placed on the wardroom table. Doc conducted a first-aid ABC examination. The patient's airway was open. He was breathing, but respiration was rapid and shallow. Circulation was adequate, but his pulse was rapid and thready. Still in his soaked poopie suit, Doc inserted a saline IV and used a pneumatic cuff to immobilize the broken leg.

As he viewed the pilot, lying on the makeshift operating table, Doc worried. He had done all that he was trained to do with this type of injury, but his years of experience told him that something was still wrong, very wrong. The pilot was not exhibiting the responses that Doc expected from the injuries that he could see. He had slipped in and out of consciousness several times as he was being treated. His respiration was becoming more irregular, short and shallow.

Doc sat slumped in one of the chairs and thumbed through the thick medical text, frequently stopping to check LCDR Jones' symptoms. *Something didn't add up. He just had to find it.*

27

23 Jun 2000, 1245LT (0445Z)

The two OSPREYs flew low over the horizon. They headed directly toward the island. After a quick pass around the remnants of the airfield, the two birds shifted to a hover fifty feet above the field. A squad of Marines, clad in cumbersome full NBC protective clothing, fast roped out the back of each. They rushed to set up a protective cordon around the landing zone. Both OSPREYs gently touched down at the end of the pockmarked runway.

As the OSPREYs landed, the SEAL platoon and the hostages broke free from the tangled jungle at the far end of the runway and ran toward the waiting planes.

When they were about a hundred feet away, Roland raised his hand, stopping the on-rushing group. He yelled out, "Hey Marines, glad you could make it. Now that the action is over. Password is Sierra Six."

The senior Marine signaled them forward with a wave and yelled good naturedly, "So you SEALs need to be picked up again."

"My Chief is hit bad," Roland panted. "We need an IV and a doctor real quick!"

"We have stuff onboard the bird," the Marine answered, jerking his thumb toward the lead OSPREY. "There'll be an IV in there."

Passing through the Marines' protective cordon, the SEALs and hostages ran straight to the planes and climbed aboard. The Marines followed, keeping a careful watch on the tree line.

The planes were seriously overloaded. Lifting off in the hot air with all the extra passengers was problematic. The SEALs and the Marines stripped the plane of anything that wasn't absolutely essential. All the gear and most of the weapons were dumped onto the ground. The planes lumbered down the cratered runway and finally lifted off with just inches to spare.

As the last OSPREY went feet wet and cleared Nusa Funata, the pilot radioed a report from Roland that all SEALs and hostages were safe and accounted for. Almost as a postscript, he added that all facilities on the island were completely destroyed.

23 Jun 2000, 1430LT (0630Z)

"XO, get into radio and get SUBPAC on the horn!" Hunter yelled frantically. "We've got to tell them that the mission was completely successful! Make it a Flash Priority message and Code Word it "Golden Dawn." God, I hope we're in time!"

"Skipper, calm down. I'll get it out right away," Fagan answered.

He had been in control, but hurried to the CO Stateroom when he heard the Skipper shout.

"In time for what?"

"XO, I can't tell you. It is that Special Appendix that I couldn't show you. Just get the damn message out as fast as you possibly can. As soon as you get it out, get COMSUBPAC on Secure Voice. I need to talk to the Admiral. Use every precedence you can think of to get through. This is really, really important!" Jon Hunter was so excited he was shaking.

23 Jun 2000, 1515LT (0715Z)

The return flight, although flown down on the deck and all-out, was uneventful. As the two grey birds passed over the *ESSEX*, the passengers fortunate enough to be seated by the small porthole like windows saw that the deck was cleared. There were neither helicopters nor people on the flight deck. All the external doors and hatches were shut, too. For a warm tropical morning, this was very unusual. Normally there would be a dozen or more helicopters parked topside, some being readied to fly, some parked there for rapid use if needed. There would be dozens of crewmembers in brightly colored jerseys moving about the flight deck, each performing some vital function in the operation of this sea-going heliport.

Vulture's row was empty. The bridge and the Flag Bridge were both closed up. If they could have seen inside the *ESSEX*, they would have been even more surprised to find that Condition Zebra was set. All access to the outside was secured. The atmosphere inside the ship was being maintained at a twelve-ounce overpressure so that any air leakage was from inside the ship to outside. The only air entering the ship passed through several levels of filtration and was monitored continuously to make sure it remained pure.

The OSPREYs swooped down and squatted for a landing on the empty flight deck. They taxied so they were parallel to the island and parked nose to tail. As their massive turbine powered propellers spun to a stop, sailors in full NBC gear raced out of a large set of double doors in the side of the island, dragging a large plastic tent-like structure from the door to the side hatch of the forward OSPREY. They taped the plastic decontamination chute to the plane, forming an air-tight seal. The chute made a plastic tunnel all the way from the plane to the island doors. As this was happening, another group of NBC-clad sailors, standing at a discreet distance, continuously hosed down the first set with a mist of clean seawater.

Finally, the sailors stepped away from the plane. Only then was the pilot told by radio that he and his passengers could deplane. The aircrew and Marines, who had all stayed in their NBC clothing for the entire ordeal, left first. They entered the island and were directed through a series of chemical showers before they were allowed to remove their protective clothing. Even then they were isolated in a separate, sealed contagious disease ward in the ship's hospital.

When the last of the NBC-clad crew departed, the hostages and SEALs walked down the chute. Roland and Jankowski gently carried the stretcher bearing Boats.

They were sent through a different path. Two NBC-clad corpsmen relieved Roland and Jankowski of the stretcher and carried Boats into an isolation ward operating room where surgeons were waiting to attend to his wounds.

The rest walked into shower facilities. They disposed of all their clothing into plastic burn bags. They then showered, scrubbing vigorously with harsh antiseptic soap. As each emerged from the shower, they were given a hospital gown, several shots and directed to a bed in a second isolation ward.

When the last person on the first OSPREY had entered the island, the chute was collapsed, sealed shut and placed in a barrel for disposal. Another decontamination chute was rigged to the second OSPREY. The whole procedure was again completed.

When all the new arrivals were safely inside the ship, one of the deck crew entered each plane and disengaged the wheel brakes. The crews then pushed each plane over the side, into the water.

High up on the island, out of sight from the flight deck, Admiral Schwarz and General Kendall observed the operation. As the OSPREYs splash into the three-mile deep Timor Sea, General Kendall commented, "There go two $25 million-dollar birds. How are we going to explain this back in Coronado?"

Admiral Schultz shrugged and replied, "It was a deck handling accident. They weren't properly secured and rolled off the deck in heavy seas. That's the way it will be logged and that's what the investigation that I am about to start will find."

23 Jun 2000, 1520LT (0720Z)

"XO, we have a problem," RMC Tyler said over the 21MC to Fagan, who was standing in control. "We can't synch with the satellite. We're troubleshooting, but I can't find the problem."

"Did you get the message out?" Fagan queried.

"No, sir. We're down on all satellite channels. No SSIXS, No Satellite Voice, nothing," Chief Tyler replied. "Looks like it is going out. Standing wave on the BRA-34 looks good. Could be the satellite is down. Could be the cesium clock is out of spec. I just don't know."

"Do we have communications with anyone right now?" Bill Fagan continued his questioning.

"Only voice with those F-14's. The OSPREY's are over the UHF horizon and everything else has been satellite. How important is this message, anyway?" Chief Tyler asked.

"Chief, the Skipper says that it is as important as you can get. We need to get it to SUBPAC anyway that we can. Let me tell him the problem," the XO answered.

He had just turned to walk to the CO's stateroom when he saw Hunter maneuver through the door into control.

Hunter stepped to the periscope stand, saying, "I heard that. This is Murphy's Law at its worst. We have to have that message to SUBPAC immediately. We have less than half an hour. Chief, have you tried switching masts, transmitters and cesium clocks?"

Chief Tyler answered, "Yes, sir. I've tried every possible combination." The tone of his voice said that he was hurt by the Skipper's implication that he might not have tried the most basic troubleshooting.

"Figured that you had, Chief," Hunter answered in an attempt to smooth the Chief's ruffled feathers. "Had to ask to make sure. Are you sure that the only circuit is with the F-14? Long haul HF won't work?"

"Skipper, I checked the propagation charts," Chief Tyler answered, even more in a huff. "There is a point three percent probability of reaching the HF relay station on Guam. That is the highest. The F-14 is it," He said with finality.

"OK, Chief. Get that F-14 pilot on voice. He is about to get the biggest surprise of his life," CDR Hunter said. "I hope that the *NIMITZ* comm center is up to snuff and has a circuit that works."

Hunter grabbed the red secure voice phone and started talking.

Doc Pugh walked into the control room. His patient was not responding to anything and was rapidly deteriorating. If he didn't get help soon, Doc was afraid that he would lose him before they had any hope of reaching a medical facility. The only help within several thousand miles was onboard either *NIMITZ* or *ESSEX*. If he could just talk with one of their doctors, maybe they had the answers.

"Skipper, I need to talk to you," Doc Pugh said as he stepped up to the periscope stand.

"Doc, if you are up here to tell me to take it easy, I don't have time right now," CDR Hunter retorted with exasperation. "I'm a little busy."

Just then the F-14 pilot that he had been talking with on the secure voice circuit asked for yet another repeat of the message. The two Lieutenants flying in that bird were in way over their heads with this situation. The comms center onboard the *NIMITZ* wasn't helping matters any either. Hunter was growing increasingly frustrated.

"It's not that, Skipper, but it's really important," Doc continued. "I need to talk with you."

"Doc, talk with the XO. I really don't have time right now," Hunter said with finality.

Doc Pugh turned to the XO, who had been standing beside the Skipper listening in utter disbelief to what Hunter was telling the pilots. It was an absolutely unbelievable, horrible story. He tore his attention away from the radio interchange to listen to Doc Pugh. "OK, Doc. What is it?"

Doc Pugh opened his medical text to a marked page and began to talk, "I have been trying to figure out what is wrong with my patient. He has not been responding to the treatments I have been giving him. His symptoms are pointing me here."

The paragraph that he pointed to started out with, "The meniges are the three membranes that encase the brain and spinal cord, the pia mater, arachnoid, and the dura mater."

"I think that we have a problem with either a subdural hematoma or a subarachnoid hemorrhage. You can see the list of symptoms here. I discounted the headaches and nausea. After all, he did punch out of a jet at 600 knots and swallowed a lot of seawater when he hit it. He complained that he was dizzy, but I discounted that, too. What I can't write off to the expected effects of the crash are a couple items. First, he complains of tingling in his right arm. His motor responses show a partial paralysis in that arm. He also has some selective amnesia.

"I can't tell from the symptoms which problem we have. I don't have the equipment or training to tell them apart. Now look at this," Doc Pugh concluded, pointing at the final paragraph of the explanation for subarachnoid hemorrhage. It said:

"About one-third of all patients die from the initial hemorrhage, and a further 15 to 20 percent die within the next month. It is therefore necessary to locate the area of bleeding as quickly as possible. Neurosurgery may repair the damage"

"I need to talk with those Doctors on *NIMITZ* and find out what to do" Doc said as the XO looked up from reading the troubling words.

Bill Fagan turned to CDR Hunter, "Skipper, we need to use that pilot as soon as you are done."

22 Jun 2000, 2045LT (23 Jun, 0745Z)

Admiral O'Flanagan threw down the flimsy sheet of paper and grabbed the red phone from his desk. He hurriedly dialed a well-remembered number as he glanced anxiously at the wall clock.

The Chairman of the Joint Chiefs answered the secure phone, "Schwartz here."

"General, they did it! Everything. Call off the special mission. We only have a few minutes. I'll give you details when I have them," COMSUBPAC reported.

General Schwartz yelled across his desk at the National Defense Command Center, deep in the bowels of the Pentagon, to the Flag Watch

Officer, "Call them off. God, this is cutting it close. Their launch window opens in thirty seconds!"

Admiral O'Flanagan, in Pearl Harbor, turned to his Communications Officer, "Get another satellite overhead down there. I don't care if we lose coverage on the whole rest of the Pacific! I need comms with *SAN FRAN-CISCO*. Now! Damn it!"

23 Jun 2000, 1450LT (0750Z)

The B-2 came around to a launch course that pointed directly at Nusa Funata and came to a launch altitude of 10,000 feet. The mission commander began the pre-launch checklist. He took the unlock codes envelope out of the pre-sealed safe resting just outboard of his station. Both crewmen broke open the envelope and checked that the codes matched the ones on the message that they had received less than an hour ago. All that was left to do was to load the codes into the missiles, verify the targeting data and launch the first nuclear strike since World War II.

The pilot brought the ungainly black bird around to fly in the launch parameter envelope as the mission commander finished the pre-launch sequence. The bomb bay doors rumbled open and the rotary launch magazine lowered enough to expose one AGM-86B nuclear cruise missile to the slipstream.

The command radio crackled alive as the mission commander lifted the red launch cover. "Gold Eagle, this is Knee Cap. Mission Abort, Repeat Mission Abort! Authenticator Lima Zulu Six Tango Gulf. You are directed Romeo Tango Bravo. Report status. Over."

National Command Authority had just canceled their mission. The pilot swung the bomber around and climbed as the bomb bay doors rumbled shut. They were headed home.

23 Jun 2000, 1640LT (0840Z)

LCDR Jones lay unconscious on the wardroom operating table. His leg was splinted and the gash on his forehead now sported a neat row of sutures under the gauze bandage. But he had slipped in and out of consciousness repeatedly since they had pulled him from the water.

"Doc, we have Dr. Morgan from the *ESSEX* on satellite voice," Chief Tyler said over the MJ phone. "We've patched it through on the 21MC box to the wardroom for you."

Chief Pugh, this is Dr. Morgan on the *ESSEX*," the box on the bulkhead squawked. "I have reviewed the information that you relayed to us. Has there been any change in the patient?"

"He is currently unconscious," Doc Pugh answered. "Blood pressure has been one-six-zero over nine-five. There has been recurring emesis. There is evidence of anisocoria. The right pupil is dilated considerably larger than the left. When the patient was conscious, he complained of a severe headache. The onset of cephalalgia, together with the other symptoms point to a subarachnoid hemorrhage. The other possibility is a subdural hematoma. Both are way beyond my capability to treat."

Dr Morgan responded, "Chief Pugh, it sounds like your diagnosis is on the spot. You know your stuff. Is there any sign of opisthotones?"

Doc Pugh answered, "No sir, the neck is stiff and he resists movement but no sign of opisthotones."

After a brief pause, the 21MC again squawked again as Dr. Morgan answered, "Well, I think that we have a Grade IV subarachnoid hemorrhage. He needs to be moved to a neurological unit as fast as possible. The nearest one appears to be in Jakarta. Can you get him there?"

"I'll have to talk with the Skipper," Doc Pugh replied. "We're a long way from Jakarta and I'm not sure how friendly they will be. What do I do in the meantime?"

"We've got to relieve the intracranial pressure, relieve the swelling. You have mannitol and dexamethasone in your AMAL." Dr. Morgan's voice crackled over the circuit. "Administer an injection of mannitol and continuous dexamethasone through the IV. That will reduce the swelling and buy us a few hours. Place the patient in a cervical collar and catheterize him. Measure the urine output and give me the numbers every hour."

Dr. Morgan prescribed a regime of analgesics, nimodipine and anti-hypertension medications to combat the symptoms and to make Jones as comfortable as possible. That was all that they could do for the injured flier until they could get him to a proper hospital.

22 Jun 2000, 2220LT (23 Jun, 0920Z)

"Have they gone nuts on *SAN FRANCISCO*!" Admiral O'Flanagan ranted. "What's this crap about attempting to rescue the survivors from that frigate? There are probably two to three hundred of them. *SAN FRANCISCO* doesn't have any place to put them. They'll be stuck on the surface, sitting ducks. And, worse, they will blow cover for any deniability in this. Get me General Schwartz on the red phone, again!"

After a brief pause to establish the communications link, COMSUBPAC was speaking with the Chairman. He first briefed the General about the activities of the night around Nusa Funata. He then launched into an explanation of the intentions on *SAN FRANCISCO*.

General Schwartz warily questioned, "What are the alternatives here? As I see it, we can't leave them in the water. The nearest land is Nusa Funata. If any make it that far, they'll die of the smallpox with the remaining terrorists. There are no other ships in the area. If we leave them, we have a couple of problems. Just for a start, it violates international law."

Schwartz paced the length of his desk, turned and paced back. The red cord for the handset trailed behind him. "*SAN FRANCISCO* can do the rescue with little risk as long as we can keep air cover over her. More importantly, when word gets out that we sank that frigate and then left the survivors to die, we have a huge black eye. On the other hand, if *SAN FRANCISCO* pulls it off, we lose all deniability."

"My sense is to go for it. Keep as many topside as they can. Don't let any of them have any hard information that *SAN FRANCISCO* is a US sub. Anything they can hand over to CNN." General Schwartz concluded.

23 Jun 2000, 1710LT (0930Z)

"Come around to two-one-seven and go to *Ahead Full*. I want you to get over to the area where the frigate sank and start a box search for survivors," Jon Hunter directed, his voice weak and scratchy.

He had returned to the conn and was slumped down in a fold-down jump seat behind the periscope stand. The flushed skin and sunken eyes spoke volumes.

"COB, make sure that there is nothing on the mess decks or anywhere near there that says "*SAN FRANCISCO*". No ball caps or insignia on any uniforms. That includes dolphins. Station guards at the forward and aft end of the mess decks. I don't want any of our guests wandering around."

"Aye, sir. It's a good thing the weather is reasonably calm. As long as we keep the speed down, a lot of them can stay topside," the Chief of the Boat replied.

"That's my intention," Hunter said. "Until we fill the space topside, I only want the injured below decks."

"Skipper, the EMT team will set up a triage in the mess decks, but I'll still need to use the wardroom as an operating room and I will probably need to use the twelve-man berthing as a hospital ward for the seriously injured," Doc Pugh stated. "The EMT team will have to handle the initial diagnosis and treatment. I still have LCDR Jones to worry about and I expect that there will be some seriously injured people in the water."

"OK, set it up with the Chop and the COB. Keep guards on the spaces that you use," Hunter replied. "And, COB, I want at least two armed men topside. I'll have an additional one up on the sail. I want everyone searched and anything that could be a weapon seized. That includes any injured men. I don't expect any trouble, but better safe than sorry."

"Yes, sir," the two chimed as they departed control to get ready for their guests.

23 Jun 2000, 1740LT (0940Z)

The black sub raced all out across the crystal blue sea, leaving a wide, frothy white wake behind it. The sooner they arrived there, the better for the survivors' chances.

Jonathan Hunter and Jeff Miller, both with 9 mm Berettas strapped to their hips, stood together on the bridge. Seaman Lipinski, carrying an M-16, joined them.

Overhead, a pair of S-3B Vikings from the *NIMITZ* made lazy circles in the cloudless pale blue sky. Higher still, a pair of F-14s orbited like sea eagles looking for prey.

Below decks, the sub was ready to receive their unexpected guests. The question still remained unanswered of what to do with them after they were plucked from the water.

"Captain, JA," the 7MC blared, disturbing the stillness on the bridge.

Hunter picked up the handset and said, "Captain."

"Captain, this is Durstin Turnstill. I know you don't think much of me, and with good reason. What you are doing for these people is great. I want to help. I speak Bahasa, the local dialect. Let me be your interpreter."

Hunter thought for a minute. The Australian cost them valuable time and had been of no use so far. Maybe he would be useful after all. But, could he be trusted?

Finally Hunter replied, "OK Mr. Turnstill. Tell the Chief of the Watch to get you a harness and deck traveler. Report to the COB topside. And thank you."

As they approached the site, the sub slowed. Miller ordered, "Lower the outboard." He would use it to maneuver in close to survivors and to protect them from being hit by the great bronze main screw.

The COB led the search and rescue party as they rushed topside. They hurried to lay out their equipment, ready for instant use.

The plaintive cries from men in the water slowly became audible above the slight wind as the first of the flotsam drifted past the boat.

As Miller carefully maneuvered the sub through the remains of the frigate, they came upon a group of ten survivors huddled together, floating in their life jackets. The shipwrecked sailors eagerly paddled toward the waiting submarine and attempted to pull themselves onboard with the lines thrown by the SAR party. Most were too weak from their harrowing experience to actually get aboard without help. Seaman Osterburg led the rescue swimmers into the water. Together with the SAR party topside, the SAR swimmers helped the bedraggled survivors aboard *SAN FRANCISCO*.

Turnstill shouted encouragement and instructions to the men in the water in both Bahasa and English.

As each new survivor was plucked from the water, they were given a cursory check for major injuries and a more careful search for weapons.

The injured were then carefully lowered through the hatch to eager hands below waiting to aid them. The EMT team treated those with minor injuries and worked to stabilize those with more serious problems.

The submarine quickly became the center of a mass of survivors, all clamoring to be pulled aboard. The process worked reasonably smoothly. The severely injured, primarily burns, concussions, and broken bones from the explosion, were triaged topside and treated in the wardroom. Everyone else huddled just aft of the sail, topside.

The beds in the twelve man berthing area were soon full. Wardroom berthing, and then the chiefs' quarters, were pressed into service as additional medical wards.

Every crewman with even the most rudimentary medical experience was busy. Seaman Martinez found himself in the Engineer's stateroom administering IVs to three badly burned survivors. Chief Jones and three of his ETs were in crew's berthing watching twelve patients with a variety of injuries, from broken bones to saltwater ingestion.

The mess decks were filled to overflowing. Soon, every available square inch was in use. Those with relatively minor injuries filled the passageways. The uninjured filled topside.

The SUCAP S3-Bs were pressed into service as longer range SAR birds. The combination of their advanced forward looking infrared sensors (FLIR) and inverted synthetic aperture radars (ISAR) were very effective in finding isolated survivors, particularly as night began to fall.

28

23 Jun 2000, 2336LT (1536Z)

As the last of the survivors was being pulled aboard, Fagan climbed to the bridge.

"Skipper, we've got two hundred and forty survivors onboard. The mess decks and all the middle level berthing are crammed full. We have over a hundred topside. Doc reports that he is almost out of medical supplies. He has ninety-four patients, all in fair or better condition and nothing he can't handle. Burns, broken bones, salt water ingestion, a couple of concussions, some lacerations and bruises.

"The crew has been doing a great job. Everybody's pitching in to help. Even Turnstill is finally being useful. Don't know what we would have done without him interpreting."

Hunter commented dryly, "About time he did something besides eat, breathe and sleep."

Fagan continued, "More interesting, the CO was in that last bunch. He's not a happy camper. Demanding an explanation of why his ship was attacked in sovereign waters and making all kinds of dire threats. He's been using Admiral Suluvana's name liberally. He evidently is a close follower and supporter of the admiral."

"Interesting," Hunter replied, scratching the stubble on his chin. "Any clue of why he was in these waters? He give you any ideas?"

Fagan replied, "No sir, but I bet it has to do with the island. They must be here to escort the delivery ship."

"Maybe they are the delivery ship," Hunter mused. "Pick-up was supposed to happen last night if we believe that comms intercept. Have you seen any other ship anywhere close?"

He gazed out over the water for a few moments and then said, "Here's what I want you to do. Isolate that Skipper in the Chief's quarters under heavy guard. No one is to say anything to him. Find out who his leading quartermaster is and interrogate him. Take Turnstill with you.

"I'm betting that only the Skipper and maybe a few of his senior officers are in on this. The leading quartermaster will know the planned routing and schedule. He probably doesn't even know that it is anything but a routine port stop.

"We'll use that against the Skipper to pump what he knows out of him. Get a message drafted to SUBPAC giving them the status of the rescue and telling them we have the Skipper. Let them know that we suspect that the frigate was the pick-up ship and that we are planning to interrogate the Skipper. Also find out what they have done to help us off-load our guests. By the way, do we have that Skipper's name?" Hunter asked.

"Sure Skipper, his name is Balewegal, Commanding Officer of the Indonesian Navy Ship *SAWAL*," Fagan replied as he started to lower himself down the long ladder to the control room.

23 Jun 2000, 2325LT (1725Z)

CDR Hunter stalked into the goat locker with Turnstill close behind him. Hunter glared down at the seated Indonesian Captain. "Well, Captain Balewegal, you should be happy to know that we have two hundred and forty of your crew safely onboard. They are being given medical attention, food and dry clothing. From your recent activities, though, I doubt that you care.

Turnstill translated Hunter's statement into Bahasa.

Balewegal angrily responded, in English, "I don't need the services of this spy dog!"

Turning to Turnstill, he continued harshly, "So, you have returned to your masters. Our money was not enough for you. You take American money, too. Do your American masters know all that you have done for us? Do they know about the drug smuggling?"

Turnstill lunged at Balewegal, his face contorted with rage. Hunter slammed him back into the bulkhead before he could reach the seated captive. Balewegal attempted to jump up to defend himself, but the COB shoved him back down.

Hunter yelled, "All right. That's enough!" while jamming the still struggling Turnstill into the corner.

Turnstill slumped down into the corner and held up his arms defensively. "Enough! I've had enough."

Balewegal started, "Captain, maybe you don't know that Turnstill was the top heroin smuggler in Java. That's how we found him, or rather rescued him. I'm afraid that our Courts are much harsher with drug dealers than yours. He was caught trying to sneak in a boatload of pure heroin. Sentenced to beheading. Admiral Suluvana saw some use in this mangy mutt and had him released. He has been importing items for us ever since."

Turnstill looked up at Hunter. "I was framed. Suluvana and this bastard set me up. I didn't know there were drugs on that boat. They told me it was a load of fertilizer and farm tools."

Hunter replied, "I don't give a damn. We'll sort that out later. Right now, I have more important things to worry about."

Hunter turned to Balewegal. "It seems that you have considerable explaining to do. Admiral Suluvana is in custody and is singing like a bird. The lawful Indonesian authorities are demanding that we turn you over to them for prosecution. They sound distinctly unhappy with your activities of late."

Hunter crossed his arms and looked down at the seated captive. "Using one of their frigates to transport a deadly biological agent for a known terrorist and shooting down an American aircraft will not endear you to them. And, of course, losing your ship is not a career-enhancing move.

"You know, of course, the facilities on Nusa Funata have been captured and destroyed. I'm afraid that some of the smallpox virus may have leaked from the ruptured containers during the fighting. Our forces have been evacuated and the island is quarantined."

Unblinking, Captain Balewegal stared back contemptuously, "Captain, it is you who are the criminal. You attacked my ship without provocation in Indonesian territorial waters. I do not recognize the ones that you call the lawful authorities. I demand that you release my crew and me immediately!"

The short, paunchy Captain raised his fist and attempted to rise. The COB slammed Balewegal forcefully back in his seat, again.

"Captain," Hunter continued dryly, "I don't think that you fully understand your position. We will happily release you within swimming distance of Nusa Funata. You can go there and share the fate of your fellow terrorists. I already know that your crew was not part of this plot. They will stay here and be turned over to your Navy."

In a more conciliatory tone, he continued, "If you choose to help us, maybe I can arrange for our senior people to intervene on your behalf. As I understand Islamic Law. That's what the Indonesian law is based on, didn't you say? The penalty for treason is death by beheading. Sounds pretty final. Think it over. If you want to talk, tell your guard. He will get me." Hunter turned and stepped toward the door.

"Wait," the Indonesian Captain started hesitantly. "I'll help you. What do you want to know? Just don't turn me over to them."

All right, start talking," CDR Hunter said, taking a seat across the table from the Captain. "I want to hear everything." Captain Balewegal began to relate a tale of deceit, bribery, terror and treason.

24 Jun 2000, 0647LT (23 Jun, 2347Z)

"Captain, message from Chairman of the Joint Chiefs. It's marked "Personal for" and addressed to you. I'll bring it to the bridge," Chief Tyler announced over the 21MC to the bridge cockpit.

"Very well, Chief. Lay to the bridge," Hunter replied.

Chief Tyler made the long climb to the bridge and handed the

Commander a stainless steel clipboard prominently labeled "TOP SECRET, SPECIAL CATEGORY" in inch high red letters.

The Commander flipped up the front cover and read the flimsy message form underneath.

TOP SECRET, GOLDEN DAWN, Special Handling required
    EYES-ONLY: CO USS SAN FRANCISCO
    From: Chairman, JCS
    To: CO USS SAN FRANCISCO
    Subj: Survivors INS *SAWAL*, LIMDIS
    BT

1. Proceed best surfaced speed to vicinity 114.30E 07.45S to rendezvous with units of Indonesian Navy for transfer of survivors. Advise expected ETA soonest.
2. Transfer Captain Balewegal in prisoner status to Senior INS Officer Present.
3. Transfer LCDR Jones for treatment. Advise any other immediate medical requirements for transfer.
4. Well Done!
5. General Schwartz sends

    BT

24 Jun 2000, 0620LT (0320Z)

The cell phone began its annoying buzz, disturbing Mustaf from his reverie. He angrily grabbed the offending device and growled a greeting. Who would dare call him on this number? Only three people had access to it.

"Mustaf, this is General Schwartz." The gravelly voice was unmistakable. "Your operation has been totally destroyed. Have you made your peace with Allah?"

How did he get this number? What did he mean by totally destroyed? None of the operatives had reported in. The silence was most disturbing, and now this mysterious phone call.

"What do you mean, General? I have no operation. I am a peaceful businessman dealing in the trading of commodities. I have always been faithful to the teachings of Allah, why do you ask?" Mustaf countered calmly, but his mind was racing.

"That's good," the General responded, "because if you step outside that tent and look to the East over that anti-aircraft gun emplacement guarding your commodities, you will see your trip to Paradise coming over the ridge about now. Good-bye, Mustaf." The line went silent.

Mustaf stepped outside as the General had suggested just in time to see four small, low flying missiles clear the horizon. All were pointed directly at him. He stood rooted in place, unable to even shout a warning. They rapidly grew from hummingbird size until they seemed to fill his entire vision. Three of the missiles made minor course corrections and crashed into other parts of the encampment, causing tremendous explosions. The last one continued directly at him. His mind told him to run, but his legs would not respond. It was too late, no time to run. What was that horrible screaming? What coward feared death so? His last conscious thought, just before the blinding flash, was that it was his own voice.

General Schwartz replaced the receiver and noted with grim satisfaction that the satellite intercept of Mustaf's cell phone was located exactly in the center of his tent. Too bad that he was such a creature of habit. The first flight of four Tomahawks launched from the *PITTSBURGH* would be arriving right now. The next four would follow in thirty seconds and the final four would be thirty seconds behind them.

29

The sun was just peeping over Koko Head, the ancient volcano marking the windward end of Oahu. The lights of Honolulu shone brilliantly from Waikiki up the twin mountains of Tantulus and Round Top. Jon Hunter was alone with his thoughts, sitting on the ice cap for the number one BRA-34 antenna, on top the sail of *SAN FRANCISCO*. Jeff Miller stood in the cockpit, a few feet forward of him and directed the ship toward the entrance to Pearl Harbor, a couple of miles ahead.

They had surfaced shortly after midnight and steamed through the remnants of a beautiful, star-filled tropical night. Hunter usually relished this time, alone under the stars, just he and the sounds of the sea. That time was drawing to a close. Soon they would be steaming into Pearl Harbor to all the tumult a homecoming brought. It should be a joyful time, sweet to contemplate. Returning to family, the mission successfully completed. Back to the day-to-day routine.

Hunter was troubled and angry. He held the offending message tightly wadded in his hand. Admiral O'Flanagan had sent him a "Personal For" message last night that recounted the terrorists taking Peg and the girls hostage. It told of the rescue and reassured Hunter that his family was safe and healthy. The closing paragraph ordered Hunter to not divulge any of this. The story was to die behind a veil of secrecy.

Hunter breathed deeply. The warm air tinged with the scent of land calmed him. On the one hand, his family was safe. That was an immense relief. On the other, the fact SUBPAC had waited three weeks to tell him was infuriating.

"Captain, XO on the JA," Jeff Miller turned around and handed Jon Hunter the handset.

"Skipper, Harbor Control has requested that we stay out here for a couple more hours. They request an ETA at Papa Hotel of zero-eight hundred," Fagan relayed from control.

Papa Hotel was an imaginary point outside the channel entrance to Pearl Harbor. It had been established in the late 60's after the *QUEENFISH* had run aground on the coral reefs returning from an important mission on Christmas Morning. Papa Hotel was the final checkpoint before entering the harbor. The ship had to be completely ready for navigating the narrow entrance channel and had to receive permission from Harbor Control before venturing beyond Papa Hotel.

"Alright, XO. We can kill some time out here. Come on up and enjoy the view. Send the messenger to get a couple of cups of coffee," Hunter answered. He needed to talk to someone and forget that message for a while.

Fagan made the long climb up to the bridge and took a seat on the Number 2 BRA-34 ice cap. The messenger delivered the steaming coffee in large white Navy mugs.

Together they gazed out toward the dimming lights of Honolulu and the blazing orange-red sunrise. After a long pause, Hunter commented, "We've learned a lot on this time out. It's time for both of us to move on. You're ready for your own boat. And, it's time I went ashore for good. When you have your own boat, remember this. Enjoy the moments, it doesn't last forever."

13 Jul 2000, 0800LT (1900Z)

The immaculate white barge, really a thirty-foot motor launch but nautical tradition dictated that an admiral's boat be called a barge, flew a blue pennant with two white stars. It lay quietly waiting for the approaching submarine, bobbing gently in the swell. Two side-boys in dress white uniforms stood at parade rest against the stern rail. Rear Admiral O'Flanagan and several of his senior officers stood in the covered cockpit, behind the coxswain.

As *SAN FRANCISCO* slid alongside, Hunter could make out a yellow sundress peeking out from under the awning. Then he could see Peg waving gaily. It was good to be home.

The barge picked up speed and matched *SAN FRANCISCO*'s progress. Hunter could see a line being tossed from the barge. The COB caught and tied it to the number three cleat. The crew on the barge passed a short gangplank over to *SAN FRANCISCO*. Rear Admiral O'Flanagan charged across the gangplank, pausing at its end to salute Old Glory, flying proudly above the submarine's sail. His staff and, finally, Peg along with the XO's and COB's wives followed him onboard the sub.

As the sub entered the confined dredged channel through the coral reef, CDR Hunter saw that Jeff Miller and his lookout were struggling with something being pushed up through the bridge hatch. A large duffel bag was slowly emerging. Reaching down, he grabbed a handle of the bag and chided Miller to pay attention to where the sub was going.

As he opened the duffel bag and handed the lookout one end of a long rope with cloth flowers tied along its length, he asked, "Can you imagine the headlines, "Sub runs aground while Skipper and OOD tie Lei around Sail"? That wouldn't look very good for either of us. You drive the boat. We'll handle the lei."

Hunter saw a flash of yellow coming up the ladder to the bridge. Unfortunately it turned out to be Admiral O'Flanagan's gold shoulder boards and not the pert yellow sundress that he had hoped to see emerge from the hatch.

"Jon, damn good work. Welcome home," the gruff admiral growled through the unlit, but well chewed, cigar as he climbed out of the bridge cockpit to join Hunter on top the sail. "Sure hope you're not planning on spending much time at home. You're scheduled to give your post patrol debrief to the Joint Chiefs and SECDEF in five days. Beautiful morning up here, isn't it?"

Hunter greeted the admiral heatedly, "Sir, I don't know whether to welcome you aboard or to tell you what a cold son-of-a-bitch I think you are. It'll be a while before I can forgive you for not telling me about Peg and the girls being hostages. Damn it, they're my family. I should have been told."

Admiral O'Flanagan took the cigar out of his mouth and jabbed it toward Hunter, "Just a minute, Jon. I understand you being upset. Look at the big picture. There was nothing you could do but worry. You had a job that had to be done. It wasn't an easy decision, but it was the right one."

Hunter, the anger still hot in him, growled, "That's bull-shit. You took the easy way out. You were being PC, just like the rest of the flags."

"Jon, that's enough!" O'Flanagan warned. "Shut up before you say something you'll regret. It's over. You and I both have to live with it. Face facts, the way they are. Your family needs you and ranting doesn't help anyone."

Hunter sputtered some, but he had to admit that the admiral was right.

The two were silent. Admiral O'Flanagan looked out over the approaching tropical landscape for a few moments.

Up ahead, alongside the Hickam Officers Club, sat the waiting harbor tug that would escort them to the pier. Draped across the side of the tug was a huge cloth banner. Flanagan chuckled and grunted, "Jon, you really have to do something to control the wives on your boat. How is a picture of that sign going to look on national news?"

The huge banner said, in letters over three feet tall, "Caution, horny wives ahead!" The tensions of the moment were broken.

As if an afterthought, the admiral said, "Oh, by the way Jon, there is someone down in control waiting to see you. Why don't you have her come up here? She certainly deserves to have the royal ride into port as much as anyone."

This time, the flash of yellow that he saw really was the sundress. Having her up on the sail with him made the homecoming complete.

EPILOGUE

14 Jun 2000, 1830LT (1030Z)

The Super Puma helicopter flew in low and fast. It bore Indonesian Navy markings along both sides. The two passengers in the back sat silently. Not a word had been exchanged between the two since they had taken off from Surabaya over an hour ago.

The pilot brought the small helicopter to a hover only ten feet above the waves. Nusa Funata sat menacingly just a few hundred yards to the East. Dark storm clouds formed an ominous crown over Mount Guishu. A surreal blue haze surrounded the rest of the island. To the West, the sun was setting in a glorious explosion of colors.

"It's time," Admiral Mengatiz said. "Get out."

He pointed a wicked looking Beretta 9mm pistol at the other passenger. Admiral Suluvana offered no resistance. He rose, stepped out the door and dropped into the water below. As the helicopter disappeared over the horizon, he began the laborious swim to the land. He didn't know why he even bothered. He could so easily just slip beneath the waves and end it here. There was no one left on Nusa Funata and there wouldn't be for many generations. The smallpox NX had finished Aswal and all the remaining people there. Now it waited for him.

14 Jul 2000, 1500LT (15 Jul, 0200Z)

Hunter and Fagan sat back in their lounge chairs. The hot Hawaiian sun beat down on them. Drips of sweat trickled down the sides of the cold beer bottles on the small table between them.

"Seaman Martinez came by the boat this morning. He was looking for you. He had his GED and his new wife. You have never seen a guy so proud. Looks like you steered that one right," Fagan said as the two sat under the great Banyan tree in Hunter's side yard. "What's next? Are you still planning on retiring after this?"

Megan sat just above them on the branch of her banyon tree, talking to Sally on her new cell phone. Maggie sat on her Dad's lap. They both still had nightmares and didn't stray very far from Peg. Now that Jon was home, Maggie seemed to need to constantly hold on to him. It would take a while for them to forget that awful day.

"Bill, my relief has been named and will be aboard in a couple of weeks. Not much left for an old sailor to do but retire. You saw the Captain's List. I wasn't on it, so I can look forward to meaningless desk bound jobs ashore if I stay in. That's not my style, so I'll go ahead and retire. I've found a new challenge to conquer. I think that I'll work on cleaning up Wall Street. That's a real nest of vipers, much worse than anything we've faced," Jon Hunter replied.

"Besides, there's this," Hunter added, reaching for an envelope on the stand beside his lawn chair. "Results from some tests that I had before we left. Seems that I have a problem with my heart. Something called mobitz type II heart block. Something to do with the way my heart is wired. That was the cause of the dizzy spells. It means that I need a pacemaker. Relatively simple operation, but it will leave me medically disqualified for submarines."

Bill Fagan sat back in the lounge chair, took a deep breath and replied, "Jon, my orders to the next PCO class were in today's mailbag. I'm thinking of turning them down and resigning my commission."

Jon Hunter stared across the water toward Ford Island for a long moment. "It's the *KILO* thing, isn't it? That could have happened to anyone.

You have no idea how scared I was. Now you know what it's like and how to handle it. You won't freeze next time." Reaching for his beer, Hunter added, "Besides, the Navy will always need at least one CO crazy enough to do what we did."

FINAL BEARING
George Wallace and Don Keith

"This team spins a great tale." —*W.E.B. Griffin, author of the
bestselling* Brotherhood of War *series*

Commander Jonathan Ward and his crew on the old attack sub Spadefish
are on one last mission. A US Navy SEAL team is inserted into South
America. Their orders are to destroy the secret laboratories of the world's
most notorious drug cartel, and the Spadefish has been sent to provide
assistance.

But Juan de Santiago, the violent billionaire drug lord, has an entire private
army and a futuristic new mini-submarine of his own. He will do anything
to protect his empire.
And he knows the Americans are coming...

Final Bearing is the first book in The Hunter Killer Series.

Get your copy today at
severnriverbooks.com/authors/george-wallace

ACKNOWLEDGMENTS

As with any work, there are people who volunteered their time and expertise to help me write this book. My frequent co-author, Don Keith, and old friend, Jack Gobbell, are largely responsible for introducing me to the fascinating idea of story-telling. They are both far better at it than I am, but I thank them for the lessons they have taught me.

Two other old friends helped with advice in areas that I have more limited experience. Dr. Denny Vidmar, CAPT USN MC (ret) provided key advice for the medical parts of the text, particularly with Jon Hunter's mystery malady and in dealing with Red Dog Jones' injuries. CAPT Duncan Smith, USNR, was invaluable in getting the SEAL team tactics and weapons right. I could handle describing submarining and SEALs on submarines from personal experience, but once they left the hatch, I was dependent on Duncan's experience.

Last, and certainly not least, I have to thank my wife, Penny, who has patiently lived with this consuming passion. She has diligently (and sometimes persistently) been my chief proofreader and copy editor, as well as toughest critic.

Any success that this story might enjoy is largely due to their efforts. Any mistakes and shortfalls are entirely my responsibility.

ABOUT THE AUTHOR

Commander George Wallace USN (ret.) served in the US Navy for twenty-two years as an officer on nuclear submarines. After receiving his commission through Naval ROTC at The Ohio State University, he served on two of Admiral Rickover's famous "Forty One for Freedom", the USS JOHN ADAMS (SSBN 620) and the USS WOODROW WILSON (SSBN 624). Commander Wallace served as Executive Officer on the Sturgeon class nuclear attack submarine USS SPADEFISH (SSN 668). Spadefish and all her sister-ships were de-commissioned during the downsizings that occurred in the 1990's. Reflections on the passing of such capable "boats" inspired his first novel, the National Best Seller, <u>Final Bearing</u>, co-authored with Don Keith. Their second novel, <u>Firing Point</u>, is in production as a major motion picture.

Commander Wallace commanded the Los Angeles class nuclear attack submarine USS HOUSTON (SSN 713) from February 1990 to August 1992. During this tour of duty, he worked extensively with the SEAL community developing SEAL/submarine tactics. Under his command, the Houston was awarded the CIA Meritorious Unit Citation. Commander Wallace and his wife Penny live in Alexandria, Virginia.

Sign up for George Wallace's newsletter at
severnriverbooks.com/authors/george-wallace

Printed in the United States
by Baker & Taylor Publisher Services